CARTEL PUBLICATIONS
PRESENTS

RAUNCHY3
JAYDEN'S PASSION

T. STYLES

NATIONAL BEST SELLING AUTHOR OF *RAUNCHY*

Library of Congress Control Number: 2012946636
ISBN 10: 0984303073
ISBN 13: 978-0984303076

Cover Design: Davida Baldwin www.oddballdsgn.com
Editor: Advanced Editorial Services
Graphics: Davida Baldwin
www.thecartelpublications.com
First Edition

Printed in the United States of America

CHECK OUT OTHER TITLES BY THE CARTEL PUBLICATIONS

WWW.THECARTELPUBLICATIONS.COM

Acknowledgments

I acknowledge all T. Styles fans near and far.
I Love You.
I acknowledge everyone who lent their names, not their likenesses,
to the characters within this book, for my contest.
Thank You.

Dedication

I dedicate this to my grandbaby J.R.
Thanks for reminding me to take time to love.

What's Poppin' Fam,

We hope you have enjoyed the roster so far this year! Although, I am a little sad that with this year's releases comes the end of era's like, "Shyt List 5" and the current novel on deck, "Raunchy 3: Jayden's Passion", I THOUROUGHLY enjoyed this one! In true "Raunchy" fashion, T. Styles DELIVERS! Jayden is on some whole other shit! Get ready!

But before you go, keeping in line with Cartel tradition, where we honor an author whose journey and literary work we admire, we would like to pay tribute to:

Miss KP

Miss KP is the author of, "The Dirty Divorce 1, 2 and 3"! This series was her first and for a new author, she came on the scene kicking! If you have not read her work, do yourself a favor and cop it!

Ok, I'm out; ya'll go to it! You will not be disappointed!

Much Love,

Charisse "C. Wash" Washington
Vice President
The Cartel Publications
www.thecartelpublications.com
www.twitter.com/cartelbooks
www.facebook.com/cartelcafeandbooksstore
www.facebook.com/publishercharissewashington
www.twitter.com/CWashVP

"Be sure, beautiful.

Because the moment you shake my hand, and look into my eyes…I own you."

- Jayden Phillips

PART ONE

PROLOGUE

Spring of 2002
Houston, Texas

The summer heat coughed in thirteen-year-old Jayden Phillips' face, as he burst through the doors of the school's cafeteria. Air raced through the grooves of his cornrows and he bucked against the wind. Turning around momentarily, he could feel the anger steaming from the kids chasing him. They carried matches and they were ready to cause permanent damage. A quick count would end at ten and they all were gunning for him. Jayden fucked up royally and he knew it. He needed to catch wheels cuz if the mob caught him, he would be beat into a bloody pulp.

"You stole my money, boy! I'ma kick your ass when I catch you too!" Yelled Sandy, the prettiest and angriest of the bunch. Jayden wasn't much on girls, but if he had to pick one his selection would be smooth. Sandy had it all. Beauty, big pretty eyes and most of all money. "I'ma put gum in your hair and burn it to your scalp!"

Thunderstorms kicked up inside of his chest with the news of her threat. If only he hadn't crept into her purse spider-like, to steal the twenty-dollar bill that stuck out of the edge, none of this would've happened. It didn't matter that he dropped the money some ways back. He reached into her shit, and for that she wanted to hear him cry. Before he stole it his decision made sense. He was broke, hungry and tired of not having money to wash his clothes and Sandy was so caked up he thought she wouldn't miss it. He was dead wrong.

Jayden twisted in and out of the cars in the school's parking lot, hoping to tire a few of them out. But five could go three more miles on pure hate alone. The worn out white Converse he wore offered little comfort when his feet struck the concrete. Pain shot up his backbone and he contemplated giving up and getting his beat down over with.

Things looked bleak until suddenly one of the kids fell face down like a domino, followed by another. A smile stretched over his face when through the crowd, he saw the brim of his brother's black baseball cap. When it came to running not too many people could fuck with his twin.

He was rebellious, a fighter and most of all he loved him. Once again, Madjesty saved the day.

When Madjesty caught up with him, Jayden noticed the grin on his face and the slyness in his eyes. He lived for this shit, Jayden was sure of it. "What you do this time, little brother?" He laughed, as he kept up with him on his quest. It was as if they possessed the same getaway plan because they switched from left to right simultaneously, neither having to update the other.

"Little brother? First of all, you was born only a few seconds before me." He said out of breath. "And second, I didn't do nothing," he looked back at Sandy who's pace seemed to simmer. A little. "You know how they be fucking with us at school sometimes. I ain't about to hit no girl though."

"Speak for yourself. If you put your hands on me, I'm breaking skin. Girl, boy or animal," Madjesty said, mostly out of breath. "Go up there," He pointed to a red brick dwelling with shattered windows, graffiti walls and trash in the yard. The fucked up thing was, people actually lived there. "In that building."

Without hesitation they dodged into the property that was known to sell everything from pussy to ice cream. The moment they were inside, they looked out of the window on the door to see if their pursuers were still hot on their trail. The walls were gray and heaps of pink gum stuck to the floors like dried lumps of concrete.

Out of breath, Jayden was able to see Sandy and her friends look at the building and slowly back away. Angry or not, they knew better than to go inside the death trap. If the Phillip boys wanted to be stupid enough to risk their lives, that was on them. It didn't take long for the horde to dissipate but Jayden knew he would see her pretty-angry face again.

"What was that shit about?" Madjesty asked, slapping him on the back as they flopped down on a step. His black jeans were so tight they would've been skinny jeans if it were the right era. The hallway was dank and smelled of hot compost but neither seemed to notice. "They not gonna be after you like that for nothing." Madjesty controlled the dirty white laces on one of his shoes, by taming them into a bow.

"She got mad because I asked for her friend's number. I think she like me or something." To cool down, Jayden pulled a few times on his white T-Shirt with the permanent yellow stains in the pit area. He stood up and walked toward the door again while brushing off the back of his already dingy jeans. "But, I ain't worried 'bout it though."

"I don't believe you." Madjesty stated. "I mean, I don't believe you like girls."

Jayden's face-hardened and he wasn't sure why he lied about snatching her money. Part of him considered how the world viewed thieves. Sure they'd stolen from the store at times in an effort to survive. That type of thing was commonplace but they never stole from someone they knew. There were rules with that shit.

"I don't know why you think I'm lying. You know how them bitches be at school." He wiped the sweat off of his forehead. "They all freaks."

Madjesty eyes seemed to brighten with his response. "So you really like girls now?" He smiled and leaned his upper body against the wall. "Because you never fuck with bitches at our school. Every time we talk about them you always saying how nasty they are and shit like that."

A lady walked out of her apartment and Jayden, always the gentleman, rushed to open the door. "I like girls, Madjesty. I might not kiss 'em and stuff like that, but I like 'em." His lies tasted like dirty pennies in his mouth. He didn't like girls and he couldn't explain why. When he was next to them his body said it was wrong and he couldn't make it right. "If I get with somebody, I gotta like her a lot but you don't care who you go with." He swallowed air to allow his mind a chance to pause.

He hated how Madjesty bombarded him with questions like, 'Is this girl pretty' or 'that girl cute.' Jayden was only interested in what they could do for him. What they could give him.

"Jayden, I think you gonna turn out to be gay." He kicked a roach out of his path, which was threatening to fuck his shoe. "That's why ma be keeping a close eye on you."

"I don't like how ya'll be talking about me behind my back sometimes." He leaned on the door. "You supposed to be my brother, Madjesty, not ma's. Plus you don't even fuck with her like that and she don't fuck with you. She be telling people all the time how she only got one son, and you know which one she chooses," he points to himself, "me."

Madjesty pushed the hurt down into the pit of his stomach, where he kept the rest of his disappointments. "You telling me something I already know. I don't fuck with that bitch now and never will." He pulled his cap further over his eyes. He loved her deep down inside and felt weak for it. "You the one who always making her out to be more than what she is. I had one conversation with her recently and that was the night she got up complaining about niggas stealing her dirty panties."

Jayden frowned. "What that got to do with me?"

"Nothing, I just wanted you to know where my loyalty lies. I wish I can say the same about you."

"My loyalty lies with you, Madjesty. You know that." He paused. "I just want the three of us to be family. Without stabbing each other in the back. Don't you?"

Madjesty stood up, removed the cap off of his head and wiped his damp face. Their musty odor contributed to the rancid smell of the hallway. "Don't play with me like that, Jayden." He hit him softly on the shoulder. ".........don't you?" He put his cap back on.

Jayden tilted his head. His hearing failed him again. "What you say?"

"How come you act like you can't hear sometimes? Just keep it real and say you don't feel like listening."

"I'm not ignoring you." Jayden tugged at his right ear and seemed to go elsewhere in his mind. "Madjesty, have you ever done it with a girl before?" He focused on his lips.

"Uh…yeah…I fucked lots of girls before." He lied.

"I'm serious."

"It don't matter if I fucked girls or not, I kissed a rack of 'em."

Jayden didn't understand sex nor did he care as much as his mother or his brother seemed to. He was all about having money to eat, wear clean clothes and having a place to live.

"Anyway, where were you at lunch time?" Jayden inquired.

Madjesty's grin got larger. "Remember the girl Rocket I was telling you about? We were kicking it in the girl's bathroom."

"What ya'll talking about in there? You coulda got in trouble if a teacher caught you."

"You scary as shit. We were talking about the field trip. She was asking me if I was going and stuff like that." Jayden thought about how badly he wanted to go but knew it wouldn't be possible. "I think she was gonna let me kiss her if I asked." He paused. "She kept saying, 'get out of here boy! You gonna get me in trouble.' But Jayden, I think she wanted me in there." He grinned at the thought. "You should see the way she be talking to me all close and shit. I'ma make her mine, watch."

"Like you did Tisa? Right before she dumped you for the boy who kept hitting you in the back of the head with the encyclopedia?" Jayden combatted. "The girl didn't want nothing to do with you, Madjesty, and Rocket probably don't either. Anyway don't she go with the boy Baisley? Who play football?"

Before he could respond, a door opened upstairs. Three male teenagers appeared from an apartment, leaving the door ajar. They wore expressions of satisfaction and for some reason they grabbed Jayden's attention. He watched them jog down the steps two at a time as they moved toward the exit.

"Man, that shit was wild!" The shortest of them said. "Can you believe she in there getting it in like that?"

"Believe it," the other said groping his dick, "nigga, I was there!" He gave him dap.

They laughed as they swooshed past the twins before disappearing outside. Curious, Jayden approached the opened door. The incident called him and he pushed forward. Madjesty was right behind him.

Inside the unknown apartment, the first thing he smelled was smoke and unclean sex. The air was also thick and for some reason, Jayden felt at home. He approached a sofa and it all made sense when he saw the back of a woman's neck. Her hair was swept to the right and her head hung frontwards without support. On the floor were empty beer bottles and used condoms filled with creamy froth. Slowly Jayden walked around the front of the couch and his heart sank when he saw her face. It was his mother, Harmony Phillips.

Things got worse when Jayden felt another presence in the room. By the time he stared into the murderous gaze of a man, the eyes of his double barrel shotgun was pointed in Jayden's direction.

RUN DOWN SOUL

Jayden and Madjesty were enveloped in partial darkness. Mama didn't pay the light bill yet again. This type of shit wrecked Jayden's mind. Why couldn't she do the basics to see that they were safe? Jayden sat in a plastic yellow chair, across from his mother's inebriated, half naked body. A candle's radiance spotlighted the thick vomit in the corners of her mouth and the stern expression on her sleeping face. She looked a fucking mess. She was so wretched death didn't want her.

Jayden placed his hand on her warm thigh, hoping that like in the past, she'd bounce back and come through the episode alive. Even a hopeless drunk, a worthless mother and a monster, deserved love. Didn't she?

"I don't know why you bother with that bitch." Madjesty declaimed, as he leaned against the dirty wall of their apartment. The candle beside him threatened to burn out for good. His arms were crossed tightly against his body like a lunatic wearing a straight jacket in an insane asylum. "Just let her kill herself so we can finally be free." He tugged at his baseball cap, masking the pain in his eyes. He was tired of his mother fucking with his mind. Playing games with his heart. If she wasn't going to take care of them, DIE ALREADY was his chant. "At least she can't hurt...."

Jayden couldn't hear him clearly so he tugged his right ear, held his head down and eyed the wooden slats on the floor. He could see his boyish reflection in them, which he loathed. "She's our mother, Madjesty. We only get one." He inspected his twin's eyes, the only person on earth who accompanied him in her diseased womb. "She gonna stay sick if she don't have our love." He sipped the flat orange soda that sat on the table. When he was done, he placed it back next to the permission slip for the field trip, which Harmony constantly ignored like everything else. He knew he wasn't going. How could he? She didn't even pay the light bill.

Madjesty pushed his body off the wall and stomped toward him. "Did you just say love?" His eyes formed tiny slits as he pointed at Harmony's limp body. "What the fuck this bitch ever teach us 'bout love? Huh?" He stood over Jayden demanding answers. The wrong response might make him snap and he knew it. "I'm the only one who loves you, Jay. Not this whore faking like..."

Jayden didn't catch the entire sentence, but he heard enough. "Don't put me in a position where I gotta choose you over her, Madjesty. Because I would never do that to you."

His voice lowered. "And I would never do that to you either. Unlike her, I love you." He traipsed back to the wall and slid to the floor. "It's just me and you against the world. Plus she will never be who you need her to be. Ever. And one day when you need her the most, she'll let you down. I put my life on it. I just hope it won't be too late."

Jayden was still looking at him when Harmony stirred. It took a few seconds for her to open her red eyes. When she saw her twins examining her, she placed her hand over her face to cover her shame. "What ya'll doing now, talking about all the things I did wrong again?" She laughed at her own joke. "If you are, save your fucking breath, I already know."

Madjesty peered at the worn out cream slip Harmony donned, which exposed the darkness of her full breasts and extra hairy pussy. Then he observed the loaded frown lines on her forehead, which resembled the bark of an old oak tree. Oh how he hated that bitch. His twin was different. Jayden chose to focus on the way the candlelight touched her eyes, turning them into caramel candies. And the way her head tilted to the left, causing her cascading black hair to dangle over her shoulder, just above her breasts. He saw beauty in the beast. He saw a mother he adored. Despite the burning hate she had for him inside.

"You think its funny don't you?" Madjesty raged. "That we don't have lights in the house? Or no food?"

"I do what I can. If you can do better than me I won't stop you. You'll be old enough to get a job soon anyway."

"You don't do shit but drink, fuck and sleep!"

"Watch your mouth, nigga. Before I crash your teeth into your tongue."

Fed up with Harmony's raunchiness, Madjesty leaped up and trekked toward the door. "Jayden, I'm going to Mrs. Brookes house. I think Promise coming home today. Meet me there when you finish with this zombie."

Before he could depart, Harmony's legs flung around in front of her, planting her feet to the floor. It was becoming harder to control him. So she planned to murder him and be done with it for good, until the contents of her stomach swirled, causing a putrid cream liquid to splash out of her mouth. The meat soaked mess slapped the floor and Jayden's permission slip on the table. After a few more gags she wiped her mouth with the back of her hand and said, "Aren't you gonna ask me if you can go out?" She breathed heavily due to the pain in her gut. "I am your mother, Madjesty. One day you will realize you love me and it will be when you least expect it."

"The day you die will be the day I dance on your head." He stormed out, slamming the door behind him.

"I hate that bitch!" Harmony yelled. Her attention moved to Jayden, who always seemed to be there when no one else was. "Clean this shit...!" Her speech was broken. Jayden tugged his ear. "It stinks! And stop fucking with your ear all the time. You look stupid."

He sprung up, grabbed the candle along with his permission slip and moved to the kitchen. He wiped the paper off before returning to the living room with a rack of newspapers to clean the vomit.

"How did I get home, Jayden?" She laid back down, face up. "And why aren't ya'll at school? I don't want them people calling me about you fucking up again. If they do I'ma hurt you."

He sat the candle on the table. "We had a half day." He lied, sitting the permission slip next to the candle. "And that man who's house you were at drove you home in the back of his pickup truck. We sat back there with you." He paused his next statement because Harmony hated people in her business, even if she put them there. "And he helped us bring you in the house."

"You let somebody in my fucking house? I told you not to let nobody in here, Jayden!"

He refused to roll call the twenty men who'd already been in their home that week. It wouldn't matter anyway. Harmony was far from reasonable. "Ma, you wouldn't wake up. And we couldn't carry you. Madjesty and me tried, but you were too heavy. We needed his help."

"Humph, well, I'm surprised he bothered to do anything. He's a selfish bastard." She reached for the vodka bottle on the table, sat up and poured it into her mouth. Most humans needed oxygen, her slutty ass needed liquor.

"He was gonna shoot us until we told him you were our mother." He wiped up the muck as best he could from the floor, but the skanky smell still ruled the air. Since they didn't have any cleaning products, the scent would have to die with time. "But I think some boys raped you. I didn't want to do nothing until you got up but you want me to call the police?" Jayden walked into the kitchen and threw the soiled newspaper in the trash.

Harmony laughed at his statement. "I can't believe you actually that stupid." She looked at him as if he were a pathetic dog with two legs. "Ain't nobody rape me and don't go making up lies, Jayden." She drank more vodka. "People get killed for less."

He sat directly across from her in the chair. "So you let them do stuff to you?"

"What stuff you talking about, little boy?" She closed her eyes. "What you know about what happened to me? You wouldn't even know what to do with a pussy if one rubbed against your nose."

Yuck! Harmony was correct. Jayden knew nothing about a woman's body or what to do if he ever decided to sleep with a girl. He certainly didn't want their lady parts on his nostrils.

"Ma...I don't understand...you said he was mean. So why..."

She shook her head and interrupted his statement. "Jayden, it's a lot about life you don't understand." Her eyelids lowered again. "And I don't have enough time to teach you."

He looked at the dying candle. He thought about the milk and eggs in the refrigerator, which would be foul before long, since the electricity wasn't on. He thought about the dirty clothes piled mountain high in his room. He had so many questions but didn't know how to articulate them. If he was going to shoot the short version, he didn't understand how she could give her body to so many men, yet didn't have money for food or the bills. He reasoned if she was clean, she could get a job and all their problems would go away.

"Ma, I want you to get some help. Old Lady Cray down the street drank a lot but now she clean." Hope was heavy in his voice. "Maybe I can ask her how she did it and we can be happy and you can get a job and stuff like that."

"Jayden, don't be an idiot your whole life." She paused. "Old Lady Cray a dyke. If I gotta eat pussy to get better, I'd rather roll over twice with six dicks in my mouth."

"I didn't mean it like that. I want you to live, mommy. I want you to get better. So we can be together forever."

"My life...my life is so hard."

"I know, mommy but we love you. Very much."

"I don't deserve love! I deserve death."

"You don't. You deserve to live and be happy. With us!"

Jayden was relentless with his expression of love and then suddenly, something happened. He witnessed a tear materialize in the corner of Harmony's eye. After all this time, he finally got through to her. It wasn't until the water rolled down her cheek, leaving a slick trail in its wake that he was sure it was real. He wished Madjesty could be present to share the moment...he'd never believe him. His body trembled because it was a sign that Harmony's soul was somewhere in that decrepit body. It was a sign that she wanted to change and be free.

"You don't have to cry, mommy." He dropped to his knees. "I'll help you get better." He rubbed her bare leg and salty tears oozed into his mouth. "You just have to try. Maybe not drink so much. I love you."

Harmony sat up and stood over him. For a moment, silence stood between them. "But I don't love you. Never have. Never will."

Jayden's stomach felt as if he'd swallowed a bowling ball. He knew what was coming next. Boldly he proclaimed, "That doesn't change how I feel."

Jayden's love was too strong. Too much for her to bear. Why did he insist on making her feel? Why did he insist on caring about her? So she reacted the only way she knew how, with extreme violence. No longer feeling the hangover, Harmony rose and slapped him in the face. Possessed with the demons of the past, she slapped him again. Jayden went through this before, so he remained in his seat and turned the other cheek, until a closed fist struck his eye, causing blood to rush to the surface. On hands and knees now, he curled up into a ball while Harmony beat him unmercifully. She beat him for not being the son she always wanted. She beat him for living. She beat him for his unconditional love.

When she was tired she stood over top of him, breathing heavily. Sweat weighed on her eyelids and popped up on her nose in puddles. "You don't know shit about my life, Jayden!" Spit escaped her lips and sprinkled on his messy cornrows. "If love could've saved me, my father would be alive today! So don't tell me shit about love!"

When he was certain the abuse subsided he rose slowly and sat back in the chair. Trembling he asked carefully, "Mommy, if you really don't want to be here," soft sobs accompanied his words, "are you gonna make us watch you die?"

She thought his question strange but she went a different way. "Do you really love me?"

Jayden's words seemed to pour from his gut. "More than you know, mommy. More than you know."

Harmony wiped the tears from her eyes and leaned closer to him. "When I've made your world a living hell, where you don't want to see another day, express your love for me then. Maybe I'll believe you. Now get the fuck out of my face. I want to be left alone." Defeated, Jayden stood up and slogged toward the front door. He was almost there until she said, "And unless you can come up with some damn money, you not going to no field trip. Get the fuck out of my face."

Irritated, Jayden pulled open the door. When he did, Todd Craig, who belonged to a woman by marriage next door, was there. He would only visit on the days his wife worked at the soup kitchen or the nights she prayed at the church for their souls.

Holding a vodka bottle dressed in a brown paper bag, he said, "What happened to your face?"

Jayden was beyond angry. He was there to fuck his mother and all he brought was liquor. Nothing for her kids, ever. He was nothing like Mr. Nice Guy. "Why you worried about it? You don't care anyway."

He laughed. "You right, kid. Now where's your mother?" He looked past him. "I ain't got all day. I gotta talk to her about something."

Jayden wiped the tears off of his face and said, "I wonder what your wife would say, if I walked down the street to that church she be at and told her you were here." The man was frightened. "I bet she wouldn't like it at all...would she?"

He removed his yellow glasses and tucked one of the temples into the neck of his shirt. "What you just say to me, kid?"

Jayden's heart rate kicked up, but he was angry. He was hungry, dirty and tired of not having enough. Yet these men, the ones who crept into his apartment like roaches, had it all. They brought her bottles of liquor, kept her drunk and in the end stole her attention.

"You heard what I said. Let me go see how your wife feels with you being over here," Jayden walked around him when he was suddenly yanked by his braids and pulled back into the apartment.

NIGHTMARE ON EAST 40ᵀᴴ STREET
SOME NIGHTS LATER

Jayden hustled through the rain on the way to Mrs. Brookes house with a ball of gum that tasted like wax in his mouth. The drops dampened his hair and brought with it the smell of sour milk. The sky was lavender and the darkest part of night was threatening to greet him. He wanted to be as far away from the dangerous Houston streets before it happened. Usually Madjesty would walk with him but he was already at Mrs. Brookes, not wanting to spend more time than he had to at his house.

Since Madjesty took a liking to girls, they didn't share the same pleasures anymore. Madjesty preferred to hang with tough neighborhood kids who had cute sisters with big titties, while Jayden preferred to sit on the porch of his building, daydreaming about one day having the good life.

Jayden was almost at Mrs. Brookes when he saw a green Honda Accord stop abruptly a few feet in front of him. The smoke from the exhaust pipe pumped out a thick gray fog and the passenger door flung open. A short woman wearing a gold sequin dress flew out in a panic. Even under the darkening skies, the streetlights lit up her outfit as if she were performing on stage. Since an idle mind is the devil's workshop Jayden was drawn to her immediately.

A shorter man standing five-foot-five if he stood on the curb, grabbed the woman by the brown bun on top of her head and drug her a half a block. When he finally stopped, she fell face first and curled up in a fetal position like she was born again. A few pieces of her natural mane, which were snatched from the roots, grazed the streets before flying into the wind.

"Where's the money, Armanii?" he grabbed her hair so that her eyes were peering into his. "You been ducking and dodging me all day and I'm tired of fucking around with you."

"Daddy, its like I told you, I spent some of it. I" Her smile was as stiff as a dick. "I just needed a little hit because I wasn't feeling too well and you know how hard I work." She gripped at his pants leg and begged for *mercy. "Please, let me get my purse out the car and I'll give you all I got."*

"All you got already belongs to me, bitch."

The woman tried to rise but his brown dress shoe added weight to her chest keeping her where she belonged...down. "Daddy, today was rough and I didn't make much. But I promise, if you let me work on my day off tomorrow, I can make you the money plus double."

He simpered and pulled her to her feet; her ankles scraped the pavement, wiping some of her brown skin with it. "Armanii, I don't want to hurt you." He looked down at her legs. Blood traced from her thighs to her knees. "Look at what you made me do. Every time I see you beat up I feel pain. Why you make me do this?"

"Because I was wrong. I deserve it; daddy and I don't want you to suffer for my mistakes. That's why I work so hard for you."

"Glad to hear that because I'll be by to get my money tomorrow." He reached into the car, grabbed her black leather purse and slapped her across the face with it. A red gash ran across her upper lip giving her a bloody mustache. The sly smile he wore during the entire process would stay etched in Jayden's mind forever. "Don't fuck with me again, Armanii. I don't want to discover that you're worth more to me dead than alive." He jumped into his car and sped off.

"Short dick bastard!" Armanii said under her breath before wiping the blood off of her lip. When he was totally gone she really started feeling herself and flashed her ass cheeks before throwing a FUCK YOU sign in his direction.

Jayden didn't realize he was still gawking until she said, *"Now you know if somebody stares at me as hard as you, I usually charge them."* She picked up her purse, grabbed a cigarette pack and freed one along with a lighter. *"You gonna help a bitch out or what?"* She held out the lighter.

Jayden rushed toward her almost knocking her down in the process. She placed the cigarette between her pouty pink lips and waited. He did his best to activate the orange cream-colored lighter but it wasn't working. This was his first time. He was humiliated, until suddenly an orange flick glowed, showcasing her angel like face. Outside of the residue from an old blackened eye, and the fresh scar running across her lip, she was stunning. Like a movie star.

"Sorry to stare at you." He handed her the lighter. *"I just ain't never seen nobody as pretty as you before."* Harmony use to be the baddest but years of dick licking and bottle sucking had taken its toll on her features. So he was being honest.

She grinned, smoothed the tentacles of her bun, with the hand holding the cigarette. "Flattery these days will get you anywhere you want." She sighed. "I guess that's my problem." As if she remembered something she asked, "You got money?" She raised the edge of her dress slightly. "Wanna have a good time? I'll make that little dick of yours skeet in under ten seconds."

He shook his head so quick from left to right, that he got dizzy. "No! I...I don't want to do nothing like that."

Her eyes narrowed into tiny oval slits. "Well the way you looking at me, I know you want something. Spit it out, kid. What is it?"

Jayden was no match for this woman of the streets. She was cunning, charming and calculating. Armanii Rhoades sold her body to her brothers at the age of twelve and to anyone with five dollars up until her eighteenth birthday. Afterwards, she left her mother's tiny apartment and decided to take her show on the road as a free agent.

It took Carol Rhoades three days to realize her daughter was gone, and another three to alert her father who was doing life in federal prison for murder. Incarceration didn't stop him from reaching out on the streets to find his only child. He sent his best friend, Joseph Goss, a man who unbeknownst to him, had stumbled his way into the Pussy Game. The first bitch on his roster? His friend's only daughter and the rest was pimp game history.

Jayden walked slowly beside her, careful to keep his distance. "Are you hurt?" He popped the tasteless gum. "Your leg is bleeding a lot."

"Not more than my heart." She looked over at him. "So are you gonna walk a bitch to safety or what?"

Jayden knew if his mother sobered up and went to Mrs. Brookes' house, and he wasn't there, it could possibly spawn a series of events, which might result in his lips getting snatched off his face. But Armanii was mystical, and for some reason, he wanted to be around her. He nodded and replied, "Okay."

She looked him over, like something was off with him. Jayden figured it was his feminine mannerisms and he tried to add pep to his step but he could never master his swag like Madjesty. He compensated for his failures in other ways. Like by telling girls they were pretty, when they looked like circus monkeys. Or by opening doors to anyone with a purse, or a pair of high heels, even if they were rough around the edges and could lift small cars. He went overboard and because of it, he constantly felt fake.

"My apartment's in there." She pointed at a well-kept building. "All the way at the top. Where I keep most of my dreams." She took the dead

cigarette out of her mouth, and crushed it under her gold pump. She blew out her last puff and it smacked Jayden across the nose.

He rushed to open the door and when Armanii approached, limping, he offered his shoulder for support. They were about the same height so the deal worked out fine. Her wet armpit rubbed against his shoulder but he didn't care. As they walked up to the top floor, Jayden could not keep his eyes off of her.

That is until a man walked out of his apartment and into the hallway and said, "Little boy, you better not be caught up with that woman!" The top of his head shined like a marble and gray hair ran across the back of his head from ear to ear. "Her and her pimp are not nice people. Get away from here! Now!"

"Get the fuck in the house, Bert!" He quickly slammed the door leaving them alone. Jayden looked over at her. "Look, I'm not holding you hostage. If you want to listen to a crazy old man, that's on you. So are you coming with me or not?"

Jayden answered by walking with her to her apartment even though his stomach ached and he sensed danger. It wasn't until she opened the door, that he found a new source of amusement. The apartment was neat enough, with a large suede coach and matching ottoman in the middle of the floor. But it was the woman in the scantly clad jean shorts, which were close enough to her pussy to be panties, who stole his attention. She was stretched out on the couch, wiggling her fiery red toenails and eating butter pecan ice cream. The soles of her feet were as black as her eyes. She was singing with the TV until she saw Armanii's bloodied legs.

"Oh my, God, Sweet Licks!" She sat the ice cream down on the table. "Not again!"

"Don't call me by my street name when I'm home." The door closed behind them and Armanii plopped to the sofa. "I told you I don't like that shit. I don't know why you acting dumb."

"I'm sorry, Armanii." She rushed to the kitchen and returned with a damp paper towel. "Can I get you something? A cigarette? A hit?"

"We got company, Myter." She looked over at Jayden who was entranced. Her voice was soft and sweet so he tugged at his ear.

"Oh I didn't see him at first." She smiled at him. "He's one of your new clients?"

"He's a kid, Myter." She responded as if she didn't offer to suck him like a straw a few moments ago.

"And?"

"Please go sit down somewhere, you giving me a fucking headache."

Myter threw the paper towel on the table and stomped toward the back stopping short of her exit. "Maybe Joe wouldn't beat your ass so much if you knew how to talk to people, bitch. I'll be in the back in case you give a fuck." She disappeared into her room.

Armanii was enraged but she kept it together. She knew firsthand what she gave up to be with Joseph, only for him to abuse her and never love her in return. She certainly didn't need it from her sister who ate ice cream and played with her pussy all day long.

"Is she your roommate?"

"She's my sister. We're both what you may call ladies of the night." She paused and focused on Jayden's eye. "What happened to your face?"

"Same thing that happened to yours I guess." He said under his breath. "Somebody hit me in it." He decided not to tell her that his mother was an abusive-stank-hoe-drunk, with nothing else to do with her time but beat her kids.

"Come over here, and sit next to me." She placed her hand in the position she wanted him to occupy on the couch, and rubbed it softly. Jayden obeyed. "What are you doing out by yourself?"

"Not sure." He shrugged.

"You know the only thing out here this late at night, is pussy, dick and trouble. Which one you want?"

Jayden had so many questions running through his mind. He wanted to know what a lady of the night was. He wanted to know who she was. Needing to soothe his nervous ticks, he grabbed the damp towel and did his best to clean her wound. He had practice having nursed every bruise Harmony ever developed on her pathetic body, as well as a few of his own.

"How come you gave him your money? After he beat you?"

Armanii snatched the towel from his hand and tended to her own sores. "It's rude to ask a bitch about her paper. I see the sugar in your walk," she lashed out, "but if you ever want to have a chance at having a real woman, you'd better learn some manners, faggie!"

She was cold and quick, and Jayden was suddenly nervous. Maybe the old man in the hallway was right. He looked at the door, just to make sure it hadn't moved. Something about her energy said she was deadly but he was too bored to heed the warning. "I'm sorry. I didn't mean it like that."

"Yes you did and sorry ain't never enough." She threw the bloodied paper towel on the table. Nursing her wounds was useless. She would be back outside tomorrow night, on her knees again. "If you must know, he offers me stability."

"What's stability?"

"I don't have to worry about my lights going out, getting hurt by another man or not having a place to sleep or eat. As long as I have him, I'll always be taken care of. Kind of safe."

Jayden immediately wanted stability too. As a matter of fact, stability would be his new favorite word.

"So tell me about your life." Armanii continued. "Whatever it is you want to talk about is okay with me." She rubbed one of her feet. Her feet were callus and looked like white powder was spread over them.

"I'm thirteen years old, my mother doesn't love me and I don't know how to make her." He grew tired of chewing the gum, so he set it on top of the bloody paper towel on the table. "She loves her boyfriends more than me and my twin brother."

Armanii seemed to come to life with the news. "I'm sure that's not true." She stopped massaging her feet.

"It is. The other day I was in the hallway and she pulled me by my hair back into the house. Just cuz I threatened a man who was at the door to see her."

"You don't like the man?"

"Not really. My mother is sick and I want her to get better. He was over there to have sex with her and he never gives her nothing nice."

"Your idea of nice and your mother's may be two total different things." She smiled. "What does he bring?"

"Liquor and stuff."

"Not sure I agree with the way your mother runs her pussy business, but it's still her business."

"Pussy Business?" Jayden frowned and tilted his head.

"Yes, all girls have a pussy. Some profit from it by charging straight out and making a few dollars, some hold out in the hopes that they'll get married and others just like to fuck. Maybe the latter is your mother."

Jayden was missing the jewels she was dropping. All he cared about was the men trying to get her bottle sick. "But they don't care about her. They want to see her die. How come she let them do that?"

When Jayden looked at Armanii, for some reason she was crying. "Jayden, in order to get a bitch to do whatever you want, all you gotta do is get into her head." She returned to the question Jayden asked regarding why she gave Joseph her money when he assaulted her. "Your mother favors the liquor, some favor love."

"I don't understand."

Frustrated Armanii continued. "To capture a mind, find out what she wants and provide that for her. You'll have everything she owns, including her pussy and heart."

"What if a person wants more? Like money?"

Armanii saw the twinkle in his eyes. "You're straight to the point, I like that. Well, if you're really good, you can get all she has left, even her money. Make her dependent on you and you'll have her soul." Her words seemed heavy and when Jayden investigated her arms, he noticed raised holes in her flesh. Armanii was a world class heroin addict.

"But how do I do that? I mean, get their souls and stuff."

"You gotta observe people. Not by how they move but by what they try to hide. Nobody is ever really good at hiding their intentions, desires and dreams. People are needy. They need love. They need acceptance and they need to feel wanted. Observe more, talk less, and the rest is easy."

Jayden didn't know why he was so interested but he wanted more, although he wouldn't dare push. Instead he dropped to his knees and massaged her feet, hoping she'd offer more. They stank to high heaven, like boiled bologna, eggs and old cheese, but he was use to this level of wretchedness.

She looked down at him and grinned. "You catch on quick." She wiggled her toes. "I like you." She was thrown off at how good he was. His fingers were magic and she wondered what else he could do with them. "I also see something else in you, I just don't know what it is."

Stroking her toes he asked, "Can I come back over here?"

"Sure, kid. Why not?"

"When?"

Before she could reply, Myter came out of the back of the apartment with a loaded .45. "They back, Sweet Licks," she said disrespecting the request to call her by her name, "They pulling up in the parking lot right now."

Armanii jumped up and fear took over her disposition. "Jayden, you have to go. I'll get in contact with you when I can."

Selfishly he asked, "But how? You don't have my number. And when can I come back?"

Armanii hooked her hand under his pit and pulled him toward the door. When he didn't seem to be leaving on his own, she opened the door and pushed him in the back of the head sending him flying down the stairs. When he turned around the door was slammed in his face.

DIRTY JAYDEN

When Jayden woke up, the gum he kept in his mouth overnight was broken up and felt like rubbery strings all over his tongue. Madjesty didn't wake him up again and wasn't in the room. He was hungry, frustrated and lonely.

He eased out of bed and stood in front of the cracked mirror inside of his bedroom, with the best clothes in his wardrobe on the chair behind him. His life was dogged, yet he tried to make the best of it each day. It was hard being the butt of everyone's joke at school. It was difficult waking up hungry and without a meal. Jayden wasn't smart by a long shot, but if he learned nothing else, he grasped the fact that he never wanted to live life like this again. Then there was something else going on with him, something that he battled with everyday...his identity. A few of his features told him he was a boy but his body longed to be a girl. Why? He couldn't share his feelings with anybody because Harmony would crack the glass in his eye and Madjesty was so masculine, that the thought of being anything other than a boy was unfathomable to him.

He stared at his reflection. His cornrows were now transformed into a thick mane of untamed, curly hair which fell at his shoulders. He ran his fingers over his bare chest and could've sworn he felt two bulbs sprouting beneath his skin. When he squatted, he looked down at the hairy softness between his legs. Was his dick big enough if he were to have a girlfriend? He didn't think so. Although he was ignorant in the ways of the body, he wondered why he had to be a boy.

With time running out, he decided to get dressed and brush his hair into a smooth ponytail. In his opinion he resembled a girl more than ever now. What he wouldn't give to wear tight jeans like the girls at his school, or carry the latest designer purses. Instead he was resigned to filthy jeans that did nothing for his figure and swallowed up his hips.

School was in two hours, and although he didn't want to go, he didn't want to be home either. So many things were circling around in his head. He wondered if his new friend Armanii was okay and if Sandy was still interested in starting a bonfire in his hair.

When he looked out the window, he saw Madjesty in the front of the building, talking with his new friends. He always met people more easily *than Jayden, and he wondered how. They were twins so what made them so different? He tried to play ball and catch with them, but his limp wrist always ended up being the topic of discussion.*

Jayden was about to meet him outside, when he heard heavy pants within the house. He placed his blue book bag over his shoulders and eased toward the front of the apartment. On the way out, inches away from his mother's room, he heard a man's heavy moan. When he sniffed the air he could smell Dooway's cologne. It was the only time the house smelled fresh. He was his mother's ex-boyfriend's son yet they carried on like long lost lovers.

From the cracked doorway, Jayden observed the arch in his mother's back and the sheen left from the sweat on her skin. She illuminated. She moved her body like a wave, as Dooway pushed deeper into her mound from behind. Her plump round ass slapped against his dick filling the room with rhythmic sounds. He surveyed Harmony's moves and the look of admiration, which held Dooway's face. Nina Simone was a prolific lyricist and Di Vinci was a great artist, but Harmony Phillips was the ultimate lover. The ultimate seducer. A Siren.

As if Dooway couldn't get enough, he ran his tongue from her neck to the musty spot between her legs. Harmony pulled his head closer to her spot and maneuvered her waist like a belly dancer. The slurpy sound of her wet pussy and the lapping of his tongue filled the bedroom.

Jayden hated to admit but a familiar tingly sensation attacked the softness between his legs. Usually the feeling confused him, so he never explored it because it made him feel dirty. But now, with the stress of the day ahead of him, he reached into his pants and massaged his space. He wanted to feel good. Feel a little better.

After a few swipes between his legs from left to right, as he observed the scene through the cracked door, he was overcome with a feeling so sensual that he knew he would pleasure himself this way on a regular. He bit down on his bottom lip and worked himself harder before finally climaxing on his fingers. But when he came down, and the feeling was over, he was ashamed. He reached his first orgasm in the throws of his mother's love making session and that made him feel naughty.

When he dropped his head, he saw her yellow panties on the floor. They were balled up in a pile. Soiled. And in the middle of the doorway. With his foot, Jayden eased them into the hallway and stuffed them into his pocket. Walking backwards slowly, when he was further enough away, he dashed into his bedroom and closed the door.

Quickly he removed his jeans and dirty boxers. Naked from the waist down, he held the laced panties in his hand. His heart danced happily in his chest as he slid them onto his body. They looked so right against his skin. His dampness pushed against the seat of the underwear and he loved every minute. His fantasy came to a crashing halt when he heard footsteps moving in his direction. He didn't want his mother to find out that he was the one who'd been stealing her underwear all along, simply because he had a need to be feminine.

Quickly he removed them, opened the bottom drawer of his dresser and stuffed them into a white grocery bag filled with the rest of Harmony's panties that he'd stolen over the years. When he was done, he got dressed and went outside to meet his brother.

●━━━━━━━━━━━━━━━━━━━━━━━━━━━━━●

Jayden followed behind Madjesty and his friends on their way to school. In the past they would be heavy in conversation, talking about life and their mother's drunken bullshit. Now that he had them, it was as if he didn't need him anymore.

When they reached a crossroad, Madjesty turned and addressed his brother. "We 'bout to cut school and go to Mrs. Brookes' house." He paused and stuffed his hands into his pocket. "You rolling with us?"

"Why you not going to school?"

"Because I know enough." Madjesty said tugging on his cap. He was dumber than a doll but you couldn't tell him shit. "So you going or not?"

Jayden walked closer to him and whispered. "Can you walk with me instead?" He looked at his friends. "Alone? I kind of want to talk to you about some stuff."

A worried expression covered his face. "Is everything okay? Ma hit you again when you were upstairs?" He shook his head. "I told you to leave out the house when I do but you act like you never wanna go. Like you like being around that bitch."

"Naw, it ain't nothing like that."

"Well talk to me about it later then, unless you want to skip with us."

Jayden's head hung. "Naw, I'm cool. I guess I'll see you later." His heart ached and it was starting to feel like there was no one in the world in his corner. Madjesty went in the opposite direction, while Jayden went on to school.

When he trudged through the school's doors, he observed his project quietly from afar. She didn't know he was watching because she was involved in a heavy conversation with her friends. But once she was alone, he approached silently. He walked up behind her at the lockers. "Can I talk to you for a moment?"

She turned around and smiled until she saw who it was. "Ugh, what you doing in my face, boy?" Sandy yelled, smacking Jayden in the nose. The pain felt more like an itch and rushed to the middle of his forehead.

"You stole my money and now you got the nerve to say something to me? What the fuck is wrong with you?"

Jayden rubbed his face. "I wanted to say I'm sorry and that I think you're the prettiest girl in school." He backed away, keeping his eyes on her the entire time. "That's all." Embarrassed he turned and walked away.

"Jayden," she yelled, stopping his motions, "I don't know what the fuck is up with you, but we not friends. Don't walk up to me like that again at school. If you do, I'ma get my brother to fight you. He's a Blood." She slammed her locker closed. "Remember that shit."

●━━━━━━━━━━━━━━━━━━━━━━━━━━━━━━━━━━━━●

Everyday after their encounter, Jayden would approach her at the same place anyway. Even though she would reject him, over time, her responses were less violent. Besides, Jayden was a cute boy with smooth hair and wild eyes, even if he didn't wear designer clothes. Sandy started to secretly look forward to his attention as long as her friends didn't see her with him. Not only was he a looker, he was bold and that alone was a turn on. It was obvious that he was determined to win her over whether she wanted him to or not. On the fourth day, which happened to be a Friday, Jayden saw Sandy fussing at her boyfriend in the hallway.

"Why you do that, Derrick?" She sobbed, her nose as red as a hickey. "Everybody saw you two together! You made me look so stupid."

He frowned. "What the fuck are you talking about, baby? It wasn't even that deep. We were just playing."

"You let the bitch sit in your lap! In the cafeteria! I even saw you kiss her on the neck."

Derrick tried to grip her by her Louis Vuitton belt, to pull her toward him but she slapped his hand away. "You making it out to be more than what it is. She's a cheerleader so we was just playing, Sandy. That's all." He paused, "Ain't nobody trying to fuck with that fat bitch like that."

"But she's my friend."

Derrick wanted this episode over. Sandy wasn't giving up the pussy anyway but her friend was. Suddenly Derrick grew angry and he clenched his fist. Instead of hitting her with it, he came down on her face with his forearm, banging the locker beside her with his other fist. "Bitch, I'm not trying to hear this shit. Fuck you, it's over anyway!" he stormed away.

For a second Sandy stood stunned in the hallway rubbing her face. It was obvious that she was waiting for him to come back and apologize, it never happened. Humiliated, she stormed into the restrooms and Jayden patiently waited.

When she came out, Jayden was still there. He approached her cautiously. *"He's a loser. I saw the whole thing from over there."* He pointed where he stood, as if she gave a fuck.

For the first time ever she smiled at him. *"What do you want from me, Jay? You could never be with somebody like me."* Sandy observed his second-hand gear. *"I mean look at you, you don't even know how to dress."*

"Close your eyes."

She frowned. *"Boy, why?"*

"Just close 'em for me."

She looked around and when she didn't see anyone looking, she shut her lids. *"Now what?"* She crossed her arms over her chest.

"Imagine me in whatever you want."

She grinned. *"Okay now what?"*

He raised his arms. *"Open your eyes?"* She did. *"How I look now?"*

She smirked and shook her head. *"You don't even want to know how I think you look."* She strolled away and Jayden rushed to open the door for her.

"Can I hold your book bag for you?"

"Whatever." She threw it into his arms and he caught it.

"Anyway I just want to be your friend, Sandy." He tried to stiffen his steps by not moving so freely at the hips. *"Everybody needs friends."*

"I have enough friends."

"Not as cute as me."

Sandy smiled again. *"I wish you just leave me alone. I mean don't you have something else better to do? Somebody else to bother?"*

"I'll leave after I ask you this one question. You going to the field trip?"

"Yeah." She wiped a few tears away that crept up on her face. She was thinking about the forearm abuser again. She sure did love the bum. *"You?"*

"Yeah. I turned my field trip slip in today." He didn't need to tell her he forged his mother's signature, or that he didn't have the money. He came up with a plan. *"Maybe we can see each other there or something."*

"I can't hang out with you. My friends would laugh at me."

"Why?"

"Because we not in the same league." Jayden shook his head and smirked. *"What's so funny?"* She asked.

"At first I thought you had your own mind. Guess I was wrong." They approached the public bus stop. She sat on the bench and he sat on the bench's back.

"I know what you trying to do, Jayden, by being nice to me." She snatched her book bag away from him. "I'm not that stupid. I won't let you finger fuck me so you can tell everybody at school."

Jayden's stomach juices swirled due to the implication. He wasn't interested in doing what she was talking about. In fact, he didn't know what finger fucking was. "Look, you let a nigga talk to you like he crazy, hit you in the face with his arm and then you blame me for being nice? What's wrong with you?"

"So what he accidently hit me. You stay coming to school with bruises on your face. You don't hear me saying nothing about that."

Part of him was embarrassed and the other part didn't know she noticed. Her comment had him wanting to hurt her but he remained quiet until the anger went away. "Okay, I won't give you another compliment maybe you deserve somebody like him."

Jayden got up to walk toward his house when she yelled. "You wanna go grab something to eat? Maybe get a sandwich? With me?"

Before turning to face her, he smiled slyly like he saw Joseph do when he took Armanii's money on the street. "Cool with me."

●━━━━━━━━━━━━━━━━━━━━━━━━━━━━━━━●

The air conditioning felt good against Jayden's skin as they sat in a booth inside IHOP (International House of Pancakes). "So you got a girlfriend?" Sandy bit into her cheeseburger and wiped the corners of her lips with the paper napkin. "I know you do." She eyed his cute face. "I mean somebody gotta like you at school."

Jayden placed his arm behind her neck and rested it on the chair like he saw the man across the way do. "A lot of girls like me but I don't like everybody."

Something in Sandy's eyes told Jayden she was relieved. "Is it true what they say? That you might be gay?"

Jayden shifted in his seat. "If I was, would I be here with you?"

"I thought you said you wanted to be friends."

"Yeah, but I still like my friends pretty."

She smiled again. "Can I ask you something else?"

Jayden plopped a fry into his mouth, it was the best food he had all week. "Go 'head."

"Why did you try to steal my money?"

He coughed up a bit of fry and wiped it off the table. He knew this question would come up sooner or later, so he prepared for it. "Your favorite color is purple. You wear it on Thursdays because you and your boyfriend have the same class. You always look so pretty in it, but he never notices. On Tuesday you wear yellow because it matches his uniform on the day he has football practice, but he never notices that either."

She seemed irritated and plucked out a few of her lashes. "Are you gonna get to the point already?" She blew them away.

"I took the money because I saw this and I wanted you to have it." He went into his pocket and handed her a picture of a purple and yellow Shamballa bracelet that he clipped from an ad. "I know it's a sucker move because the money was yours, but I was gonna pay you back for it later. And I didn't have none on me at the time." A smarter girl would have laughed him out of America.

She looked at the picture of the bracelet and smiled. "You were gonna get this for me? For real?"

"I wouldn't lie. I really wanted you to have it." He looked into her eyes and was certain she was getting weak. "If I had the money and you were my girl, I would do more for you. The bracelet was just to make you smile." He sipped his coke and rested his case as if he already bought the gift. "Anyway, I'm gonna get a job next month. The store down the street from my house said they would hire me, if I get a work permit."

She smiled wider. "So you do want to be with me? Like more than just friends?"

"No. I want to only be your friend. I told you that." Sandy looked insulted and confused. "Don't take it that way, I didn't mean to hurt your feelings or nothing. I'm just into older women."

She glowered. "Why?"

"I like stability," he said throwing his new favorite word around, "and older chicks believe in taking care of their boyfriends too. Young girls don't want the same things. They take more than they give. I want somebody who will hold me down when the time gets rough like I would them. You know?"

"I guess." She shrugged. "I don't know how I would feel about that though."

"I understand why...look at your boyfriend. He does stuff for you but then he feels like he can talk to you any kind of way. Kiss your friends in front of you and all that. I would never be so mean. If you had your own shit to bring into the relationship, then he would have to respect you." He paused eating the last of his meal. "Look, you go 'head home, I'm gonna pay for the food."

"How?" She looked confused. "You don't have no money right?"

He sure didn't. "I got some today. I'll meet up with you later...cool?"

Sandy sluggishly eased out of her seat. Her steps were slow before stopping all together. As if she remembered something, she turned around, dug into her purse and pulled out twenty dollars. "This one is on me, Jaydèn. You get next."

Mission accomplished Jayden grinned and said, "That's a bet."

● ━━ ●

Confident he finally understood girls, Jayden knocked on Mrs. Brookes' door eager to tell his brother about his ventures. He had taken advice from Armanii and it finally paid off. Nothing could make his day better, than sharing the news with his twin.

When Lakisha Brookes finally appeared, a smile dressed in ruby lipstick spread across her face, as she scanned over him with judgmental eyes. Although Mrs. Brookes favored the barbershops by sporting a low cut, her beauty could not be masculinized. Her smooth brown skin, and natural lengthy eyelashes, softened her features. Her face wasn't the only thing that captivated upon first sight; her curves went on for days.

"Hi, Mrs. Brookes," he stuffed his hands into his pocket like he did the first twenty times on the way over her house, to be sure his money was in place, "my twin here?"

"You know that brother of yours practically lives here. Come on in, baby."

Jayden and Madjesty had been coming to her house for the past few months, ever since Harmony realized she would feed them and keep them out of her way leaving her with plenty of time to fuck. She was for anything which left more money to buy booze in her pockets too. By the time they'd get home, they would be ready for bed and that worked just fine for a mother who hated her children anyway. There was one problem, some homes shouldn't be allowed to entertain children, and Mrs. Brookes' house was such a place. It was a perverse heaven where kids could act out everything they imagined and pick up a few habits their young minds should never know. Out of all of the surprises she had in store for underage striplings, there was no sneakier treat than her ten-year old niece, No-Boo-No.

Mrs. Brookes backed up so he could enter her bungalow and Jayden caught a whiff of her home. Her house always smelled of hot meals, fresh baked bread and sweet incense.

"Madjesty, your brother's here!" Mrs. Brookes called into the house. "You can go sit in the living room with No-Boo-No and your brother. Promise is with his father so he ain't home right now. I gotta finish up dinner for you guys." Mrs. Brookes strutted toward the kitchen.

Jayden's heart was always filled with jealousy when he saw the furnishings and observed the way she cared for her home. Harmony needed to take notes but he knew she'd never be interested. This was the life Jayden wanted, full of stability and promise.

When he bent the corner he saw Madjesty spread out on the sofa, flipping the channels on the large screen TV. No-Boo-No, who was given the nickname because she broke all rules, was sitting on the cream carpet, legs agape, as she played with the contents of her brown purse between her legs. For a thirteen year old she was too grown and there was nothing anybody could do to change it. The damage done to her mind was stuck like titties to a woman and her raunchy life would simply have to play out with time.

"What you looking at, retard?" No-Boo-No teased Jayden, as she sprayed an adult scented perfume over her chunky brown arms and legs. "I ain't the TV you know."

Jayden trudged further into the living room, bringing his musky scent with him. She pinched her nose.

"Why don't you Phillip boys ever wash your clothes?" She sprayed more of the cheap scent in his direction, making the space suffocating.

"Why don't you suck my dick?" Madjesty interjected, never breaking his stare off of the television. "We here to see your cousin not you, bitch."

No-Boo-No blew a kiss in his direction to be irritating. "So let me get this straight, you talk to me when your brother gets here but when I wanted you to play in this pussy earlier," she opened her legs, revealing her cotton white panties with the yellow piss stain in the seat, "you acted like you were scared." She laughed and her chubby jaws bounced.

"Why I want to play in that funk box?"

Her face reddened and she felt degraded. "I asked around about you, Madjesty," she looked at Jayden, "and your brother, and I can't find nobody who you been with. Why is that?"

Madjesty was growing furious. In front of his brother he faked like the man and now his cover was being blown. "I keep telling you, you don't know shit about me."

She was getting to him and decided to hit home. "Yes I do, Madjesty. I hear when you're offered up, you fake out. What you scared of girls or something?"

Madjesty's secret came crashing out and Jayden found it hard to look at his twin. Outside of kissing a girl or two on the cheeks, truth was he was horrified about going to the next level. "Like I said, you don't know nothing 'bout me."

"Oh I don't?" She put her hand on her hip. "Then prove it, walk with me in the bathroom right now and let me see that dick of yours. I'll give you a treat you never had before. Ask my cousin Promise how I roll." She licked her lips and crawled toward him.

He took his foot and kicked her in the shoulder, forcing her backwards. She rolled over and hit her head on the edge of the glass table. "Ouch!" She rubbed her fresh knot.

"Man, shut the fuck up. I wouldn't fuck with your ass if you begged me."

She sat up and rubbed her head. "I'ma tell my auntie you just kicked me. And she not gonna let you or your brother come over here anymore."

Madjesty dropped the remote and sprung up. In seconds flat, he was over the top of her head like mistletoe. "Bitch, you can tell her whatever you want. I don't give a fuck! But if she put me out, I'ma come up to your school and wait for you out front. And when I catch you, I'ma break every bone in your face before I move to your arms."

She stood up, wrapped her arms around him and said, "Stop being mean, Madjesty. You know I like you. I wouldn't tell my auntie you kicked me, if I do how else will I see you?"

"Well you shouldn't have said it then." He pushed her off of him.

"At first I was talking to your brother until you jumped in. You shoulda let him take up for himself."

"Well he's my twin, so if you talking to him, you talking to me too."

Jayden heard enough of her pathetic plea. "Madjesty! I don't wanna go home right now. Just leave her alone. Plus I gotta tell you something." He put his hand on his brother's back and led him into the foyer. When they were alone, he reached into his pocket and pulled out the money. "Look what I got."

Madjesty couldn't believe he was holding. In a heavy whisper he said, "Wait, how you get that shit?"

"Sandy gave it to me." He left out the part where he took the money from the table that was used to pay the check, leaving the bill unpaid.

He frowned. "You talking about Sandy Reynolds?" He didn't know his brother to be a liar but for some reason he didn't believe him. "Why she do that? Not too long ago you told me she was mad cuz you asked for her friend's number."

Jayden's lie felt stupid coming out of his twin's mouth. "Because she like me I guess." He shrugged. "I told you that in the hallway."

"Yeah right. Bitches like me too and ain't none of them ever gave me money before."

"Maybe you didn't ask."

Madjesty never thought about it that way. They were just about to go back into the living room when there was a knock at the door. "One of ya'll get that for me." Mrs. Brookes called out from the kitchen, wiping her hands on an apron.

When Jayden opened the door, he saw Harmony standing on the other side with a look of displeasure on her face. He could've dealt with that, but the person she was with made Jayden want to shit on himself. "Ya'll get your stuff right now! It's time to go!"

FAIR EXCHANGE IS NO ROBBERY

Jayden's limp body sat on the edge of a chair, across from Sandy and her father who were sitting on the sofa. His right foot moved rapidly and wouldn't stop no matter how he tried. The sound of dripping water in the kitchen sink, banged against a dirty pot that had been there for weeks. He could bet money that his mother would be doing something any minute to embarrass the hell out of him. The only bright side was that the lights were now on. Literally.

"Like I said, I wasn't there, but if my son says she gave it to him, how you know it didn't happen?" Harmony asked looking at them both. The blue dress she wore was more presentable than her usual tasteless selections, but still revealed a smidgen of her brown areolas.

"I know because when my daughter came home she was in tears." He said, stealing a look at her breasts. He was disgusted. "She would never do something like that. As a matter of fact, this young man was the same one who tried to steal money out of her purse some time back. Did he tell you that?" He caressed his daughter's knee. Harmony and Jayden thought that was weird.

"Get to your point." Harmony responded.

"I guess he finally got away with it. Sandy had just enough money for lunch for the week...nothing more. My wife has a debilitating disease and we can't afford to give her twenty dollars to be giving to her friends." Both Jayden and Harmony eyed the Louis Vuitton belt on her jeans and wondered how much of that was true.

Jayden didn't like him but he wondered how it felt to have a father, something he always wanted.

"Your sick wife is not my problem and neither is your lying daughter." He looked at the way his hand rested on her knee. "And judging by the belt on her jeans and the way you're rubbing her leg, I guess she's able to come up with the money to trick on my son somehow."

He removed is hand. "What are you trying to imply?"

"What you already know."

"Ms. Phillips!" Mr. Reynolds yelled, playing with the hair on the back of his right hand. He twisted a few strands, before moving to the next group. It was as if he was trying to hold himself back from some-

thing. *"You are being rude and unreasonable. Now I'm sorry to say this but unless you can give me another reason, I'm going to be forced to call the authorities."* He looked at Jayden. *"Now what do you have to say for yourself, young man?"*

Jayden remained silent. This was ridiculous. He slicked her out of her money straight up so why was Sandy lying? Instead of answering, he stared at his shoes and then his hands. *"She gave me the money, sir."* He looked into his eyes. *"That's all I can tell you."*

"Well where is it now?" he asked, his voice shaky and unsure. Age looked horrible on him.

"I don't have it. She bought me food with it."

"Where?"

When Jayden didn't respond, Harmony slapped him in the back of the head, forcing his forehead frontwards. When his head rose, the first person he looked at was Sandy. She was nothing but a pretty faced liar. He looked at the belt again and wondered how much boys would pay to fuck or kiss her.

"Where did you go to eat?"

Jayden didn't feel like talking to him anymore and he could feel the money burning a hole in his pocket. But it belonged to him, and he didn't want to give it back. As far as Sandy knew, it went to the waitress at IHOP.

"Where did you go eat, Jayden? I want this mothafucka outta my house."

Although Mr. Reynolds was seated, he stomped the floor with his cane sending out a loud thud throughout the rundown apartment. *"Miss, you will not talk like that around my daughter."* He looked around. *"We do not come from this type of environment and I won't subject her to your foul language."*

"And you will not come over here and disrespect my son! Since Jayden was born he never lied to me! Ever! Now if he says your daughter gave him the money and they spent it on food, then that's what the fuck happened. Now unless you have something else to talk about, get the fuck out of my house." She pointed at the door.

"Please don't talk to my daddy like that." Sandy said under her breath. *"He's old."*

"Little girl, you ought to be glad I even opened the door for you and your dried up father to begin with. Unlike him, I knew you were a liar the moment I laid eyes on you."

"What kind of mother are you?" Mr. Reynolds growled. He observed the surroundings again. Dishes littered the sink and dust particles were visible on every area of the hardwood floors. The smell of unwashed

clothing and the filthy toilet made matters worse. "You don't even take care of your home and I can smell the liquor from your skin from over here. And I'll bet you there isn't a man with morals alive who would lay with you."

Jayden felt the temperature in his body rise, but remained silent. His mother was a mess but she was his mess.

"You right about that. I don't do men with morals." Harmony grinned. "I'm a drunk, Mr. Reynolds. I barely want to get up most days but how else am I gonna get my next drink?" She looked around her pathetic dwellings. "I don't clean my home and I haven't disciplined my children to be regular enough to help me out around here." She looked at Jayden and there was something loving behind her eyes. Something real. "But my son is good. And he has a pure heart." She ran to the bedroom and came back out with nineteen loose dollar bills and four quarters. "There's your money. If it will make you feel better about your daughter being dumb enough to be used, so be it. Right now all I want you to do is get the fuck out of my house." She placed her hands on Jayden's shoulder. And the pride he felt for his mother at that moment was indescribable.

Although the old man was withered, he leaped up with the finesse of an Olympic high jumper as he snatched the coins and money from Harmony's grasp. With the handle of his cane firmly in his hand he said, "I want your son to stay away from my daughter." They both moved toward the doorway.

"If I find my son anywhere near that little bitch of yours, I will kill him myself!"

When they were gone, Jayden and Harmony bathed in silence. He remained seated. She remained standing behind him. After a few more seconds, she sat on the sofa and observed him.

"You don't have to tell me she's lying on you. I already know." She twisted the cap off of a fresh vodka bottle. Where had it come from?

He shifted in his seat. "How did you know?"

"Her eyes wouldn't stay still." She swallowed the contents she poured into the top of a mouthwash bottle, because all of the cups were broken. "You tried to run game," she pointed at him, "and I get that. You forgot one thing though, if you gonna run game, you betta know what the fuck you're playing." She laughed at him. "I keep telling you you're not smart enough, you'll never be. You will always be the kind of person who has to be told what to do and think."

Jayden swallowed. His throat felt pasted together.

"When I was a girl, I was the baddest bitch alive." Harmony smiled as she stared into the grimness of the living room. "Niggas use to give *their whole lives, just to be with me," she licked her arm, "just to taste me. Nothing was off limits." She looked into his eyes. "And that included their money. I never had a problem with having cash in my pockets. Ever." She grinned remembering her patented fuck technique. "In all the games I ran nobody ever came to my grandmother's house saying I took anything from them. You know why?"*

"N-No." He stuttered.

"Because I perfected my craft. Fair exchange is not robbery. The threat of me not fucking with them, not giving them any of this good pussy, was greater than the loss of their money." She poured the vodka into her mouth. Fuck a cup. "I was a genius and master manipulator. You have to be when dealing with other peoples money."

Jayden could feel a prickly sensation cross over his skin. The next question was hard but he wanted an answer all the same. If she had so much money, why was their cupboard bare? Why were the lights always getting cut off and why did he and his brother wear holey clothing to school? "Mama, what happened?"

"I showed one man my heart and he was the only man I've ever loved. The only man I will ever love." Tears poured down her face and she swatted them away like flies. "I made a decision to stop running game and to be with him exclusively. But it was too late for my mind. I'd done too much dirt and sex was just in my bones. I had to have it all the time even if it wasn't with him. In the end I'd done so much, that he wasn't able to recognize me anymore.

"When he left me all I wanted was more sex and money became unimportant. I had to fuck in the day and fuck at night. Some people ate breakfast but I sucked dick." Jayden's skin crawled. "These days I be so caught up, I forget to ask for money." Another swish of vodka made her pain easier to swallow. "Now it don't matter to me anymore." She looked around her run down apartment. "Nothing matters to me anymore." Her eyes zeroed in on him. "Not even you."

The old Harmony had returned.

The sorrowful look on her face was replaced with rage. She sat back in the sofa and crossed her legs. "Jayden, put my money on the table before I break your neck."

"But I don't have it. We used it at IHOP."

"Sandy wasn't the only one I was observing, little boy. Although you didn't take that girl's money, you had something to do with its disappearance. I don't care how or why. I do know that if you don't put my money on the table in fifteen seconds, I'm gonna get up." She laughed. "You could never be smarter than me, Jayden. Ever."

In a quiet whisper he asked, "What about the field trip? You said if I could get the money I could go."

"Fuck the field trip."

Jayden stood up, walked over to the table and released the money. It floated down like a polluted snowdrop.

"Now get the fuck out. I want to be left alone."

Jayden dawdled toward the door. Head low. Heart heavy. Mind confused. He placed his hand on the doorknob and noticed he could still smell Sandy and her father's fresh scent in the air. "Thank you for what you did for me." He turned around and looked at her. "I'll never forget it."

"Not sure if that's a good or bad thing, Jayden. Just leave me alone. Contrary to what you believe, all misery don't like company."

●━━━━━━━━━━━━━━━━━━━━━━━━━━━━━━━━━━━━━●

Heavy music poured into the hallway of the building and rolled down the stairwell. The closer he got to Armanii's door, the louder the music rose. He'd been trying to reach her ever since she put him out and he hoped she was okay. At first he knocked in a mousy fashion and received no results. With an ounce of confidence, he knocked harder and this time Armanii flung the door open and smiled at him.

"Hi, Armanii." He waved and stuffed his hands back into his pockets. "I was coming to see if you were okay."

She hugged him tightly, with a cigarette in her hand. A stump of grey ashes fell into his hair. She wiped it away too roughly. "And if I wasn't? You gonna kill for me?"

His eyes widened. "No…I…was just…"

"I'm just playing!" She hugged him again. "Oh, Jayden, I was just thinking about you. I ain't seen you since…well…since them niggas tried to kill me." She seemed high. Real high.

"Why they wanna do that?"

She released him. "Because they said I stole fifty thousand dollars from them or some shit like that. When I was fucking one of them," She wiped the corner of her mouth. "But they gotta prove it first. Besides do I look like a girl who would do such a thing?" She spun around so he could see her body. Although she was less flashy with her red off the shoulder jumpsuit, she still looked slutty and pretty.

"How you get away? When I left they were in the parking lot."

"You ask so many questions," she opened the door wider, "but since I'm feeling good, come on in and I'll answer whatever you want to know."

When his foot crossed the threshold, he wanted to turn around when he saw Joseph sitting on the recliner. But since he didn't seem to be interested in him, he walked further inside. Joseph was packing a blunt with a pile of weed that lit up the apartment before he even fired it up.

Armanii turned the music off, plopped on the sofa and crossed her legs. "Sit right here." She massaged a place on the sofa. "Next to me."

Jayden traipsed into the apartment and sat next to her. He could feel her warm skin against his leg. "Joseph, this is my friend Jayden." She rubbed his back, "And Jayden, this is Joseph."

Jayden waved but Joseph didn't acknowledge him.

Jayden cleared his throat and asked, "So you gonna tell me how you got away, Armanii? From those guys?"

"You don't forget a thing do you?" She giggled. "That trait will come in handy later." She exhaled. "Well, as it turns out, the police was doing some kind of sting operation in the building that night. They raided five apartments that were involved in some drug operation. So, the niggas after me thought they were coming for them and rolled out. I haven't seen 'em since. I know it ain't over yet though, I'll see 'em again." She seemed scared.

He frowned and moved away from her. Armanii's leg was too close to his and crept him out. "Are you worried they might come back?"

"Don't have time for worrying when I have to live." She smashed the cigarette into the ashtray.

"And money to make." Joseph added, never looking at them.

Jayden examined Joseph again from the sidelines. He didn't seem as smooth as Pimp Fast Tony, his idol from Galveston. He seemed like a junky trying to make a come up, something he was familiar with considering his mother was one.

"So, kid, Armanii tells me you're interested in 'The Game'." He still hadn't given him eye contact. Even with his blunt completed, he just rolled it around the table. "You shouldn't ask a whore those types of questions though, she only knows what she's supposed to. What a pimp teaches her."

Jayden looked at Armanii thinking she'd be upset but instead she was smiling. He just disrespected her and she was grinning like a clown.

"Well, what should I know about The Game?" Jayden inquired.

"First you gotta know what it is. Some bitches like your friend over there, love dick. So even if she wasn't whoring and selling her funky pussy, she'd be fucking somebody, probably for free. You see in order for The Game to work, bitches gotta love what they do. They gotta love sex more than they love food. That's what keeps them out there on the cold and hot nights."

"But Armanii said you gotta get into they mind first."

"Didn't I just finish telling you not to listen to no bitch?" Joseph looked at him angrily and Jayden shivered. "To answer your question, the mind shit is bullshit. You get their mind by helping them do what they want. All whores I know on the stroll, love dick. I don't care what they say." He looked at Armanii. "That's why they so good at it." He talked mad shit for a man who only had one prostitute.

"I thought it was about the money too." Jayden combatted.

"It's about the money to businessmen like myself, but not to whores. Ask that bitch how much money she got to her name."

In a low whisper he asked, "How much money do you have?"

She smiled although her eyes said she was hurting. "None."

"Zactly. Bitches don't see the money. It comes to managers like myself. I had to check her the other night when she tried me by not handing it over. We make sure they have all they need. If you gave them paper anytime they wanted, they'd probably kill themselves." He shook his head. He was so full of himself. In all other areas of his life he was a loser. "No, the benefit for them to be in the game is the dick, that's what keeps them coming back for more." He balled up a fist. "And if they forget who's boss, you gotta make them remember."

He was a fraud, and Jayden didn't like him. He recalled the days he would look out of his window when they lived in Galveston Texas. Most of his time was spent observing Pimp Fast Tony. He remembered the women wiping the sweat off of his face, just so perspiration wouldn't drop on his suit. He never seen him strike them. They loved him. They needed him. And in his opinion, that was power.

"Oh, I see." Jayden lied. "But if they love the…d-dick so much," he stuttered, "why you gotta hit them? Shouldn't they do what you want just cuz you say it? Just cuz they love it?"

Joseph was irate. So mad, that the blunt he just rolled crushed under his fingertips. The young man called his pimp game out and he was insulted.

"Jayden, come with me in the bedroom." Armanii said, analyzing the hostile vibe in the room. "I got a TV in there."

To get out of Joseph's wrath, Jayden gladly followed her. Once inside, Armanii's room was just as imagined. Pretty red curtains hung from the windows and matched the red comforter on her bed. "Sit on my bed, but you gotta take your pants off first."

He frowned. "I don't wanna do nothing with you." Jayden said seriously. "I just wanna watch TV."

"Honey, you don't have to worry about me touching you, I'm always on the clock and anything I do to you is gonna cost." She laughed at her own joke. "So believe me when I say you can't afford me. Now take off your pants or get out of my house." She turned the TV on.

Jayden took off his pants and awkwardly sat on the edge of her bed in his boxers. Armanii eased out of her clothes and slid into a pink nightgown. Then she flipped back two burgundy sheets on her bed, before sliding into the pocket. When she was comfortable she raised an edge and said, "Get in with me."

Jayden got under the covers, lie sideways and rested his head on the fluffy pillow. He observed the wall, which held a picture of a baby in a gold frame. "That's your child?" He pointed.

Armanii came behind him and pressed her body against his. When they were close, she placed her face gently on top of his and looked at the picture with him. "You shouldn't be here, Jayden. I really want you to go." A tear fell out of her eye and wet his nose.

"But I don't want to leave." He pleaded and wiped it away. "I like it here."

"I know." She hugged him tighter. "And I like you here with me but it isn't safe. My home is no place for kids."

"Why?"

"He was taken from me, by an evil person. An evil person who still lives."

"Sweet Licks, why you lock the door?" Joseph banged jiggling the gold knob left and right. "Bitch, you crazy or something?"

Jayden jumped and pulled the sheet under his chin while Armanii got up to answer the door. When Joseph entered he asked, "So you having sex with my woman, Jayden? I invite you into my home, teach you the game and this is how you repay me?"

Jayden shook his head no.

"Then why are you in her bed?" Jayden hopped out of it and tried to leave the room. "No, you don't. You stay right there because now you owe me. Anybody who sleeps with one of my bitches has to pay."

"I just want to go home."

"Too late for that, son. Sit on the edge of the bed." When Jayden was there, Joseph undid his pants. "Come here."

"Please, I don't want to come. I just wanna go home!"

"Do what the fuck I say."

Jayden looked at Armanii for help but she looked at the floor in shame. Help wasn't coming any time soon. "You should not have come here, Jayden." Armanii cried to herself. "Now it's too late."

Joseph fished for his penis and when he finally pulled it out, Jayden was confused. If he was a man and he looked like that with no clothes on, why didn't he look the same when he was a boy? Something wasn't right.

Since Harmony didn't bother to teach her sons about the human anatomy they were totally ignorant on the subject. And with Madjesty constantly rambling about how somebody could suck his dick, Jayden figured maybe he hadn't gotten his yet. After all, he was still a child.

"Open your mouth, boy. I ain't got all day."

"Please, I don't want to do this. I just want to go home."

The mad man looked down at him. "Don't make me tell you again."

In fear for his life, Jayden quickly followed orders. At first he placed the helmet on the tip of Jayden's tongue before easing the entire thing into his mouth. Jayden squinted from the taste of salt and his jaw tired. To make matters worse, Joseph kept pushing it deeper into his throat and he would smack him every time he gagged. Before long, Jayden knew exactly what he needed to do, to make him happy. Exactly what he needed to do to survive.

"Just like that." Joseph encouraged, looking down at him. "You doing real good."

He kept Jayden in the house for three days, forcing him to perform oral sex on him almost every hour. On the first day he knew his mother would come looking for him. On the second day he was certain it would be in any minute. On the third day he understood that once again, she'd abandoned him. Madjesty was right she let him down.

Jayden was unaware that Armanii and Joseph ran this type of thing all the time on young boys. That's why she was happy when she saw him at the front door because it meant they didn't have to go any further that night. Joseph loved oral sex from young boys and would have murdered him and dumped his body like he did the others but Armanii remembered one thing Jayden said that saved his life. And that was that his mother didn't care about him. So getting caught was highly unlikely.

One day while Armanii and Joseph were still in the bed with Jayden next to him he said, "Get up, kid and go home." Just like that he released him and both of them went back to sleep.

Jayden eased out of bed and closed the door with hate in his heart. Who was he now that he was made to do something so atrocious? He put his jeans on, went into the kitchen and grabbed a fresh paper towel. Then he turned the stove on and lit the edge. The orange glow was so bright and the warmth of the fire close to his face gave him pleasure. He threw it on the sofa and watched it go up in flames. He didn't leave until it was engulfed and the smell of smoke was suffocating. When he was done, he left the apartment. He ran to the building down from Armanii's and walked into the basement. From the window, he could see the smoke *streaming from their apartment. He placed his fingers into his pants and rubbed his space, while examining the damage he caused. It got him beyond horny. When he reached and orgasm, he walked home to deal with life. Revenge turned him on. Within an hour, Armanii and Joseph would both be dead.*

━━━━━━━━━━━━━━━━━━━━━━━━━

By the time he reached his own house, Harmony was on the couch passed out and his brother was nowhere to be found. Slowly he approached the front of the sofa where two empty bottles of vodka sat next to a half full one on the floor. The pink nightgown she wore was covered with sweat but her hair was pulled back into a neat ponytail.

He was about to wake her, but the loud ring of the phone stopped him. He dashed into the kitchen and picked up the cream handset. "Hello."

"Jayden, where were you?!" Madjesty screamed. "I been looking all over for you! Why would you leave like that? You had me scared!"

He couldn't wait to tell him what happened and was relieved that he called. Although he wanted to tell him, he wanted to tell his mother first. "Was mommy scared? When I was gone?"

Madjesty sounded irritated. "Does it even matter?"

"I guess not." He paused and opened the refrigerator. It was empty as usual. "Where are you?"

"I'm at the grocery store with Mrs. Brookes. She gave me a quarter so I could call you. But are you okay?"

"I'm good, but I really need you to come home now. I wanna talk to you."

"Okay, I'll have her bring me home later tonight. We can talk then okay?"

He tugged his ear. His voice was low. "Madjesty, I need you home now."

Silence.

"Is ma there?" Madjesty asked.

Jayden looked at her on the sofa. "Yes."

"Well I'll see you later tonight. That way we can have more privacy."

Disappointed Jayden decided to keep his secret safe and said, "Okay, Madjesty. If you say so."

He hung up and walked back over to his drunken mother on the couch. He plopped in the chair across from her and observed her limp body. "Mommy, are you up?" She stirred a little. "I'm home, but I need you to talk to me."

Silence.

"Did you come looking for me?" Jayden needed to know that she cared. Needed to know that in the days since he'd been gone, that his absence actually mattered.

Instead Harmony stirred again but her eyes remained shut. She was a lifeless dummy taking up air and space. What a complete waste of a soul. This event would change things in the future if she didn't choose to be present for him. Now.

Tears rolled down Jayden's face as he recalled the horrible events in his mind. Having to perform oral sex on a man was one thing, but now he was also questioning who he was. His mind was confused and only his mother could offer him clarity.

"Mommy, some man made me do things to him, and I need you to talk to me, please. I don't know what to do." He wiped his tears. "

Harmony's eyes finally fluttered. "W-what you talking about, boy?"

He was relieved to see her eyes. "Mommy, a man made me stay in his house. That's why I couldn't come home. He forced me to do stuff to him and I'm scared." He wouldn't tell her about the fire he started. As far as he was concerned they had it coming. "Mommy, I don't know what to do."

Time was running out on her attention to him. Her eyes rolled back up into her head, before settling on his face. When he gripped her hand, she snatched it away. "Hand me…the bottle." She reached for the vodka herself but she wasn't even close. "Give it to me, Jayden."

Jayden avoided her request and anger was simmering through his blood. "Did you hear what I told you, mommy?" Her discount of his feelings injured his soul. "I need you and I need you now. Please."

Harmony might as well have farted in his face, because she went back to sleep. He felt extreme hate for her at the moment, yet there was something he needed to know. If she wasn't going to answer his questions, he was going to do the research himself. So while her eyes were closed, he raised her pink slip a few inches up her thigh. His body trembled as he looked at her to be sure she hadn't awakened. When he saw she was still sleep, he bent down and peeked at the fine hair, which covered what Jayden needed to see between her legs. Was she like him or not?

This was wrong. What was he doing? With the front of her slip resting on her stomach, he jumped up and circled the couch. He wanted to see if they were the same but was this the right way? His mind couldn't wrap around her being that deceptive. Could he be a girl instead of a boy? There was only one way to find out. He took a deep breath and prepared to go all the way. Back on his knees, he looked between her legs again. Her eyelids were still tightly closed and he saw nothing but a wild tangled bunch of hair.

His heart rocked in his chest but he pushed forward. Taking another look at her closed eyelids, he eased a finger toward her mound. The scent of her body was shocking and caused his stomach to twirl. How did men touch her when she didn't even clean her body? Jayden knew no matter what, when he was older, baths would be his best friend. He shook so much from what he was about to do, that he thought she'd wake up from the sound of his chattering teeth alone. But he was on a mission so he took a deep breath and pushed his finger into her pussy. When his finger was sucked into her dampness like a vacuum, his eyes flew open. She was both warm and wet. Just...like...him.

Frightened, Jayden scooted back as far away from her as possible. He could still smell her body chemicals on his finger. What's going on? He didn't understand. He knew he was a boy, and nobody ever disputed it. Yet in his opinion he looked just like her. Felt just like her. Did penises come later in life? After you aged? If that were the case when would he get his? His mind was wrecked and the confusion made him hate her even more. She was supposed to be present for him and able to answer his life's questions. But she was too drunk to know he was even in the building. He had no one. Not his mother or brother.

The uncertainty about who he was, coupled with the rape, made him bitter. He stood up, walked over to the couch again and stared down at her. What a bitch! What a whore! He was so incensed he was trembling. He needed to do something so he stomped toward his room and reemerged with a dingy pillow. He held onto it tightly and slumped toward the sofa. He tried to talk himself out of it but it wasn't working. Ready to make a move, he stood directly over her and pressed the pillow over her nose and mouth so he could see her eyes. So he could see her die. First he pressed hard and then harder. She was right, she didn't deserve his love. She didn't deserve life, so he would take it from her.

He resigned to murdering her, until he looked at her closed eyes. When she slept she looked like an angel. He thought about how she took up for him in front of Sandy and her father last week. He thought about her not being able to live long enough to change. And he thought about his love for her. So he removed the pillow and threw it on the floor.

She looked stiff. Like a mannequin. He killed her. He actually killed her. He was about to pass out from grief until she took one hard breath and gasped for air. For that moment when her eyes opened, he knew that as awful as she was, he would prefer her alive than dead. She closed her eyes again and went back to sleep.

Jayden's heart was heavier. And it was clear that all Harmony cared about was alcohol and sex, not even her own life. His absence for three days proved that he wasn't a factor. Harmony and Armanii were of the same family. They were filthy whores who had the powers of their bodies without the knowledge of how to use them.

Needing some air, he trotted to the front door and held onto the knob. He took his mother's raunchy scent with him. Now he would have to live with the horrible secret of what happened to him at Armanii's, for the rest of his life.

When he walked out of the door, his head was down causing him to accidently bump into the next-door neighbor who was on the way to his house. Todd never missed a chance to get a shot of pussy. A bottle of vodka dangled in his hand as an offering to Harmony. "Your mother home?" He pushed his glasses closer to his face with his index finger. After their last altercation the kid made him nervous.

Jayden wanted to hurt him. Instead he closed the door and stepped closer to the perv. "Yeah…she here."

"Well I want to see her." He stepped closer.

Jayden observed the bag and then his four eyes. "I don't drink vodka."

He grinned. All lip, no teeth. "What you mean, kid?"

"Just what I said. I don't drink vodka. What else you got?" He focused on his jean pockets.

"I think you're a little confused, son. I'm here to see your mother." He advanced forward again. "Now move out of my way."

Jayden countered his move and blocked him. "If you want to come in, you gotta pay me."

He took a step back, put a hand on his hip and laughed. "So what are you, some fake ass pimp now? You think you gonna just take my money? I'm a grown ass man, little boy, not a fool."

Unmoved he said, "Do you have money or not?"

His eyebrows rose. "Wait, you're serious aren't you?"

"My mother may fuck you for a bottle of vodka but right now she's drunk and passed out on the couch. When she's like that she can't think for herself. That's where I come in. Now do you have money or not?"

"So you're saying if I give you the money, you'll let me in to fuck your mother?"

"You can do whatever you want to her. Right now I don't give a fuck."

He was stunned. "So she's not even conscious?" He laughed. "You want me to fuck her when she's drunk and don't know what's going on? I'm supposed to pay for that?"

"Isn't she always that way?" He looked at Todd's black patent leather shoes. "I know how you like to smack her around and spit in her face while she's out. I see you all the time when you come over. You can do that all you want and I won't say a thing. Just as long as you pay."

His eyebrows rose. "You know what, I'm out of here." He turned to walk away.

"Bye."

The neighbor approached the steps and trooped down them with purpose. His mind said the little pimp in the making was crazy but his dick was already hard, just thinking about Harmony's tight pussy. He shivered a little when he thought about how well Harmony sucked a dick, with no gag, even in her sleep. Up until this point, for free. Not being able to satisfy his craving would drive him mad and he knew it. Surely he could spare a few bucks.

So he turned back around and looked up at Jayden. His ponytail made him feminine, but his eyes were as hard as stone. "Look here kid, I got twenty bucks...nothing else."

"I'll take it." He stretched out his hand and wiggled his fingers.

The neighbor walked back up the stairs, reached into his pocket and slapped the money into Jayden's dirty palm. Grabbing a second to take it all in, he twisted the cap off of the bottle and swallowed the vodka. "You smart, kid." He pointed at him. "Don't know how fucked up a life you must have, to sell your own mother but I gotta give you credit for one thing, you're bold." He shook his head. "An attitude like that gonna get you paid or killed." He placed one hand on his shoulder, walked past him, and entered the apartment to claim his prize.

Jayden opened the bill and examined it fully. A smiled spread across his face. He earned that paper straight up. His eyes never leaving the money, he walked down the steps. He wondered would his mother respect his game now. Whether she did or didn't he wouldn't give a fuck.

Something happened to him at that moment, something that would change the course of his life forever. He finally understood that as long as there were women out there who didn't care about their bodies, or their families, that there would always be someone available to profit. And to take advantage of them. Could it be him? He wasn't sure. But he could say if given the opportunity he would gladly take it. Making money was now a passion. The Pussy Game was now his life.

PART ONE

Present Day
Green Door – Adult Mental Health Care Clinic
Northwest, Washington DC

Christina Zahm sat behind her desk, irritated beyond belief with Harmony's funky-inconsiderate ass. Before the day was out she planned to ensure she was in trouble with her parole officer and thrown back in prison where she belonged. While she was sure Harmony was having a ball, probably fucking some kid, while she sucked on a bottle of vodka, she had better things to do with her time. She also had other people on her list who needed her help and who were actually trying to change their lives. She was just about to call the goons on Harmony, when she entered her office unannounced, swaying from left to right.

Harmony could never be accused of being *best dressed*, but the outfit she wore was the worst thing she ever donned. The black cardigan sweater she rocked on her frail frame had two rips in the sleeve and a loose button, which exposed her saggy breasts. Her jeans were so filthy they were wet with mud.

She leaned up against the doorway and said, "Honey, I'm home." The liquor in her system lit up the room like a scented candle.

One of her employees followed Harmony inside the office. "Christina, are you okay?" She asked looking at the inebriated mess in her office. "Want me to call the police?"

"I have it." She sighed. The woman left and Christina got right down to it. "Harmony, I know you're not stupid enough to come to our meeting drunk!" Christina got up and opened the window, even though it was hot outside and the air condition was on. She immediately picked up the phone to have Harmony taken somewhere appropriate. Hell would be good; anywhere else would be fine too. "I don't know what your problem is, but this little act has earned you a stint back in prison." She stabbed the keys on the phone with an attitude. "I hope whatever you were drinking was worth it."

As Christina held the phone in her hand Harmony asked, "Do you know what today is?" She was too busy with snitching to respond. "Today is the three month anniversary of when my son was born."

Now she had her attention. "What are you talking about, Harmony?" She held the phone firmly to her ear but curiosity was killing her. When someone answered she said, "Yes, can I have Akieon Timberlake please? I believe he is Harmony Phillips' probation officer."

"I had a son." Harmony walked further into the office and threw her limp body into the chair. "He was a cute little thing, and I got to keep him for a short time." She paused and looked into Christina's eyes. "And you know what, it was one of the best moments in my life. And a girl like me, Miss Doctor lady, only gets a few." Her head rolled around before stopping in place. "I miss him. So much."

When Akieon came to the phone, Christina examined Harmony to be sure she was being truthful. The solemn look on her face answered the question. If she didn't hear the rest of this story, she would die. "Yes, I just wanted to let you know that Harmony Phillips has been doing fine with her visits. I'll be in touch."

When Christina hung up, she grabbed her chart and sat across from her. The smell of alcohol lifting from her body was getting her drunk, but Harmony's new confession was so interesting she would endure. "You never told me you had a son."

"Not too many people know about it. I learned a long time ago that some things should be kept to yourself, and the birth of my son was just for me." She smiled crookedly before sobbing. "Only me." She placed a weak hand over her heart, which flapped in her lap.

Dr. Zahm opened her chart. "Tell me about it. When was the boy born?"

"Can we talk about Jayden first?"

Christina sighed, not feeling up for her games. But if hearing about Jayden first would open up the doorway to what she wanted to know now, she'd walk through it. "Sure, let's talk about Jayden." She scanned the chart. "When we last spoke, you said Madjesty raped her. Can you tell me what happened next?"

"When they were kids they use to call me mother monster. They thought I didn't know but I always did. But when Jayden was raped, and some other things in her life happened after that, it became apparent that I wasn't the only monster in the family."

Jayden Phillips
March of 2004
Fort Washington, Maryland

I play with my pussy too much. I play with it when I'm scared. I play with it when I'm tired and I play with it just because. It's the only thing that makes me feel better. I'm about to go at it again, until I hear something outside. I hop out of bed and look out of my window. My neighbors Sebastian and Luh Rod who live down the street, are looking up at my house. It seems like they're always around my house...watching me.

The good thing is Sebastian is so sexy he can be a model. His skin is dark chocolate and his hair is short but very curly. The thing that really stands out about him is his eyes. They're ice blue, like a white person's. I never seen a nigga with blue eyes before and I wonder if they real. Sebastian has a small lightning tattoo under his eye and since I don't talk to him outside of hi and bye, I never found out what it stood for. His brother Luh looks regular enough with his long dreads down his back. What do they want with me?

I lift the window and yell, "Can you please tell me what the fuck ya'll doing in front of my house?" My long hair falls in my face and I pull it behind my ear. "You creeping me out."

"Why, you scared?" Sebastian smiles and for some reason, my heart melts.

His thumbs are stuffed under the buckle of his belt and he stands like a cowboy. No matter what day it is, Sebastian wears the same outfit, a white t-shirt, blue jeans and grey New Balance's. He's always fresh but also the same.

"I'm scared enough to call the police." I warn.

"Sexy, ain't nobody gonna fuck wit' you." Luh Rod looks over the mansion. "We just love to look at this big pretty house of yours that's all. Us lesser people gotta live in run down spots on the same block. What ya'll do, have this mothafucka built or something?"

"When you gonna invite us in, Jayden." Sebastian grins. He seems wicked.

My heart rate increases. I slam the window down and rush toward the phone to call the police. With the phone in my hand I return to the window but they're gone. They're going to rob us one day, I'm sure of it. I wouldn't feel so unsafe if my boyfriend Evan or as he likes to be called, Shaggy, was here with me. I still remember the day we hooked up officially. It was right after I learned that he killed my boyfriend and his old friend, Xion because he was jealous we were together. Because I met Shaggy first, I couldn't believe he'd take a life for me and something about it turned me on.

So I went over his house, got on my knees and sucked the skin off of his dick. Believe me when I say Shaggy was whistling my name when I was done. He wondered how I did it so good but I could never tell him about what I went through in Texas. It probably wouldn't matter anyway. I had nightmares about being forced to suck Joseph's dick for three days straight, while my so-called friend Armanii watched. They got what they deserved later though and I'ma leave it like that.

Even my mother didn't know how I attained my skills when she called herself trying to teach me how to suck dick with a carrot. All she kept doing was cheering me on when the vegetable disappeared in my throat, with no gag. The only thing I hadn't done was fuck yet but I was saving the goodies for Shaggy.

Something was different though. Because over the months we'd been together, he wasn't the same. He seemed distant ever since somebody murdered his father, Paco. To hear Shaggy tell it, Paco was the strong member in the family since his mother Trip was dying from complications of Syphilis. Apparently she caught it as a kid, never got it treated and now it was too late. I met her once and she was half blind and on her last leg. I couldn't help but think that maybe if she died things between us would be better. Am I wrong for wanting him focused on me?

It was because of Shaggy my business, Thirteen Flavors, was doing well. At first things were rocky until I had him go get Passion, my star bitch, from a hotel. She was with some girl/boy probably shooting heroin. I never got all of the details on what happened to Passion's boyfriend that night but they both told me it ended badly.

I pick up my phone and try to call him and again he doesn't answer. Push a girl a little and she learns to be tough but push her a lot and she snaps. I like my life in order. I like things to move a certain way. My way. It's called stability. He knows that so why is he acting like he doesn't care? I call him once more and when he finally answers, I lose my mind. "Shaggy, why you ain't answer the fucking phone? Don't fuck with me!" My temples throb as I think about all the things I can do to him. With my bare hands if I'm mad enough.

"Baby, I had something to do. I told you that."

He sounds sincere but I'm not positive. "Are you sure?"

"Yes! What you think was happening?"

"Did I do something wrong, Shaggy? Say something wrong? Or anything like that?" I feel like I'm losing him. Everything in me tells me he doesn't want me anymore, but why?

"No!" He sighs. "Why you always think you said something wrong because you don't talk to me every hour? You know niggas after me and shit."

"I know and I want to help you."

"But you can't."

"I can. But you just gotta trust me." My body trembles. "I don't want you to leave me. I want us to be together forever. Even if I gotta kill us to make that happen."

"I won't leave you, Jayden. But you gotta give me my space, baby."

"Space?" I frown and brush my toe against the baseboard in my room. "Since when do you need space?"

"Jayden, I been meaning to talk to you about this. I mean, you starting to crowd me and I'm gonna need you to back off a little."

I freeze in place. "So you saying it's over?"

"No! I'm not saying that! I'm just saying I need a little time. Please."

He hangs up and at that moment, I want his existence crushed, the way he's trying to crush mine. So I call him back and say, "I'm gonna come over your house after my company leaves. You better be there when I knock on that door."

"Don't threaten me."

"No! You don't threaten me. You belong to me, Shaggy. That was our agreement."

"We haven't even fucked yet!"

"That's not my fault. You afraid to be around me. And when we do see each other it's rushed."

"Jayden…"

"Jayden, shit!" I yell gaining control of the conversation. "Now you said you wanted to be with me and I agreed. But now that you got my heart, nigga, you better act right. Like I said, I'ma be there when my company leaves. Don't go no where."

Shaggy has me fucked up if he thinks he can just play with my heart. That wasn't happening. I purposely shielded my feelings for fear of being thrown off. I like stability. Did I say I need stability? This kind of shit pushes a girl away. Makes her crazy.

When I hang up on him, I wait for my sister to call back. It had been a while and finally we would see each other again. Things got so crazy since the last time I saw her. For starters, our aunts and mother were fighting over who owned Concord Manor and now that the courts were involved, only they could decide who was right and who was wrong. To make matters worse, my mother had to register as a sex offender and wasn't allowed near small children because of that boy she fucked in the bushes in front of our house. My own personal world is being rocked too because although Passion was back on my clock, she was constantly asking for me to release her from obligation but I can't right now. I need her.

When my sister finally arrives, I open the front door and look at her for a moment. The jeans she's wearing drowns out her body and removes her curves. She looks like a boy to me. I think I even see a bulge between her legs. What is that? Why she wanna be that way when we were lied to for so many years? I want a girly twin, who I can do makeup with, go shopping and stuff like that. And what's up with the red curly hair? The shit is creeping me out. When I move closer, I try to look into her eyes to see how she feels about me but they're hidden more than usual with the brim of her baseball cap. Something doesn't feel right.

Yeah I could've gone to see her when she was in the institution, but life got too busy. So overwhelming. My mother is drinking so much, the hallway stinks when she pisses. And I need to make money to keep the bills paid around here. So what could I do? I couldn't leave.

Trying to ease the tension, I walk up to her and wrap my arms around her but she doesn't hug me back. "Still mad at me?" I ask separating myself from her before closing the front door.

"Naw. Been through a lot." She walks around me. "I see ya'll really fucked up this house. Where's all the furniture?"

"Aunt Ramona and Aunt Laura sold it. It's a long story." They said that although the house was in dispute the furniture belonged to them. "Well come up to my room. So we can talk."

Madjesty follows me upstairs. "Where is Harmony? I got to see her before I leave."

She sounds angry. Ma's life is already fucked up; she doesn't need Madjesty making it worse right now. "Why?"

"Don't worry about all that," Madjesty smiles and it looks weird. "Just know that before I leave, I got to see her. Cool?"

"Cool." We make it to my room and I sit on my bed and rub a place for her to sit next to me. Like Armanii use to do before I killed the sick bitch. "Sit down next to me."

She stuffs her hands into her pockets. "Naw. I'll stand."

I place my hands in my lap, my nails are chipped and need to be done. "So what you been up to?" My feet swing under my body. Why does being around her feel so awkward?

"You mean besides losing one of my best friends, getting raped, shot and being committed in a crazy house for a month?" She laughs.

My eyes widen in shock. I don't think that's funny. "What?"

"Yeah. Life for me was fucked up!"

Her lips say one thing but her expression says another. At the moment, she looks anything but bothered by the incident. How does she do that? I think about what Joseph did to me almost everyday. It's tough keeping secrets but I guess with anything, you get better with time.

"I'm so sorry, twin." I stand to hug her and again she rejects me and backs away. "Why didn't you call me, Madjesty? I told ma over and over I wanted to talk to you. I knew she knew where you were but she was keeping that info top secret."

"She never told you I wanted to talk to you?"

"Never." She looks like she doesn't believe me and it hurts.

"Where is your father? You guys still close?"

"We're close but a lot of shit been happening between your father and mines so I've been seeing him less these days. I've been busy anyway." I shrug. "So it's not too bad."

"Shit going on with our fathers like what?"

"I don't really want to talk about it." I tell her in a low voice.

"See…that's why we'll never be like we use to be." She points at me. "Ever."

"Don't say that." I wrap my arm around her shoulder, trying to calm her down. But when she shoots me an evil look, I move away. "We…we gonna be close like we use to. We just have to work on it."

"You mean how we were working on it before I left?" She's being sarcastic. "Because if I can recall whenever I reached out to you, you never had the time. And then when you made the time you would take it back by standing me up."

"That was then! I think we can be better now. I think we can be like the kids we were in Texas."

"Never." Madjesty says playing with the perfume bottles on my dresser. "Things will never be the same."

"Okay…you want me to open up?" I have to make this connection tighter between us because she isn't helping me. "And keep it real with you?"

"I want it if you want it. But I'm not pressing you no more." I can tell she's given up and it's like I don't matter now.

"I want it." I insist, wishing I hadn't let so much time come between us now. "And if we gonna be close, we have to stay out of our fathers' business. Their beef has torn us apart."

"I don't have a problem with staying out of their business."

"Okay...tell me where you been?"

"Before I do that, answer my initial question. What kind of beef do our fathers have?"

"Okay...I'm gonna trust you first. My father is after yours because he thinks he kidnapped his friend Antoinette."

She looks guilty. "Tell me something I don't know already."

"Okay...well your father has admitted to having her but now he's changing the game. He's saying if my father doesn't pay him five hundred thousand and hand over Shaggy, Paco's son, then he's going to kill her." Just the thought of losing him makes me sick.

Madjesty grins like she's proud of Kali. "So why doesn't he do it?"

I frown and try to conceal my disgust. "He's torn. Because Shaggy is my boyfriend and I love him. I don't want to lose him and don't even understand why Kali wants him." Madjesty's pushiness is irritating. "You see?"

"You know Shaggy like that? I mean, I know you knew him, but when shit get there?"

"Why?" What difference does Shaggy make to our situation? "I just said he's my boyfriend. Do you know him, too?"

"Yes."

"How?"

"Well, let's just say that he raped me. He raped me and sucked on my chest in front of my girlfriend before he took her away. And when he was done, he shot me in my arm and left me for dead." Madjesty laughs insanely. Again.

When her statement exits her lips, I'm dumbfounded. This doesn't make sense. "You were the boy/girl they were talking about?"

"I guess." She pauses and an insulted look covers her face. "I don't know what story you were told. But then...check it...I get to the hospital and I cut my breasts off." She lifts her shirt to show her mutilated chest and I back away against the wall. I know my sister wants to be a boy but would have never thought she'd go so far.

"...they thought I was crazy so they committed me." I tug my right ear. "Can you believe it? They thought I was crazy because I didn't want any part of my body that he touched. They couldn't understand that so they said I'm crazy!" She laughs harder and I think she's been released from the institution too soon. "Well maybe I am!"

I rub my temples. "I...I don't understand. You...you were Passion's boyfriend?"

"Yes."

"They said they killed some dude/girl but...but I didn't know it was you." I pause to analyze everything Shaggy told me about that night, against everything she's telling me now. "Had I known it was you I would've never told Shaggy to kill you." I know she doesn't believe me but I'm being honest. We have our shit between us but she's my sister and I love her.

"Hold up." she moves closer. "You gave the order for him to kill whoever she was with didn't you? Because that's what he said."

"Yes. But I didn't know it was you. I would've never given the order for some shit like that! Ever. Think, Madjesty, how would I know you were posing as a boy? And how would I know you were with Passion? I never saw you guys together at school."

"That's because I never went to school and neither did she."

I have a moment of clarity. She came to hurt me. "More shit happened then I know about in that motel room. So let me go make us something to drink so we can talk about all this shit and get it out in the open. Sit down, sis." She does. "You still drink Henny?"

"That's all I'll ever drink."

I smirk and say, "I'll be right back."

I can tell in her eyes that she means to do me harm so there's one thing I can do to protect myself, and that's tell my father where she is. If he has her in his possession, maybe Kali will leave my boyfriend alone and let us go on with our lives. So I go into the kitchen to make *the* call.

"Hi, Kreshon. When you talk to my father can you tell him to call me back? She's here but I'm not sure how long I can keep her! I'm sure Kali will give Antoinette back now if my father kidnaps Madjesty. Then maybe Kali will leave my boyfriend alone too."

"Okay, Jayden. I'll tell him." He says. "Just keep her there."

I feel like a traitor after I finish the call but I did what I had to. I know he won't hurt her. He'll probably negotiate with Kali and maybe all this will be over sooner than later. Once upstairs, I hand her the drink. She downs it as if it is cold water and she hadn't had any in days. "Thanks, sis." She grits her teeth.

"No problem." I look pleased. "I love you so much, Mad. I'm so glad you're here."

"I love you, too." She steps close to me and out of nowhere, crashes the glass against my left ear and knocks me to the floor. "Oh, I'm sorry." She stands over me. "Did I just cut your pretty little face?" My blood is everywhere. I see it. I feel its slickness. "The funny thing is, you really look like mama now."

My face is warm and sticky and the pain isn't as bad. It just feels cold. But then, well then the pain turns blinding. It hurts so badly now my face feels like it's burning. "Why did you do that?" I ask from the floor.

Madjesty drops down to her knees. "So what's the plan? To get back at my father you decided to sell your own sister instead?"

I always had problems hearing out of my right ear. People would call my name and think I was ignoring them when I couldn't hear the best all the time. But now it sounded like water was in my good ear because I could barely hear her voice. I focus on reading her lips.

"You love him that much more than me?" She asks.

"I don't want Kali to kill Shaggy. And if Jace has you, he won't do it. I love him and you know Jace would never hurt you." I'm so scared now. I feel helpless.

"Now he's Jace, huh? Not daddy?" She hates me. I made her hate me. "So you would trade me for Shaggy?"

"I really am sorry, Mad." My face is in pain but it doesn't hurt more than my heart. Although she's angry, I feel awful that she knows I betrayed her. And if she gives me another chance, I plan on proving to her how much I was wrong. "Don't hurt me anymore."

Her eyes get dark and she jumps on top of me. "You know, Harmony told me not to trust you but I didn't believe her. Matter of fact, I don't believe shit that bitch says. But what do you know, for the first time in her life she was right."

Placing her weight on top of me, she raises my dress and pulls down her jeans. What's happening now? What is she…my statement is cut short when I feel her ram something into my pussy. I try to fight her by punching at her back but she's stronger. Angrier. Madder. Whatever is inside of me tears at my flesh and places me in extreme pain. It's hard and cold at first. My face burns. My vagina is on fire and my heart is broken. My sister is raping me. My flesh and blood is raping me.

"How does it feel, sis?" She pounds harder. Like she's making love to me. Like she's enjoying it. "How does it feel to be violated, huh?"

"Stop!" I beg as I move wildly under her trying to get free. "Please stop, Madjesty. It hurts."

She moans. "Does it? Because that's how it felt to me when your boyfriend took what he wanted. He didn't give a fuck." She pounds me repeatedly as she widens my legs to push into me deeper. "I bet you were saving this pussy for him wasn't you? He wanted to be the first to hit this, huh?" She laughs never stopping her flow. I wonder how Mr. Nice

Guy feels about this, as he looks down at us. "Well guess what; tell him an eye for an eye!"

I focus on the picture of us on my dresser. We were happier when we had nothing because we had each other. All that has changed. Maybe I do have a little energy left. Maybe if I fight harder I can stop her but I don't because I'm heartbroken and crushed. I forget my pain, forget the blood dripping between my legs and forget she is my sister. I feel hate and I check out mentally. I also notice the world around me seems quieter but I can smell her sweat and feel her hot breath against my cheeks. She's stealing everything from me and I will never be the same. It wasn't enough for her to rape me, she gotta kiss me too. Like a woman would a man. My skin crawls and I try hard not to throw up. If she felt anything like this when Shaggy raped her, I understand but it doesn't make me despise her any less.

When she's done she lets out one last moan. It was stronger than the ones leading up to that moment. I know what happened without her telling me. She came. How did she do that? Why do I turn her on? When she's done she stands up and I finally see the thing she used to assault me. It's plastic, brown and has vein-like lines running alongside it. It's also covered in my blood. It's a dildo but the way she stuffs it back into her pants I know it's her dick. She finally got one.

When she's presentable she stares down at me with an evil expression. Zero love. "Sneaky, bitch!" She yells.

I pass out.

⚫——————————————————————————⚫

When I come too, she's gone and dried blood is on the inside of my thighs. I have a headache and my vagina is throbbing. Madjesty is dead to me. If I see her on the street, I can't say what I might do to her.

After crying uncontrollably, I'm finally able to lift myself to my knees. I lean on the bed and pull myself off the floor. Cramps run up and down my lower stomach and the gash on my face aches. While on my feet, I make it to the mirror to check the damage. I put our picture face down. When I look at my reflection, I'm relieved it isn't as bad as it feels. That is until I see glass hanging out of my ear. Carefully I take out a piece and it falls to the dresser. Followed by another, and then another. I'm enraged. The pain can't be described.

When I see my phone light up, I see Olive's name flash on my caller ID. Although she had become a good friend to me, I don't feel like talking to her. All that's on my mind is leaving my room without having to see my mother. I don't want her to see me like this. I don't want anybody to see me like this. When my phone lights up again, I see my father's name run across the screen. But why didn't I hear it ring loudly? Why is the sound so low?

I answer and my heart beats in my chest. "Hello." The handset shakes in my hand. "Daddy…are you there?" I can barely make out what he's saying. Anger washes over me like a warm blanket. "Daddy, I think something is wrong with my phone." I lie. "But if you can hear me, I need you to have somebody find Madjesty. She was here but she left. And when you do, daddy, I need you to…well, I need you to kill her."

"Baby girl, don't talk all wild on the phone." He pauses. "Where do you think she's going?"

"Could be anywhere. She's supposed to be in the institution…maybe you should look for her there."

HARMONY
JANKY ASS BITCHES

One minute I'm walking into my house and the next minute Madjesty's crazy ass is running down the stairs like she just committed murder. I'm thinking we're cool since I was the only person going to see her half titty ass and she tries to kill me. I didn't even know she was in the house because she wasn't supposed to be released from the institution. When my sisters Laura and Ramona went into their rooms, after saving me, I decided to go outside to get some air. Based on Madjesty's conversation on the phone, she was going to AMTRAK and to be honest, I hope I'd never see that bitch again.

When my doorbell rings and I open the door, I see someone I hadn't seen since my childhood, Ebony. And who does she have with her? Half dead ass Trip. She's wearing a pair of dark glasses, I guess to cover her bug eyes and she's walking with a cane. The way Trip moves it looks as if she'll blow over at any minute. A certified mess. Is she here because she knows that her son is fucking my daughter? I knew the moment I saw the boy sniffing around Jayden's pussy that it would bring up blasts from my past. Ebony, on the other hand, looks like she had work done on her nose and they'd taken too much off the tip.

"Hi, Harmony." Ebony smirks looking back at her homie. "You remember Trip right? Shaggy's mother?"

My heart rocks in my chest yet I pretend as if I'm not scared. Of course, I remember Trip, I remember that bitch too. When we were kids, I stole Ebony's earrings by stuffing them into my panties after she invited me to her party. Me and Trip had history because I fucked her boyfriend Paco and gave him a fresh case of syphilis. Something tells me they aren't here to thank me.

"I know who both of you are." I place my hands on my hips and frown. "Now what are ya'll doing here?"

"We came to see you." Ebony responds.

I roll my eyes, tiring of the games already. "How did you know where I lived?"

"I ran into Mrs. Duncan." she smiles weirdly. "She came to my wedding and I couldn't believe my ears when she said you said hello. You gave her your address when she was taking you home and she gladly gave it to me." *I hate that teacher.*

"So now we're here." Trip says. Although she is the cripple out of the crew, she looks the most dangerous.

"Well I'm busy."

"Nonsense...we have a lot to talk about." Ebony pushes past me as Trip follows. They stroll into the living room and sit on my sofa. "I see you have done well for yourself, Harmony Phillips." She looks up at the vault ceilings. "Or did you steal this place too. After all, I heard you can stuff everything in that big black hole between your legs."

I courtesy laugh and remain in the doorway. "This is all mine, baby doll. I don't have to steal shit."

She looks at Trip and breaks out in laughter. "Are you sure about that? Because if my memory serves correctly, you stole my earrings, the ones my father gave me." *I know that's why I stole them dumb ass.* "And when I approached you at the Burger King about it to fight you square up, you ran and told the security guard at the restaurant like a punk."

"Ebony, I thought you were some big shot attorney now. We were fucking kids when that shit happened. I mean you can't be serious about coming up in here with all of this foolishness."

"I'm very serious!" She stands up and prowls toward me. My door is open and I contemplate pushing her out but then what was I going to do with Trip? Shoot craps with her blind eyeballs? "My father gave me those earrings and he died a month after you took them from me."

"And my father died way before that and guess what, I'm still alive!"

"You are so careless and inconsiderate." She sits back on the couch, the only furniture in my house since my sisters sold most of everything else. "And then I'm hearing that you fucked Trip's man. I also heard you were the reason Constance killed herself because you were fucking Kreshon too behind her back. Damn, Harmony, is no man belonging to your friends off limits?" She digs into her purse and pulls out a cigarette and lighter. "Come sit down." She lit it. "The quicker we talk the faster this will all be over."

I hang by the open door. "Maybe I didn't make myself clear." I roll into the living room. "You two bitches are not welcomed in my home. We're not friends anymore. We're grown ass women with new lives. So live yours and leave me the fuck out of it."

When I say that, Trip stands up using her cane. "I'm dying, Harmony. I can barely see and my days are numbered. And you know what," she pauses, "there's not a day when I don't think about you and all the things I wanted to do to you if I ever saw you again." If she comes any closer, I'm gonna kick the hell out of the cane sending her crashing to the floor. The bottom line is, what do they want from me?

"Trip, you need to..."

She places her dry finger over my lips. It smells like raw potatoes. "There's no need in you opening the mouth you suck dick with to say anything to me. I know you fucked Paco and I also know you gave him syphilis. The fucked up part is, I didn't know I had it until it was too late. You have taken everything from me." She removes her hand and I wipe my lips. YUCK! "Look at my body, Harmony. This is part your fault."

I laugh. "It's my fault you didn't use a condom?"

"So the shit is funny?" Ebony asks standing in front of me.

"No, this shit is hilarious." I say holding my stomach. "You come over my house and accuse me of being the reason you're half dead and blind." I point to Trip. "And you got half a nose." I point at Ebony. "You bitches need new earrings, a dick and a life. Get over it already! It wasn't my fault Paco couldn't eat enough of this pussy. Use your head, Trip, he wanted me I didn't hold him between my legs at gunpoint. I couldn't keep him out if I set a trap for his ass. This juicy had him coming back for more. Literally. You didn't stand a chance."

Trip frowns. "You really are the worst fucking human being I've ever known."

"Tell me something I don't know already." I go to pour me a glass of vodka in the kitchen, secretly hoping they'd be irritated and gone by the time I get back. When I return, both of them are still there. "Can you tell me what you two Mindy's want now?"

I see Trip moving toward me quickly but I can't react. Before I know it, she's in my face hitting me all over my body with her cane. She's moving so ridiculously that at first I can't help but laugh, until I feel a searing pain in my stomach and another in my back. I fall to the floor to protect myself, but the blows won't stop. She's trying to kill me. She's actually trying to kill me.

"Oh my, God! What are you doing, Trip! I'm going to lose my job! I can't be involved in no shit like this!" Ebony yells. "We were supposed to talk to her. Let's talk to her!"

Before long it feels like hot iron pokers are sticking me everywhere. And then I feel myself pulling for air and having a difficult time breathing. Oh shit, not again!

MADJESTY
EVIL OF THE UGLY KIND

I'm evil.

And I can't believe what I've done. Krazy K stole his foster mother's small blue Kia Sephia to help me get away from it all. It's stuffy. Too many of us are inside. I feel like I can't breathe. Krazy is behind the wheel, Kid is riding shotgun and Sugar and Dynamite are in the backseat with me. As he drives in fast motion, I lean up against the door and stare out the window. Wild thoughts roll around in my mind and I don't recognize myself anymore.

From my house to the train station, all I did was cause havoc and it wasn't my plan. When I went to the house to talk to Jayden, I had no idea she was fucking with the nigga who raped me. I went over there to find out why she abandoned me when I was in the mental institution. I wanted to know why she hadn't called, or come to see me. I mean I knew Jace was after me because he knew me and my father had something to do with the disappearance of his fiancé, but I never thought she'd get involved. So when I picked up the phone in her room, only to hear her telling one of Jace's niggas to come pick me up, I felt betrayed. I wanted her to feel an ounce of what I'd gone through. So knowing she was a virgin, like I was before I was violated, I raped her. I raped my…

I shake my head to get the thoughts out of my mind. I hope God can forgive me, because I'll never forgive myself. I know at that moment I don't deserve love. That's probably why Denise and me didn't work. I don't even deserve happiness and I will avoid them both at all costs.

"Madjesty, you scaring the fuck out of me," Krazy says as he maneuvers down the streets. "Can you tell me what the fuck is going on?" He looks at me through the rearview mirror and I turn my head. "The way you left out of that train station wasn't normal, man." The back of the white t-shirt he's wearing is wet with sweat. He must be nervous.

"Yeah, you scaring me too," Sugar responds as Dynamite just stares at me like I'm going to die any minute. Sugar places her hand over mine. Her fingers are trembling. "Is there something I can do for you?"

I take three quick breaths. "Ya'll gotta let me get my head together. I can't think right now. I can't do anything. I'm fucked."

"Why don't everybody just leave my nigga alone," Kid adds. He reaches into his jean pockets and pulls out a stuffed blunt. "I know what he needs." He holds it up. "You trying to hit the wire?"

"Later for that shit, Kid." Sugar smacks his hand. "You always wanna do some dumb shit when things are serious. You act like you don't give a fuck about nobody but yourself sometimes!"

He looks back at her. "Bitch, I will slap the shit out of you if you ever tell me I don't care about my nigga. You know how fucked up I was when I saw Mad's face just now. I thought he was shot or something!"

In a serious voice Krazy says, "I wish you would put your hands on her." He looks over at him. "Playing or not." Kid shakes his head. *What's up with that shit? No one defends Sugar.*

"Madjesty," Sugar says softly, "I'm just saying this shit looks weird right now. Look at your clothes." I observe my dirty jeans. "One minute you tell us to drop you off at Concord Manor and the next thing we know, we picking you up from the Amtrak station." She pushes her red eyeglasses closer to her face. "I'm not trying to get into your business but you gotta tell me something! I'm worried about you."

"You do look fucked up, man." Krazy is spying on me from the rearview mirror again.

Yeah I'm fucked up. Plenty fucked up. I look at the small drops of water that suddenly dress the window. It's raining. How did it know to rain on one of the worst days of my life? Was I really fucking crazy? Was I really far gone? Not only did I rape my sister, I also tried to throw myself in front of a moving train.

"Turn the air up, man." I say. It's too hot in here! I can't breathe. He doesn't do it quick enough so I roll the window down and feel my stomach juices swirling. I stick my head out of the window and rain sprays against my face in the wind. Releasing whatever I had in my belly, it splashes against Krazy's car and smacks the shiny black Mercedes behind us.

"Pull over, man." I say in a low voice. When Krazy doesn't stop I get louder. "Pull over unless you want me to fuck this car up!"

He turns the wheel hard to the right and glides in front of two passing cars before parking on the medium. The moment the wheels stop, I push the door open, fall on my knees and throw up everything I have in my body. I didn't eat anything that day so it was mostly liquid. It isn't until Sugar touches me softly on my back that I realize I'm crying.

"Oh my God, Krazy! I never seen her like this before. Do something to help her! Please." Her hand trembles as she keeps it firmly on me. "Can you tell me what's going on, Madjesty? I'm dying right now because I can't help you. Who hurt you? Talk to us!"

The sound of Krazy's shoes pressing against the wet dirt is all around me. When I look at him I see he's pacing. "I'm not gonna keep taking nothing's wrong as an answer. You my nigga and you have to kick it to us straight." He stops and stands at my other side.

When I look over, I see Dynamite in the car. She seems scared. I took her out of the mental institution when I escaped earlier today, only for her to see me like this. She probably thought that when we left shit would go smoothly. Me too. I guess she was wrong. We both were.

"Say something, Madjesty!" Sugar screams.

"I wish ya'll stop pressuring him!" Kid yells. He kicks a few rocks and one of them accidently hits me in the forehead. "He'll tell us what's wrong when he's ready." I hear the flick of a lighter and see a cloud of smoke hover over my head. "Here, Madjesty hit this."

I swat his hand. "I'm not feeling that right now and I don't know what's wrong with me. I did some shit I can't take back, ya'll." From all fours, I look at them seriously.

"Like what, homie?" Kid inquires. "What could you have done that could've been worst than some of the shit we seen? We got secrets we're taking to the grave." I remember the girl I killed in the motel. To me this is worse.

"Think of the foulest thing you can imagine."

"Rape?" Krazy guesses immediately.

Silence.

"Whatever you did, I'm sure it was warranted." Krazy continues with the usual scowl on his face. "I know you, man. You hit the bottle hard but for the most part you a good dude."

"I'm with Krazy," Sugar adds. "You don't do shit unless somebody got it coming."

She knows that's a lie. I know they mean well but they can't begin to understand the day I had. If only Denise was still in my life, maybe this would be easier to deal with. She told me she would run away with me to Texas and when I waited on her at the train station, she didn't show up. The next thing I know, I'm witnessing three men die after trying to prevent me from jumping in front of a moving AMTRAK train.

"I gotta go back to the hospital ya'll." My stomach feels like its pulling and pushing at the same time, and things were starting to sway. Shit like cars and people and the ground beneath me. "Take me back, Krazy. Take me to the place you found me. I don't need to be out here, man. I'm dead serious." The four of them look at each other.

"Madjesty, I don't wanna go back there. I can't deal with it again." Dynamite says to me out of the window. "Please don't go back." It was the first thing she said to me since I got in the car from the station.

Krazy adds his piece. "I don't think you need to be in no place like that either." He looks at Dynamite and nods his head in her direction. "You not like them."

"You're right." I stand up and brush my pants off. " I'm worse. Now take me back to the spot. I gotta get my life together."

He takes a deep breath and raises his hands in defeat, before dropping them at his sides. "You got it, homie." He looks at everyone else and says, "Everybody get back in the car or get left. We out of here."

●━━━━━━━━━━━━━━━━━━━━━━━━━━━━●

When I wake up I'm back at the mental institution. Sitting up straight in the bed I stare at the room. It's drab and cream colored. It feels lifeless and makes me want to leave all over again but I made a decision to stay. Hopefully they can fix me. I told everybody about what happened at the Amtrak station and they all blamed my mother. Maybe they are right.

"How are you, Ms. Phillips?" A white man asks holding a clipboard. White dandruff particles cling to his hair and the shoulders of his medical jacket. Nasty mothafucka.

His presence makes me uncomfortable because we're alone. Where is the nurse? I pull the sheets up to my chin and look around the room for something to protect myself with in case he tries to hurt me. "My mother's name is Ms. Phillips." I frown. "I go by Mad."

His face turns red but he maintains his cool. "Okay." He clears his throat. "Mad, let's talk about what's going on with you." He flips a few sheets. "For starters you're pregnant. And because you're pregnant, we have to keep an eye on you and the medicines we provide. You were also very dehydrated, so we had to give you fluid intravenously." He points to the bag. "There's nothing in there that could be harmful to you or the baby though. Please don't worry."

The room seems to tilt. "What you mean I'm pregnant?" The I.V. sticking in my arm starts to hurt. "I can't be pregnant...I don't understand how that would..." The moment the statement leaves my mouth, I know how it's possible. Shaggy. But why hadn't the people told me when I was first here? They gave me all types of shit to keep me doped up and out of their way. Maybe the baby is dead already. Or worse, maybe he'll come out like me. Psychotic.

"You're carrying a child, Ms. Phillips." I want to drop his ass. "I mean, Mad. Now I was told that you were lesbian, did something happen that we need to be aware of?"

"First off I'm not a lesbian. Second of all I told the people when I got here that I was raped. They should've told you since you're my..."

There is a loud commotion outside of my room. I hear threatening voices. *What are you doing in here?"* Someone yells in the hallway. *"You can't be in this part of the hospital without authorization."*

"We're just looking for somebody," the man says. *"When we find her we'll leave."*

"But you all do not have authorization to come back here! I'm going to call the..."

When a few screams ring out, the doctor in my room says, "Stay right here. I'm going to find out what's going wrong." He looks so horrified I'm sure he'll run in the opposite direction of the trouble. I can't see him playing hero.

He leaves without another word and I hop off of the bed. Something tells me that whoever is causing all of the commotion, is trying to get at me. Wearing only a hospital gown, I jump down, grab the I.V. machine and roll it with me to the door. I rise on two toes and look out of the window on the door. I can't see anybody so I open it slowly and peak out. I spot some people on the other end of the hall but they don't see me. They are busting in patient's rooms and throwing shit around the wing. When I see Kreshon leading the pack, I know exactly what the deal is now. I pull the tape off of my arm and snatch out the needle to the I.V. I run out of my room and make a beeline in the opposite direction.

I hope they don't spot me but my wish doesn't come true when I hear, "There she go right there! Hey, Madjesty, we not going to hurt you. Come here so we can talk to you for a second."

"Leave me alone!"

"Jayden want's to rap to you and we're just here to get you, that's all. So ya'll can talk."

"Is that why you busting up the hospital and shit?"

Quick footsteps moved in my direction but I'm gone. There's no way I'm going to let them catch me. I figured Jayden told Jace what I did to her and now she wanted me dead. Maybe I should lie down and get it over with. The only thing that stops me from giving up is the baby. If I'm pregnant, I need to protect it despite the father.

With them still hot on my trail, I break right and then left. Thinking they're probably moving off of sounds to find out where I am, I slam a door leading into the stairwell loudly and duck into an office on the opposite side. I peak out of the window on the door and don't see them yet.

A black lady is on the phone and I think the nametag on her desk says, *Maureen.* She doesn't seem too happy to see me. "What are you doing in here?" She hangs up the phone. "You're not supposed to be here. Who is your doctor?"

"Please keep it down, I have somebody out there who's trying to kill me and if you make too much noise, they gonna be successful."

She stands up and approaches but I want her to sit down. "You're not answering me! What are you doing in here?" Her questions get louder and I search for something I can bust her in the forehead with.

When I spot a silver letter opener with a leather handle on her desk, I pick it up and point it in her direction. I can penetrate some organs with this shit. "If you don't shut the fuck up, I will stick this in your throat until it comes out of the other end of your skull. Do you understand me?" Her eyes widen and focus on the door. When I look to see what has her stuck, I see the doorknob move. I guess it's too late for me now.

JACE

HOT BODY

Jace's room is extra cool but he barely notices because of the warm legs wrapped around him under the black thick comforter on his bed. The young treat with the soft pussy had been trying to get with him for the longest, but with Antoinette being in his life and the pursuit of money always on his mind, he didn't give her the time of day. Although circumstances changed slightly, he still had a lot to deal with. Antoinette was still held hostage by Kali and he wasn't trying to hand over Shaggy, plus he worried about the well being of his daughter.

When she told him to find Madjesty and kill her, he knew something was seriously wrong. From the moment he met her, it was apparent that she adored her sister. Their love was the only reason he didn't hurt her to get at Kali early on. To make matters worse, Jayden didn't seem to trust him enough to tell him what went wrong between them.

"Jace, why is your body so hot?" She coos. "You always feel like you got a temperature and stuff. My father had the same thing and something was wrong with his liver. You better get that checked out."

"I'm not sure why I'm so hot, Phaedra." He winks at her. "Maybe you do that to me." She giggles and Jace appears to go elsewhere mentally. Like he always did.

"Where your mind at?" The brown-skinned beauty places her head on his chest and runs her finger through the ripples of his muscles. He can feel her toasty breast against his body and his dick stiffens. "Cuz it don't seem like it's with me." She looks up at him. "And if that's the case, I'ma have to work harder to make that change."

Jace wipes the long strands of black hair out of her face and peers into her brown eyes. There is no doubt that she is beautiful, but so is Antoinette. "Don't worry about what's on my mind. You didn't come all this way for that shit anyway."

"You're right about that." She wiggles closer to him and her pussy rests against his thigh. "So tell me, what did I come all this way for?"

"You already know." He covers his mouth and coughs a few times. "Excuse me, baby. I must be coming down with something."

She hesitates a little. "Jace, you been doing that all day. You sure it's just a cold?"

"What you talking about?" He pauses and runs his hand alongside her face. "Why wouldn't I be sure?"

"I don't know." She shrugs. "A hot body plus a consistent cough sounds strange, that's all."

"Wait, you think...I got something else?"

"I didn't say that." She got up and leaned on her side, facing him. "But I did have a cousin who died from pneumonia."

"Well I don't have pneumonia." He coughs again. And for some reason, his mind floats to Harmony and the last time they'd been together. It had been weeks and he still regretted the day he fucked her raw. Even if she did have something, could he be impacted that quickly? When he thinks about how she burned him as a kid he shakes his head. "I'm good. What, you worried about catching something from me? If you are, it's a little too late for that."

She climbs back on top of him, gropes his warm rod and places it inside of her body. Her moistness sucks him in. "Ask me that question now."

He holds onto her waist and pumps into her. "I can never get enough of you but I know you know that don't you?"

When she kisses him softly on the lips, he pushes deeper into her flesh. He's always amazed how no matter how hard he fucked her, the pussy always tightened when they went the next round. She knew the code to make him bust so just when she clicked her hips to the left followed by a hard right, it was over. To enhance his experience, she places his wet dick into her mouth and sucks him dry, just the way Harmony use to do. His juice oozes down her throat and she doesn't stop until she swallows every drop.

Mission completed, she wipes the corners of her mouth and looks up at him. "Did I make you happy? Because you know I tried."

"I'm not into telling you shit you already know."

"Well did I make you happy enough to put a few dollars in my purse over there." She points to her white Michael Kors bag on the dresser.

He shakes his head and grins. "Always the gold digger."

"You sell drugs, I sell pussy, just on a long-term basis."

"And what is that supposed to mean?"

"I don't lease my body out to more than one nigga at a time, Jace. You know that. So as long as you take care of me, I'm all yours."

"Well I'm not sure if I want to make the purchase."

She giggles and says, "Well how about we go again and..."

When his phone rings, he stops her in midsentence by reaching for it on the dresser. It's Jayden. "Baby, we found out where that package was but stuff didn't go as planned. Are you still sure you want me to do this? Because once I do, there's no turning back."

"Daddy, I'm having trouble hearing you."

He speaks louder. "Where have you been? I been calling you for two days straight. You had me worried sick."

"There's something still wrong with my phone. Remember I told you about it when you called me a few days back?" She pauses. "Anyway, I haven't had a chance to buy a new one so I'm gonna talk but I might not be able to hear you unless you yell." She sniffles. "I need to see you. I had a bad dream about you. That you were going to die and I miss you so much."

He pushes Phaedra out of his way and sits up straight in the bed. "I'm fine, Jayden. And I been coming over there for days but nobody answers the door!" He yells as she requests. "Not even your mother."

"I know, somebody stabbed her and she's at the hospital." He shakes his head. Harmony lived in the hospital. "I've been spending a lot of time there with her too. Maybe when you came over, that's where I was." She pauses. "I'll tell you what happened when I see you okay?

Phaedra touches his arm and he slaps her hand away. It's as if she'd stolen some of his oxygen just by being in his space. "Jayden, I haven't been this scared in a long time…"

She cuts him off with a quivering voice. "I'm sorry, daddy. I guess what I'm trying to say is, come see me. I need to be around somebody I love. That's all."

"I'm on my way."

JAYDEN
DOCTOR'S BAD NEWS

The office is too cramped. The bitch next to me must've bathed herself in the cheapest perfume she could find because I've sneezed ten times since she walked in. I hate coming here. But more than anything, I hate that the volume in my world seems to have been turned down since I lost some more of my hearing. The best part about today was seeing my father. Although I wish he didn't keep asking me what was up with my face and if I still want Madjesty dead, his company was what I needed. I made my decision and I wanted it carried through.

My mind is rushing. I'm nervous about what the doctor has to tell me about my hearing. So I press my two fingers between my legs and cover my lap with my brown leather purse to hide my nastiness. I work my fingers left and right and up and down, until I feel the sensation I'm looking for. Tingly. Relaxing. Calming. Once I cum I smile and I feel better already.

When I look at the counter, a chick with bright yellow hair and big blue earrings keeps looking in my direction. She's eating ice cream too. I wonder if she sees me so I remove my hand and sit them both over the top of my purse. Embarrassed, I focus at the Vibe magazine cover with Beyoncé on the front. But when I look at her again, she's still staring at me. What does this bitch want? It takes me a minute to see she's mouthing my name and she looks irritated. How long had she been calling me?

I rush over to her, stepping over a soiled pamper that was thrown on the floor. "I been calling you for five minutes." She's lying and her exaggeration makes me want to hurt her.

I look at her dry lips. "Sorry."

She waves at me like I'm wasting her time. "You got insurance?" She scoops a spoonful of chocolate ice cream out of a container and puts it in her mouth. She keeps her jaw slightly open and I notice it sits on her tongue like she doesn't want to swallow. *Gross ass bitch.*

"I told you I have insurance."

"Well how come I don't see your information here?" She flips open the yellow chart with my name written in black.

I glance down at it. "I don't know why you don't see it." I shrug. "I don't work here."

"You know what, just give me your card. I don't have time for all this other shit." She rolls her eyes and holds out her hand. Then she looks at the two employees with cartoon scrubs standing behind her.

I reach into my purse, slap my Medicaid card into her palm and turn my head to see who else in the lobby is looking at us. Everyone is. "It's right here."

She looks at the employees again, holds my card in the air and laughs. "I asked her if she got insurance and she gave me this shit." They hold their stomachs and burst into laughter.

"You wrong as shit for fucking with that patient, Charisma." One of them says.

"Shut the fuck up, Tena."

Because my hearing is not the same, their voices sound low and it irritates me. When she's had a good laugh, she looks back at me. "Sweetie, this isn't insurance."

I can feel my throat dry up and I swallow air. I want out of here. "I been here before," sweat rolls down my face, "and Dr. Takerski accepted my insurance. I don't understand what the problem is now."

"I didn't say we didn't accept it. I'm just saying this ain't insurance. This is welfare." She makes a copy and hands it back. I feel faint. I walk away from her, sit down and wait for my name. I hate how people look down on you just because you need a little help. My money game is on pause right now since my hearing is fucked up but soon I will be back on top.

Five minutes later a big girl walks in with a large brown bag. She sits it on the counter and everybody including Big Earrings tears into it, removing meals in white containers. I want out of here, which is why I'm relieved when Big Earrings mouths my name again. I quickly walk past the bitch and toward another girl holding my chart.

She takes me into Dr. Takerski's office, hands him my file and strolls out. He looks over my chart and a sour looks spreads on his face. He removes his gold-rimmed eyeglasses and motions for me to sit down across from his desk. I do. "Jayden, where is your mother?"

I clear my throat. "She wasn't able to come, she's sick. But she asked me to get as much information about my situation as possible." I lied. I didn't tell anybody about my weakness so they wouldn't use it against me. And that includes my mother. Plus she was cut up in the hospital with troubles of her own.

"Okay, we have a problem but I need to be sure." I can hear him clearly, which means he must be yelling.

"I don't understand. What do we have to be sure of?"

Although I think he's Pakistani, his dark complexion turns slightly red. "Jayden, it appears you're going deaf in both ears. The left drum was ruptured but the other looks like it has been damaged for a long time." He sighs. "If we're going to save your hearing, you must undergo drastic surgery. The longer you wait, the more irreparable damage may occur. The problem is, Medicaid won't cover all of your expenses."

The room feels like its spinning and I hold onto the arms of the chair for support. "So I'm going to be deaf? Permanently?"

"You very well could be." I want to cry. "Now there are many opportunities available for the hearing impaired, Jayden. Life isn't over just because you have a handicap."

"I don't want many opportunities! I want my hearing! And you're making it sound like I've lost it already."

"I don't want to jump out there and tell you something without verifying first but if you don't get your hearing under control now, you'll lose it for good." He tears off a paper on a pad. "This is a referral to an ear nose and throat doctor. He's going to run the final test necessary for me to be sure. Give this to your mother." He hands it to me. "This is one appointment you don't want to miss, Jayden. Are we clear?"

I want out of there. I rush down the hallway with the referral balled up like trash in the palm of my hand. Fuck the world! I'm about to pass the counter when I see that bitch again, the one with the big earrings and wide mouth. She's sipping soda before she places it back down on the counter. I guess she just finished eating.

I walk up to her. She's laughing with her co-workers until they point at me. She turns around and faces me, with a smug look on her face. I grab her cup off the counter and pour the soda all over her head. Her whack wig flattens on the top and ice cubes smack against her nose. She's yelling something but I'm already out the door.

●————————————————————————————●

I hold onto the white plastic bag in my hand. Standing in the doorway of her hospital room, I gaze at my mother. She looks bad. She's hooked up to machines and I wonder when I can take her home. I'm so use to seeing her in the hospital though, that it isn't that scary anymore. She survives everything.

I walk over to the bed and place my hand over hers. She drinks so much these days that her face always looks ashy gray. "Ma," I say in a low voice, "are you up?" She doesn't respond. I sit the bag on the top of the white cotton blanket over her body. I open it and remove a pair of white cotton briefs out of a pack before raising the blanket to her thighs.

She turns her head and looks at me. I focus on her lips so I won't miss a word she's saying. "You could've just spent the money on liquor you know. I don't like panties."

I laugh. "I know, but I didn't spend it on just liquor."

She smiles and looks at my face. "What happened to your ear? And the side of your face?"

"Nothing." I lie.

She doesn't press the issue. "How long have you been here?"

"Not long." I place her foot into the left and then the right holes of the underwear. She lifts her waist when I reach her butt and I slide them in place. They never gave her panties or maybe she keeps taking them off. "I been here every day though." I place the covers back over her legs, grab the bag and walk to the head of the bed. "Do you remember telling me that auntie Laura and Ramona stabbed you? Did that really happen?"

Her lips turn up like the edge of an old rug. "I told you they stabbed me because they did. Why would you ask me something like that anyway?" her voice is low and I step closer to hear her.

"I'm sorry, ma." I rub her dry hand. It feels cold. "I wasn't trying to say it didn't happen. I just never thought they'd go so far." I sweep my hair across my left shoulder and it falls at my breasts. She rolls her eyes like she's jealous.

"Well they did go that far. Spanish bitches are always vicious." She's serious but something in her voice tells me she isn't telling the full truth.

"Wait, aren't you half Spanish too?" I tug my right ear. It doesn't work anymore. I'm fucked.

"I got more black in me then them." I laugh. "But, Jayden I have to tell you something and it's kind of important."

"What is it, ma?" The tone in her voice makes me anxious. "Are you okay? Did the doctor say something else is wrong with you?"

"Outside of the stab wounds being inches away from my major arteries, I'm doing relatively okay for a bitch who was almost killed." She says in a low voice. Something is wrong. "That's not what I wanted to talk to you about." She looks into my eyes. "When Madjesty was last at the house, she seemed upset."

My nervousness turns into anger. "And…what that got to do with me?"

"She didn't seem right." She leans in closer. "Did something happen between you and her? That I should know about?"

I feel my stomach turn sour and I rub it. "Ma, I don't know what you getting at. Madjesty got shit with her and that's all I'm gonna say. Anyway I'm tired of worrying about what she's doing and if she's safe. It's time for me to start caring about myself."

She throws her weight back into the bed and the headrest rocks. "I hear what you saying but I have to get a hold of her. Do you know where she is?"

If my father handles business she'll be dead soon. "Ma, like I told you, I don't keep up with Madjesty anymore." I swallow. "Anyway that's your job not mine."

Her eyes narrow. "Since when have you two not kept up with each other?"

Since she raped me. "Ma, I have a lot of things on my mind. Problems of my own and Madjesty is not included. That's all I'm saying. Okay? Just drop it."

"Did you know she was pregnant?"

She didn't even ask what my problems were. I guess I shouldn't be shocked, she's just as selfish as usual. "No, I didn't know. But how could she get pregnant?"

The moment I ask I know the answer. Shaggy is the father. He had been calling me saying he needed to talk to me but I didn't have shit to say to the nigga. Not now anyway. Madjesty didn't have to rape me but he didn't have a right to rape her either. I wanted something done to him. Something final.

"She was raped, Jayden. Not sure if she's keeping the baby or not even though she shouldn't. She'll probably be the worst mother if she does." *You should know.* "I mean can you imagine her walking around with a big ass belly? And what about when the kid is born? How he gonna call her mommy when she's dressing like a man?" She shakes her head. "It's so ridiculous that I hope she doesn't go through with it."

"Whatever she decides, it's her business." If she does keep it I know the baby will be beautiful. I hate thinking I would never have a relationship with my niece or nephew. But it's Mad's fault not mind.

She looks at me. "One day I'll get to the bottom of why you two aren't talking." She pauses. "Anyway, I'm really worried about her and I need you to find her for me."

Stop the press! I look into my mother's eyes. Although I want to believe her, I'd known her long enough to know when she was lying or hiding something. It doesn't take me long to figure out the truth. "The social worker came by again didn't she?"

"Jayden…"

"Ma, I don't feel well so please just be honest with me. Did she come by or not?"

She exhales. "She found out I was in the hospital again. I think she was checking on another one of her clients, walked past the room and saw me in bed. Anyway, she said she checked up on both of you at school and that you haven't been doing well. She also mentioned that you haven't been going." She's irritated. "I need you to get it together, Jayden. And I need you to go back to school. You might not look at it like it's a big deal because I know you've been bringing a lot of money in the house but that's yours not mine. I rely on those welfare checks. I didn't go after your father for child support like I could have, so all the money I get from them is for me."

I roll my eyes. She's tripping. "Ma, the money is supposed to be to take care of us."

"You know what I mean."

"Anyway, that little bit of money you get from them checks ain't doing nothing but getting me embarrassed." I say, remembering the girl at the doctor's office, "and why didn't you tell her that Madjesty was committed? That way she'll leave you alone about her."

"Because they'll cut my checks! I don't see you doing extra around the house with your cash."

"That's a lie. And you can't knock me because I've been taking care of you too."

"I'm not saying that you aren't doing nothing but if she wants, she can take you away from me. And when that happens you'll end up in foster care. I'm telling you now, you don't want to go to those types of places. Dykes will look at that pretty face and that fat ass and be in the bed with you making you do all sorts of things."

You mean like my sister? "Why do you keep threatening me, mommy? The shit is old now."

"Because I'm telling you the truth, Jayden and I want you to understand. Do you want them to take you from me? Is that you're motive?"

"I don't." *I could always stay with daddy if they did, though.* "I just can't deal with Madjesty and her shit right now. And you know I haven't been going to school, I mean, how many times have we gone to the movies together on a weekday?"

"Jayden, please."

"I'm serious. I'll try to slide to class a few days out of the week but that's all I can promise."

"I guess I don't have a choice," she sighs, "but we're going to have to think of a plan for Madjesty's disappearance. This Katherine Sheers bitch means business. I'll call up the institution again but I doubt she's there. She was committed voluntarily." She looks at the plastic bag in my hands. "Anyway thanks for the underwear but did you bring what I really want?"

I open my purse and remove the scissors. Then I walk over to the I.V. bag, connected to the veins in her arm. I cut a small slit at the top, where no liquid is present. I take the bottle of vodka from the bag I brought in and pour a little inside. I could've let her drink it but she said she didn't want it on her breath. So the doctors won't smell it. I know the real reason was she got higher this way. I know its fucked up that I'm helping her shoot liquor in her veins but she looks so bad when she doesn't have it. I was afraid that if I didn't give it to her, she'd do reckless things to get it that might get her killed.

A minute later her eyes are drowsy. She seems like she's in heaven and I wish I could join her. Once she's sleep I walk over to the wooden dresser next to her bed and pick up a piece of paper. I see the hospital emblem but I can't make out all of the words. I'm really going to have to teach myself to read better especially since my hearing was a mess. Although I can't understand everything, I do read my mother's name and the letters AZT in parenthesis along with HIV. *What the fuck!*

KALI
STEALING ATLANTA

The rain is knocking against the windows so hard, that the blinds hang a little to the right inside the luxurious home were Kali and Antoinette were living. The weatherman called it a rainstorm but to the residents in Atlanta it resembled a hurricane.

Kali sits on the edge of the king size bed with his phone pressed against his ear. The hatchet on his back rests in its brown holster; he didn't go many places without it. His forehead is creased and it is apparent that he isn't in a good mood. That didn't stop her from fighting to get his attention.

Carefully and bravely, Antoinette eases behind him and rests her chin on his shoulder. "What's wrong, Kalive?" She kissed him gently on the ear. "You seem out of it tonight."

Without looking at her he frowns. "Why you say that?" His voice is plain and void of emotion. "Just cuz a nigga don't feel like watching Sex and The City wit' you?"

She removes her chin. "No, it's because one minute we're making love and the next you zone out on me. I mean, was I that bad?" Her joke was met with silence.

Finally he looks at her with an evil glare. Sometimes Antoinette's presence made him feel like he was wearing an Eddie Bauer coat in the summertime. "I got some shit on my mind." He shakes her away from his space and she backs off. "Nothing you need to worry about."

"Well how come you won't talk to me? I'm here for you to use, Kali. Not just when we fuck."

He exhales. She's working the last of his nerves. "I can't find my boy, Antoinette and I'm not feeling good about it. I don't feel like talking."

She sits on the edge of the bed next to him and her feet slap against the floor. "Your boy? What you mean...you can't find a friend of yours or something?"

"I don't have any friends, Antoinette. I'm talking about my son."

She laughs heartedly. "When are you gonna realize you have a daughter, Kali? At first I thought it was a joke but everyday you're with the, 'my son this', and 'my son that'. You don't have a son, you have a daughter."

"What the fuck's that 'sposed to mean?'"

"Kali, calling her your son probably caused her to cut off her own breasts. You gotta know that whatever she's thinking in her head is real. It's not healthy to be roaming around saying your one sex when you're another. You better get that in your head because I think things will get worse before they get any better with her. Hopefully she'll get more help."

The moment she threw the secret he shared with her about his daughter cutting off her breasts, he cursed the day he ever opened his mouth. It wasn't like they were real lovers. Kali kidnapped her for a debt that Jace, her fiancé, owed him. She was his captor not a friend. Maybe if he had her gagged and tied up like she was in his mother's house in D.C., she'd know the difference. Luckily for her Kali enjoyed fucking her. That one privilege gave her the faulty notion that she was his equal.

Rotten bitch. He thought. Disrespecting my kid. How wrong he felt for betraying Madjesty's trust. He understood how it felt to be one thing when every fiber of your being said you were another. And he didn't take kindly to outsiders analyzing them and making assumptions about the people they were.

"You really need to cut it out, Kali and start facing reality. You're not contributing to her mental well being is all I'm saying." Antoinette continues. She's on a roll with her reckless lip game.

The moment her lips close, they fly back open as she attempts to gasp for air due to Kali squeezing her windpipe. "So what am I contributing now by choking the fuck out of you? Huh? Tell me, bitch since you know so fucking much!"

"Kali, I can't breathe." She softly touches his offending hand. "Please, let me go. You're going to kill me." There wasn't any life behind his eyes. He blacked out a long time ago so she closed her eyes to express what was about to happen if he continued. He would kill her.

Her action worked because he drops his hand and walks over to the window. Her coughs and gasps for breath sounded in the background but he didn't care. *Rotten bitch. Maybe next time she'll think straight before she violates.*

He parts a few slats in the blind and observes the pouring rain outside. "When I was a kid nobody understood me." He opens the blinds fully to see better. "I had to deal with life on my own. I didn't have a mother or even a father to look out for my well-being. My grandparents tried their best but they were too old to control me, eventually they were put out of their misery. That's one of the reasons I'm the monster you see *before you today. But I won't do that to her. I mean I won't do that to him. No matter what she was born as, I will always treat her as she wants. Always." He turns around to look at her. "So if I say its my mothafuckin' son, then you better hear me before I forget that nigga owes me and dump you where you belong. In the gutter."*

Kali walks over to the edge of the bed and picks up his cell phone. It rings a few times before the person he wants answers. "Jace, do you have my daughter?"

His voice is thick with sleep. "I don't know what you talking about." He coughs three times. "What do you want?"

"You heard me, nigga. I been trying to get a hold of my kid. How come I haven't been able to reach her?" He looks at Antoinette and she's rubbing her neck. Drama queen. He thinks.

"You got it confused," Jace responds, "my kid's the one who doesn't look like a nigga. You better get a hold of Harmony's ass, I'm not little dude's mother."

He laughed although he didn't like Jace's joke. But he was right, they had business that had nothing to do with Madjesty. "Did you think about your decision yet?" He looks at Antoinette again and she's lying on the bed crying softly. "Time is of the essence if you ever want to see your bitch alive again."

"I don't know where Paco's boy is, Kali. I been looking for him everywhere but he's never where they say he is. I can get you your money but I don't know about him. Let's just make the exchange and put this shit behind us."

"That's not part of the deal. I told you what I want! Five hundred thousand and Shaggy. I don't want one without the other."

"Well you gotta give me some more time to find him, Kali."

"How much more time you need?" He paces the luxurious bedroom carpet. "I told you this mothafucka raped my kid. This ain't a game to me! I want his head!" He looks at Antoinette. "Or would you rather it be your bitch's instead?"

He walks over to her and lifts her head by the chin. She knows immediately what to do. She releases the belt on his jeans and pushes them to his ankles. Then she covers his rod with her warm mouth. It was amazing; she doesn't look sad anymore.

"As I'm looking at your bitch now, she's bound and gagged."

Thinking she is somewhere tied up with a sock in her mouth, Jace grows angrier. "Don't hurt her, Kali. Like I said, just give me some more time. I'll get you Shaggy."

"You got two days." He feels a nut coming on as her tongue slithers around his dick. Jace's nervous breaths in his ear only brought him closer

to ecstasy. *"After that, the bitch is dead."* He fills her mouth with nut and despite being scared she swallows every drop. *"Am I understood?"*

He exhales. *"You got it."*

When he ends the call, he steps out of the jeans which hold his ankles hostage and kicks them across the room. *"Go run me a bath, Antoinette."*

She wipes the corners of her mouth. *"In there?"* She points at the bathroom.

"You heard me."

Antoinette tromps to the bathroom. She was in there for five minutes before coming back out and throwing up in the bedroom trashcan and carpet. *"Your water is ready."* She wipes her mouth with the back of her hand.

Kali saunters toward the bathroom. *"Clean that shit up. And when I'm done, you get in after me. I want that pussy clean before we go at it again."*

When he walks into the bathroom, he steps over the married couple that he hog-tied and murdered on the floor. They were the real owners of the house that he and Antoinette took over. After getting undressed, like they weren't even in the room he slides into the water and goes to sleep.

MADJESTY

AT ANY COST

I hate white walls. Cream ones too. Even though they're bright, they never seem to make me feel any better. Sitting on the floor in my room, inside of the mental institution, I hold something in my hand I'd just taken. I remember how my life was *almost* stolen from me. Had it not been for a doctor walking into the room, instead of one of Jace's goons, I would've been dead. God knows the nurse whose office I busted into would not have cared less. When the cops got there Jace's men made an exit. I gotta get out of here. I can't take a chance of them getting at me again but they took everything I owned. Plus I need to talk to my sister. I need to apologize for doing what I did to her.

Standing up, my toes press against the cold hardwood floor. I increase my height by rising on my toes to look out of the door's window. I gotta get out of here. I need something to drink, to stop my mind from moving around. And then I remember, I'm carrying some kid in my belly. Why would he want to be in me? Using a dog's womb would've been a better choice of entering the world.

When I look out of the window, across the way I see a family. Looks like a father, a mother and their son. He looks a little younger than me in the face, even though we're about the same height and build. I wonder who is crazy in their family and did they still love them?

When one of the nurses walk over to the family, the mother and father hand their son a portable video game and walk away. I open the door, look both ways and walk over to him. The air rushes through the back of my white gown and I remember I'm wearing nothing but panties and a t-shirt. I hate panties but they won't give me boxers. They think if I wear them I'll not want to be a boy. Stupid idiots.

I'm standing in front of him for thirty seconds but he doesn't notice me. He's too busy with the game. "Hey, what game you got?" He doesn't answer. I take the seat next to him. "You here to see somebody?"

He looks at me. He seems sad. Then he looks at a door to the left, I guess it's where his peoples went into. "I hate that bitch." He tells me before focusing back on the game.

I laugh. "I feel you. Who you came to see though?"

"My sister, she use to cut my dick with my mama's pussy razor. She keeps it in the medicine cabinet." *What the fuck?* "She only does it when I'm asleep. Said she had to take the skin off of it so it wouldn't eat me." He examines my gown. "She wears one of those. Are you crazy, too?"

"Do I look like it?" I smile. I feel fake. I hate feeling fake.

"No, but neither do my sister."

I stand up and walk toward my room. "You wanna hang out in here with me?"

He shrugs and stands up quickly. "I ain't doing nothing right now." When he walks into my room, he looks at my bed. "My mother had one of those beds in the house. She use to strap my sister down so the devil wouldn't get her. I think the devil fucks her too because in the middle of the night she always screams his name." *This kid is sick. He should be in here with me.* "My sister would cry when she's been in there for too long and mama would let her out."

"If she lets her out when the devil comes for her, why she strap her down? So she couldn't kill herself?"

"So she couldn't kill us." He pauses and looks at me again. "Does it move up and down? The one in our house did. I use to get on it all the time when my sister didn't use it. I wish they hadn't sold it for mommy's candy."

"Candy?"

"Yeah, she puts it in her candy cane and pulls. Smoke comes out and everything."

Oh. The bitch is on crack.

He walks closer to my bed. "Can I sit on it?"

"Go for it." He's on his way but I stop him before he jumps on it. "But you gotta take your clothes off because I don't want my bed dirty." I slide out of the gown I'm wearing. He eyes my baggie panties and the white t-shirt covering my scarred up flat chest. I throw the gown at him and it smacks him in the face and falls to the floor. "You gotta put this on though. To make it real."

The kid must've been pretty bored because he wastes no time coming out of his clothes and putting on my gown. His blue jeans and yellow Star Wars t-shirt lay in a puddle on the floor. I tried to pretend like they didn't interest me. Like I walk around in my t-shirt and panties everyday on a natural. "Thirsty?" I walk over to the juice in the cream container on my dresser. "It's fruit punch."

"I guess."

I pour him some. Out of his view I pop the pills in it. The thing is, I really like him. Sounds like he comes from an addict mother like me. It makes us brothers. Which is why I feel bad stealing his clothes after giving him the medicine I swiped from a nurse who thought I was cute. While she was in my ear telling me I had swag, I was fingering her pussy and in her pocket grabbing meds.

It wasn't like he didn't have fun before he passed out. I activated every function on the bed for him while he acted like he was on a ride at an amusement park. By the time his parents would find him, he'd be sound asleep in my room. Dressed like me.

⸻

After leaving the hospital and jumping out of a cab, I ended up over Bernie's house. Although she wasn't a good grandmother, she was the only one I had. I guess I didn't know where else to go. The last time she saw me she learned that I was her granddaughter and that she'd been fucking her own son. I think about that wild shit all the time. How can you look your son in the face and not know it's him? I mean how high does a mothafucka have to be? That could never be me. Ever. I would always recognize my child.

There's no guarantee that she would help me, or no guarantee that she would let me stay but I have to try. I would've called my friends but I didn't want them to see me pregnant. It took them forever to accept me as I am. This kind of thing would set our friendship back ten years. So with nowhere else to go I knock on my grandmother's door, hoping she'll accept me.

It doesn't take long for a light-skin woman with a short Afro and gums for teeth to answer the door. A cloud of smoke escapes from behind her and brushes my face. It smells stinky sweet. Not like weed. I see a pipe on the table and know what's up. They too old for this shit. Aren't they?

Mrs. Afro wears a serious look on her face. Stabbing her fist into her pudgy waist she says, "Either you're the first boy to ever get pregnant or I'm high. You tell me…which one is it?"

"Arizona, what you hollering about? And who the fuck is at my door?" Before she can answer, my grandmother appears. She looks harder than she did the last time I saw her. And the gold wig she always wears looks extra crunchy. I want to turn around and bounce but I don't have no place to go. "What the fuck are you doing at my house, nigga? I don't want you around here." She looks behind me.

"Pops ain't with me."

I don't think she believes me. "Then what do you want?"

"I came to see you. I…" I couldn't finish my sentence because she slaps me. It wasn't as strong as Harmony's strike but it cut me just as deep. "Get the fuck away from here before I put my hands on you!"

Wait…if she didn't just put her hands on me, what the fuck was that? I don't budge. I can't move.

"Get on from around here, dyke." She points to the left, away from her house. "And I never want to see you around here again because if you come back, I'm shootin' to kill. You hear what I'm saying? Tell your father that too."

I feel angrier than I have in a long time.

"Neicy, why did you just hit that child?" She points at my belly. "She's pregnant! Look at her."

She looks at my stomach in the yellow Star Wars shirt I'm wearing. My belly pokes out a little but the rest of me is slim. How could she know I was pregnant? I didn't.

"Arizona, if you got a problem with anything I'm doing in my house, get the fuck out of my house!" Her attention focuses back on me she says, "Leave, now! And never come back here again. I'm not fucking around with you."

My last hope is gone. Nobody ever did anything for me just to be doing it. I'm starting to really hate the world around me. Like really, *really* hate it. I didn't know I was walking away at first because I was moving backwards. I was in my head, trying to figure out what the fuck I would do now. Tears fill up in my eyes and I hate myself for thinking she would want me. Thinking she would help me. I'm almost out of her walkway, when I spot a brick next to her mailbox. I pick it up and smile. She's too busy fussing with Arizona to see me approaching at the fastest speed I can. When I'm close enough, I lunge it at my grandmother's dome. I aim for blood. A red swirl moves over her head but she ducks just in time. The look on her face is priceless.

"Bitch, are you that fucking crazy that you would throw something at me?"

My fists ball up in knots and I feel like hurting both of them. "I don't have anywhere else to go!" I cry. "I don't have anybody else to help me! I'm pregnant by a man who raped me. And because I hated my body when he was done with me, they threw me in a fucking mental institution." I move closer to her. "You were a bad mother! I know something about that because I had one just like you who raised me. But it don't have to be that way now." I'm probably making things worse instead of better. "Since you couldn't help my father in his life, the least you can do is help me! Please."

Arizona walks inside the house shaking her head. I don't know if what I said got to her, or if she's more interested in finishing up her high. Before my grandmother follows, she looks at me with hate in her eyes. But she pushes the door open wider before disappearing inside. She doesn't invite me in but I take it as an invitation anyway. Besides, where else could I fucking go?

JAYDEN
HEAR NO EVIL

I'm standing in the window, looking at the world. I can't hear it the same. No matter how different my life is right now, there's one person I need to see A.S.A.P. and he's doing his best to dodge me. I pick up the phone and make a call. I look at the .9 mili on my dresser my father gave me for protection and pick it up. When my call is answered I say, "Shaggy, where have you been?"

"Around."

I know that mothafucka. "I really want to meet up with you okay? How come you not trying to come over?" He's talking low and I can't hear him. "Can you speak a little louder?"

"I said, I'm not going to lie, I want to come see you but you don't sound right. It's like you mad at me. Is there something I should know? Just keep it real with me."

I sit on the edge of my bed and try to disguise the hate in my voice. "Why you say that, baby? I mean, it's been almost two weeks since I've seen you and you may hear my anxiousness." I lick the barrel of the gun. "If I'm wrong for wanting to be with my man call the sheriff. Now come over here...please."

He laughs. "I wish I could believe you, babes. I really do. But if my father taught me nothing else before he was murdered, he taught me to sense danger. And right now the feeling is off the charts."

I laugh. I'm tired of playing games with him anyway. "You want to know what's up?" I put the gun on my dresser. "I know you raped my sister and when I see you I'm gonna make you pay for that shit. It's gonna be nice and slow too, just like I know you like it."

"What, bitch?"

"You heard me," I pause, "and just so you know, the reason your father is dead is because of what you did to Madjesty. You not going to be able to hide forever, Shaggy. I'm gonna see you hogtied and in the back of a trunk if it's the last thing I do. Think about that while you're still breathing, nigga."

I hang up, throw myself on my bed and look up at the ceiling again. I don't come out of the room much unless I'm getting something to eat or sleep. It's not like the house is busy. I'm mostly alone since my aunts Ramona and Laura were arrested for stabbing my mother and she's still at the hospital recovering. It doesn't help that the mental institution keeps calling to say Madjesty has escaped. After the fifth call, I pretended to be my mother and told them she was here and that I would complete the paperwork to release her since my mother committed her voluntarily initially. I gave them to my mother to take care of. This shit is getting ridiculous.

When I feel a strange vibration, I look over and see the *other* cellphone on my dresser moving slowly. It's the phone I used for Thirteen Flavors when I was running my business. Even though I haven't been fucking with it, that doesn't stop it from blowing up. I hate that perverted ass men call the line all hours of the night wanting something. They don't give a fuck that my life is about to change probably for the worse. I could give it to Passion and them but I don't want them to have it either. They were blowing my phone up for work but I wasn't in the mood. After awhile I'm so irritated with it going off, that I open my window and toss it outside.

I'm tired of being helpless, so yesterday I had my father bring me over some books. Books with large letters and big pictures so I can teach myself to read. If I'm going to go to school, and get my life together, I need to be smarter than I was. Since I couldn't hear, I had to be smarter than everybody around me.

I know what I need. Easing out of my jeans, I stand in the middle of the bedroom with my red silk panties. Then I ease onto the edge of the bed, open my legs and place two fingers inside of my pussy. From the mirror across my room, I can see my pink center and the cream spilling over my nails.

Hornier than ever, my tongue runs over my lips as I move my fingers in and out of my cave. For the first time ever, I want dick. I want the touch of a man on me and inside of me. When my mind flashes to Madjesty I feel my stomach churn. She was the last person to touch me and sooner or later, I will need somebody to come behind her to erase that memory. The way I was craving sex lately I wonder if this is how my mother feels. If it is, the late night fuck sessions we watched in Texas make sense.

Trying to take my mind off of things even more, I lean back, place a pillow over my face and press my fingers deeper inside of me. I push my hips toward my wrist until I can feel the unevenness of my flesh. After five more presses, it doesn't take long to reach an orgasm. Needing some air, I throw the pillow on the floor. When I rise I see my father in my room.

"Daddy," I grab my jeans and cover my pussy. "What are you doing in here?" He's talking low but I can't hear him clearly. I focus on his lips but I'm so nervous about what he saw, or what he may be thinking of me, that it isn't working. "I'm sorry, daddy. I didn't hear you come in."

"What are you doing?" His voice is loud and filled with disgust.

My heart does the 'Stanky Leg' in my chest. "I was taking a nap. And I...didn't know..."

"You're going to be like your mother aren't you?" He says it in a way to make it clear that he hates me. "A fucking whore!"

"Daddy, I'm so sorry. So fucking sorry." Tears roll down my face but I can't move from my bed. I know I look like a slut and I feel terrible that he has to see me like this.

"I got the car for you." He's still angry because his eyes never produce the warm look he usually gives when he first sees my face. "Hurry up and come down stairs." He coughs a few times, grabs a piece of the Kleenex on my dresser and covers his mouth. It turns red in his hand. I leap in my jeans and rush toward him.

When I reach him, he extends a hand to keep me from touching him. He hates me. "Daddy, are you okay?"

"Be downstairs in a few minutes..." He turns and leaves.

My life keeps getting shittier. I grab a black plain Polo t-shirt that hugs my upper body, revealing just a little of my belly, Then I slide on my flip-flops. When I'm done, I grab my purse and run downstairs. When I get to the bottom of the steps, I see the back of a woman. She slender and her long brown hair is swept over her shoulder. When she turns around to look at me, I finally see my father's legs on the floor. My chest tightens and I find it hard to breathe.

"W-what's going on?" I ask her. "Why is he down there?" She ignores me so I walk around and see his eyes shut and blood oozing out of his mouth and nose. It takes everything in me to stay conscious.

●━━━━━━━━━━━━━━━━━━━━━━━━━━━━●

The hospital room is packed with some people I know and others I've never seen before. At first everyone was talking until the outsider walked in...the doctor. My father is hooked up to a respirator and he looks bad. In the brief time I've known him, I've never seen him look like this. Whatever is going on with him, I hope he'd hurry up and get well. I think I'm losing my mind and I won't be able to take more of this. First my mother and now my father.

Right next to him is the woman who was at my house earlier. Her light skin looks flushed and her eyes very dark. She's beautiful. I think she's about thirty something but she might be older. To her right is

Kreshon and he looks like he's been crying and my heartaches. His tall body hangs over her shorter one and his hands rest on her shoulders. Were they together? For some reason I didn't want them to be. He always looks so good whenever I see him, like his clothes were made out of one hundred dollar bills. The only thing is, he acts like he never notices me. So I open a few buttons on my shirt, now he's looking.

When the doctor leaves, my father removes the oxygen mask from his face. Everyone looks at him and I wait for his word. I focus on his lips and he says, "I want to be alone with my daughter." The crowd doesn't seem too happy about leaving. "I'll call you back in when I'm done with her."

Everyone is about to go until he grabs the lady's wrist that was at my house earlier. "Jayden, this is Metha. I came over to introduce you to her earlier but some things happened." *Yeah, you caught me playing in my pussy.* "Since you don't have a license, she's going to be your new driver. She'll take you wherever you want to go and I'm giving you my truck."

If he gives me his truck what will he drive? "But I don't want your car, daddy. What are you going to have, when you get out of here?"

"I'll buy another one." He smiles and I don't believe him.

He turns his head and says something else to her but he's speaking low and I can't read his lips. Whatever he said got her upset enough to run out of the room with tears rolling down her face. When she's gone, he rubs the edge of the bed for me to sit down. I quickly do and he places the oxygen mask over his mouth for a few more seconds and it fogs up.

He takes it off. "First, button your shirt." I do it quickly. I know he thinks I'm totally freaked out now. "Now, she has been working for me for over a year and I can honestly say, next to Kreshon, she's the only one I trust."

"But you said I shouldn't trust no one."

He grins a little. "You're right, baby girl, but every rule has an exception. She and Kreshon are it."

"Okay, daddy, if you say so."

"And baby, I'm sorry for what I said to you in your room. It just…caught me off guard to see you like that. You're not a whore and I don't want you to think I think of you in that light because I don't."

I'm red. I'm frozen. I don't want to talk about this. "Okay, daddy."

"It's time to get serious now so put on your big girl panties." I frown. I'm not wearing any. "Jayden, I have AIDS and I'm having complications."

"Complications?" My eyes widen. "I don't understand. When you came to see me the other day, you were fine. You had a cold but that was it."

"It wasn't a cold, it was a symptom of a much bigger issue. If you learn nothing from my situation, learn that you have to always protect yourself." He steals some more oxygen. "I have so much to be grateful for though."

His positivity is making me angry. "Daddy, I'm confused and if you have AIDS I don't understand what you have to be grateful for. You're about to fucking die!"

He glares at me. "Honey, I'm blessed enough to know that I'm dying. And that I'll be able to spend some quality time with the one person I love before I go." He coughs a few more times. "Now I know you're hurt, but for me that's the brighter side to this shit. If I don't have it I'll go crazy."

I exhale. "So how long? I mean…what are they saying?"

"I have pneumonia and the doctors doubt I'll live out the week. Had I known I was HIV positive, I could've used medicines like AZT to help bring this shit under control. Now they'll give me a few things to keep the infections down but it's mostly too late."

AZT? I saw that before when I went to visit my mother in the hospital. The room is spinning and my head is throbbing. I can't believe this is happening to me. Some of my salty tears fall into my mouth and I wipe the rest away, "This is so fucked up. How did you get it?"

He stares at me. I know he will never tell me but I know my mother gave it to him. Suddenly blinding anger consumes me. I want to ask him when was the last time he slept with her but it doesn't matter. He won't stay with me on earth no matter what the answer.

"Don't be angry, Jayden. I'm a grown man and I've made a lot of bad decisions. But guess what, I stand by every one of 'em." He breathes in more oxygen. "But I want to talk to you about something else, I know your hearing has gotten worse. Hasn't it?"

How did he know that? I never told anybody but the doctor. My mother lived with me for years and the only thing she ever told me was to stop tugging my ear. This is why I love him. He cares enough to notice me. "Why you say that? My hearing is fine."

"There have been so many times I've called your name for you not to respond. I even knocked on the door before I came into your room today." He frowns and I can tell the area is still soft with him. "I never said much about it before because I thought it wasn't serious." He touches me weakly on the face. Like he didn't have enough energy but needed to do it anyway. "I'm right ain't I?"

I guess my tears answer his question.

He reaches over to the nightstand and grabs some keys. He places them in my hands. "I want you to go to my house." He's breathing harder, like he's been running around all day. "When you get there, go downstairs into the basement, you know where you usually sleep when you come over."

I nod and I think my mouth says, yes.

"Good, in the bathroom, inside the shower stall, is a safe. Go by yourself, Jayden. Don't take anyone with you inside, not even Metha. I trust her, but even she may be tempted when faced with fruit."

"Okay, daddy." I feel like I want to die.

"To get inside the safe, pull the hot water lever down instead of turning it to the right. The safe will open. Inside you will find a half of million dollars. I was supposed to give it to Kali for Antoinette but he won't be getting it now. Besides, one of my business associates in Atlanta said they spotted them together and she didn't look like a hostage. I wasted so much time on that bitch. That I couldn't spare. " He frowns. "Anyway that money is for you now."

"Daddy, I don't want it."

"Jayden, please just listen to me." He breathes some more oxygen and removes the mask again. "I want you to take some of that money and do whatever you can to get your hearing repaired. Maybe if you do it now, you'll be restored. The rest I want you to put up for college. I want you to get an education, the best that money can buy."

"Daddy, please don't leave me."

"I need you to focus because although it's too late for me and your mother, it's not too late for you. Get an education and do what you have to, to make a better life for yourself."

"The money doesn't help me if you aren't in my life."

He looks frustrated. "Jayden, please, do this for me. I want you to promise me that you are going to stay out of trouble, take care of your health and go to college. It's my dying wish for you and the only way I'll be able to rest in peace. Now I want you to take out your cell phone."

"For what?"

"Just do it." I do as I'm told. "Good, you have a recording feature?"

"Yes."

"I want you to activate it." I do as I'm told. "Now I need you to record yourself right now, the promise you're making to me."

I nod. I want to stop reading his lips but am afraid I'll miss something.

"Do it, Jayden. I want to hear you say what you're promising me."

I place the phone to my lips. "I promise to stay out of trouble, take care of my health and to go to college."

"I love you, Jayden. Always." He coughs. "You can end the recording."

I'm crying so hard now, I can barely breathe. I press end and place my phone in my purse. "Stop that," he wipes the water off my face, "now I want you to play the promise whenever you're about to break it. Okay?"

"Yes, daddy."

"There's something else I want you to do." He pauses to place the mask on before finishing. "I want you to stay away from the street life. It ain't for you. It wasn't for me either. I guess I knew it all along because I made some decisions that got my fiancé caught up. But I'm smarter now and if I had it to do all over again, I would not have chosen the drug life." He pauses. "The best part about any of it is being able to take care of you financially. I lived the life on the streets so you don't have to. That's what the money is for. You understand?"

"Daddy, I'm not selling drugs."

"Never said you were but I know about the business you were running with the girls, Jayden. Word got back to me and I denied it until somebody showed me this."

He reaches into his dresser and shows me the first postcard we did for the fake babysitting service. The card shows Passion, Foxie, Na-Na, Gucci and Queen with three neighborhood kids. They were wearing tiny jean shorts with colorful t-shirts and each of them held an ice cream cone in their hand. The message on the bottom of the card reads, *'Let us tame the bad boys and girls of your life. Thirteen Flavors Babysitting Service, Our girls are available anytime of the day or night.'*

I'm beyond embarrassed because it's clear from the card that the only thing we were selling was pussy. The kids in the picture look like they have attitudes. I know at that moment that I'm giving up the lifestyle for good. Seeing the disappointment on his face makes me feel cheap. "You're right, daddy. I can do so much better and I promise to get an education and make you proud." I feel like I'm about to cry again. "Even if you can't see me."

He smiles. "I'm going to always see you." He promises. "And baby girl, we couldn't catch Madjesty." Now I'm disgusted. "I don't know what you two need to do to make it right, but it must be done. She's your flesh and blood and you need her because if I'm sick, chances are your mother is too." He admitted that she gave it to him even though I know he didn't mean to. "Can you make me the promise to at least try?"

I love my daddy but there are some things I simply won't do.

I'm looking out the window of the black Escalade my father gave me. For some reason, I can feel Metha staring at me and she looks like she has an attitude. She's such a boring bitch. I can tell. "What's wrong with you?" I focus on her lips. "My father's dying, not yours." I roll my eyes.

She wipes the tears off of her face and I wish she stops crying. Her sadness makes me feel worse about mine. "I'm sorry, I had something on my mind. And I kept asking where you wanted to go," she wipes more tears off, "but you didn't answer me. I figured you were ignoring me or something."

"So you're crying?"

"I wasn't crying about that. Like I said, I got a lot on my mind."

"How do you even know my father?"

She exhales. "I was an alcoholic and your father gave me a chance when nobody else would."

"Look, even if I was ignoring you, you don't have to look like you got an attitude." I say, overlooking her announcement. I knew alcoholics all my life, so her story was no big deal to me. I am going to have to remember to watch everybody around me though, if I'm going to keep my illness a secret. "Take me to my father's house." I look out of the window once more, before focusing on her again. "And for future reference, whenever you're around me, don't talk to me unless I'm looking at you."

She grips the wheel tighter and says, "Okay." She's a bitch. I can already tell. "Good because my father may have vouched for you, but he'll be dead soon. And depending on how you act will determine if you're services will be needed. At some point, I do plan to get my license you know?" She quickly pulls over to the side of the road and throws the car in park. My neck snaps back and then forward before my head crashes into the seat in front of me. "What the fuck?"

She looks back at me and says, "Listen, I love your father and there isn't a thing I won't do for him, but you're not going to disrespect me and think shit's sweet. Now he may be your father but I'm losing a good friend in that hospital. I'm emotional right now because he told me he's dying and I can't take a lot of shit from nobody, especially not some spoiled little bitch." She pauses, "Have some respect instead of talking to people like they don't matter. It'll go along way."

I rub my head and she pulls back in traffic without my response. I can't believe she spoke to me like that and suddenly I believe she's more interesting than I thought.

When we get to my father's house something feels wrong before I even step out the car. For starters when I open his front door, I'm met by a growling gray and white pitbull. I didn't even know he had a dog and I start to back out. But something about his eyes tell me he's more scared of me than I am of him. I don't leave, plus I need that money. So I drop my hands by my sides, to show him I mean no harm. The dog walks around me and smells me. My heart sways in my chest and when I look down, I can see it moving. After he takes his nose and presses it against my ass, he walks away and leaves me alone. I think I'm good to go.

I walk downstairs, and it follows me. Before I make it completely inside of the basement, I see everything is broken and fucked up. I can't believe daddy left his place like this and then it dawns on me, he didn't. Walking further into the basement, I can barely move without stepping over things lying on the floor. That's when the hairs on the back of my neck rise. Either somebody was there, or somebody had been there.

I pick up a bat that's lying on the side of the wall, and move slowly to the bathroom. When I get there, my fear is realized. The safe is open and the money is gone. Damn!

JACE
DEAD LOVE

Jace holds the phone to his ear, barely having the strength to keep it in place. When he finally hears her voice he says, "Harmony, how are you?"

"Jace...uh...Jayden isn't here with me." She's shocked to hear from him and is certain he's preparing to tell her how much he hates her guts...once again. "If you leave a message I'll tell her you called. She said she was coming back to check on me later."

"I know she's not there, Harmony. She just left me not too long ago. I can't imagine what she's going through with both of us being in the hospital. We're lucky to have her."

She's nervous. What does he want? "Well how did you know I was in the hospital?"

"Jayden told me."

His heavy breathing takes Harmony off guard. She never heard him sound so weak before. And her heart sings whenever she hears his voice. "What's going on with you, Jace? I mean, where are you?"

"In the hospital too."

"Why?"

He places the oxygen mask on his face, removes it and says, "Do you remember when we were kids and I was bouncing the ball with Brittany that day? I think you were getting the mail or some shit like that."

Harmony didn't know where he was going. "Yes. I think so."

"Did you know that I use to stand outside in front of your house everyday, hoping you'd come hang with me?"

She pauses. "What do you mean? You were always playing with Brittany. I figured the last thing you were thinking about was me."

He chuckles. "Naw, Brittany use to come out to keep me company but my motive was to always see your face, Harmony. Always. That's why I was psyched that you moved back to the neighborhood when you left Concord Manor."

Her jaw drops. "But you seemed so uninterested."

He laughs lightly. "How you sound? I use to ask you where your uncle was all the time. I think I asked you where he was that day. That nigga didn't fuck with me and I didn't fuck with him. I heard stories about the shit he might be doing to you in that house."

She remembers. "Stop playing, boy, you acted like you didn't like me. And when I did talk to you, you never said much. It was always like I was bothering you or something."

"I was a kid, woman, my game was off. But I loved you from the moment I saw your face." He inhales some more oxygen. Despite his condition he admits, "I still love you now."

Harmony cries although she's determined not to let him know. Why was he calling her with all of this emotional shit anyway? Her heart or body couldn't take it because despite everything, he was the love of her life. "Jace, I remember that day all too well. It was the same day my grandmother slapped me down the steps after I promised to come back out and play with you." It was also the first day her grandmother forced her to perform oral sex on her but she would keep that part to herself. If she did anything in life, she would never forget that afternoon.

"I remember that. When she hit you, I sent Kali over there to handle that shit for me. Shirley was always a fucking bully. She use to throw the rocks in her garden at us or leave her gate open so her dog Dingo could bite us."

Harmony was stunned. "Wait, you sent Kali to help me that day? I thought he came over on his own."

"Fuck no, I sent the nigga." He continues to set the record straight. "Your uncle threatened me and said I couldn't be anywhere near the house. He was going to call the police and I was young so I believed him." Since he was raping her, it all made sense to Harmony. "That's why I use to ask you where he was all the time." He pauses to catch his breath. "Naw, Harmony, I paid Kali five bucks to steal the shit out of your grandmother and he was going to do it, but she went back in the house before he handled business." He inhales more oxygen. "I never wanted to tell you but I hated that old bitch. I know she was a female but anybody who lets a pedophile around her granddaughter was not worthy of my respect."

"You couldn't hate her more than me." She remembers the years of sexual abuse she endured. "No one could."

Harmony considered that day again. The recollection about Kali had her stoned. Him coming to her rescue when Shirley hit her that day sealed their bond. As a matter of fact, had he not stepped up, she would have never slept with him later on in life. And if that hadn't happen, she and Jace would've probably been married with more kids right now. The thought fucks her head up. Instead they were both dying.

"Harmony, I need you to get your health checked out."

She immediately grows offensive besides; she'd just gotten her results. She was HIV positive and refused to acknowledge it. And she refused to take medicine. "What are you talking about, outside of the stab wounds I'm fine." She lies.

"I…I don't know if that's true or not, but you need to get yourself checked out anyway."

"Why?"

"Because I have AIDS Harmony and I'm dying." He coughs. "I'm not on the phone to point fingers at you because to be honest, I don't even care anymore. I got to meet my daughter and I love her more than anything. After spending so much time with her, I think she loves me too. Now you led a fucked up life, but she has all of her fingers and toes and for that I thank you. I'm just asking you not to put so much pressure on her by getting drunk, hurting yourself and shit like that. She thinks she can save you but we both know she can't."

"Jace, I don't want to hear this shit."

"Harmony, I need you to be there for her. I need you to stop drinking and be the mother I know you can be. She's going to really need you but only if you in the right mind. I see something in her eyes that doesn't rest well with me. Something you'll have to get under control before its too late. She's dark and very dangerous."

"Jace…"

"And the way you help her is by pushing back on the liquor," he interrupted, "and taking care of your health. My daughter needs your strength right now."

She grows ignorant. "Just because you're dying doesn't mean I have the shit too. And I'm tired of you trying to tell me how to raise Jayden! I been doing it on my own for years."

"Are you that fucking selfish?!" He yells, causing his heart rate to kick up faster than it should. He was dispensing energy he couldn't spare. "I mean really, Harmony! Are you actually lying to me even though I forgave you for ruining my life! I'm dying! I probably hurt some other people too by fucking you and still…I'm not pointing fingers." Now he's angry. "But you gotta think about someone other than yourself." He pauses. "I forgive you, Harmony. Do you hear me, baby, I forgive you." She weeps harder but covers the phone so he can't hear her. "And all I'm asking is that you get focused. She's going through some things right now that are heavy and she needs a mother. She needs you. Can you be there for her? Please."

Harmony waits until she isn't crying anymore and removes her hand from the receiver. "You should've treated me right when I begged for your love, Jace. Consider this as payback. Die a slow death!"

MADJESTY

SLICK AND WET

When I come upstairs from the basement, I'm happy to see my grandmother is nowhere to be found. I guess she's in her room high, since it's one o'clock in the morning. When I see the keys to her car on the table I think I'm seeing things because she never leaves them there. She must stuff them in her asshole when she doesn't use them. She always talking about her car this and her car that and even threatened me a few times saying if I took it, my dyke ass and baby would be out on the streets. But I'm so bored right now it's a chance I'm willing to take.

I scoop them up and head for the door when I hear, "Madjesty, is that you in the living room?" I don't say anything. "I don't know what you doing in there but you better not have anybody in my house. I'm serious."

I try to sound sleepy. I yawn and say, "I'm just getting some juice."

She's silent and I figure she dosed back off. When I get outside and into her car, I'm amazed at how clean it is. Everything is in place. I don't get how she can be so ratchet in every other area of her life but keep her house and car on point. When I drive down the street, I almost slam into somebody on the back of a motorcycle, when I see a cute girl in some tight pink sweatpants and a white t-shirt. She don't look too classy but she phat to death. I'm trying to have some fun so I pull up on her and roll the window down.

"Can I holla at you for a minute?" I smile at her. She's a cutie.

She almost trips over nothing when she sees me. "You talking to me?" She points to herself.

"Who else would I be talking to?" I wink at her. "Get in...I don't want to be alone."

She pulls the car open so hard my grandmother's handle comes off. FUCK! Now she gonna know I was driving this bitch. "I'm sorry," She says getting in. She hands it to me. "I didn't pull it that hard." I throw it in the back.

"It's cool." I lie. "So what you about to get into?"

"I was waiting for my boyfriend to come pick me up." She runs her fingers through the short cut she's sporting. "Why…what you about to do?"

That pussy. Normally I wouldn't be interested in somebody with a nigga but I don't care anymore. It had been awhile since I fucked and with me being pregnant, I figured I'd better get some now before I started really showing. "Can I drop you off somewhere?"

"I can't go home now because I'm late. So I'm trying to stay out until the morning that way I can sneak in. You got somewhere for us to hang?" She smiles real wide and I see her brown teeth. I shake it off. Her mouth is ghetto.

I know I'm pushing the limits but I say, "Yeah, I know a spot."

⚫━━━━━━━━━━━━━━━━━━━━━━━━━━━⚫

She's lying on my bed on the floor, naked all over. I take my jeans and my boxers off and stand in front of her. I'm wearing nothing from the waist down. "Oh shit, I thought you were a nigga." She looks at my joint.

"Got a problem with that?" I don't give a fuck if she does. She can always walk home. I'm tired of apologizing for who I am.

To my surprise she says, "I'm cool with it if you are. It'll be my first time."

Lies. I get on top of her so that my space is on her pussy. I move around slow at first so I can grind into her. She's gripping my back and pulling me into her. It ain't even five minutes and she's so wet I can barely stay on because she's so slippery. "Hmmm…you feel so good. I never fucked a girl before." She tells me.

"It's cool." I say trying to concentrate. The less she says the better.

I lift her shirt and suck on her titties. She smells good. Like coconut or some shit like that. Her nipple in my mouth tastes like perfume and I ease my hand behind her ass cheeks and pull them toward me. Now I'm pressing so hard against her clit that if I keep this up I'ma cum. "Turn over." I say. I want the feeling to last.

"What…why?" She whispers.

While she's asking questions, I flip her over like a pancake and spread her ass cheeks apart. Then I stick my clit into her asshole and move up and down. This bitch feels so good I'm not going to be able to hold on. I lick her back and then bite her shoulder before easing my fingers into her cave. She's wet. The kind of wet that gets me going.

"Fuck me just like that," she wiggles her waist and I push my fingers deeper into her. "Please." I'm about to cum." *I don't give a fuck if she does or doesn't.*

Truthfully I wish this bitch shut the fuck up before my grandmother comes downstairs. Where is the mute button on this slut? I can feel the pressure on my stomach and I ask my kid to forgive me until I can push this nut out. When I finally cum I fall into her back and breathe heavily.

When I'm done I say, "Where you want me to take you, baby?" I stand up and get dressed.

She pulls her clothes up. "You don't like me or something?"

I look down at her. "It ain't that, but you got somebody right? I thought we were just kicking it."

"I don't really like him like that. Plus he was supposed to come get me tonight when I met you and he didn't. So as far as I'm concerned he's cut."

"Look, you been real cool," I say grabbing my grandmother's keys, "but I really gotta take you to your spot so I can get back home. I'm kind of tired." I yawn for special effects and wipe my eyes. This bitch can't be here when my folks get up. That's all I know.

"But I want to stay here with you." She pouts and that's when I see the crazy. "I'm not ready to go home."

"Listen, you cool. Real cool. I like you but not in that way."

She stands up and walks over to the television on the dresser and knocks it down. It crashes at my feet and I jump back. Did I miss something? The noise in the quiet house sounds like a gun going off in church. "What the fuck you doing?" I yell looking at the mess.

She doesn't waste anytime going to the pictures on the walls and pulling them down too. The frames shatter and I'm about to shit on myself when I hear footsteps from upstairs. "Please...please don't do anything else." I say softly. "Let's talk about this."

"You don't like me! You fucked me and now you don't like me." The fucked up part is back in the day I would've went for a bitch like this. "Why you bring me hear to treat me like this?"

The doorknob turns. "Madjesty, what the fuck is gong on in there?" I hear my grandmother say. "And why is this door locked? I don't like locked doors in my house." When my father was here he kept locked doors all the time so she's lying.

"Grands, I'm not feeling good." I lie. "I'm sorry about the noise. I got sick and fell."

"Well open the door so I can make sure you okay."

"I just want to get some rest." I look at the girl and beg her with my eyes not to say or do shit else. "I'll see you in the morning. I'm sorry for making so much noise."

Silence.

"You don't have nobody in my house do you? You know I don't play that shit."

"No. I'm just trying to get some sleep." My heart is kicking up hell in my chest.

She walks back upstairs and I don't move until I hear her bedroom door close. Focusing back on Nut Job I say, "I'm sorry 'bout how I treated you. The only reason I carried shit like that was because you said you have a man. But if you trying to see about me, I'm trying to see about you too." I was lying. After what I did to my sister and losing Denise, I didn't want to be in a relationship. I didn't want shit but sex. And even if I did, I didn't want her. "You sure I can't drop you off somewhere and take you to breakfast in the morning? So we can start all over?"

She smiles and walks over toward me. The glass from everything she broke crushes under her feet. She hugs me and says, "You can take me back to the group home I live in now. It's late enough and the Resident Assistant should be sleep by now."

"I'm with it."

"But can you stay with me until the morning?" She looks at me. I swear I don't feel like this shit.

"Anything you want." I try to smile by my cheeks are wiggling. I feel like stealing the fuck out of this bitch. Now I was gonna have to find a way to replace everything down here.

I sneak out of the house and take her where she lives. And I spend the next hour spooning a bitch in the bed I wanted to get away from, while her roommates look at me and smile. The moment I hear her snoring, I jet. Now on the road, I'm sleepy, tired and noid. My mind is all over the place and then I feel queasy, like I got to throw up. When vomit flies out of my mouth, I bend down and let it all out. I end up crashing into a stop sign and the hood of my grandmother's car flies up. It's totaled. I know it.

I leave the scene taking nothing but her car keys. When I make it back home without her knowing, I place them exactly how I found them. I was so nervous I didn't leave the basement until I heard my grandmother crying about somebody stole her car. And even though it was me, it would be a secret I'd take to my grave.

JAYDEN
DIED TO SOON

It took some months and now he's gone. At least sunlight's coming through my bedroom window. Today will be a pretty day to bury my father, a man I barely got to know but love anyway. I think about him all day. I know it's mean but all I want to do is put him in the grave and go on with my life.

Since someone stole all of the money daddy left for me, I didn't have enough for his funeral. Who did it? He didn't know either before he died. I'd spent my own money on furniture for the house before I even knew he was dying, so I was broke too. Thank goodness for the funeral director, Mr. Grover. He was kind enough to allow me to pay after the service was over. Had it not been for him, I would've been lost. If I had Thirteen Flavors my problems would be over but I was done with that lifestyle. The square life is going to be hard to live by but I made a promise to my father to get an education and to do better, so it's a promise I'm going to keep.

The clock says 7:00 am when I first look at myself in the mirror. But when I check again, although I hadn't moved from the mirror, it is now 7:30. *Daddy's dead.* I need to eat. I'm losing too much weight. My body doesn't move the same. *Daddy died on me.* My hair is long and straight, all of my curls ironed out. I like it this way. I didn't wear makeup, mainly because I wasn't sure if I'd cry and ruin my face. *My daddy died. Daddy died. Why did he have to die?* The dress I chose is all black, strapless and long. Not sure if it's appropriate, maybe I should change.

There's a sinking feeling in my gut. And I feel alone. All alone. Where is my sister? Where is my twin? I need her here with me. Oh I forgot, she raped me and I never want to see the bitch again. My world is a mess. A fucking mess!

I need to get rid of this headache. I walk to my bathroom and pull up my dress. I'm not wearing any panties. I never do. I sit on the toilet and nestle my feet into the mint green bath rug. With my legs spread, I run my finger over my button. It tingles slightly, but not enough to give me a release. I rub it again. *Tingle.* And again. *Tingle.* Yeah, that's good.

When it's warmed up, I make small circular motions on my clit. Light and consistent. *Tingle.* I can feel the pain leaving already.

Now I'm so slick, I can apply more pressure. I bite my lip and move rapidly over my clit again and slip my finger into my pussy. *Tingle. Tingle Tinnnnnnngllle.* This is the best feeling in the world, which is probably why I do it all day. Everyday. If my father is watching me, will he think I'm a pervert? Oh wait, he saw me do it already.

I shake my head to get him out of my mind. I'm so wet now, there's a slick trail from my clit to my cave. When I raise my finger, a long glistening string of my syrup dangles from it. I wonder how I taste. Probably sweet. I stick my finger into my vault, coat it with cream and place it into my mouth. Yummy. A few more quick-fast motions and I finally get what I'm going for. *Tingle. Tingle. Tingle. Tingle* ....Mmmmmmmmmm. My headache is gone. Now let me get this shit over with.

●———————————————————————————————————●

I had Metha drive me in my truck, so I could be alone. I rest my head against the window, and watch all life pass me by. I wasn't about to sit in a limousine with a bunch of people I didn't know even though Kreshon begged me too. When we reach the funeral home, a smile spreads across my face. I'm overwhelmed with love, when I see all of the people out front who came to honor him. "Daddy, must've been a popular guy." I say to no one in particular even though Metha is in the truck with me. "I wish I got to know him longer."

My hearing hasn't gotten better. So I look at her lips to see if she's talking. She's quiet but her eyes are locked on the funeral home. She seems confused. Not as appreciative of the turn out as I am. Her lips start moving. "I don't know, Jayden, but I think something else is up." She parks in a spot available for immediate family members only. "You want me to go check it out? While you stay in here?"

"No. Let me see what's going on, too."

I jump out and approach the home, she follows me. On the way, I move closer to a sea of people dressed in dark colors with long faces. Some I recognize, most I don't. When I make it to the door, I see Kreshon grabbing his cell out of his dark blue suit jacket. I can't get over how handsome he is. Why is he so attractive, even at this age? If he's my father's friend, doesn't it make him one hundred or something?

"Jayden, come here." I quickly follow his orders. He smells of mint. Maybe it's the white thing riding the wave on his tongue when he speaks. He reaches out his hands for me. I accept and feel safe with him. When I see the way Metha gives me a certain look, now it feels wrong. They have history I can tell, but what is it? I focus on his lips. "I was just calling you. They saying we can't have his funeral." He holds me like I'm going to break. Maybe I am. "What you want to do?"

I feel my forehead tighten. I'm embarrassed. Hurt. "Where is his body?" I look around as if it would be out here with me. "They said I could pay later. They said I had time."

"He's in there." He releases my hands and shakes one fist in place. He seems angrier than me and it makes me feel better. "I swear I feel like blowing this mothafucka up. I ain't never have no shit happen like this before." He moves in closer, so that only I can hear his words. "They said give them the money now, or leave the premises."

I observe the people observing me. They look at me with pity. I hate pity. If I could've made a living off of the people who have felt sorry for me in my lifetime, I would be a millionaire. "How much is he asking for?"

He looks at someone behind him. A man I never met with an equal disgruntled look. "They asking for ten grand."

"Please tell me you have it, Kreshon." I'm pleading with him with my eyes but if I could've gotten on my knees and kept my dignity, I would've done that too. I don't have anywhere near that amount of money. The only change I have is enough to buy food and a few things around the house.

"Jayden, I ain't got shit. You should've told me you needed it and I could've helped you raise it. You said you had it when we talked earlier." His face distorts and I can tell he is embarrassed that he can't come through. "When Jace took that hit, we took it too. There was some money in another portion of the house that belonged to me that he told me about. I lost out big too." I think he's telling the truth, but I can never be sure. I feel out of place. Out of my league.

I step a few feet away from him and look down at my shoes. The black Christian Louboutin peep toes I just had to wear. It's amazing, you can look like a million bucks but be worth none. I feel lightheaded. I'm just a kid. Why was I going through all of this alone anyway? I'm about to fall out when the funeral director pulls up in a red Mercedes. Through the dark tint in his windows I can see his face. He's probably in his late forties and the car color is over the top for his age.

I push through the crowd and approach him at his car. He has a grin on his face, which is different than the one he wore when he helped me plan the service. '*You need the best casket, Jayden. You need the best limousine. You need the best headstone. And if you're having a repast, which we can also help you with, you need the best food too.*' I didn't know my father for a long time, but the time I did was special. I wanted him to have the best but I didn't know I couldn't afford it.

Mr. Grover, has extra thick eyebrows and a long face. He eases out of his Benz and walks straight up to me carrying a black shiny cane, with gold posts at both ends. His eyes roll from my feet to my breasts and stay there. "Ms. Phillips, Ms. Phillips," he grins again and grabs both of my hands, placing them into his. "Why do you get more beautiful each time I see you?" His comment is out of place. "Mighty, mighty refreshing you are."

My voice is calm. "Mr. Grover, I think there's a problem. You said I could pay you for the service after it was over. If I'm not mistaken, you said you'd give me a month."

He looks confused and pulls his hands away from mine. I'm glad. They're wet. "I never said anything like that." He chuckles, shaking his head from left to right. "I'm running a business, beautiful." He places his hand over his chest. His pinky finger sports a ruby gold ring. It's too tight and his finger looks swollen. "Not a charity." He's lying. Why?

"So where the fuck did she get that from then?" Kreshon asks with a stern voice above my head. I didn't know he was behind me, but I'm glad that he is. "Now we got friends and family out here," he steps between us, "and this is disrespectful to my nigga's legacy."

Mr. Grover appears to be irritated by his presence. "And it's disrespectful to my legacy for you to think I'd do a funeral for free." He removes his black suit jacket and throws it over his arm. "I mean have you had a chance to look in there? Everything is beautiful!" He looks at me again and I finally see his snake-like eyes. How did I miss them before? "Now you know, there are ways to work it off. A body like yours can earn a few bucks."

I squint. "You better slow down," I warn him. "Slow way down."

He blinks rapidly. "Well either come up with my money, or take your dead father with you. It's entirely up to you." He walks away leaving us alone.

Kreshon follows him at first like a shadow, until I pull him back. He steps in front of me and rubs my shoulders. My head is low because my heart is heavy. "I'm sorry about this shit, baby girl." In a less defensive voice than he used with Mr. Grover he says, "Jayden, we may have to plan this for another day. I don't think this dude is budging." He's talking to me but looking in his direction. I can feel his malice. "Fuck!" he yells and I jump a little. "I feel like hurting this dude!"

I look up at him. The sun stands behind him like an intimidating bodyguard, forcing me to squint. "Then do it."

The anger drains from his face. He looks at me seriously. "Jayden, don't give me an order you don't want carried through. I'm not that kind of man."

I swallow. "I want him held up and those doors open. Whatever you gotta do to make that happen, including taking his life, I'm with that shit."

●━━━━━━━━━━━━━━━━━━━━━━━━━━●

Kreshon makes it happen. Not sure how he did but he does. When we finally walk into the home, just as Mr. Grover said, everything is beautiful. The flowers. The decorations. It's breathtaking. Better than I could've imagined. My only nervousness at this point is seeing his casket again. I don't have the strength to do this alone and I miss my sister more. I hate myself for being weak for her.

I smooth the back of my dress and am about to take a seat in the back. Kreshon sees me from the front, looks puzzled and moves my way. When he reaches me he says, "Your seat is up front, Jayden. You gotta go up there."

I sit down. "Why I gotta go up there?" *Who are you my new daddy or something?*

"Because it's what a person does when a member of their family dies. People want to offer you their condolences. They can't do it if you're sitting back here." He takes my hand. He's acting like he's my father but I was about to bury mine. "Now come with me up front."

I ease my hand out of his and I think he's confused. The fact that I'm a child stops at my age. I'm being forced to make grown woman decisions and I want grown woman respect. "You know what I needed," I look up at him, "for people to offer me their money. They can keep their condolences." Surprisingly he looks like he understands. "Anyway I prefer to sit back here for many other reasons too."

"Like what?"

"I want to see who's really here for him and who's here just to be nosey. You be surprised what you learn about people when you quietly watch." I give him a look so that he knows my statement is meant for present company included. I remove my stare and focus on the area my father will be in a little while. "I'm not going up there, Kreshon. So how 'bout you hold that front seat down for me."

"Alright, Jayden." He looks frustrated and is about to walk away.

"What happened? To the director?"

He stops and walks back over to me. "You really want to know?"

"I wouldn't ask if I didn't." I hate when people did that type of shit. Just tell me.

"Me and my mans sat him down and had a conversation with his face. After that, he made a call to his employees so that they would know the funeral was back on. Needless to say he was mad, so to cool him off a little, we left him in the trunk of a car away from the funeral." I smile and watch him stroll off. I like him. A lot.

Before long the place is jammed pack. I can't believe how many people are here and more are coming. Things are fine until Metha dashes up to me and says, "Jayden, somebody just dropped some trash out front. We tried to get him to take it with him but he refused. Some disrespectful type shit."

I stand up and move in the alley of the home, bumping an older woman walking inside in the process. "What are you talking about?" Not more drama. I tug my right ear. I guess out of habit.

"Let me take care of it. You been through too much already." She dips before I get an answer.

"I'm going with you."

Once outside, she immediately jumps in a bald-headed man's face, who is sitting out front in a burgundy Toyota pick up truck. "Why are you leaving this shit here! Take it with you!"

"Look, I'm just doing what she asked. I spent too much time here as is. I gotta go home to my wife." He speeds off, almost crushing Metha's toes under his wheels in the process.

While Metha curses at his license plate, I search for the trash everyone is up in arms about. Wherever it is I'm sure we can find a dumpster for it out back. I spot it some feet out, in front of the sign that reads, *Jace Sherrod's Homecoming Service.* Now I see why Metha is mad. It's huge and right in the front. When I walk closer, the trash moves and I jump back. It isn't until it rolls over that I see my mother's face. I run up to her. What is she doing out of bed? She hasn't fully recuperated from her recent stab wounds yet.

"Mommy, what are you doing here? You're supposed to be in bed!" She's drunk and probably unaware of how terrible she looks.

She reaches out for me. "Jayden, h-help me up."

This is Déjà vu. I had taken care of my mother all of my life and am at it again. I extend my hand and she stands up. Barely. "Mommy, why did you come here like this?" I look around to see who is watching. Everyone is. "You can't be here."

Her face is ash gray and she's wearing a silver dress under a men's oversized black suit jacket. "Jayden, remember when you were a kid and I asked you to tell me you love me after I've made your life a living hell?"

I nod. I think about that day often. Instead of giving her a lot I say, "Yes."

With tears in her eyes she says, "That day has come." She smiles but it isn't complete. "I need to hear you love me even though I've taken your father from you." My nose itches. I want to cry. I want to slap her in the eyes.

"So you're admitting that you're infected?"

She nods. "Yes. Do you love me now?"

I try to say I love her but at the moment I hate her. The kind of hate that makes you violent. It's the same feeling I felt when I burned Armanii's house down. But I want to prove her wrong more than anything. I want her to know that despite all she's done, I'm still here for her. "Ma, I told you there wouldn't be anything you could do, to make me hate you." I swallow. "I love you and I meant that."

She hugs me and I breathe in her earth smell. She wipes her tears away. "Please take me inside. I gotta see him." She's sobbing and my heart rips into pieces. I can count the times on my fingers where I saw her cry. "I need him to know that I'm sorry and that I always loved him too."

Too? Had he professed his love recently? "Mommy, you can't go in there like that. I'm sorry." I think about all I went through today, to make things perfect. Everything I endured. I didn't need her being loud and ridiculous and ruining everything. "I'll give you one of his programs or something."

She looks directly into my eyes and I can finally see she's broken down. "Please, Jayden. I gotta be in there with him."

When I turn around everyone is still staring at us with their judgmental eyes. Out of spite, I put my arm around her, walk her inside and she sits next to me in the back. Who were they to judge? Some of the mothafuckas in here might be murderers. My mother isn't the best. She isn't even decent but I'm alive and as long as I live, I'll never abandon her.

We are sitting down for a few minutes before Kreshon pushes an attractive man up to us in a wheelchair. Kreshon was looking at my mother but she's so drunk she focuses only on my father's picture in the front. "Jayden, this is Tony Wop, your father's cousin."

I smile and extend my hand. He doesn't accept.

"He's not well mentally." I drop my arm. "He was poisoned at a party we threw for your father a long time ago," Kreshon looks at my mother again and I wonder why. "They put him in a mental institution because he was never the same after that shit and took a hammer to his head. He got into his skull and almost died. I just wanted you to meet him." They roll away.

All he did was embarrass me. If he can't speak, why bring him back here? When they finally bring the casket inside, I feel my body tremble. It's silver and black and is beautiful. When I hear loud rattling, I look over at my mother. She's shaking so hard, the button on the men's jacket she's wearing knocks against the wooden bench. She's a wreck. I need her to be there for me, to be a mother, yet here I am having to play mother to her.

I feel alone until I smell a strong scent of weed and someone places their hand on my shoulder. I turn around and see Olive's naturally curly Afro and those signature long eyelashes. She's drop dead sexy even though she's high. Everything about her is real and that's why I fuck with her. I immediately feel bad for ignoring her calls because all she wanted to do was be there for me. Her legs are crossed and she's playing with the two silver balls I always see her with. They go in and around her fingers and she smiles at me.

To her right is Passion, who grins weakly. She brushes a few tentacles of her long black hair away from her face and places her hands in her lap. She looks clean, like she isn't using anymore. Now I can see why Madjesty's attracted to her and the thought makes my tummy sick.

"What are ya'll doing here?" I ask Olive. I'm smiling for the first time all day.

I read Olive's lips. "You wouldn't answer the phone, Jayden. So I found out about what happened to your father and came to support you. Are you alright?"

"I'm fine." I lie. "I just want this to be over." Her being here is some real shit. I had been avoiding her since Madjesty raped me and yet she came anyway. "Thank you for coming." I look at Passion and say, "you too." Even though I don't know Passion's motives. They sit back in the seats behind me and I smile again. I know Olive is here so suddenly I'm not alone.

As I focus back on the casket, I feel extreme warmth over my hand. When I look down, I see my mother's hand over mine. Her nails are dirty and her fingers feel gritty. But I don't care. It just feels good to be touched by her, even if it's because she's scared.

Service is moving along swiftly until someone kicks open the doors and yell, "Where is that bitch? Where the fuck is she?" She's angry and the mood changes immediately. I guess you can't have a black funeral without drama.

Everyone in the funeral home turns around to investigate the owner of the voice. It comes from a big woman wearing a long turquoise Muumuu. Her hair is wrapped in the same material. But it's the knife in her hand that has my attention. "Where is that slut?" Tears pour out of her eyes as she looks around. "I want to see the bitch who killed my nephew now." The hair on the back of my neck stands up. She wants my mother.

I look in the back to find an exit but someone in the front points my mother out. When the yeller spots her, her anger goes to the next level.

"Who is that, ma?" I ask her. She doesn't respond. She just seems stunned to see her.

"I warned my nephew to stay away from you." The woman rants as she slowly approaches. If she comes over here, I don't have anything to defend myself. To defend us.

"I tried to tell him you would be the death of him but he wouldn't listen." She points at his body in the casket. Why is she doing this now? Even if you hate her, couldn't this wait?

"Now look at him!" She continues. "Not even forty, yet he's dead!"

Kreshon walks up behind her and catches a slash to his new suit for his efforts. "Ms. Karen, please don't do this here." He asks, keeping his distance. He places his hands up. "This day is for Jace. You wrong for this shit."

She faces him and I'm not sure if she'll try to stab him or not. "What do you mean this day is for him? Every day of his life should've been for him! But fucking with this whore stole that."

I heard enough. I'm on my way to put her in her place, when a man flanked with four other men walk through the door. He's dressed in all black and the way he looks at my mother, tells me he doesn't feel any better about her. Now what?

HARMONY
FREAK ACCIDENT

I'm riding the hell out of a man who looks familiar even though I can't remember where I know him. I have a bottle of vodka in my hands and I pour it over my nipples. He licks the liquid off my stomach and rises up to suckle my breasts. We been having hot nasty sex all day! I feel shivers. Everywhere...but especially my pussy. I can feel him about to shoot when I stir my hips like a spoon in melted chocolate. I want more. I need to feel close to someone even if it's a stranger. I just saw Jace get buried and my mind is heavy. I'm such a fucking failure unless I'm in the bedroom. That's the only time I shine.

I still can't believe Jace's aunt was about to kill me at the funeral. That hating ass fat bitch never liked me! Had it not been for Rick, Jace's father, who came in last when she was about to cut me, I would've gotten stabbed up again. Bitches loved poking holes in me. After we left, Jayden was too busy wondering why Jace didn't tell her about them. Who cares? She kept promising to find out why when I wanted her to leave the shit alone.

He looks up at me and I say, "Tell me you love me."

He grins. He likes games I can tell. "I love you, Charlotte."

My eyebrows rise. He calls me by the wrong name but I don't care. All this shit is fake anyway. I get up and stand over top of him on the bed. It moves a little but I keep my balance.

"Do it." He begs. I inch up over his face and piss all over his chin and chest. He's in awe. He jerks his dick so hard it looks like he's pulling up weeds in a garden. Before he rips it off and wastes my time, I jump back on it and buck wildly. Shit is all good until he throws me off of him and my head hits the TV stand on the left side of the bed. I'm about to curse him out until I turn around and look at the door. We are no longer alone.

A brown skin woman stands in the doorway. She's chunky but has a very pretty face. "Not again, Dalvin." She's real calm and walks out of the door. And then I remember, Dalvin lives a few houses down from me. He's my next-door neighbor. The one who grabs my ass every time I walk by him on the block. But who was she? I never saw her before.

I stand up and say, "Who was that? Your sister?"

He's frozen and doesn't answer my question. "You gotta go." He gets louder. "Now!"

"Fine with me, but are we gonna finish the bottle?"

"If you don't get the fuck out of here, you might not be able to make it out alive."

I heard that before. "Why?" I ask, putting on my panties. I grab the bottle because he won't be drinking this now.

"Because that was my wife. We were separated but now we're back together." *I can't tell.*

If that was his wife it didn't look like he had any problems. She seemed easy does it. The moment I think that, I hear an engine revving up outside of the window. When I look out of it, there is a pickup truck coming full speed ahead in our direction. I don't get a chance to warn Dalvin until it's too late. The truck comes barreling into the bedroom knocking the wall down and pushing the mattress into the next room. She ran into the fucking house! This bitch is crazy. She backs out.

I grab my pants and don't bother putting them on. I hear her revving up the engine again and know what time it is. I pick up my shoes and carry them in my hands. Before I can put them on, she comes into the house at maximum speed again. The front wheels of her tires are on Dalvin's body and his blood is everywhere. He's gone I know it.

I run outside as fast as my legs will take me. I don't have anything but panties on from the waist down and I know it's over. That is until I see Metha, Jayden's driver pulling up. I flag her down and I see Jayden in the backseat. The moment I'm safe and inside I say, "Take off." I look behind me. The truck and house are still one.

"Ma," she looks back at our neighbor's house. "What is going on?" She looks at my lips.

"I had a situation back there." I drink the rest of the vodka and throw the bottle on the floor. "Ain't nothing for you to be worried about." I put on my pants and then my shoes.

"How come you always into stuff? Please say you not fucking that woman's husband. When you know you're positive! That is so wrong."

"Jayden, relax!"

"You being reckless! Damn, we just buried my father!" Silence. "This shit is killing me, ma. I mean, I want to help you but you won't let me."

I sigh. "Why do you feel I'm your responsibility? I'm your mother, not the other way around."

"Because you aren't responsible and somebody has to worry about you! You run around town fucking people's husbands and you're going to get yourself killed when they find out you got that shit. If you don't slow down you're going to get me killed, too." She grabs my hand. "Ma, I'm trying to take care of you, but you gotta meet me halfway."

I look over at her. Her makeup is perfect. Her body is flawless. She's being chauffeured by a driver and she has her father's Escalade. A man who's dick I sucked most of his teenaged years. She doesn't know the first thing about struggle. I snatch my hand away from hers. A little over a year ago she thought she had a dick instead of a pussy and now she wants to tell me about life? Yeah right!

"You got money?" I say.

"For what, ma?"

"Because I'm asking, or would you rather me sell myself to get it instead?"

She looks at the woman in the rearview mirror who shakes her head at me. Fuck her too. Eventually Jayden reaches into her wallet and separates a one hundred dollar bill from a stack. She gives it to me. "Be careful, ma." I leave without responding. The last thing I wanted to be was careful and she and I both knew it.

JAYDEN

EVERYTHING CHANGES

"How are you for real, Jayden?" Passion asks me as I focus on her lips. I don't want to tell her about all the wild shit my mother has been doing. And how it has me about to pull my hair out. And how she's throwing her diseased pussy around the neighborhood like the Washington Post newspaper. So I keep it to myself.

"I'm good." I shift in my chair.

"I hear you, but you've been quiet ever since Olive got up and went outside. Still mad at me or something?" We're in the doctor's office as I wait for my name to be called to find out the status of my hearing tests. I'm nervous.

"Why are you here, Passion? Just keep shit for real with me." I look into her eyes. "I know you don't fuck with me like that. You never did."

She looks away and then back at me. "That's not true, Jayden. I mean, we had our problems but I always looked at you like a friend. I guess we don't do good working for each other, like that anyway. But I'm still trying to be in your life."

"It ain't like I'm holding you hostage anymore. Thirteen Flavors is done with, you're free to do you. I'm never going back to that shit. I made a promise to my father."

"But I'm still your friend whether you want me to be or not." She drops her head. "Do you want me to be?"

"That's on you." I look at the kid with the boogers in his nose. I'm tempted to pick them out. "I'm going to focus on me and I'll leave it as that."

"You talk to your sister?" She asks me.

"No I haven't and right now, all I'm thinking about is me." I think I understand the reason she's around me now, to get closer to Madjesty. If she's waiting on that she'll grow a dick first.

"I hope she's okay." She sits back in her chair and looked at the ceiling. She looks like she wants to cry. "I been worried sick about her."

Olive comes into the waiting room with a cloud of smoke over her red Afro. The entire room smells like weed now and a few parents frown.

She's smiling at me through squinted eyes and I can't help but grin. She sits next to me, grabs my left hand while Passion grabs my right.

"You just had to get high didn't you?" I ask. "At my doctor's appointment at that."

Passion leans forward. "Yeah, Olive, I really wish you would've waited to do that shit when I wasn't with you. You know I don't want to be around that stuff anymore. If you were trying to stay clean I would respect you."

"Well I'm not."

"I'm serious!"

I learned after the funeral that Olive and Passion were friends through Shaggy. And even though he'd been ignoring them too, they maintained their friendship.

"Listen, bitch, I'm not the one who decided not to get high no more." Olive tells her. "If you wanna hug some trees and save the world then that's on you. Just don't knock my flow." She plays with the silver balls in her other hand. "I swear you were more easier to be around when you were on heroin. I'm just being honest with you."

"That's some ignorant shit to say." She exhales.

Instead of calling Metha, we drove in Olive's 15 passenger van which she uses for the airport taxi business she ran on the side. She'd just finished a job but wanted to go with me to this appointment and I was glad she came. I always wondered where she got her money because she smokes so much weed and popped so many pills, she had to be able to support her habit some how. I'm sure we looked like three lesbians holding hands but it didn't matter. I needed their support.

I'm about to call my mother to make sure she's okay when I feel Olive's hand brushing against my thigh. She claimed she wasn't gay no more but every time I turn around she's touching me. I wish she stops because every time she does it she makes my skin crawl. "Olive, I'm still not fucking you." I push her hand away. "So I wish you quit that gay shit."

"I'm not gay anymore." She laughs, sits back in her chair and crosses her legs. She's always hornier when she's high.

"Can't tell, when I slept over last night, I woke up with your hands on my breasts." Passion shivered. "That's some gross ass shit, Olive. Contrary to what you believe, no means no."

"Because you don't get high anymore, I'm not gonna bust your little bubble too hard but I will say this. You were with a bitch for two to three months, so you can't say shit to me about being with a woman."

Passion turns red. "First of all I didn't know she was a bitch and second of all we didn't have a relationship like that. We weren't eating each other's pussies, she was doing me." She looks at me and I look away. "The entire time we were together I thought she was a nigga. Honest."

"Sure you right." She laughs. "Nobody is dumb enough to believe you can be with a woman for two months and not know. Save that shit for somebody who believes you."

"I'll never tell you anything in private again."

"Promises, promises."

Every time anything pertaining to Madjesty comes up, I want to skip the subject. "Olive, I know you not gay anymore, but how could you fuck with a bitch? The shit's so nasty to me." I think about how juicy my pussy gets when I get horny and can't imagine tasting another female's.

"So you really think eating pussy is nasty?" Passion and me nod our heads yes. Olive leans out and I focus on her lips. "Okay let me ask you this, do you really believe eating pussy is disgusting, no matter who the pussy belongs to?"

I frown. "Yes."

"So why should a nigga eat yours?" She's wearing a conquered look on her face.

"What, I'm confused." I say.

"Me too, Olive." Passion adds. "You gotta give us more than that."

"Listen to what I'm saying, if eating pussy is so nasty, niggas who love it gotta be gross too right?"

Passion shakes her head. "Naw, that's different. They supposed to do that shit."

"You not making sense. If it's so gross its gross. It don't matter who does it."

"Olive, shut your gay ass up, you a little too high right now." I respond. "I don't care what you say, there's nothing in the world you can tell me that will make me want to eat another bitch's pussy. I don't care if they clean that mothafucka everyday with bleach."

"Whatever, bitch," she waves me off, "but listen, what's up with that kid Sebastian and Luh Rod? They seemed real strange to me, the day we came back from your father's funeral and they were hanging in front of your house."

"On everything I love I said the same thing. I think they may try to rob me or something." I think about how broke I am. "They're going to be mad if they do. Outside of the little money I have saved for a rainy day, I'm dead broke."

"Ya'll better get an alarm," Passion says, "all that house ya'll got and anybody can walk in there anytime they want. That's dangerous. You never know which creep may be waiting to take advantage of you."

"Right now we can't even afford that shit. I'll worry about that when the time comes."

When I look up at the counter, I see a new girl who doesn't seem nicer than the one I threw the juice on. She acts like she doesn't want to be here either. I hate bitches like that…just quit. She's waving at me and I stand.

Passion grips my hand. "You want me to come in there with you?"

Since they don't know the entire secret I say, "No, I gotta go alone."

"When are you going to tell us what's wrong with you?" Olive asks. "It ain't like we not here to support you. Are you burning or something? If you are it happens to the best of bitches."

"Don't be ridiculous. Ain't nothing wrong with this pussy." *Ask my sister, she knows.* "I gotta go at it alone." I walk to the doctor's office and he's waiting with a smile. He never smiles so I know immediately something is wrong.

"Where's your mother, Jayden?" He looks behind me and I take my seat.

"She couldn't make it." I shrug and flash my teeth. I feel so stupid. "She's ill again. It's okay though, I can tell her whatever you want me to know."

He takes his glasses off and looks frustrated. "I really want to speak to her this time, Jayden. You are a minor and I can't keep discussing this serious situation with you alone." He picks up the phone on his desk.

I lean forward. "What are you doing?"

"What's your home number?" His finger hovers over the digits. "I have to call her."

"Dr. Takerski, please don't. I can handle whatever you gotta tell me." I want to cry but don't know if it will help. "My mamma be busy these days. She don't have time for all that. So much has happened in her life."

His expression is stone. "The number, Jayden."

I rattle off the home phone number and hope the man upstairs won't remember how I told him to fuck off and to go to hell. I need his help right now. I don't want my mother speaking to him or anybody else about my business. Even now when I go to school, I put in every effort to be the best I can just so she won't have to crawl out of the hole and embarrass the shit out of me.

The phone doesn't ring too long and once again the fake ass God upstairs let's me down. "Yes, may I please speak to Harmony Phillips please?"

At first I'm trying to read his facial expressions, until he looks like he's seen a ghost. He presses the speaker button on the phone and the office lights up with the nastiest words ever. *"I don't know who the fuck you are but I don't get up before five in the evening! Who the fuck do you think you are calling me this time of day? Huh? Huh?"* She sounds like she's drinking in her sleep. My mother is the worst.

He clears his throat and wipes the sweat off of his forehead with a stiff hand. "Mam, this is Dr. Takerski and I'm calling because your daughter Jayden is here in my office," he looks at me, maybe to see if I left him alone with the drama, "and I have something very important to tell her and you."

"Well shit, if she's there, what do you want from me?"

He looks at me as if he feels sorry for me. I hate that look. "She's a minor and she's been coming here alone lately. Did she explain her situation to you?"

Click.

He looks at the phone. "Hello." He presses the speaker button again. "Ms. Phillips."

I'm beyond embarrassed. I can't believe she couldn't come out of her drunken status for a few seconds, to be a parent to me over the phone. She didn't even have to get out of bed. "I'm sorry, sir but like I told you, she's not feeling too well."

He's still staring at the phone as if she'll call back and say she's just playing. It never happens. He clears his throat and says, "Jayden, I'll get straight to it. Do you know if your mother was using drugs when she was pregnant with you?"

Probably. "I don't know about drugs, sir. But she keeps a bottle in her mouth at all times." I move in my seat.

"Well the issue in your left ear came as a result of glass rupturing your ear drum. But the condition in your right is as a result of a birth defect that I usually see in children who are born to parents who abuse drugs or alcohol." He seems mad.

"I have a twin sister and she seems to be okay." *Well she did rape me but that's another matter all together.*

"She may be suffering from other defects that you aren't aware of. I really need to see her too."

"Humph." I whisper.

"Chances are your hearing has always been lower than people who don't have your effect and had you come sooner, like when you were a toddler, we could've addressed it right away and corrected the issue. Now, well now your hearing is deteriorating rapidly. The specialist you went to said if you don't do something now, you'll be permanently deaf." He pulls a sheet of paper off of a yellow pad. It has numbers on it, which includes lots of zeros.

I know what this is about. "How much?"

"The surgery will cost $50,000. That's $25,000 per ear. The problem is, Medicaid only covers your medicines and aftercare. Which means you'll have to come up with the rest on your own."

As he gives me more bad news I finally get it. God doesn't fuck with me at all. "Where am I going to find that kind of money? I'm broke." Maybe he knows of some charity program for kids with drunken-whore parents like me.

"I'm afraid that's a problem I can't help you with, Jayden. This is why it was so important for me to talk to your mother." He brings her back up and it makes me feel worse. "Now I have something I would like to give you for now. But you must understand that it's only a temporary situation. After a while, these won't work either."

He gets up and walks toward me. I smell the stink of his breath and my stomach churns. For some reason I focus on the bulge of his pants and notice he seems to be packing more than a doctor should. My pussy jumps. Maybe if I fuck him he'll help me out, its certainly worth a try.

He sits a white box on his desk and removes two brown C shaped devices. They were the ugliest things I'd ever seen in my life. "These are hearing aids." He sticks one behind my left ear and then the right. "Can you hear me clearer?"

I can't believe how bright his voice sounds. I can even hear the clock ticking on the wall, although faint. My hearing isn't back to the way it use to be but it's better than what I'd been dealing with since Madjesty hit me. I feel a smile stretch across my face so long I think my mouth will crack at the edges. I quickly take a mirror out of my purse and hold it up to my face. And then I see what I look like. A freak. Sideshow Jayden. Like one of the kids at my school with the big block shoes. I can never walk around like this.

"Jayden, can you hear me?" He asks. I hear him just fine.

I place my mirror back in my purse, remove the hearing aids and throw them in there to. They take the sound with them immediately.

"Why did you take them off?" His voice sounds lower again.

"Because I want to adjust them better when I get home." I stand up. "Dr. Takerski, when is the appointment you scheduled for my surgery?"

I watch his lips. I've become a pro and wonder if I can get paid for it. "The earliest I could get it is in six months."

I frown. He calls that quick?

"But, they'll want half down in two months just to secure your appointment. You think you and your mother can come up with the money by then?"

I look up at him. He doesn't understand the life I lead. I need to hear. I need to be a part of the world. So not coming up with the money was not an option. "In two months you'll have your fucking cash. Thanks for nothing."

●━━━━━━━━━━━━━━━━━━━━━━━━━━━━━━━━━━●

Trouble don't stop. Because when I get home, the windows to my house are busted open and the door kicked in. I walk through the place where the door should be. Shocked, I can only move slowly at first until I see the TV is gone and everything looks destroyed. I just bought that TV.

"You already know who I think did this shit." Olive says. "Old blue eyes himself."

I'm so mad I can see my nostrils flaring. Olive and Passion hang in my background as I walk further inside. I can only imagine what their faces look like now. Sebastian and Luh Rod definitely did this shit, I'm sure of it. I'm wondering when this happened until I think of my mother. She has so many enemies that this could've been an attempt on her life too. At the funeral last week the lady I found out was my aunt tried to kill her. And what about my grandfather, he seemed like he hated her, too. And then there was the next-door neighbor's wife. As terrible as my mother is, it could be anybody.

I dart up the stairs on a mission to find her. I call her name throughout the house. When I finally reach her room, my heart trembles the vessels in my body. I'm rocked with complete fear. I can feel Passion and Olive right behind me so that gives me the confidence to go inside. I touch the doorknob and slowly open my mother's bedroom door. She's lying on the floor, naked; a half empty bottle of vodka is in the palm of her hand.

Worried, I rush to her, drop on my knees and rub her back. If I lose my mother too, I'm not sure how I will react. She's the only family I had in the world since I'd written my sister off. "Ma," I say softly hoping she'll come around like she normally does whenever she has too much. "Are you okay?"

It takes a minute but eventually she rolls over, looks into my eyes and throws up right where she lay. It splashes on my hair, shirt and jeans. I hate when she does that shit. I jump back in anger and fall into Olive's legs. I'm frustrated with everything.

"Jayden, you want me to call the hospital?" Olive asks with concern all in her voice.

I watch my mother roll over and grab her head, not letting go of the liquor bottle once. "No, she'll be alright." I stand up and then I remember the little money I had saved is in my room. I rush toward my bedroom, knocking Olive into Passion in the process. Unlike my mother's room, my door is wide open. I didn't even have to step in fully to realize everything worth money was gone. My TV, my clothes, my purses, and my jewelry, everything I worked hard for and bought in our short time here in Maryland was taken. I fall to my knees and cry again. I'm so tired of crying but I don't know what to do.

"Jayden, please don't cry!" Olive runs to the bathroom and comes out with a damp cloth. It's the one I use to wipe my pussy real quick when I play with myself. She *would* pick up that one. She wipes my mother's vomit out of my hair and does her best to do the same to my clothes. "It'll be okay. You can get everything you lost back plus some."

"But how?" I ask seriously. She doesn't answer.

"I'm going to get you something to drink." Passion says. She seems rattled by all of this.

"Why is all of this shit happening to me? First my father dies and now we've been robbed." I rub my temples to relieve some of the pressure on my head. It doesn't work. "I don't know what to do anymore, Olive. I'm handling all of this alone."

"What's up with your mother? Is she always like this?"

For the first time ever, I'm honest with one of my friends. "All the time."

She rubs my back and sighs. "I'm so sorry, Jayden. I can't imagine what you're going through right now. It's no wonder you're not in a crazy home." I think of Madjesty. "You're stronger than I would be if this was me."

"You know I watched a TV show some time back that says if Black Widow Spider handlers are bitten a lot, they develop a tolerance against the venom. I think that may be what's happening to me now. I'm so sick of this shit, Olive. I'm starting not to care anymore."

Before she can respond, Passion is backing into my doorway. At first I think some niggas are still in the house, about to finish us off. It only takes me seconds to figure out its much worse. Mrs. Sheers, my social worker, walks into the doorway and a look of shock covers her face. "Jayden, what is going on around here? The house is a disaster." She doesn't walk all the way inside of my room, I guess to keep her distance.

I stand up and dust off my wet jeans, damp with my mother's vomit. "I...we..."

"Where is your mother?" She interrupts. She's a bully. "Is she okay?" Her question sounds more like a statement. If ever I needed my mother to stay where she was, now is it. If Mrs. Sheers sees the condition she's in right now, she'll probably throw me in a foster home in a hurry.

"She's fine. She's just..."

It's too late, my mother comes yelling out of her room and into the hallway. I can't see her yet, but I can only imagine what she looks like because Mrs. Sheers covers her mouth with her wrinkled pink hand. Now she joins me and my friends in my room as I wait for my mother to appear in the doorway. I shake my head when I finally see her. This is the final straw I know it. Mrs. Sheers will remove me now. And where will I go? My father is dead and I don't have his financial support anymore.

My mother obviously doesn't understand the severity of the problem. Why else would she come out of her room holding a man's sock between her legs to cover her stank box? She doesn't bother to protect her breasts, which swing like they own the place. The scars from all of the wars on her body stand out like constant reminders that she shouldn't have children. And most of all, she shouldn't have me.

"Ms. Phillips!" Mrs. Sheers yells observing her bareness. "What is going on around here? What kind of home are you running?"

My mother lifts the bottle to her lips and drinks what's left. Some of the vodka rolls down the sides of her cheek and it appears like everyone including me, stands by for her drunken response. "I'm in my house, bitch," she slurs, "what the fuck are you doing here?"

My eyes pop open and Mrs. Sheers looks back at me and then at her. "Its obvious things are worse here, more than I thought."

"What the fuck is that supposed to mean?" My mother asks.

"It's clear you have an alcohol problem and your home situation must be reevaluated." She looks at her again. "And I also went to the children's school, Ms. Phillips and I didn't like what I heard. Because although Jayden is doing better now, Madjesty seems to be missing in action. To make matters worse, I came into your home to see the door kicked in and things all over the place. Not to mention I almost slipped on this envelope." She's holding a piece of paper.

"That's a paper." I say, wondering where the envelope is.

She clears her throat and says, "I meant paper." I know the bitch opened our shit. She wiggles it at my mother but she prefers to suck the air out of the bottle than to take the paper.

I look at what she's holding and snatch it from her. On the top were the words, *District Court Of Maryland.* Although they used a few large words throughout the document, it doesn't take me long to get the gist of what's going on. I throw my weight on the edge of the bed and look at it again. Then I stare at my mother with disgust. Apparently there was a court date regarding who was the rightful owner of this house. And since my mother failed to show up and state her case, the judge made a decision in her absence. Basically he said that she had to put the house up for sale and split the profits with my aunts Ramona and Laura or buy them out for $250,000. I figured my aunts were out of jail now and fighting with vengeance. I guess her lies about them stabbing her came back to bite. I don't know who stabbed her, but it definitely wasn't them.

My mother had six months to come up with that amount of money. With this news I finally know what I have to do. And there was no wasting time in the process. Either I get money now, or lose the life I was starting to love in the process. But first I had to make a few stops.

SHAGGY

GLORY, GLORY, GLORY

"How much is the cover tonight?" Shaggy asks the man at the door. The rundown club smells so bad inside, he contemplates leaving.

The big-legged bouncer looks him over. "Are you buying or drinking?"

"Both?" Shaggy says.

"Then it's five dollars." He gives him the money and moves toward the bathroom. There's a line around the corner and he figures the main attraction is performing tonight. When he's next, his heart is in his chest. He came to this place at least three times a week to satisfy his sick thirsts. Ever since he raped Madjesty and Jayden was acting weird, the only thing he could do was bust a nut to clear his mind. He could get bad bitches but he enjoyed freaked out shit. He loved it so much that he did it regularly. When the dude before him comes out of the bathroom stall excitement stirs through his veins.

He steps inside and locks the door. He looks at the toilet and frowns at the shit, piss and toilet paper circling around inside of it. He gets his mind right when he sees the hole on the side of the stall's door. The wall has graffiti everywhere but he could care less. He pays his fifty bucks, unzippens his pants and sticks his dick through the dark hole. After a few seconds he feels a warm mouth on his stiffness. He can't see who is putting in work because that was the power of glory holes. It could be a man or woman. You could get your dick sucked by a bitch you didn't know. If your imagination was proper, the person blowing you off could be anybody you want. From Beyoncé to Janet Jackson, the choice was yours. But in the case of Shaggy, he imagined it being Madjesty Phillips.

"Keep that shit right there." He encourages pushing his lower body into the wall. He places his hands on the tops of the stall's walls for leverage and pushes his waist deeper into the hole. Whoever is on duty means business because in less than a minute, he busts his juice everywhere. He doesn't stop gripping the top of the stall until he's empty and when he's done, he pulls his pants up and exits the bathroom without a thank you.

He's almost to his car until he sees his distant cousin. He fucked her one night at a club when he didn't know they were related. These days they acted like it didn't happen but both of them knew the truth and would take it to their graves. "Hey, cuzo." She says, wiping her finger through her treated red hair. "What's good with you?"

"Everything. How 'bout you?" He says, trying not to remember how soft her titties were.

"Some bitch name Jayden been asking around for you. She been telling everybody in the family that you not trying to see her in person. That you scared and shit like that. I was going to tell your mother but since she's been in the hospital, I left it alone." She looks around. "Well, let me get to work." When he thinks about her possibly working in the Glory Hole he shakes his head. Had he patronized her before? He'd been in there so much that it was possible. "I just wanted you to know."

Shaggy felt his blood pressure rise thinking about Jayden and decided to see that bitch on her own turf.

●━━━━━━━━━━━━━━━━━━━━━━━━━━━━━━━━━━●

Jayden was in the driveway, looking at her social worker leave when Shaggy pulls up. He parks his car and steps so closely too her, they kiss. Literally. "Listen bitch," he says in her ear so that the white lady eying them doesn't hear what he has to say. "If you want me, I'm here." He pushes her with his chest. "Ain't no need in going to my folks house asking about me. I'm right here beside you…right now. What you want to do?" He looks at her but she doesn't move, yet he sees the danger in her eyes. Still, the last thing she wants to do was alert Mrs. Sheers about their scenario. "That's what the fuck I thought. Stay out of my lane before I run you over, and that's on everything."

He leaves her to her thoughts before pulling off.

JAYDEN
MAJOR HANDOUTS

I wanted to kill Shaggy so I had to get away. He got that one but he'll see me again. Now I'm sitting in my father's old house in DC. I can feel his presence everywhere. Pictures of him are all over the walls and it's evident that his aunt Karen loves him very much. I stand up from the table where we just finished eating dinner and walk toward a picture in a gold frame on the fireplace. I've been looking at it all night. It's of my mother, my father and the man I saw in the wheel chair at the funeral. The eerie part is, my mother looks just like me. Like we could be identical twins. I guess I see why she hates me so much.

"You look just like her," Karen confirms as she walks up behind me. Luckily I hid my hearing aids under my long hair, so I can hear everything they're saying. "This was the last time Antonio had a clear mind. He looks so happy." Her expressions alternates from love to hate as she eyes the photo. It doesn't take me long to see that when she looks at my mother, the love goes away.

"Antonio?" I frown. "I thought the person in the picture is called Tony Wop."

She sits the photo down on the fireplace although she keeps staring at it. "That's his street name." Her lips curl up. "I hate that the boys were determined to follow in Jace's father's footsteps. I love my brother, but Rick can be a selfish ass bastard at times. Watch him, honey. Watch him with both eyes. That's all I'm going to tell you."

Wow. "When was it taken?" I can't stop looking at my father and mother together. They look so happy. They look so in love. I'm sad that I never got to see them like this.

"Somebody snapped it on your father's eighteenth birthday." She looks at the picture with pity again and I really want her to sit down. I want this moment alone. "The night had so much promise. Unfortunately it ended with tragedy because of the poisonings."

I have so many questions. "I thought you didn't like my mother?"

"That's true. I don't."

"So why is her picture here in your house?"

She exhales. "As a reminder of what life was like before their lives were altered by her the night of the party." She shakes her head. "They were young black men with so much promise. And women too. All gone because of her." She shakes her head. "It just hurts my heart...you know?"

I just stare at her.

"You said their. Are you saying the poisoning was my mother's fault?"

"Let's just say that a lot of young people were killed that night." She pauses. "Twenty to be exact because the alcohol was tainted." I look at my mother again, she doesn't look like she could be so vicious. Suddenly she's more interesting than I thought. "It's rumored that Massive, your father and grandfather's enemy, was involved with their deaths too but it was your mother who led him there."

"Why are you telling that girl those scary stories again?" My grandfather says entering the room. He's short but handsome and his accent screams Spanish. "You're going to scare her away before we even get to know her." He grabs his jeans at the thighs to sit down comfortably at the table.

She glares and I can't tell if they like each other or not. "Quiet, Rick. I'm just giving her a little history. She's old enough to hear the truth anyway. I can tell her whatever I want."

He seems frustrated. "How about you give me a little tea like you promised after the meal. I have to wash that awful beef-whatever you made for dinner down my stomach." He laughs. "After all this time, you still can't cook."

I thought the food was great. "Fuck you, you always liked my cooking when we were kids and you know it." I wonder how they're related because I can barely see the black in him while Karen screams it with her African garb. "You need to be thanking God I even let you back in my house."

"Karen, stop being so serious. You're worst than a catholic priest." He taps her on the arm. "And I still love your cooking. Now go," he points to the kitchen real bossy like, "let me speak to my granddaughter." She looks at me and I can tell she doesn't want to go but she does. When she's gone he says, "Sit, beautiful."

I sit in front of him. "You look so much like your mother, it's disheartening."

"Disheartening?" My eyebrows rise. "Why?"

He sits back in the chair and crosses his legs. "Your mother is very beguiling and she's broken a lot of hearts in her days. From what I'm told, some of the stronger men have fallen under her spell. That makes her dangerous."

I swallow. "I get that."

"I didn't know about you." He skips the subject. "Jace never told me I had a granddaughter. I wish he had, I really do." He shakes his head. "I heard about the funeral expenses, don't worry about it, I took care of everything with Mr. Grover."

That's good for the funeral director but I could care less. I'm mad he's still alive.

"You mean we took care of everything." Karen returns with the tea and I can tell Rick is irritated. It's like she doesn't want us alone. "I overheard your conversation about not knowing about you. Your grandfather was in Mexico hiding but I was always here. I can't believe Jace didn't tell me about you."

"Stop your lies, woman. I've never hidden a day in my life."

She grins. "Don't forget who you're talking to, Rick. I know about your gambling problem, although she doesn't." She looks at me. "Like I was saying, I wish I knew why your father didn't tell me about you."

"Well after what I saw at the funeral, maybe he had his reasons." I whisper.

Karen sighs. "I'm sorry about that, Jayden. It was so out of character for me to be that way. But I lost someone I raised as a child. You have to understand how I felt, when I learned he was dead from AIDS. He had his whole life ahead of him."

"But he wasn't your child, Karen. He was mine."

"But you never treated him that way. He was constantly trying to prove how much he loved you. How tough he was. But none of it was ever good enough for you was it? Jace could've been anything he wanted in the world, but you stole that from him. And now he's gone."

He takes the teapot and pours himself a cup, no sugar. "You're wrong for what you're doing right now but I forgive you." He looks back at me. "I'm sorry you have to see us like this. Let's just say we have our disagreements on how Jace should've been raised."

"No disagreements." Karen interrupts. "Your problems became his. He was a child yet he had to deal with grown man issues." *Like me.* "Had you never killed Massive's daughter at her graduation, maybe he would not have gotten involved in the drug lifestyle."

He slams his fist on the table. "Jace died from AIDS, not drugs! Don't confuse the two."

I want to get out of here. This meeting is not going how I expected. I decide its best to tell them why I'm here. "I need help."

Ricks eyebrows rise. "Sure, honey, what do you need?"

I didn't know if I could hit him for two hundred fifty grand, so I decide on the fifty instead. "I need money. Fifty thousand." Karen gasps but Rick keeps a straight face. "It's for surgery." I lift my hair and show them my hearing aids. "Without it I'll be permanently deaf. Can you help me?"

"I can have the money to you by tomorrow." Rick promises and smiles. A rich grandfather is just what I needed. "I'm doing better now financially. A lot better."

"What you really mean is that you're back selling drugs again." Karen walks up to me and moves my hair to look at my ears. "What happened, baby?" She moves my head from left to right and I smell the honey from the tea on her clothes.

I didn't want to tell them that Madjesty damaged one ear so I went with the story about the other. "My mother drank when she was pregnant and now I have a defect."

Karen shakes her head and laughs.

"What's funny?" I ask with an attitude.

"I don't think your situation is funny, please forgive me, honey. But I told your father to stay away from that bitch. If only he would've listened."

"You could've told him to stay away all you liked, if the pussy called him, he was going to answer. The boy was a grown man and you had to let him make his own decisions."

"At the expense of his life?"

"You are not his mother. She died while breastfeeding him in the park in case you forgot. Remember?" He yells. " You can't make a teenage boy and definitely a man do anything he doesn't want to do. He loved Harmony and he paid for it with his life. It's over anyway…just leave it alone."

"You really don't care do you?"

"It doesn't matter now does it?" Rick says. "Harmony's a drunk who will meet her fate soon enough. Who cares whether it's now or later. Eventually you will get your wish for her…death."

As I look at them disrespect my mother, like they're better than her, I realize I can't be here anymore. I feel disloyal. I stand up and say, "On second thought, I don't want your money."

Karen walks over to me. "What…why?"

"Because you're talking about her mother in front of her." Rick stands up and walks to me too. "I knew you would scare her away."

"I can come up with the cash, I got a money plan in mind that's fail proof." I brag. I don't want them thinking I'm all the way fucked up because I'm begging for a little cheese.

"I believe, you, but why don't you let me help you?" Rick says.

At this moment I wish I didn't wear the hearing aids because I wouldn't have to hear this shit so clearly. "My mother is a drunk and she's also HIV positive, but she's my mother. And as long as I live I'm not going to stand by and watch you or anybody else disrespect her." I grab my purse. "It was nice meeting you both." I lie. "But it was wrong for me to come here."

●━━━━━━━━━━━━━━━━━━━━━━━━━━━━━━●

I walk down the street with knife in hand, pointing low and to the right. When I get to Sebastian's house, I plan to carve out those blue eyes, cut off Luh's dreads and make them give me my shit back. After the situation didn't go as planned with my grandfather and aunt, I figure I have to at least get the money I saved to buy food and stuff for the house. I know exactly where to go too. The niggas who took it.

When I make it to his block, I hear music rattling my hearing aids. They must've been having some sort of party. I'm happy shit is sweet for them because my life couldn't be more wicked. The closer I get to his crib, I see colorful balloons hanging off of the trees and bushes in front of his house. It doesn't take me long to see Luh Rod on the porch with a beer in his hand. He's talking to some light skin girl with a fat ass and big legs. If she gets in my way I'll slice her face in two.

I almost reach him when someone sticks their foot out sending me crashing to the ground face first. The knife flies out of my hand and my teeth stab my upper lip. Someone roughly rolls me over like dough and when our eyes lock, I can tell he wants to kill me. "Who are you, Money Mike from Friday After Next?" I didn't get the reference. "Who you came to cut?" He's keeping me on the ground by pushing my shoulders down.

He's Pakistani or Arabian, either way he's beautiful. That doesn't stop me from yelling, "You better get your fucking hands off of me!" I wiggle strongly under him but I don't budge. "I'm not fucking around. If I get up I'ma hurt you." If only my strength could match my threats.

When I see Luh Rod's dreads partly covering his face as he stares down at me, I try to pop up again. I want his blood. I want his small children. I want his life. "Easy, sexy," the Arabian says, "You gonna hurt yourself." This mothafucka's crack head strong and it's making me angrier.

"Fuck wrong with you, girl?" Luh says, "I know you ain't coming all this way about that shit at your house. It ain't that deep."

My eyebrows rise. "So you admit you did it huh?" I huff. "Just tell the fucking truth." I'm too excited and want to hurt him. He's actually admitting to taking my shit to my face.

"Man, fuck this bitch." Luh says, walking away, leaving me alone with the strange nigga. I try to squirm from up under him again but I can't move. How does he do that shit?

When I hear a car pull up and see a pair of grey New Balance get out of it and walk toward me, my heart drops. "What the fuck is she doing down there?" He asks. It doesn't take long for those blue eyes to investigate me from the ground. "Pick her up, man."

"You sure, Bass? This chick was coming down here to do damage to somebody and I still haven't found out who." My head rises and my eyes zero in on Luh Rod. He looks like he's upside down from the ground and I'm breathing so hard, I can smell my own breath. "Judging by the way she's cooking, Luh must be the object of her satisfaction."

"Let her go." Sebastian says. "I got her."

The moment I'm released, I charge Luh Rod but Sebastian lifts me in air. My feet kick wildly as I'm taken to a white box-like house on wheels that's parked on the curb. I didn't even see it there. I'm thrown inside and Sebastian who rushes in and closes the door behind him blocks my path when I try to leave. I attempt to knock him down to get at his kid brother, but I'm pushed to the floor. My ass bounces twice before stopping. When I fell the floor sounded so weak I thought it would break. The place is small but neat and has a kitchen and living room area. Mostly everything is brown but it smells like somebody takes care of the space in here. "Who the fuck lives here?"

"Me." He says dryly.

"Well why am I here? And what is wrong with you for bringing me in here like that?" I yell at him. "I got business with your brother. Let me at him."

"You sound stupid." He huffs. "Picture me letting you get anywhere near my brother."

I'm pacing the area. "You don't have nothing to do with why I'm here." I stop. "Or do you?"

"Jayden, I don't know what's up with you but whatever happened, you got the wrong person. I suggest you go home before shit gets serious."

"Shit *been* serious and it ain't no need in you lying! I already know he did it, Sebastian, he half told me before you came out and ruined everything." I pop up but he pushes me back down.

He's breathing heavily and his hands are on his hips in a big man way. Like he just finished running and needed to catch a few breaths.

"Can you slow down and tell me what the fuck you talking about? How 'bout we start there."

I look at him. "Can I stand up first please?" I try to seem defenseless but my heart feels strong.

"If you act right." His blue eyes mean business. "Because I don't have time for the rest of this shit."

He's so sexy. Wait, why am I even thinking about that right now? These niggas broke into my house and took everything I loved. As I look him up and down, I wonder if he wears the same thing everyday to bring attention to his eyes. They're so pretty that he doesn't need to wear anything special, they're attention getters alone.

I carefully stand and spot a knife on the kitchen sink. I'm going for it the moment I can. When I'm on my feet, just as I planned in my mind, I rush for it when all of a sudden I'm hit in the back with a blunt object. Now I have a mouth full of rug and I turn over ready to beat his ass.

"So what, now you hitting girls?"

He doesn't like my comment, I can tell. "Jayden, I want you to go home. I'm not fucking around." He's scaring me, but my anger doesn't stop my mission. I want my stuff back. "I don't have anytime for this shit right now."

This is stressing me out. I need to play with my pussy. "Not until ya'll give me my money and the rest of my shit back."

"We don't have any money of yours, Jayden. I don't even know what the fuck you talking about. Now either go home, or I'ma have my girl cousins come in here and put hands on you. You already made me do more than I usually do when I hit you in the back just now with my fist." *That was his fist?*

I feel like I want to cry but I don't want to do it in front of him. I'm broke, I feel ugly wearing these hearing aids and I think I forgot to wear deodorant today. My life is so dry right now. Brillo pad dry. I'm a mess. "Can I stand up again please?" He nods.

When I look out of the window to my left, I see a sea of beautiful people. His people. They have to be Arabian and also pretty shades of African American. They are all eyeing the wheel house but especially the girls. I'm outnumbered and I decide that now is not the best time to fight this battle. I will be back though. I'm about to surrender when I notice the sign over their heads outside. It reads, *'Welcome Home Luh and Bass.'*

Even though I don't care I ask, "Where are you coming from?" I point at the sign.

"Jail." I swallow. *Oh shit.* "How long were you locked up?"

"For the past two weeks." I swallow again.

My eyes roll everywhere. I'm embarrassed. "When did you come home?"

"Today."

"Luh too?"

He nods. "Yes."

I'm not a genius but it doesn't take me long to realize he could not have robbed my house and be in jail at the same damn time. He's still breathing heavily and he looks like he wants to hurt me. I probably ruined his surprise party. But then...well...there's something else behind his eyes. Those blue eyes are so fucking sexy but they also creep me out.

He steps closer. "Take your jeans off, Jayden."

I step back. "Sebastian, I don't have time for this shit." *So why am I coming out of them?*

"Go over there, on the couch." He points behind me.

I dispute him again but my half naked ass is already seated. He stands over top of me and looks down at my pink thongs. Thank goodness I wore panties today. My yellow legs shake and I place my hands on them trying to slow them down. I feel his eyes everywhere and I match his stare by looking at him too. I can't look away and I feel so cheap. But I would be lying if I said I didn't want this.

He eases on his knees and places his hands on my legs. I smell some type of cologne and never thought he could be this fresh. Prior to now I looked at him like a thug. The boy that stands outside in front of my house scaring me along with his brother sometimes. "Why do you stand in front of my house sometimes?"

"Because I like you." That's weird.

"How old are you?" My question sounds dumb.

"Eighteen." He's older than me. Wow.

"What does the tattoo stand for? The lightning one on your face?"

"My mother and father died when lightning struck a tree and fell on our house." He points to it outside. "That's why I don't stay in there."

I'm nervous and feel the need to talk but I don't know what else to say. I want him to say something stupid so I can get out of here. So I can have an excuse to leave. He reaches for my panties and I rise up to help him take them off. He places them on the arm of the couch and opens the drawer beside me. He takes out a condom and places it on top and I figure he fucks bitches here all the time but I don't care.

His hand brushes across my leg. My breaths are heavy. I'm about to fuck Sebastian in the wheel house and I don't even like him. He's not even my friend. I want to tell him to stop but maybe this will erase the last memory I had of having sex with my sister. He pushes my legs apart and his face moves toward my box like he's about to kiss a small child. I push my ass back into the cushion and extend my hands to shove him backwards. He's heavy on the weird already.

"What are you doing?" He doesn't respond. "Sebastian, I don't know about this. I never did that before." He doesn't respond. Why isn't he talking to me?

I make a decision to leave, until I feel my syrup oozing between my legs. I want this, I just didn't know it. He grabs my waist and pulls my pussy toward his face. His tongue softly touches my clit and I cum instantly. "Oh…oh my Gawd." I cover my face. "I'm so sorry."

He chuckles a little and I learn I like his laugh. "Damn, you didn't even let me get started. I thought I was the nigga just coming home from jail. You must've been backed up, too."

I'm too embarrassed to speak. I'm such a whore. Such a freak. Just like my mother.

He stands up, grabs the condom and eases it on. When I see how big his dick is, I wonder if I can take it all. And then I remember, thanks to Madjesty I know I can. I'll be glad when my sexual encounters aren't fucked up by what she did to me. It would be so nice.

"Lay the long way." I move quickly so he doesn't throw me out. He places his body over top of mine and kisses me gently on the neck. My body jumps and I move my waist toward his dick like I'm doing waist lifts in exercise class. "Slow down, ma. We 'bout to do this easy."

My ass crashes into the sofa and I'm impatient. I wish he hurry's up. Inside I'm screaming fuck me now but I keep my mouth closed. He smells so good and he feels so warm. I can do this every… *Wow*. He enters me slowly and I fill up quickly. He strokes me softly, massaging my thighs at the same time. He's so considerate and passionate that I can't imagine him being the same person standing outside of my house.

"Jayden, you feel so good, baby." His dick brushes against my clit sending trembles throughout my body. This is how it should feel. "Why your pussy so wet, girl? You're dripping everywhere."

I don't care to respond. I place my hands on his lower back and pull him toward me. Closer. My hips do a dance and I feel a familiar sensation between my legs. I'm about to cum again. Me and Sebastian do good together. A smile of pleasure is on my face until he pulls out of me. I eye his dick and can't imagine at some point in my life, I thought I had one of these. His helmet presses against my clit before pushing back into me again.

When he looks at me I realize I love his face too, not just his eyes. Before I know it we're locking lips and I'm in awe of the emotions I feel right now. Kissing. Hmmmm. It stings a little due to my teeth crashing against my upper lip outside and I wonder if he can taste my blood. He doesn't say anything if he does. The kiss is so nice. His tongue plays in my mouth while his dick plays in my pussy and I want to be nastier with him. I want us to be rougher but I don't want him to think I'm a freak. If we play again I'll let him know how I like it. Slow at first and then rough, almost violent-like.

I kiss his shoulder until I feel him panting heavily. "Jayden, oh Jayden, I'm almost there. Damn, baby."

Worried he's about to get his and leave me stranded, I wind into his dick until I rub out my last orgasm. I know we're in the same place when he looks at me with heavy breaths and smiles. Those blue eyes. That dark skin. He's perfect.

Things are going smoothly until he says, "You got a hearing problem?" He points to my hearing aids.

I'm mad. "You can get up now." I tell him.

The smile is wiped off of his face. I scramble to put my clothes on and walk to the door without so much as a thank you or a response. I don't look at him after our bodies disconnect. I can't. With my hand on the doorknob I say, "I like how we move together. I can do that with you anytime you want," I look at the door harder, "a lot if you got the time. But that's all I want from you. Cool?"

I leave.

•——————————————————————————————————•

I walk into the house pussy tired but with a smile on my face. That is until I remember; fucking Sebastian doesn't take away my problems. The moment he lifted off of my body, I realized I still had to deal with the world alone. I want to keep my promise to my father but I need stability too. Leaning against the closed front door, I look up at the crystal chandelier and the vaulted ceilings. All this house and we still broke. This shit is comical.

I walk into the kitchen to make me some hot tea and milk. I remember that I still have a beautiful tub in my room and decide to give myself a bath. I try to move quietly in case my mother's home. I want to be alone and don't need her negative energy right now. I have to come up with a plan to save us all. I need two hundred and fifty thousand minimum to make our problems go away.

I always work well when I've had a good orgasm. I smile when I think how I'm going to play with my pussy in my bathroom and listen to the radio, as I replay what I just did in my head with Sebastian. Sebastian, my new black and Arabian mixed sex buddy. Mmmmmmmm.

I put the pot of water on the stove and lean against the refrigerator remembering how he felt inside of me. Suddenly things don't seem so bad. That is until the lights go out. I know right away my mother didn't pay the light bill again. I can't count on her for shit!

FUCK!

MADJESTY

FIGHTING BABY
SOME MONTHS LATER

I'm sitting on the light colored carpet, looking at my grandmother and her friend Arizona. I don't know why I'm sitting on the floor, I guess I don't want to be near her although I want to be around somebody. I learned quickly she was a super addict. Addicted to everything that could get her high, from alcohol to heroin, which is why it always amazed me why her house was always so neat. Not a thing was out of place; accept the vodka bottle, pipe and syringe needles on the glass table.

Since I'd been staying with her, I was learning a lot about myself too and I guess I'm stronger than I give myself credit for. It had been 8 months since I had anything to drink, and it was the hardest thing I ever had to do in my life. Not a day went by when I didn't want to taste Hennessey or smoke with my friends. But I was pregnant and although I always imagined my wife giving birth to my baby instead of me, it was still mine and I wanted it to live. Healthy. Fun would come later, for now I would have to wait.

"What you over there thinking about, boy?" Arizona asks, glass in one hand and a crack pipe in the other. It's like she's trying to decide which one to do next. "You been staring at us for hours. Give your eyes some rest, we ain't no TV show."

I crack a half smile for charity.

"How many times I gotta tell you, bitch, that ain't no boy." My grandmother pulls her wig down a little by the bang, forcing it up in the back. "It's my granddaughter. Say it again and I'm gonna throw you out on your tailbone."

"I hear what you saying," Arizona responds, "but it sure looks weird to see her dressed in baggy jeans, t-shirts and hats while she's sporting that big ass belly. If you ask me she got twins in there." I shiver. "Either that or a fat boy."

"I don't give a fuck about none of that shit you spitting, you heard what I said." Bernie retaliates. "She's a girl...address her as one."

Pressed for the last word she says, "It just looks like a boy, is all I'm saying."

In a whisper Bernie says, "Okay, how 'bout I bust both of your eyes and you can tell me what she look like then."

"Fuck you!" She chuckles stuffing the pipe with crack.

As Arizona pulls and Bernie drinks, there's a knock at the door. "Who the fuck is that?" She yells slamming her empty glass on the table. She stares at the door with violent eyes. "Did you hear me? Who the fuck there?" No one answers.

Hoping it's my father, I hop up as fast as I can with my belly. When I pull it open, I see my friends standing on the other side. I grin when I realize how much I miss them. Krazy, Kid Lightning and Dynamite eye my belly like I'd stolen it from somebody. It isn't until I look to my right, that I see Sugar. Something happened to her since the last time I saw her. Something that I can only describe as a total transformation. She's still wearing her red glasses but her brown chest seemed to fill out more in her shirt. She's never been a big girl but the extra pounds she took off did wonders for her frame. All and all, she's sexy as hell.

"Who is it, Madjesty?" Bernie yells. "You making me nervous."

I hold the door open and look back at her. "I told you to call me Mad and my friends are here. Give me a second."

"Well I don't want nobody in my house, so go talk to them outside." *I bet if they had rock you'd let them in, bitch.*

Embarrassed, I step outside and subject myself to more of their scrutiny. "Yo, you really pregnant?" Kid asks looking me over. "Like, you really got a baby in there and shit?" He touches my belly and I jump back. Still wasn't too keen on having niggas touch me, friends or foe.

"I told you she was pregnant, punk!" Krazy replies. "You ain't believe me when I said I saw her at the store the other day and followed her here. I want my fifty bucks too, I don't care how you get it."

"Suck my balls." He fires back.

I look at Dynamite and she waves. Can't believe she's still with them after all of this time. I figure Dynamite had to be at least 21 years old, but she never told me about her life. Our friendship started and ended so quick. "I see you still have her with you."

"Fuck yeah!" Kid says. "Man, you scored big time with bringing her from that institution. She can pick locks to everything from a car to a safe." He pauses. "No way we letting her out of our sights that easy."

"How you doing, Mad?" Sugar says softly. She even talks different. "I know you ain't want this." She steps up and points at my belly. "So I'm so sorry you have to go through it alone. Do you know what you gonna do about it? You look too far along to have an abortion."

"I'm fine, I guess. And I'ma keep the kid." They all frown.

She steps back and stumbles on the brick I threw at my grandmother months back. Bernie didn't bother moving it, so I figured she wanted it there. Maybe as a reminder to throw me out later. When she's about to fall, Krazy catches her and touches her softly on the back. He looks into her eyes and says, "Be careful, baby. Don't be breaking your stuff all up. You too pretty for that shit."

Sugar smiles. The kind of smile a girl could give you that would change your world. "Stop, baby, you embarrassing me."

I know instantly they are together and for some reason, it makes me want to hit him, or do some harm to his face. "What are ya'll doing here?" I sound madder than I intend to.

"Just checking up on you," Sugar responds with love in her voice. "Since you tried to write us off we had to put the dogs on you. I worry about you everyday, Mad. I'm glad to see you fine." *Yeah right. After or before you have Krazy's dick in your mouth?*

"Why you worrying about me?"

"Because you're my friend and no matter where you are, I'm going to always be the one to find you. Like I said, I just wish you didn't write us off."

"I'm not writing you off. I'm just not in the mood for company right now."

"Why you carrying it like that?" Kid asks. "You know we don't care about you being pregnant if that's why you hiding. We brothers, man."

"Yeah...real niggas do real things, including getting our homie's back." Krazy adds. "But we don't know it's a problem, if you don't tell us. We could've found a place for you to lay up. I thought you didn't fuck with your grands like that. You probably in there catching a contact and shit." He looks at the door. "What about the baby?"

"My grandmother is fine." I lie. "And you don't have to get my back. That's what I'm trying to tell ya'll." I look at all of them. "I'm good over here." I'm so jealous. Why am I so jealous? It's a weak emotion and I hate myself for it. All they want to do is be here for me but I can't accept their help right now.

"So what, we not friends no more?" Sugar inquires.

"I'm not saying that...all I'm saying is give me some more time to get my mind right. I promise I'll get up with ya'll when I can."

"I don't know why you're doing this but I can't get you to change your mind either." Krazy says. "Had it been one of us breaking Mad Max up, you would've lost it. It's cool though." He taps Kid and Dynamite on the shoulders. "Come on, ya'll, let's leave Ms. Prego to it."

They're just about to leave when Kid turns around and says, "Oh…I saw your sister at the cemetery a while back when I was visiting my brother. Not sure if you know this or not, but her father died. You may want to see about her, that is if you care about anybody other than yourself." I'm stuck. I didn't fuck with Jace, but I knew Jayden did. And how did he die? There are so many things I want to say to her. I just don't know where to start. I don't even know how to start.

As if Kid just told me regular shit, he and the crew get in a black truck and pull off, with Sugar eyeing me the entire time from the window. I wonder if she still likes me. If she still cares. Or if seeing me like this made her realize how dumb she was for trying to get with me in the first place.

I walk back into my grandmother's house, fucked up about what he said and worried about Jayden. "What you looking so crazy for, girl?" Bernie asks me when I walk through the door. She can be an insensitive ass drunk when she wanted too. I guess that's why Kali hates her so much. And where is my father? I still haven't heard from him. Did he have something to do with Jace's death? "One minute you smiling and the next you looking like somebody slapped your best friend. What's on your mind, honey?"

I look into her eyes trying to figure out if she's really concerned about me or not. Half of her eyeballs are hiding under her eyelids and the other parts are red and glassy. She doesn't give a fuck about me. "I wanna be by myself, Bernie. Thanks for asking though."

I walk downstairs where my father use to stay and ease on the mattress on the floor. I wish I could talk to him. I wish I could ask his advice. Knowing him, I'm probably the last person on his mind. It wasn't like we were so close that he had to look out for me. He didn't owe me shit but life.

Jayden's face comes to my mind again. She was the only person who cared about me and I ruined it all. Everyday that went by and we weren't in contact, reminded me of the mistake I made. I still can't believe I…

Wait a minute.

A pain ripples across the bottom of my stomach that stops my thoughts. What's going on? I turn face up on the bed and look up at the light on the ceiling. I feel a warm liquid splash between my legs. I roll over and crawl on my hands and knees to the bathroom in the basement. Some kind of way, I take my jeans off, pull myself on the toilet and sit down. I'm there for five minutes trying to figure out what's going on. To make matters worse, suddenly I feel like I have to shit. Sitting on the cold toilet, I press down as hard as I can but this pain is different. Like nothing I ever experienced. And then it hits me. I think I'm about to…I think I'm about to have this baby. I fill my chest up with air and yell, "Bernie! Help me! Please!"

When I hear two sets of footsteps rushing down the stairs I'm relieved. But the pain. Oh my God the pain. I ease off of the toilet and my knees slam against the cold floor. I grip the bottom of my stomach tightly, because the pressure is heavy. My baby. I'm about to have this baby!

●━━━━━━━━━━━━━━━━━━━━━━━━━━━━●

I feel like I'm floating. Like somebody removed all of the furniture, the floors, and even the walls. I'm in space, accept everything is white. My arms are flying by my sides and my legs are hanging loosely under me. And then someone shakes me. Real hard.

"Wake up, Madjesty! You have to wake up." It's my grandmother's frantic voice. She seems scared and I don't know why.

I pull my eyes open and she's staring at me. Her expression is hard, like the worst thing in the world has happened. The floor under me is uncomfortable, and air rushes up my wet legs. I don't have any clothes on below. Why am I half naked, lying on the bathroom floor? I place my hand on my stomach. It's flatter than it was the last few months. Where is my baby? I know immediately something is wrong, and then I see the police. Three of them, wearing scowls on their faces like thugs.

My grandmother throws a towel over my legs. *Thank goodness.* "You gotta get up, baby."

"Where is Cassius?" I named my baby Cassius after Muhammad Ali when I was pushing him out. I made an announcement to everybody because he was a fighter and somebody told me he wasn't breathing at first. Wait a minute, is he dead? I look around. "Where is my baby?" No one speaks. "Where is he?"

My grandmother stoops down and places her cold hand on my arm. She doesn't seem so mean now. Just sad. "He's fine." I smile in relief. "But...well..."

Fear takes over me. "If he's fine, what the fuck is going on?" I look at all of them. Somebody had better tell me something before I flip the fuck out.

"It's Arizona. She...she took your baby."

JAYDEN
PUSSY GAME REWIND

I make a decision to sell pussy again but it wasn't going to be mine. Then again, it never was. Nighttime falls on Maryland and Metha is sitting in my truck, looking at me scan through the bushes under the window outside of my house. I'm searching for something I lost a long time ago. Something I thought I would never need again. I was wrong. I've been outside for fifteen minutes and had been bitten by at least twenty mosquitos all over my back and arms. I keep tugging at the red tank top that keeps rising in the back, but it doesn't stop them. If I can't find that phone, I won't get my clientele back and will need to start from scratch. I feel so fucking stupid for throwing it out in the first place. But why isn't it still here?

Mrs. Sheers made it clear that some things needed to change in Concord Manor. First she ordered my mother to alcoholic treatment, with regular meetings to check her sobriety. If she doesn't push back, after her last butt naked session, she won't hesitate to yank me out of my house for good and put me in a group home. She also kept talking about Madjesty and how she'd be back soon to make sure she was there and okay. I'm going to try my best to help my mother stay sober but I had no idea what I was going to do about Madjesty. To make shit worse, since the lights keep getting cut off at the house, I need to come up on some cash quick.

Defeated, after not finding the phone, I slip back into my truck. "Just drive, anywhere." I tell her. She eases into traffic and I throw my body into the plushness of the seat. Since he left me the title, maybe I can sell this.

I want to get Thirteen Flavors back on track but I need money to make money. Still it's my only plan. I even sat my mother down and told her some things would be changing around the house. She fought about it at first, when I didn't give her details but realized she didn't have a choice.

My life is so shitty. I don't have a dime to my name, I'm hungry and I'm over my head with my mother's responsibilities. I'm too young to get a *decent paying* job and even if I could, Mrs. Sheers said she would be stopping by the house regularly and checking on me at school. So it's impossible for me to get a job and make good grades too. My temples throb until I remember Kreshon. He said if I ever needed him, I could call his name. I hope that's true.

I lean up and look at Metha. She's wearing the same mean expression she always does. I hate this bitch most times. She doesn't say much to me and I don't say much to her. I guess we work better that way. I wonder all the time why she's still around. My father must've looked out for her majorly and if I ask, I doubt she'll tell me. "Metha, you know how to get to Kreshon's house?"

She places her hair behind her ear and I focus on her lips. No hearing aids today. They hurt sometimes and give me headaches. "Yes. I think I remember." She looks at me through the rearview mirror. Her lips tighten and she rolls her eyes. "He don't live too far from here. Why?"

"Can you take me there? I got to ask him something and it's kind of important."

"Jayden, what did your father say about Kreshon?" She doesn't look at me this time, just focuses on the road.

This bitch's job is to drive, not question me. "What do you mean?" I smack my tongue. "And what does that have to do with you taking me to his house?"

She looks out of the left window and back at the road. I'm irritating her I can tell. "Kreshon can't take a lot of stress. I know he seems cool and most of the time he is, but you have to be careful with him." She looks at me seriously. "A young girl like you shouldn't be connecting with an older man like him anyway. Hang out with kids your own age. He can be dangerous."

My forehead crinkles. She's working my nerves beyond belief. "First of all what is he like, thirty something?"

She scratched her nose. "Yes. Why?"

"Well as far as I know that doesn't make him mad older than me. Second of all before my father died he said there was one person I could trust and that was Kreshon." He actually said I could trust her too and the fact that I leave her out seems to hurt her feelings. "So what you need to do is steer this truck and let me tend to my business."

She shakes her head and waits until I look at her to start speaking again. "I'm not saying that you can't trust him, Jayden but everyone has limits. Some more than others. Please be careful is all I'm saying to you. I know you don't like me and I feel bad that we got off to a bad start. But you're Jace's daughter and I'm worried about you." Her expression tells me she's telling the truth but I need money. In a hurry. So unless she's taking me to the bank, she can swallow the words she's spitting and choke on them for all I care.

"Metha, I'm confused on why you feel it's any of your business. My father didn't leave you as my guardian angel he left you as my driver until I get a license. That's why we're always going at it, you don't know your place."

She shakes her head again. "First things first, the only place I have is home. Secondly I'm this way with you because I know your past. Jace and I spoke a lot." She looks like she wants to cry again. *Oh brother.* "I know a little about your mother too and I know she's not the best woman. Remember I saw her running out of her neighbor's house naked." My jaw tightens and I want to punch her in the back of the head. "I'm not judging her because like I said I came from a fucked up life too." She scratches her nose. "If I could take back half of the things I did, I would. But I don't have that option anymore, Jayden. You do."

"What part of this got to do with me?" I ask.

"You have to be a bitch everyday don't you?" I stay silent. I guess she knows the answer already. "When I see somebody going down a path that might lead to a dead end, I have to say something. Nobody did that for me until I met your father. He cared enough about me to invest some time by helping me with my alcoholism. I'm trying to pay it forward with his daughter and I wish you give me a chance."

What is she talking about? I wish this bitch just kills herself in a car accident and save me the trouble of her mouth. "You use to fuck Kreshon or something? I mean tell me the truth, is that why you coming at me sideways?"

She frowns. "Not even close, little girl. I don't even know why you would ask me something like that."

I fan her away with my hand. "If you didn't use to fuck him, why do you care what I do with him? It's not your business. You act like I make you ride us around while I fuck him in my truck. Relax."

"I'm done." She spits.

She proceeds on the way to Kreshon's house. I'm suddenly appreciative of the silence. I think we're almost to his house because she slows down. I'm about to call his cell to let him know I'm close, when we reach a light. When I look to my right, I see silver Lexus pull next to us. It's Kreshon and when he looks at me my heart melts. He can be my stability if he wants too. I wave excitedly, hoping he's happy to see me too. Instead of matching my happiness, when the light turns green, he pulls off. *What the fuck was that about?*

"Metha, isn't that Kreshon's car up there?" I point at his license plate. His brake lights flash us.

She inspects the car and says, "Yep. That's him." I know she thinks the shit he just did is funny. I don't.

He pulls off again. "Follow his ass!"

At the funeral he said I could call him whenever I needed him. And now he's acting like I'm not even on planet earth. As he wiggles in and out of traffic, its obvious that he's avoiding us. I'm growing angry and then it dawns on me, I never found out who took my father's money. How do I know it wasn't him? He would've been the perfect person, especially after my father gave him the stamp of approval and said I could trust him.

Although he's quick in his Lexus, Metha works the truck like we're in a Porsche. When he slows down and parks in front of a strip mall off of Martin Luther King Avenue, she pulls up behind him like police. He eases out of his car and walks toward the truck. His face is straight but he stomps toward us. I hop out of the back and meet him in the middle.

"Sorry about that, Jayden." He gazes at Metha in the truck and back at me. "I didn't know that was you following me. I got beef in these streets." He smells so good. Like he recently showered. "What's good with you though?"

"Did you take my father's money?" I didn't know I was going to ask him that. I wish I could take it back. But the question rolled off my tongue so quickly it felt natural.

He backs up and teases the pocket of his gray Polo sweatpants. They look heavy so I figure his keys are in them. "Why would you come out of your face and ask me some shit like that? Especially when I didn't have the dough to put my man to rest? You know what that shit did to me and how it made me feel? You saw how fucked up I was!" His nostrils are flaring. A lady seems rattled leaving her car. I peer at her wanting her to get away. I hate people in my business.

"I didn't mean it like that." I eye her as she walks into a store.

"Then how did you fucking mean it?" He yells and I jump back. "It's because of you I stuffed a nigga in the trunk of my car and now he's looking for me to this day."

"Then you should've killed him. That was an option too, remember?"

He shakes his head. "Something's up with you. I'm not sure what yet but something is definitely up." He looks at me seriously. I hope he doesn't hate me. I didn't even ask for money yet. "What do you want, Jayden?"

"Right now I want to know why you're running from me?"

"I just told you. I got beef. Sometimes I think you mature but when you hit me with shit like this, you remind me that you're a kid!" He looks like he wants to punch me and I wonder will it hurt. "It wasn't until I saw Metha driving that I knew it was you. So I pulled over."

I fold my arms into my breasts. "I don't believe you."

He grabs me forcefully by the wrist and Metha leaps out of the truck like a bodyguard. "What's going on, Kreshon?" When her hand turns into a fist, I know she's prepared to hit him. Suddenly I like her…for now. "You good, Jayden?"

"So you gonna step to me like that?" He studies her fist and it relaxes into a hand again. "Like you don't know me? Like we don't have a past?"

"I'm not saying all that, Kreshon. I just don't like how you handling her and I wanna make sure she alright. You cool, Jayden?"

"Jayden's rolling with me." He answers for me. "So you go on to wherever you gotta go. I'll see to it that she gets home safe."

Metha looks at me with pleading eyes. She doesn't want me to go I can tell. What is it about him that she wants me to avoid? Why doesn't she just tell me? "I'm good, Metha. You can go home and take my truck with you."

Kreshon grips my hand and pulls me to his car like I'm a kid. He walks to the driver's side and points to the passenger side. "Get in." Why doesn't he open my door? I don't bother asking, just hop inside.

The moment I close the door, a sugary fragrance hits me in the face. When I look in the back, a pink cotton garment that I can't make out is thrown over the seat. It must belong to his girlfriend but I don't maneuver it to tell what it is.

When I examine him, he's straight faced and mad. I hate that I'm the cause of his anger. We drive for about three more minutes before we pull up to another strip mall. He parks, grabs the pink thing in the back, jumps out and walks into one of the stores without speaking to me. I sit in the car for fifteen minutes, before deciding to get out. What the fuck is up with him now?

When I walk in his direction and glance at the sign over the door, I see *K's Cupcakes* in bright pink letters. The moment I switch my phat ass inside, I'm assaulted with the smells of fresh baked cakes. I smile weakly at the people looking at me, even though I'm in a bad mood. I look at the long line of customers, waiting to be served. I don't see Kreshon anywhere until I look behind the counter. He's six-foot-something and towers over everyone. Does he work here? Each one of them except him is wearing the pink garment. It's an apron.

Kreshon is organizing colorful cupcakes on the racks. When the next customer places an order, he fills it with a smile and rings up her purchase. When he's done he hands her a pink colorful box with white lace along the tips. He looks out of place and I don't know my mouth is open, until my tongue dries out. Why isn't he a drug dealer, like my father, instead of working at some cupcake factory? What a waste of thug.

When the customer leaves, he waves for me to come in the back. At first one of his employees blocks me, until he touches her on the shoulder. I follow him into an office and he throws his keys on the desk and flops in a leather seat behind it. He seems happy with himself until he looks at me. "This may be funny to you, Jayden, but it was always a dream of mine." He moves some papers around on his desk and leans back in his chair again. "It may look gay to you too, but it's my life."

"I didn't say anything, Kreshon."

"I can tell how you look that it's funny to you."

"What are you doing here? I mean, are you really a baker or something?" I observe his neat office before settling back on his eyes.

"Jayden, these cupcakes are made with my recipe." He points his index finger into his chest. It's shiny so he must get his nails done too. "And I guarantee that you won't find anything that tastes as good as what we make here. In the world."

I laugh. At first lightly until I remember how ridiculous he looked handling cupcakes out front. So female like. So danty. He definitely dried my pussy up. "Kreshon, if this is your thing this is your thing, I'm not here for all of that."

"You don't believe me." He leans forward and his chair squeaks. I'm surprised I heard it. "You think what I'm doing here can be done anywhere. Don't you?" Before I can respond, he hits a button on the phone and makes a call. "Denisha, bring in the Nightmare cupcake." A minute later a girl holding a black cupcake on a trey enters. It isn't brown or dark chocolate. It's jet black. A cloud of white icing sits on the top with sprinkles of shiny red dots. "Eat it, Jayden."

She hands it to me and I bite into it quickly. I don't have time for this shit. I need money, and if he had any, I want it now. But if it will make the process easier, I'll eat the stupid thing. While chewing it something happens. The first thing I taste is a butter light icing. It rolls up my tongue and leaves a trail of vanilla in its wake. And then there's the cake, so soft, so light, so fluffy and sweet. I'm ready to say it's the best I ever had, until I taste what I think is liquor. I never tasted anything so fucking good in all my life. I slam the rest down on his desk and point at it. "What is that?"

He grins. "It's like I told you. The best." He looks at the girl. "You can go now."

When she leaves I say, "No seriously, I never tasted anything like it in my entire life! And it has liquor in it!" I look at it, wanting to eat the rest but not wanting to look greedy. "You gonna make so much money with those shits."

He smiles proudly, crosses his arms over his chest and rocks in his seat. "I told you, ma."

I love it when he calls me that. It was very rare when my father was alive. "You gotta eat the rest though because I can't fuck with it. I have to watch my weight."

Suddenly he shoots up and knocks the cake off of his desk. It falls to the floor, top first. The white icing presses against the gray carpet on his floor. "Why you do that?" I pick it up, and throw it into the trash.

Through squinted eyes he asks, "What are you doing here, Jayden?"

"Kreshon, why did you knock your own shit on the floor?"

"Either tell me what you want or get the fuck out of my spot."

So many things run through my head, especially the conversation I had with Metha earlier. Was he crazy or something? "Kreshon, how did you get the money to open this up?"

"If you asking me again did I steal your people's money again the answer is no. This place has been open for a year. I didn't buy no fancy ass car when I was making money on the streets. I saved up everything I had so I could buy this. Had I known my man would've died, I would've put a little to the side for a rainy day. Most of my dough goes back into my business. He should've strapped up and wore a condom though." I think that's irrelevant but its cool.

I try to calculate the time he had this place in my mind to see if he was telling the truth. He was fully operational a year ago so it was impossible for him to use my daddy's money to fund it. "I'm hurting right now, Kreshon. I was robbed the other day and they took the little bit of cash I had left." He looks angry. Like he cares. "Now I'm asking you to give me what you can spare because I don't have nothing left. My mother is a drunk and she not doing right by me. Anything you can give me will be appreciated."

He shakes his head. "She's still saucing huh?"

"Yeah why? You know her like that?" I remember him gawking her at the funeral but they didn't seem friendly.

He shakes his head no. "I didn't know them peoples all like that."

"Well how you know she's a drunk then?"

"Jace told me."

My mother's antics are legendary. "If he told you about her, you know I'm telling the truth. I don't even have enough money to buy food. Now you said you cared about my father, so I'm asking you to help his daughter. Please?"

He reaches into his pocket and sits a wad of money in front of him. He grabs his keys and opens a drawer under his desk. Then he pulls out a black lockbox and sits it on his lap. When he's done, he counts both stacks and hands them to me. "That's twenty-seven hundred, the deposit for today's business. You can have it." I tuck the money in my pocket and a smile slides across my face.

"Thank you." This was more than I expected. "You don't know how much this means to me."

"Every month I'll give you a little something, not because I owe you, but because I fucked with your father. That's all I can do right now."

I jump up and rush behind the desk. I'm bout to plant a wet kiss on his cheeks, but he turns his face and I catch his lips instead. "Thank you, Kreshon. Let me do something for you." He doesn't realize it but the money he gave me will put me back on top. It's just what I needed to get my business up and running again. Pussy, pussy, pussy! Rings in my ears.

I grope his dick and slip sideways into his lap like he's Santa Claus. He smells like some expensive shit when I rest my nose into the crease of his neck. He isn't touching me, so I get up and sit face to face with him by balancing myself on one of his legs. My pussy throbs as I lean in and kiss the crease of his neck again. After fucking Sebastian, I'm trying to do the damn thing all the time. I rock on this thigh slowly to stimulate my clit. This shit feels good and if I keep it up, I'll definitely cum before he even touches me.

I forgot he's in the building until he says, "What the fuck you doing, Jayden? I don't fuck with little girls." He pushes me so hard, I fly backwards and the bottom of my back slams into the edge of his desk. I jump up preparing to hit him with anything I can find and then I remember, he's Mr. Money Bags. He has immunity.

"Don't ever come at me like that again, if you do I'ma hurt you."

He stands up and walks over to me. "You hurt?"

I rub my back because it's on fire. "I'm good." I lie.

"Let me take you home, Jayden. Don't be out here acting like a whore, Jace wouldn't approve."

It's mighty funny that he let me rub all on him for so long before he hit me with this shit. It's also funny that his dick stands out like a tent. It's cool though. We're about to walk out of the door until I stop him. I don't want to separate like this. I grab his hand and look into his eyes. My back is inflamed but I'd been beat so many times by my mother that it doesn't matter anymore. I'm tough that way.

"Kreshon, my father is dead. He's not around to look after me anymore. I'm feeling you right now, but I also realize I'm young. If you want me too, you better say something and soon. Don't wait to get my attention, because then it maybe too late."

JAYDEN
PUSSY, PUSSY, PUSSY

"Ma, I got the lights turned back on but they won't let me pay the phone bill. So I put the money on your dresser, can you remember to pay the bill please?" I ask, speaking to her on the phone in the kitchen. "They called yesterday and said if you don't pay they'll cut it off."

"Jayden, I said I'll pay it." She pauses. "Where did you get the money from anyway?"

"It doesn't matter, mommy. I got the money and all you gotta do is pay it. The hardest part is done. Why won't you get a bank so I can put money in the account and take care of stuff like this on my own? Then you don't have to worry about it."

"Why don't you get one?"

"Because I'm too young and you won't take me down there."

"I don't trust nobody with my money, especially not some big ass bank."

"But I'm putting my money in it. Not yours."

"Now you said to much, I have to go. Bye."

Click.

When I hang up the phone rings again. I answer. "Don't get too comfortable in the house little girl, it belongs to us." Aunt Ramona says. "And tell your mother she better watch her back. I might send somebody to take care of her for what she did to us." She laughs and hangs up.

Shit is getting stressful around here. My mother is working me overtime and every time I turn around, aunt Ramona and Laura was calling here threatening us. At least I'm back on top. With the money Kreshon gave me, I paid some bills and saved the rest. I'm ready to get my business up and running and I'm ready to change my life.

I even found a loophole in the promise I made to daddy. When I played the recording on my phone it said, '*I promise to stay out of trouble, take care of my health and to go to college.*' So it was my intentions to do it all. I never said anything, not one thing, about not selling pussy…on the tape anyway. If I stay out of trouble, take care of my health and go to college, daddy should be happy. Right?

A few days after hooking up with Kreshon, Olive and Passion helped me go over a few things for the business and in return I offered them both jobs. Olive was in charge of scheduling tricks and Passion was in charge of the girls, once we hired them.

When I started Thirteen Flavors back in the day, I went the fake babysitters route but since I couldn't find my phone, I needed to change things up a little. It was time to meet up with Olive and Passion again. So I went to the grocery store, bought some Brie cheese, grapes, crackers and fucked Sebastian in the wheel house. Refreshed and no longer horny, I came home eager to go over the plan.

"We need girls." I say, standing above them as they sit on the sofa. "I prefer 13 but I'm willing to start off smaller if we have to." I look at Passion knowing she always had a bevvy of freaks on her roster. "Can you help us out with that?"

I focus on her lips. "Ever since I stopped getting high, I don't hang around the same people anymore, Jayden." She whips her hair over her shoulder. "I mean, I still kick it with Foxie, Na-Na and Queen sometimes but they beefing with you because you cut them off. Queen said she tried to get you to give them the phone and everything but you wouldn't take her calls. So I'm not sure if they're down or not."

"So wait, they were mad with me because they couldn't make money and if I put them on they'll still be mad?" I ask with an attitude. "Are they getting paper now or what?"

She laughs. "Definitely not."

"So as long as they're still the same broke bitches they were when I met them, why wouldn't they be down?"

Olive touches her leg. "Listen, you said you are their friend right?"

She looks at her hand oddly. Olive never misses a chance to be fresh. "Yes. They still my girls."

"So maybe you can talk them into it. It would be a shame to waste their pussies while they're still tight and tender." Olive adds. "It ain't like they not fucking anyway. Convince them of that and you can make money too. You said you wanted money to go to college. Jayden giving you a chance to get put on. This is a full scholarship ride!"

Passion grips at the edges of her hair and twists thick strands around her fingers. "I don't know if it will work. Plus they still getting high and I'm not sure if I want to be around all that."

"Everybody gets high, Passion. Just because you changed your life don't mean you can expect everybody else too." I say. "We told you that already. Focus on your money and let people do their own thing." I'm growing frustrated and I don't have time to hold her hand through the process. I need surgery on my ears, I have to come up with a lot of money to save this house and my mother is too wretched to help me out. This is the only way I see to save us all. "Tell them I want to talk to them, Passion and I'll do the rest."

She nods and smiles. "As long as you ask them, I'll make the call."

Weak bitch. I take a deep breath and sigh. "On another note, I have to ask you something I'd been wanting to for awhile. I'm ready for the details." I rub my hands together to keep them from shaking. "And I want to get it out in the open before we go any further." I look at both of them. "I'm trusting you guys and I need to make sure you have my back, no matter what."

"You already know what it is with me," Olive says, "so I don't even know why you coming at me like that."

I turn to Passion and she looks away. "First things first, whenever you talk to me, I want you to look me in my eyes." I peep Olive. "You too."

Olive smiles. "I love looking at you, beautiful. So you won't have that problem from me." She winks. "Trust me."

I focus back on Passion. "That night I had Shaggy come find you, did he rape my sister?"

Her flood of tears answers my question. "Oh my God, Jayden, I had no idea he was a girl when I got with him. I loved him so much." She's shaking so hard, she looks like she'll explode. "I wanted to talk to you about this recently but you kept cutting me off. Mad was the first person I truly cared about and I never thought, I mean, I would've never thought Shaggy would do that to her. He was so mean and so nasty with it too. I was fucked up for days behind that shit and haven't been the same since."

I feel hot. Plain rage. I'm still counting down the days when I can find him. He showed up at my house on some big and bad shit, when I was with my social worker, but I'll see him again.

Olive seems disgusted. "I been knowing Shaggy most of my life. We were so fucking cool." Olive continues. "I should've known it was a reason I haven't heard from him. It's one thing to be a little mean at times but to rape a bitch is a whole 'nother problem."

"But please don't tell him I told you." Passion cries harder. Olive moves closer to her and rubs her back. "Mad was the reason I got myself clean." She looks up at me. "Just knowing that being high was one of the reasons I allowed that to happen fucks me up. But if Shaggy finds out I told anybody, he'd kill me. He told me and I believe him."

"Passion, the last thing you should be worried about is him. He's going to get what has his name on it." I walk closer to her and she tenses up. For some reason a part of me enjoys her fear. Maybe I hate that she loves Mad so much. And if her loyalty is tested who will she choose? "I want you to get the girls together tonight." I walk behind her and place my hands on her shoulders. I want her to have a level head. "It's time they start getting paid for what they do best, fuck." I bend down to speak in her ear. "And this time we playing for keeps."

I stand in front of her when I notice her mouth is moving. She's saying something but all I caught was, "…Gucci too?"

Enraged I look at her seriously. "What did I just tell you?" It's so exhausting when people don't pay attention. "Don't talk to me unless I'm standing in front of you. Are we clear, Passion?"

"Yes." She seems more nervous.

"Good and I'm going to need you to start being a little more loyal. In the past your loyalty lied with Gucci and them but if I even think that's the case now, I'll cut you off. For good. I need you to help me keep the girls in line but I don't want you back on call. You'll be my eyes and ears in the house. I want you to focus on your shit and to stay clean. All that shit you was fucking with ain't gonna do shit but fuck your mind up and we're business partners now. If you serious about walking straight, I want that for you." I rub her long black hair, "just don't cross me." When I can tell she understands I say, "Now, go call the girls and tell them I want them to be here in the next hour. Anybody who can't come need not waste their time."

She looks into my eyes. "What about Gucci?"

"You can hit her up too."

●━━━━━━━━━━━━━━━━━━━━━━●

An hour later, everybody I wanted to be present was there. Foxie showed up wearing a blue jean skirt so tight, the juice from her pussy stained the back of her skirt. The short gold hairstyle she sported looked over bleached and I knew right away she needed work. The good thing was her body was in tact and she was eager to get paid. Foxie's real name is Fantasia and I never understood why she wanted to be called anything else because her name is so cool. I guess if *both* my mother and father were selling ass on the streets to men, I would want a change too. The moment she gets there she sits in the chair closest to me.

Na-Na who was both Asian and African American walked in my house looking exhausted. Her eyes were mostly slanted and her skin was an even brown. She was quiet, never said too much but I knew from experience that she loved to fuck. Her preference? Fat black men with thick dicks. And although she didn't have to sell her pussy because her mother and father owned several 7-Eleven stores, she loved the excitement more than anything and felt she needed to do it to be down. The washed out black dress she wore didn't do her beauty justice because with the right clothes, baby face Na-Na was a goldmine. Her best friend out of all of the girls was Queen and where you saw one, no doubt you'd see the other.

Queen sat on the floor and leaned against the front of the couch. Every time she scratched her scrunchy black bob, it moved. I never saw her without it, which is why when she took it off, and I saw some of the prettiest brown dreads I'd ever seen in my life underneath, I was confused. Why was she wearing that hot mess when she was off the clock?

Queen came up hard because she was in the foster care system so long, she had no idea where her real family was or if they were alive. It was Na-Na and her parents who finally let her stay in there home, to give her some stability. What Na-Na didn't know was that Queen was fucking her father on a daily basis for cash. But she was stuck so far up Queen's ass that even if she found out she probably wouldn't have cared anyway.

As usual Gucci strolled in last. Her stringy black weave was missing a few too many strands and she smelled like somebody just pissed on her. But she was strikingly beautiful. The funny thing was, when these bitches was fucking with me they were making paper and stayed fresh. Now that I cut them off they looked like wrecks. Leave it to me to save a hoe. Or two.

I swore I would never fuck with Gucci again after she tried to turn everybody against me, when we all went to meet a trick one night. The trick had Foxie suck his dick and the rest of us fight each other naked, so he could get his rocks off. But the moment he bust his nut, he wasn't trying to pay us. Instead of giving us the money he owed, he kicked us out on the streets. We barely had enough time to get dressed. I exposed my weakness that night and it can't happen again. I will make whoever pay and I would be creative too.

Everybody was mad but Gucci convinced them that since I couldn't protect them, they didn't need me. The girls went for her schemes even though I gave them their money later. Secretly I also know Gucci blamed me for Passion being on heroin but it wasn't my fault. She was fucking with that shit way before me, Shaggy put me on to it. She used any excuse to go against me which is why I was trying to figure out what she was doing in my house. I must be a glutton for punishment. After all, Harmony Phillips *is* my mother.

"What's going on, Jayden? You got us here so are we about to get this money again or what?" Foxie asks looking directly at me. "Because we been trying to hit you up but you wouldn't answer the phone."

"Or give nobody the cell to make the calls on our own." Gucci adds, wrapping her hair around her middle finger. "For real for real, we were about to go at it alone. It's a good thing you called us when you did."

"Why didn't you?" I walk up to Gucci. "Let's be real, you look like you haven't had your hair done in ten years and ya'll clothes look like you just pulled them out of the donation box in front of Safeway." I turn around to look at all of them. "So if everybody could get paper on they own, why are you here?"

Silence.

I focus back on Gucci. "Listen, bitch, I'm not playing games with you no more. The Jayden you use to know vanished when my father died and my sister raped me." Their mouths drop. I didn't even share that information with Olive or Passion. I guess they know now. "I'm about getting money but I'm not about the small talk. This is my reality show and there's only one star." I look at Olive and she's smiling. "Now are you with me or not?" They all nod. Including Gucci's hating ass. "Good now before we go on, there are a few things you need to know, I don't want anybody talking to me unless you're looking directly into my eyes. Also, we not working off of the phone no more we moving on the blocks."

"What you mean? We selling pussy off 16th street or something?" Foxie inquires.

I cross my arms against my body. "Exactly."

"Jayden, that shit is dangerous!" Gucci says. "You can't just be going out there and taking over blocks. You have to have protection. We can get killed out there. Why can't we work off the phone?"

I couldn't tell them I threw it out and couldn't find it. "Gucci, I said I got you. Now if the blocks ain't for you try the door instead." A few of them move but nobody leaves. "But if you stay, unlike the girls on the blocks, you'll stand to make a lot of money with me. I'm talking about we split everything down the middle." My eyes settle on Olive and she doesn't seem happy. We discussed this part of the plan when we were alone and she said not to give the bitches shit but food and shelter. But it was my decision and I was standing by it. Plus I needed to do anything I could to convince them to stay. "Not only that, you get to live out of my house." I know where they all live and to stay in a mansion was a major come up. Even Na-Na whose parents were paid didn't own their home. They were too busy saving every penny to stuff in their graves when they died.

"So if we work with you, we get to be partners and live here for real?" Foxie asks.

"You got it, baby."

Foxie, Na-Na and Queen's faces light up. I even see a trace of a smile on Gucci's face.

"I actually get to call this home?" Queen looks into my eyes. I nod again. "Well what will your mother say?"

"What the fuck can she say?" I pause. "We making money. Anybody who can't live here, can't work with me. I can't count on everybody to be on time unless we're under the same roof. I'm not going there with ya'll again. Shit is real this time."

"Jayden, why can't we just work out of the house?" Gucci asks. "I can see this place being the hoe house of all hoe houses.

"Because I live here. Do you sell pussy out of your shoebox?"

She frowns. "No."

"Exactly." It's a bad idea to fuck with her again but it's too late now. I put her on the winning team already and throwing her out my cause the others to leave with her. "I'm going to need nine more girls because what we have right now is not enough. Any suggestions?"

Queen looks back at Na-Na but because I can't read her lips and she's talking low, I don't make out what's being said. "Maybe you didn't understand the house rules, Queen. No speaking to me or around me unless I'm looking into your eyes. No holding group conversations about my business and no betraying me." Even Olive and Passion didn't know about my hearing problem. And I was going to keep it that way. "Do we have an understanding?" Everyone nods. "With that said, Queen what did you just say?"

"I was just saying that it's about time you came back, Jayden. I was about to get up with Mr. Grover who runs them funeral Homes in DC. Good thing I didn't though, I hear he kills his girls."

GUCCI
I NEVER

Gucci is sitting on the carpet in the middle of the living room floor, naked from the waist down. Her legs are spread wide open and the members of Thirteen Flavors are staring at her laughing. She's this raunchy all the time so this type of behavior is not unusual. Everyone with exception of Passion is drunk out of their minds.

"I'm telling you right now I got the biggest clit. That's why I can cum in my pants without even touching myself." Gucci says. Jayden is jealous of the idea alone.

"Bitch, that shit is the same size as everybody's." Foxie says as she eyed her slick cave. "You ain't hardly special."

"If you got a bigger clit than me, I bet you money and I'll fuck your nastiest john."

"Gucci, go 'head with that shit." Jayden says, "Ain't nobody trying to see all of that." It was okay for the girls to have a good time but this sort of ratchet behavior made her stomach ache. The idea of sitting around looking at her girls' kitties wasn't something she wanted to do in her spare time. Jayden's tight white t-shirt was wet with perspiration and the red jeans that wrapped her body like Saran wrap was stained with the wetness from her vodka glass. This shit was too much for the second night of their living together.

"Speak for yourself," Olive says, "let the girls have their fun for the first nights in the house." She could do this type of thing all day. And although she didn't initiate the game, she wouldn't be a party blower either. She rolls the silver balls around her fingers as usual.

"Yeah, Jayden," Gucci adds with her legs still spread open and the lips to her box pulled back allowing her button to pop out, "you can't be so uptight this time around. In the past you were so dry but all that has changed. Right? We partners now remember?" She looks at Foxie and Na-Na. "Ya'll get down here and show me yours since you claim it's bigger than mine."

Foxie and Na-Na couldn't wait to hop out of their clothes like they were about to jump in a warm pool. Bare from the waist down, they flop on the floor like good little fish and spread their legs too. Olive examines all three and shakes her head. "Sorry, Foxie and Na-Na, but she got ya'll beat."

Gucci laughs hysterically. "That's what I thought, bitches." She gets dressed. Thank God. Jayden thought. The living room was starting to smell musty.

"Now both of you bitches gotta drink Tequila." They all put on their clothes and Foxie and Na-Na down their portion in the shot glasses. "I keep trying to tell you bitches, ain't none of ya'll got a more magnificent pussy than me!"

The girls were loud and boisterous and Jayden was trying to relax and go with the flow. But her teeth grinded. She knew she was being tested and that the girls of Thirteen Flavors thought she was a square. Although she was no longer a virgin, she had a class about her that was different from them. That's why she sought them in the beginning. They were whores, sluts and eager to do anything for a buck. Just like Harmony and Armanii.

"Let's play I Never," Gucci says tossing another shot of tequila. "It's a drinking game."

"I know what it is, bitch. I'm with that shit." Foxie adds. She looks at Jayden. "You playing?"

"Naw, I'm gonna watch."

Gucci stands up and pushes her arm harder than what is normally friendly. "Oh my, God! I wish you lighten the fuck up already! Damn, you always so uptight and you get mad when people don't fuck with you like that. I know you the boss and all and I respect that shit, but we about having fun too, Jayden."

Jayden observes the disappointed expression on her girls' faces. She would have to show she was part of them or else they would walk out and she'd be forced to find another way to come up with the money. "Okay, how is the game played?"

Olive shakes her head that Jayden gave in to the peer pressure so easily. She foresees the business relationship not ending well and she makes mental notes to talk to her homie about it later. In private. To run a good whorehouse the girls need to fear and respect the pimp, but Jayden was forgetting code…maybe because she didn't know it.

Gucci explains that the object of the drinking game is to say I Never followed by something that you never did. If somebody at the table has actually done that, they have to take a drink. The game works with close friends because they know their personal business and are able to call someone out who doesn't drink or who is trying to lie.

When they are all seated in the living room Gucci starts first, "I never…got fucked with a toe."

Passion who is standing over everyone turns a shade of pink. Her friends all knew for a fact she let this white man fuck her with his big toe when she didn't have money to get her car out of the tow shop. Everyone looks at her and waits for her to toss it up. "Ya'll know I can't drink. I'm clean."

Foxie shakes her head. "Then what the fuck are you doing down here then? You blowing the rest of us."

"Right, Passion," Na-Na continues, "I didn't think you were serious about that shit. You bringing my high down too." She shakes her head. "This game is not for lames. Even Jayden playing now." She points to the staircase. "Why don't you go upstairs somewhere and get the fuck out of my face?" It was clear they didn't want her to do the right thing in her life.

Passion doesn't move. Instead she starts crying. "Are you fucking serious?" Gucci laughs. "Bitch, just 'cause you clean means you turned weak too? What did you do to my girl, Jayden?" She shakes her head. "Jayden, please send her upstairs, she's irritating the rest of us. And you already know how important it is to keep your girls happy. Don't you?"

Jayden looks at her friend. She wasn't trying to rock the boat and if sending Passion away would make things cool, she was with it. "Passion, go upstairs, you don't need to be around all of this. Get some rest."

Passion jots up the stairs crying the entire way. Olive peers at Jayden, she's disappointed that she seems delicate around the girls. She's the boss not the other way around. So why was she letting Gucci carry shit like this? One minute she was checking her ass and the next she was bowing down. It was like they were taking turns on who was in power. "I'm going upstairs too." Olives says with an attitude. "I'ma leave ya'll to it."

"Fuck both of them," Gucci continues fanning her hand. "Anyway, let me go since Passion couldn't play. I never…fucked three niggas at the same time."

Everybody took a drink but Jayden. Gucci laughs. "It's your turn, Jay."

"I never…been jealous of my friend."

Everybody took a drink but Gucci. Which was comical since she was the most envious of the bunch. She knew what Jayden was trying to imply and she wasn't feeling it one bit. "My turn," she says, "I never…took my girls to fuck a trick and left without getting paid."

Jayden's face reddens. Nobody took a drink but her. "You not gonna let the shit go are you? You really are going to hold onto this shit forever. I didn't know he was going to do us like that. But everybody got their paper later didn't they? Don't I get credit for that?"

"It's just a game, Jayden. Lighten up." Gucci drinks from the bottle. "After all, we're business partners now. What's done is done. Just as long as you know going forward we looking for a leader not a follower. If you understand, everything should be as right as rain."

HARMONY
STRANGE NUTS

Me and a nigga I won't remember in the morning are getting it in on my bed. Shit is going good until my bedroom door flies opens. "Ma, can I talk to you for a second?"

She loves cock blocking. Since she was my fake little boy. "You can talk to me all you want after I finish doing what I'm doing." I kiss the nigga's dry lips. "Now beat it."

"I'm serious, ma! I gotta talk to you and I gotta talk to you now." She holds the door open.

"All I wanted to do was have a little fun. But now I'm out of here." The dude says as he stands up. He swerves frontwards, grabs his pants and the bottle of liquor he promised we'd split and rolls out of the door. I'm so mad I want to kill Jayden but I'm too tired to move.

"Now that you've ruined my night what the fuck do you want?"

"Ma, do you even care what's been going on around here? Aunt Ramona and Laura threatening you and somebody keep throwing piles of shit at our windows. You leaving me to handle all of the bills and responsibility on my own. It's not fair! Either you start pitching in or you gonna be by yourself."

I laugh. "You really are feeling yourself aren't you?" I shake my head. "Jayden, there's nothing neither of us can do to save this place. It's a wrap. And you might as well start to understand it." I throw the covers over my head but she doesn't leave. I take them off and look at her. "What now?"

She looks at me. "I know you think I'm dumb, mommy. But I'm going to come through with a plan for both of us. And when I do, I want you to eat your mothafuckin' words."

JAYDEN

RED OLIVE

I open the door to my bathroom and slip some olive oil into the warm water in my bathtub. Then I throw my pink washcloth in the tub and watch it darken in the water. Before long, we're going to hit the stroll and I can't lie, I'm worried. Worried that I don't know what I'm doing and worried that I won't make the money I need. I allow my lavender bathrobe to drop to the floor and ease my achy body into the water. The olive oil coats my skin and makes it sparkle. I'm immediately at ease. With a house full of girls, I quickly realize that the only time I can get privacy was in the bathroom. That is until there's a knock at the door.

"Who is it?" I yell.

"It's me, Olive. Can I come in?" She's screaming so I hear her clearly. How did she know to do that?

I fish for my washcloth and cover my wet breasts. "Come in."

Olive eases inside, sits on the edge of the tub and looks down at my naked body. I focus on her lips. "Can I talk to you for a second."

"Are you gonna talk to me or look at my pussy?" She's so freaky, it's hilarious to me. She claims she doesn't fuck bitches anymore, but every time I turn around she's touching somebody too much when they ask her how they look in a certain outfit, or if they seek her advice. Most of the girls don't seem to mind, she's stunning.

"I'm not going to fuck with you." She looks at me seriously. "Unless you want me to."

"Olive, what's up?" I rub my breasts with the rag. "I'm tired."

She sighs. "I see how close you are with the girls and I wanted to tell you that I think it's a bad idea."

I fucked with Olive no doubt, but she's going to have to realize I'm the boss of this shit not her. "Olive, I got this business. What you fail to realize is that I did this fine before you came along."

"And I'm not trying to get in your way, Jayden. All I'm saying is that you're treading the water too close for business. If you want the girls to respect you, you gotta make sure they have a reason. They have to know who's in charge at all times and should never, *ever*, mistake you for a friend. Weakness is not a good trait in this business."

I hear her, but there's nothing she can say that's of interest. I'm running this thing, and until I see a reason to change, I won't. "Right now I want to relax but before you leave can you get the box from up under my bed?" She leaves and comes back with it. "Open it up."

She takes the first thing out. "A wig?" She shakes it like she's expecting something to fall out of it.

"Yes, to be used whenever you hear the code word *maroon*. The other code word you need to worry about is *thirteen*." She looks confused. "Look at the sheet in the box, it explains it all." She takes it out and reads over it. She grins. I spent a lot of time going over the plan after realizing my mother really wasn't going to help me. If she didn't have HIV, I would put the bitch on the clock.

"You thought about it all haven't you?"

"I might be young but I'm smarter than people think. I'm not doing this shit just to sport fly clothes and to eventually by a nicer car. This is my life and one of these days you'll respect me for the battles I win instead of the ones I walk away from."

It didn't take me long to find the rest of my team. After cruising a few clubs in the Washington D.C. and Baltimore area, I was able to get the perfect mix of misfits. Johnna, my first white girl, with the strawberry birthmark on her face, was halfway out of the pussy game when I met her. She worked for Mr. Grover, the same mothafucka who told me I could pay him later for my father's funeral, only to change his mind the day of the service. When I found out she belonged to him, I couldn't wait to snatch her up and bring her into my fold.

It wasn't like he made it hard. He almost put her eye out with the retractable blade that came from the end of his cane. All because she couldn't work with the broken arm she'd gotten that same night from him. If Metha and me hadn't pulled up on her when we did at the restaurant, he may have killed her. He saw my face and I think he decided after what Kreshon did to him, that it was in his best interest to leave me alone. I'm not naive enough to think I won't see him again though.

Then there was Blaq, who I met at an all you can eat restaurant. She was a hostess and I thought she was the most beautiful woman I'd ever seen in my life, until she opened her mouth. It was then that I noticed that although she had a face as beautiful as Kerry Washington, her voice was as strong as Barry White. Without a doubt he could fool the straightest of men and his need to be something other than what he was born as, reminded me of my sister. For a brief moment it was the one thing I hated about him, until I remembered this was all about money.

Our relationship had benefits because Blaq needed cash for his sexual reassignment surgery, and if he worked for me, I could help make that happen. On one condition, that he stripped himself of all the makeup, hair and dresses. Why? So men who were interested in him could know what they were getting. I already had bitches that looked like bitches. I wanted a gay man to fulfill my homosexual customer requests. He refused at first, but it didn't take him long to realize I was his best bet after hearing Passion roll down how we split the pot evenly amongst everyone.

Then there was Jackie, a beautiful Asian girl who went by the name Jay-O. She was taken from her home as a child and sold into sexual slavery in America. When her owner died in a car accident when she was thirteen, she took to the streets alone. When Passion approached her at the bus stop, the only thing she had to her name was a navy blue back pack which was full of holes. Passion brought her to meet me in the truck, and when she saw the smile on my face and the girls in my truck, she was happy to join our sweet team.

Hadiya was by far my favorite. She always seemed to stare at me, like she was waiting for me to give her orders. She was a beautiful Indian girl who went out her way to make me happy. If I wanted a cup of coffee, she knew it before I had a chance to ask and that's probably why she and Foxie bumped heads all the time. I found her and Catherine, another one of my girls, at a local bar not to far from Concord Manor. All they needed was a little guidance, and I was ready to give it to them. Provided they would suck a dick and take it in the ass whenever asked. Needless to say it wasn't a problem.

Unlike Hadiya, Catherine, a cute black girl, was extremely loud. Mostly because she was recently released from prison. She walked around like she was tough and was always talking about how she wouldn't be punked by nobody...even me. Although she was rough around the edges, she told me there wasn't a thing she wouldn't do for money. And since Passion wasn't working anymore, I needed a bitch like her on my roster. A stone cold freak.

There was one problem, the bond between Passion, Catherine and Tabitha, a young girl I met at a bowling alley, was tightening. It looked like it might be dangerous. Because of their bond, the house was divided. As long as the relationships didn't fuck with my paper, I didn't care what they did.

Now Tabitha's mind was weak and it was easy to manipulate her. She was a beautiful black girl who had a passion for designer purses without a means to get them. With promises to get her bag game up if she could take dick to ass, she eagerly joined my squad. All the members of Thirteen Flavors up to this point needed to belong. They needed a place to stay. They needed stability and I provided that for them. That is until I met my final girl.

I wanted her above them all. It was obvious that wanting and getting her were two different things. I met Tywanda at a cheap clothing store when I was getting my girls outfits for their first night on the stroll. I hadn't planned on connecting with any other girls, until the money came in and I could afford to have them around. But the moment she walked past me, I knew I had to have her. Tywanda was black but her even skin tone made her look Brazilian. Her hair was cut low like a boy's but instead of dying it blonde she made it dirty brown. Her lips were pouty and pink and her breasts were round and firm. I thought I seen the best of her beauty, until she turned around and I got a look at her ass. She was perfect. Thick like a black girl and toned like an athlete.

Passion was with me the day I decided to bring her into the fold. "Go get her." I said, counting the money in my mind I would make off of her alone. "That bitch is gonna get us paid."

Passion quickly hustled up to her, as Tywanda thumbed through a few cheesy dresses on a rack. It was the only place I could buy my girls an outfit for under twenty dollars. I positioned myself so that I could read their lips and see everything they were saying.

"You are so beautiful," Passion told her, "but I'm sure you hear that all the time."

The girl smiled. "I don't hear it often, but thank you anyway."

Passion moved closer. "My boss wants to know what you're going to do with that body of yours." She pointed at me and I winked at them. "It would be such a shame to let it go to waste."

Tywanda blushed a little and shook her head. "I'm not into girls, if that's what she means."

"She's not gay either." Passion said with a straight face. "She is about her money though and she would love to make a little with you. If you're up for it. Why don't you let me take you over there to meet her."

Tywanda glared. "If she got so much to tell me, how come she won't say it to me directly? Why she gotta send you?"

Passion gave me the wave and I walked up to them. The closer I got to Tywanda, the prettier she became. "My name is Jayden," I said, looking at the product before me, "and I would love to work with you." Passion stepped away but remained close in case I needed her.

She blushed again. "What kind of stuff you do?"

"I sell pussy." I didn't want to beat around the bush because I didn't have time. And anybody who wasn't interested in doing what needed to be done, wasn't useful to me.

She frowned and stepped back. "I...I'm not a whore."

"Never said you were. And since when does getting paid for what you possess, make you a whore? If you ask me, it makes you a business person."

She shook her head no. "I can't do what you're asking. I'm sorry." Although I was irritated, I smiled at her and waved at Passion. She came back over and I said, "Give her your number and when she's ready she'll call me."

They exchanged numbers and I spent the next day waiting for her call. The phone never rang. I guess she wasn't interested in fucking, sucking and licking to make her money after all. It was weird because something in her eyes told me she was ready. Like she needed to give herself permission to be bad. They told me she was born for that shit.

And then one day, I was chilling in my house getting my feet rubbed by Hadiya. My mind was on my money and our first day on the stroll. It was raining hard outside and there was a knock at the door. I didn't hear it but Passion looked at me and told me. Before the knock she was on the floor dancing with Catherine and Tabitha in the middle of the living room. She went to answer it, and when she did, Tywanda was standing at the doorway with a brown suitcase in her hand.

I tried to hide the pleasure on my face. This moment told me that I knew exactly what I was doing. And that I could read people even when they couldn't read themselves. If Armanii was alive she would be proud. Tywanda placed her suitcase on the floor but she remained outside the house. I hadn't invited her in yet. Her face was dripping wet and her full pouty lips were turned upside down into a frown. Her sadness excited me and I examined her fully.

"You want me to let her in?" Passion asked.

I didn't want her to at the moment. Instead I observed how the white t-shirt she wore clung to her wet body revealing her round nipples. She wasn't wearing a bra. The shirt was short enough to showcase her pierced bellybutton which blinged with a hoop diamond ring. The expression on her face was heavy and it looked like she was running from something, or somebody.

"Let her in now, Passion." I finally said wearing my game face.

As if she was on an audition, Tywanda glided slowly into the house. I watched the way one leg crossed in front of the other, like they were one. She moved like she was on a runway and I enjoyed every minute of it. Her hips elevated up and down and didn't stop until she was standing directly in front of me. She would be one of my top earners, I knew it. I'm so excited I can barely stay still. The best thing about it all was that she made the thirteenth girl to complete my team. My lucky number.

"Hello, Jayden." She looked me in my eyes. "I was wondering," she wiped a few raindrops from the top of her breasts, "well I was wondering if the position you were offering was still available. I kind of need the work and a place to stay, badly."

I pointed to the floor and she slid to her knees and rested at my feet. The other girls stood behind her as if they were waiting to see if she would be accepted, while Gucci looked jealous. I was dragging things out because I knew my answer the moment I saw her face. But I wanted her to remember this day in case she ever got the idea to fuck me over or play games with my money. When I was certain she suffered enough, I lifted her chin and said, "Be sure, beautiful. Because the moment you shake my hand and look into my eyes, I own you."

Without hesitation she extended her hand, and signed over her life.

Present Day

Green Door – Adult Mental Health Care Clinic
Northwest, Washington DC

Christina sits across from Harmony breathing heavily. She was by far her most pathetic patient, but she'd be lying if she didn't say she was also the most interesting. Flipping through the notes in Harmony's chart she asks, "So basically you think Mrs. Sheers was the person who catapulted Jayden into the sex industry?"

Harmony heard the condescending tone she was famous for and rolled her eyes. "Yes."

"If that is true, which we both know it isn't, what part of Jayden's path in life do you own?"

"I'm still working that out, Miss lady bitch, that's why I'm here. You tell me, you get paid the big bucks to answer my questions don't you?" She rubs her arms for warmth. The air conditioning is on too North Pole.

"Your daughter had to make major decisions, Harmony. In most of what you told me, I don't think she had a choice. Being forced to come up with $250,000 in six months? That's insane! Some people don't see that amount of money in a lifetime."

"I didn't know about the fifty thousand dollars. Jayden never told me she couldn't hear."

"Would you have cared if she did?"

"We'll never know now will we?"

Christina shakes her head. Harmony was still drunk and totally disrespectful. She could've thrown her out on her ass because of her condition alone but in her opinion she seemed more honest now. Also there was something dark about Harmony's presence today, something that seemed final.

Christina read one of her notes. "You mentioned Jayden was a monster."

"She *is* a monster."

"Okay, you mentioned that she *is* a monster but outside of cleaning up your messes and taking care of the responsibilities you should have been charged with as a mother, I don't see how she's so bad. If anything she should be commended even though I don't condone exploiting young girls for their bodies."

Harmony shakes her head. "Do you like cubs?"

She shrugs. "I'm not much for baseball but my boyfriend seems to like them okay."

"You really are the whitest woman I know."

Christina gasps and turns an interesting shade of red. "What do you mean?"

"I'm talking about lion's cubs not the baseball team. Do you like cubs or not?"

An expression of recognition takes over. "Oh, yes, they're adorable." She slaps her hands together. Now she's giggly. "I take my step children to see them all the time at the zoo."

"Good for you." Harmony yawns. "Anyway cubs are precious in the beginning. They have the big black eyes, short ears and yellow fur you white people fall all over for." Christina sighs. "All you want to do is pick them up and hug them don't you?"

Get to the point. "True."

"Well what happens to those cubs after they turn about ten months old?" She pauses. "They're still young but now their body weight increases which gives them the ability to rip that smug face of yours clear off your clavicle." Christina rubs her shoulders. "They are cute but they are killers. Smaller replicas of their parents but killers all the same. The best killers move slowly and are amongst us in the community. They blend in with everything and everyone."

Christiana focuses on the cougar across from her and says, "Tell me about it."

"They are calculating, slow and exact. And I'm telling you that whether you believe me or not, Jayden is the same way."

Christina sits back in her seat. "Okay, I'll let you finish your story but at some point today, I want to hear about the child you gave birth too."

"At some point today you'll hear everything I have to say, because after this I'm done. I can't live this life anymore." Her body slinks down into the chair and she wipes the mist out of her eyes.

"What do you mean you're done?"

Silence.

Christina leans forward. "Harmony, what do you mean you're done?"

"Do you want to hear the rest or not?"

Worried she replies, "Carry on."

PART THREE

JAYDEN
BLUE EYES

I don't know why but it seems like making money and being horny goes hand and hand with me. So I bring Sebastian home to play a little with him. The moment he comes through Concord's doors, everybody is fussing about how cute he is. I'm not going to lie, he ain't my nigga, but I'm not sure how I feel about other bitches looking at him either.

"Oh my, God, them Blue eyes are so fucking sexy! Are they real?" Gucci says.

"Don't fuck with me, ma. They all real." Sebastian glares.

"Jayden, is he yours, because if he ain't I will fuck him for free? That's on everything."

"Well that makes you stupider than I thought." I snap. I take him by his hands and whisk him upstairs. Away from the bitches who enjoy fucking off duty. I guess Joseph was right after all.

We eventually make it to my room, and the moment he's inside, I push him to the bed and take his shoes off. "Let me holla at you for a minute. Are you sure you like just fucking each other? This sort of thing is good for you?" He's looking through me.

"Yes, why do you want more?"

"I'm not in the business of wanting more if the girl I'm chilling with isn't."

I think about it. I'm still waiting on Kreshon so I tell him, "Naw, I'm good with our arrangement for now. Let's just enjoy each other…life is so rough without a good fuck."

Before he can dispute anymore, his feet aren't even good and out of his socks before I'm sucking on his toenails. When I see his expression changes, I know he loves it. When I've sucked each of his toes clean, I remove his pants and his boxers. He tries to grab me and take charge but I push him on my bed and drop to my knees. I handle his dick like it's delicate chinaware at first, before stuffing him into my mouth like toys in a Christmas stocking. When I hum, I can feel the tip of his dick in my throat. I think I'm starting to love this shit. He grabs the back of my head and wipes forward, causing my long hair to spread out on his chest.

"Damn," he says pushing deeper into my throat. "How do you do that shit?"

I don't answer, instead I spread my jaws wider and softly place one of his balls into my mouth. I've learned overtime to spread my jaws wide. "Are you serious?" He looks down at me. "How the fuck…"

Before he can finish his sentence both of his balls along with his dick is in my mouth and I'm moving my tongue like a wave. When I feel his goo roll down my throat I'm ready for part two. That is until I see his blue eyes turn gray as he looks over me. I take him out of my mouth and turn around to see what got him shot. That's when I see somebody at my door I don't recognize.

"My bad, I'm here with Gucci and them." He looks at me on my knees and licks his lips. "I'ma leave ya'll too it though. Handle your business, partner. She's a bad, bitch!" He closes the door.

"Who the fuck was that?" Sebastian asks. When I look at him, he has his gun firmly in his hands and he's dressed. What the fuck? How did he do it so quickly? I'm up on my feet trying to pull myself together. I wouldn't know the nigga who walked in my room anymore than I would a roach in my house. And that bothers me.

"I don't know, but I'm about to handle it." I quickly get dressed. On my way downstairs I see somebody in the main bathroom. I go into it and the same nigga is in the tub with Gucci. A cigarette is burning on the tub and now it's stained. "What the fuck is going on?" I throw the cigarette in the tub and it sizzles. "I didn't authorize you to have niggas in my house."

"Jayden, you said this is our place too. Lighten up."

"Fuck that shit, I don't want mothafuckas in my house!" I still don't know who robbed me, I don't want it happening in the future.

"Baby girl, I'm just showing my lady a nice time." He says as if he just paid money for the Ritz Carlton. "You don't have to act like that."

"Nigga, this is my mothafuckin' house! And unless you selling or buying pussy, you got five minutes to get the fuck out of here before I get out of the box!"

"Jayden, that's fucked up!" Gucci says. "This is my boyfriend Tito I was telling you about."

"I don't give a fuck who he is. But I know one thing, you better roll with him or fall in line because I'm about to explode. And I'm not fucking around with you."

These sluts got me fucked up. I go into the hallway and scream down at all the niggas I see in my house now. What were they doing, having a party or something?

"I don't know what these bitches told you, but this is my house and I own them. All of them. So unless I give the say so, you don't have the right to be here. And that goes for all of you. Nobody is allowed to be in my house unless I give the okay. Now either get the fuck out, or I'm shooting anything I land on in the next five minutes!"

Respecting my threat, everyone leaves. Even Sebastian.

HARMONY
WASHED OUT

I woke up to the irritating sound of teenage girls yapping in my house. I roll out of bed and sit on the edge mad as hell with all of this shit. I can't believe Jayden would subject me to this simply because I need her help. It wouldn't have been so bad had Mrs. Sheers not made it her mission to put me in an outpatient alcoholic program. Because of that move, I had to do everything Jayden said, hoping that whatever plan she came up with worked. Maybe her father left her some money that she would use to buy my sister's out of the house. Who knows. Basically I was at her beckon call.

Mrs. Sheers claimed the program she forced me into was voluntary but I had a feeling it would be mandatory if I didn't agree to go on my own. I hadn't touched a drink or dick in days and I'm not sure if I can take it much longer. I'm having withdrawals. Most of the time I just stay in my room, listening to the world go on without me.

Life is difficult when I'm not drinking. I think about my father and how he loved me so much before he died. I think about Estelle Pointer, the woman I thought was my mother who introduced me to my first suck of alcohol. When she isn't on my mind, I think about Shirley Pointer, my non-maternal grandmother who made me eat her pussy in exchange for food and shelter. Finally I think of her son Charles Pointer, who fucked and sucked me most of my life as a girl. This is why I stay drunk, so I don't have to remember. I hate remembering.

This morning is the first time I thought about Irma while sober, the mother who gave birth to me who I treated horribly, all because she wasn't a part of my life when I was a kid. I wonder how life would've been if she was there for me, instead of the hell I called home.

I grab my blue cotton robe and decide to leave my room to get something to eat. I don't bother to do my hair I never have company anyway. Most days Jayden would bring my food up, saying I didn't have to leave the room for nothing but my alcoholism meetings. I get the impression that she's trying to keep me hidden and away from her friends. Today I want to see why.

When I walk downstairs I can't believe my eyes. Jayden is sitting at the head of the table talking to the prettiest teenage girls I'd ever seen in my life. *Fucking bitches.* They're dressed in skimpy silk pajamas and the colorful scarfs wrapped around their heads do nothing to hide their appeal. Immediately I want to throw up in my nose.

And then there's Jayden. I can't focus on her too long because her beauty sickens me. Her long black hair hangs down her back and the edges fold into cascading curls. She whips it over her left shoulder as she's talking to the girls and her light complexion is slightly bronze and free of any imperfections. For a second I see the person I'm supposed to be. The girl I was when I was partially normal. Before alcohol. Before the rape. Before the abuse.

Figuring they're about to make breakfast, I take my place at the table, opposite of Jayden. The conversation stops when they see me scoot up and fold my hands in front of me. They look at me as if I'm a human size roach, threatening to kiss them on the necks.

"Ma, what are you doing?" Jayden says with wide eyes when she finally notices me. She hops up and rushes toward me. I catch a look at the trendy blue jeans she's wearing which hug her curves, making her ass pop out like a round bubble. She tugs on the bottom of the mint green t-shirt covering her breasts which reveals her flat belly.

"Is something wrong?" She looks back at her friends and then at me. "I told you I was going to bring your food. You don't have to do anything but relax. I know it's hard being clean so I got your back. Now go upstairs and let me take care of you."

She looks like she's focusing on my lips instead of my eyes and I find that weird. "Jayden, this is my house. I can do whatever the fuck I want, remember? What…are you ashamed of me or something?"

In a low voice she says, "I didn't say that. And I'm not ashamed of you either. I'm just saying you don't have to worry about anything when you're here. I got everything." Then she lowers her head, "but the phone is off, ma, did you pay the phone bill?"

Oh shit. Here it comes. "With what, Jayden?"

She frowns. "The money I gave you."

I have the money in my purse but I'm not using it for a bill. After this shit I needed something to make me feel good. "I don't have it. You sure you put it in my room?"

She backs away and her eyes lower. "Forget about it, ma." *I already did.*

An Indian girl rushes out of the kitchen with a tray of pancakes, bacon and eggs. The smell caresses my nose and massages my stomach. I can't wait to get my hands on the food. Instead of placing it in the middle of the table, she walks up to Jayden whose back is faced towards her because she's staring at me like she could hypnotize me into walking back upstairs. I wish Jayden would get the fuck out of my face. I notice that the other girls turn their noses up at the Indian girl. She must not be a favorite.

"Jayden, your food is ready." The Indian girl says, looking dead at the back of her head. "I hope you like it."

Jayden doesn't move. Her eyes are on mine and I wonder why she doesn't acknowledge her friend. She's standing directly behind her. "Oh shit, Hadiya talking to her when she's not looking into her eyes again." The girl with a gold short hairstyle says under her breath. "That bitch kisses so much ass she's going crazy."

Jayden doesn't respond. Doesn't she hear them?

"Jayden, why aren't you answering your friend?" I point at her. "She's talking to you."

Jayden turns around slowly and looks at Hadiya. "Did somebody say something to me?" She stares at everyone but the Indian girl nods yes. Jayden steps closer to her but the girl steps back. Jayden looks like she's irritated and I think she's about to hit her. A little violence at breakfast is just what I need. She places the tray down on the table.

"I told you not to talk to her unless she's looking at you," the girl with the gold hair says.

"Foxie, shut the fuck up!" Hadiya yells. "You always starting shit." Then she focuses on Jayden. "I'm sorry, Jayden. It won't happen again but your food is ready, you want me to dish your plate?"

Jayden yanks the back of her hair forcing her to the ground. "I keep telling you to stop that shit. Don't call me unless I'm looking at you." She pushes her away and the girl scrambles. She turns to me. "Ma, you hungry? I can bring something to your room."

This shit is so weird. "I'm eating here, Jayden." I look back at the girls trying to figure out what the fuck is going on around here. Are they her slaves? She's not smooth enough to be a pimp. "Now either get me a plate or have that young bitch of yours go make me one."

Jayden walks slowly to the edge of the table. She orders the Indian girl, who seems to be moving around like Jayden didn't just yank her hair, to bring me my food. What the fuck is going on in this house? As I cut my pancakes, I notice how the Indian girl serves Jayden like she's her lover. I hope I didn't give birth to two pussy lickers instead of one.

After Jayden's and my plate is dished, the girl named Foxie reaches for the tray. When Hadiya slaps her hand away, she lunges toward her.

"Stop this shit!" A girl with a red Afro yells. I remember seeing her at the funeral. "I'm so sick of ya'll fighting each other around here. The shit is stupid and it betta stop."

"Well I didn't make the food for her!" Hadiya responds. "I made this for Jayden and if Foxie wants some, she better go in there and cook the shit herself. I heard what she told Gucci and them behind my back." She stares at her. "She said she wouldn't eat shit I made if I paid her. So since I didn't give her no dough, why she clamoring all over my shit?"

"You are such a fucking kiss ass, bitch!" Foxie yells. "It don't make no difference what you do for Jayden, she'll never eat your pussy!" *Thank God.* I think.

Hadiya gasps. "I never said she would, bitch! You just jealous of the relationship me and her have."

"News flash, you don't have a relationship with her. You work for her. There's a difference." Work for her? What could these girls possibly be doing for Jayden?

Jayden covers her forehead and she seems frustrated. "Can ya'll just stop this shit please?" She yells, looking at all of them. "It' so fucking stupid and I'm tired of breaking up fights around here!"

The girls continue to argue until there's a knock at the door. "Passion, get the door." Jayden says.

Passion answers the door and when she does, I can't believe who's walking into my house. After what Trip did to me, I'm about to run upstairs thinking he was sent to finish me off. Suddenly I'm not hungry anymore. But he doesn't look like he's there to harm me. And he looks better than I remember and for some reason, I wish I didn't wear this blue robe and I wish I combed my hair.

Kreshon walks inside and all of the feelings I had for him back in the day come flooding back...between my legs. After all, we fucked on a regular when I was a little older than Jayden and he was in love with me. We even talked about me leaving Jace and him leaving his girlfriend Constance. I talked a lot of shit but would've never been with him exclusively. Our sexual arrangement was sweet, until I gave him syphilis and his girlfriend found out about us fucking and committed suicide. I can't help but wonder if he thought about me every now and again the way I thought about him.

But instead of focusing on me, he looks directly at Jayden. He touches her softly on the shoulder and she stands up and gives him a tight hug. She beams and I take notice to the way he lovingly massages her back. Either she's in love with him, or he's in love with her. I'm beyond angry until they separate and look into each other's eyes. It was the same way he looked into mine when we were younger. I need to know what's up and I need to know now. I'm just about to ask him what he's doing with my daughter when he stuffs some cash into the palm of her hand. Like he use to do me. Wait one damn minute! Where was mine?

After they say their hellos, she grips his hand and they walk in my direction. I tug on my robe and try to rub the loose strands of my hair backwards. He smiles at me, but not in the way he use to. I feel sick. "Kreshon, this is my mother Harmony. You saw her at my father's funeral. Remember?"

"Oh yeah…hey, Harmony. You good?" He looks at me like I'm an old picture of somebody he doesn't know. Like I hadn't sucked his dick at least fifty times in my life and swallowed every ounce of his nut.

"Yeah I'm good." I look at Jayden. "It's funny that you guys are together, me and Kreshon have a past too. Tell her…me and you use to go waaaaay back didn't we?" I say.

Jayden looks at me and back at him. "Kreshon says he doesn't know you like that."

"Oh he did, did he? That's funny, because I remember having a real close relationship with him. Think harder, Kreshon. Tell her how we use to roll." *In that abandoned house in D.C.*

He swallows and takes a deep breath. "I think you got me confused, Harmony. Outside of you being my man's girl, I don't know too much about you. You sure you not thinking of somebody else?" His eyes tell me he wants me to keep our secret. He hadn't told her anything about our past. He was in love with my daughter, and he wants my blessing. The thing is, he'll never get it.

JAYDEN

THE TIME FOR THE GAMES HAVE BEGUN

It's Showtime! We circled 16th street, a well-known hoe stroll in Washington D.C, five times. I shuffle around in the passenger seat of Olive's van, getting dizzier by the moment as Metha drives. I can smell my girls' designer perfume but it's the scent of their nervousness that makes me question what I'm doing here. I can tell that they don't believe I'm up for it and if they could read my mind, they'd be right. When I look in the back, Olive and Passion who never leave my side, stare at me as if they're afraid. I put everybody together and its time to make money. The only thing is, we haven't made a dime yet. I'm procrastinating and I can't stop.

As the van crawls up and down the dark streets, I stare at the prostitutes on the block wearing high heels and higher skirts. The expressions on their faces are hard. Like they'd seen more shit than I could ever imagine. Had I not been born to Harmony Phillips, they might be true.

Focusing back on Metha she says, "You want me to drive everybody home? We been hitting the block for a while." She isn't comfortable about my choice of profession but its what I have to do.

I spot a place on the street that doesn't have many whores or cars. "Naw. I'm ready. Let me out over there." I point. "I want to check something out before I let everybody out." She pulls up and parks the van. I gaze back at my team again, put a fake smile on my face, and hop out. When I hear another door open, I turn around and see Olive and Passion.

"Where we going?" Olive asks rolling the silver balls around her fingers. "I'm ready when you are."

Sometimes she can be irritating. "Let me see what's going on first." I peep at both of them. "Just go back inside and keep an eye on the girls for me. They need coaching."

"It's your team, Jayden. And if you think we letting you cruise out here by yourself," Olive looks around, "you must be crazy. Now come on, we wasting time."

"Yeah, Jayden, Gucci and them know what time it is. So let's go get them and let them handle business. It's time to work. You ain't got to be out here." Passion says.

"This is not open for discussion." Instead of arguing, I turn my back on them and walk up the block.

I'm trying to breathe in everything around me. I guess I should've done this before getting everyone dressed and ready to work. When I walk further up the block, I stand behind a few cars and observe. I see how the johns would pull up to the girl of their choice and how she'd wiggle into the car, always with a smile on her face.

I'm still checking the scene when a tall woman with a long pretty brown weave yells, "Now you're a sexy red thing." She's with four other women, all pretty like her. Their makeup and hairstyles are faultless. "How come we haven't seen you around here before?"

I turn around to see if she's talking to somebody else but she's looking slam at me. I love her voice. So kind. So sweet. And loud enough that each word makes it to my ears. "I don't work out here. Just checking a few things out."

She walks up to me and they follow. "You not one of them documentary people are you? Always trying to get our story?" She frowns. "I hate them mothafuckas."

"Naw. Nothing like that."

"Well you better get out of here, honey." She looks concerned. "The last thing we want is somebody pulling you in a car and taking you to a place you don't wanna go. There are some crazy niggas out here and if you not smart and quick enough, you can end up in the next life."

"Yeah, my baby cousin was murdered on her first night a few weeks ago." The one with the short black bob says. "I told her I didn't want her out here but the little bitch wouldn't listen. Now she's the cause of her mother being in the hospital with a broken heart and snapped brain."

Suddenly I'm scared for my girls. "Well it's a good thing I'm not working then."

The one with the long black weave places her hand against my face. It's warm and soft, but I want her off of me so I back up. I can only imagine how many dicks she'd touch that night alone. "I'm not gonna hurt you." Her voice relaxes me instantly. "You just remind me of my little sister and I'm concerned for you that's all."

"I'm strong. No need to worry about me." I wave her off.

"I hear what you're saying but your eyes tell me that none of this is for you. So why don't you get on out of here, sweetie. The later it is the closer you get to danger." She looks around.

She's so sweet that I decide to keep it one hundred with her. "I'm leaving now, but do you think you can tell me what area would be good to bring my girls?"

"Your girls?" She grins. She reminds me of the aunt I never had. "I knew there was a reason you came out here, sunshine. So you have a little team now do you? That's good because its important for ya'll to stick together if you gonna be working the streets. The deeper you are the better."

I laugh and stuff my hands into my pockets. Then I look down the block but I was too far away to see the van. "Yeah, it's their first night on the job. I think they'll do good though. So where do you think would be a good place to set them up?"

One moment I'm looking in her eyes and the next I'm kissing the rocky pavement beneath me. My nose is inches away from her pink pumps and I can smell the musty scent of her feet. What scares me more is not that she struck me, or that I'm having a hard time getting up, but the base that suddenly rolls through *his* voice.

When I look up at him, I can finally see that what I thought was a woman, is actually a man. This happened to me one other time, with Blaq. "Are you looking down there good, sweetheart?" He says with a scowl on his face. "Because you can place your bitches exactly where you are now, right there on the ground next to you. We run this block. I be damned if you think I'm gonna let you bring some young Twinkies to move on my turf."

I rise up on my knees and look up at him. Now that he's knocked some sense into me, I can see them all for what they really are…men. Standing on my feet I look him straight into his eyes. The anger rises from my feet to my head and the liquid in my mouth shoots out and smacks him in the eye. It's over now. I just signed my own death certificate.

"Oh no she didn't spit in your face, girl!" One of them screeches. "She got it all the way fucked up! You know what you gotta do. Cut that pretty face of hers so she won't need it no more." That's an interesting idea and I don't intend on letting her do it.

Long hair wipes my gook out of his eyes and gives me a look I haven't seen since the last time I saw Madjesty. He looks like he's about to take off after me, until a silver ball smacks him dead in the forehead, leaving an ugly red mark. When it hits the ground, I see its one of the balls Olive always rolls around her fingers. When I look down the block I see Olive staring at me. "Don't just stand there, bitch, run!" Olive yells.

The last time I ran this fast, I'd stolen money out of Sandy's purse and she and her friends wanted to burn my hair. The only difference now is I have five drag queens gunning for me. "I'm going to kill you, bitch!" Long hair yells. "I'm going to beat you and that bitch's ass! You got me so mad I could probably fuck you." *YUCK!* What would that accomplish?

Olive waits until I'm close to her and we both take off. "I knew I shouldn't have left you alone!" She's breathing heavily.

In short breaths I yell, "What we going to do?"

"I got a plan!"

I look at her hesitantly and say, "That quick?"

"Just trust me!"

I follow Olive a few more feet and when I turn around, one of the drag queens has a knife in her hand. When I look at the others they seem to be clutching something in their claws too. I wasn't about to wait around long enough to find out what it was. When Olive dips behind a car and hops, I do the exact same thing. When I look down and see why she leaped, I grin.

We wait on the other side of a white car until the queen's approach. When they do, Long Hair says, "You must be dumber than you look. You should've ran all the way to the police station, now it's too late." The hairstyle that I gave her so much credit for is sliding back, revealing a brown stocking cap underneath. It was a wig. Damn that bitch is good. "Don't worry, I'ma carve some sense into you and that pretty bitch you with."

The next step he takes causes his foot to go slam into a huge pothole. He screams out in pain as the hole takes most of his foot, forcing him to fall on his face. The bone in his ankle cracks open and blood oozes out. There's an orange cone lying under the wheel of the white car next to the hole. I guess it was supposed to be covering it so people would know it was dangerous.

"Oh my God, Niecey! The bitch tried to kill you." One of them yells trying to help him up.

"Leave me alone, girl! It's cracked! I'ma be out of work for days!" She points. "Look at it!" She focuses on me. "I'ma kill you!" He promises. "Do you hear me, bitch I'm gonna see your face again and when I do I'ma kill you!" Olive and me laugh as we run away from the scene.

●━━━━━━━━━━━━━━━━━━━━━━━━●

We are on our way back to the van, when Olive grabs me and pulls me into an alley. It looks like one of us is about to serve the other the way we hang in the darkness of the two buildings. She steps so close to me, I can smell the Shea butter she uses in her hair.

"Jayden, I don't know what's going on with you and I don't care. But that shit back there was dangerous. You wanted to get into this game and I'm with you all the way but to be honest, it looks like you not ready. You let the girls talk to you any kind of way and now you're coming across as weak. You not making smart moves right now, Jayden and if they see you like this again, especially Gucci, you'll only encourage them to take over. Is that what you want?"

I can't tell her that she's right. I can't tell her that I'm scared. I can't even tell her that I need two hundred and fifty thousand dollars to make most of my problems go away. So I put on my game face and say, "Get the fuck off of me, Olive." I rise up on that bitch.

"What?" She says softly.

I look at her hands and repeat slowly, "Get...the...fuck...off...me." She removes her hands and takes a step back. Her foot lands on an opened condom wrapper. "I'm tired of you acting like I don't know what the fuck I'm doing. Yes I made a mistake tonight but there won't be too many more of them. But if you ever try to tell me how to run my shit again, we won't be friends. We won't even be cordial. Am I clear?"

"Jayden, I was just..."

"Bitch, you not listening to me, are we clear?"

She steps back. "I got it."

"Good, now lets get back to the van. I got shit to do."

THIRTEEN FLAVORS

SCARY JAYDEN

The cool October night comforted Gucci, Queen, Na-Na and Foxie as they sat on the patio smoking a blunt and talking shit. As always, Gucci made it her mission to point out the obvious. "Did anybody but me think tonight was weird?" She frees the right arm of her pink sweater. "I mean Jayden really had us get dressed and ready to work for nothing. I'm telling you it's going to be like this all the time if we continue to follow her." She scratches the red bumps that recently appeared all over her arms and neck. "She not ready for the game, she never will be."

"Gucci, I think you should ease up on Jayden." Foxie says as she drinks hot water and lemon from a yellow cup. "I don't know what happened tonight but she spent a lot of money getting us ready. So if we didn't get out there I'm sure she had her reasons."

"You are so stupid if you believe that shit! I don't know about the rest of ya'll but I'm going to keep my eyes open for any sign of weakness."

"I thought you said you were really going to give it a chance. That's why we came back." Queen says, with her legs draped over Na-Na's knees as she plays with her toes. "I like it here."

"I'm with her," Na-Na adds, never missing an opportunity to ride Queen's tits.

"And I'm not saying…" Gucci's response is broken when she sees her arch nemesis. "Hold fast everybody a spy is approaching."

When Hadiyah walks out on the patio, the cool air heats up. "Dinner is ready," she says with an attitude. She was in charge of the night's meal. Tywanda and Blaq are by her side.

Since everyone moved in Concord Manor, the house had become divided. There are the Original Thirteen Flavor girls, which includes Gucci, Foxie, Na-Na and Queen. Then there's Passion's Team, which includes Johnna, Jay-O, Catherine and Tabitha. Finally there's Hadiya's squad, which is Blaq and Tywanda. It was just a matter of time before things kicked off for the worst in the house.

"I'm not eating shit in that kitchen." Gucci says, scratching her bumps so hard they start to bleed. "Nothing you cook anyway."

"What you even doing out here?" Foxie adds. *"I'd think you'd be spoon feeding Jayden somewhere instead of coming out here bothering us. We all know you don't let her do nothing but wipe her ass when she goes to the bathroom."*

"I heard she don't even let her do that." Gucci responds.

"And I heard your ass got Chicken Pox and you in the house trying to give it to everybody." Blaq pops off. *"Infected ass, bitch."*

"I wasn't even talking to your flaming ass." Gucci says.

"I'ma tell you like this, you may can talk that shit to Hadiya but I'm not her. Believe that. Fucking with me you'll end up buried alive in somebody's yard. Next to the tulips."

"You going too far." Foxie responds."

"No, ya'll are going too far with all this hating ass shit. I'm sick of how ya'll be treating this girl just because she doing her job."

"First of all its Passion's responsibility to take care of the girls but it's obvious Hadiya is trying to take her place. It's cool with me though since everybody knows the only reason Passion is here, is to wait on Madjesty to show up." Queen adds. *"You and Tywanda always coming to Hadiya's rescue. Let her speak up for herself. Her pussy is already developed."*

"You right, I can speak just fine for myself." Hadiya says. *"If ya'll don't want to eat I'm not going to force you. But just remember that shit the next time you try to act like I'm not doing my job around here in front of Jayden."*

"You are so funny, Hadiya. I can't wait until all this fake shit is over. Because before long, you gonna see who will be running shit and it damn sure won't be Jayden. Remember that!" Gucci ends.

●───●

Hadiya, Blaq and Tywanda walk down the hallway. *"I'm telling you now at some point you gonna have to fight that bitch, Hadiya."* Blaq says. *"Just make sure that when you do, you cut her ass into pieces before she does you. I know the kind of bitch Gucci is. She's a low blower. You gotta be prepared."*

"Should I tell Jayden what she said?" She asks. *"About taking over?"*

"To be honest I wouldn't rock the boat right now. Gucci just talking shit anyway, don't even give her the satisfaction of knowing you're still thinking about her." Tywanda says.

●───●

Passion, Johnna, Jay-O, Catherine and Tabitha were sitting in the living room watching the last five minutes of a *College Hill* rerun, when

Gucci and her hating ass crew strolled in. Part of her wanted to start shit and the other part wanted to see if Hadiya told anyone what she'd just said about Jayden. The moment Passion sees her face she's irritated.

"We know ya'll watching TV and everything, but how do ya'll feel about the way things went down tonight?" Gucci asks as her crew stands behind her.

"I don't want to talk about it, Gucci." Passion says looking at the stairs to see if Jayden is coming down. The house gets mighty quiet when the boss is in the room. "Why don't you go eat, Hadiya says the food is ready."

"You really are a scary ass bitch ain't you?" Gucci says scratching her arms more. The recent rash she developed disgusts Passion and her friends. "Just cuz we live in her house don't mean we can't state our opinions."

Passion rolls her eyes. "Why are you starting shit? If you don't want to be here, go home. Ain't no bars on the doors and windows. You are free to roam around the country."

"I can't believe you talking to her like that, when we been friends since forever." Foxie adds as if she didn't wish Gucci would slow the accusations down too. "She just looking out for us. You are such the switch over bitch, its ridiculous."

When the doorbell rings, Passion damn near knocks everybody over to answer the door. Gucci and her crew are right behind her. Passion seems disappointed when she sees two pretty older Spanish women on the other side of the door, along with a black man holding a clipboard and pen in his hand. One of the women looks at them awkwardly and says, "Is Jayden here?" Passion leaves because it isn't Madjesty.

"Who is you?" Gucci asks placing her hand on her hips.

"I'm Laura and this is my sister Ramona. We're Jayden's aunts." They observe the bumps on her body. "The real question is who are you?"

"We live here."

"For now, little girl. And just so you know, you got chicken pox. You better get it checked out before you end up dead. You look a little too old for that shit."

Everybody who is around Gucci backs up and covers their noses. She frowns at her friends, rolls her eyes at the aunts and yells, "Olive, can you tell Jayden she has company!"

Jayden comes down the stairs with Olive and Hadiya behind her. When she sees her aunts she knows there's a problem. She opens the door wider. "Hey. What's up?"

"Jayden, we've been trying to reach your mother for a while."

"I know because you stay threatening us." She crosses her arms over her chest.

"That's not what I'm talking about." She pauses. "I don't know if she told you but we have a right to bring an appraiser here to check on the current condition of the house." Laura points to the man.

"Why?"

"Because sooner or later this house will be ours and when it does, we don't want it returned to us destroyed. We don't trust your lying ass mother." Ramona responds.

Jayden looks at her girls and says, "Can you give us some privacy please?" Gucci is angry that she can't eavesdrop on what was going on, but made mental notes to find out the "T" later.

When they are gone Jayden says, "I thought the judge said we have a chance to come up with the money."

Laura laughs. "Jayden, let's not be wasteful of time. We lived here for a while," her face grows dark, "that is before your mother lied and said we stabbed her. Anyway, you and I both know you won't be able to come up with that sort of cash. You on welfare. Now if you play fair, we may let you stay here to clean up our house, and clean behind our dogs but even that is up for discussion."

Jayden turns burgundy. "I'm going to come up with that money and when I do you gonna remember this shit."

"Sure we will little girl. Like I said, we're here to check on the condition of this house. If it is destroyed in any kind of way when this is all over, as I'm sure your mother has explained, you'll be held liable." She looks at the man. "Go in and do what you have to, make it quick."

As the stranger enters her home, Jayden is more motivated than ever to get money.

HARMONY
HARMONY ROULETTE

I'm walking down the street from my house on my way to get a beer from the liquor store. I can't afford vodka right now because I'm broke. The moment somebody stops next to me, I'm all the way in, willing to do whatever they want for a bottle. Things are going good, until from my peripheral vision, I see the blur of a car pull up in a hurry. I haven't been shot at before but I know a bullet whizzing by my head when I see one. I take off running as fast as I can and my feet feel like sandbags are tied to each of my toes.

Up ahead I see a house with the gate open. It's like a sign telling me to come inside. I make it to the yard but fall at the threshold. I bump my lip on the concrete and pop up like a corn kernel. Whoever was firing stopped briefly, opened his car door and fires in my direction again. Windows at the house shatter and the white fence is crumbling. Eventually I reach the backyard and over the fence. Don't know how I hopped so high but I did. When I'm done, I'm on the opposite street and guess who drives by, Kreshon.

"Harmony, is that you?" He asks pulling up alongside of me in a silver Lexus.

Even if it wasn't me, I jump in his car so fast he doesn't have a chance to change his mind. "Drive, anywhere." I look behind me for the shooter. I don't see him. "Please."

"What's going on? Somebody after you?"

I lie. If I'm going to get shot at, I don't want to be alone. "No I'm good." Something felt off. One minute I'm getting shot at and the next minute he's here. "Where were you on your way too?" I ask looking out the side view mirror.

"You really want to know?"

I finally look at him. He's wearing a black Polo shirt and he's so handsome. "I wouldn't ask if I didn't want to know. What's up?"

"I'm about to see Jayden." He turns at the stop sign and my stomach aches. Why is he trying to fuck my daughter? "Don't worry, I haven't fucked her."

"You mean you haven't fucked her yet." He shakes his head. "What are you doing with my daughter, Kreshon? Be honest. She's so young."

"Jace asked me to look after her."

"So you think I'm that stupid? Jace is dead, the nigga not giving you no medals for shit you do." He makes another left. "I know you. And you love pussy. My pussy. I also know how you look at her, she reminds you of me doesn't' she? That's why you doing it."

"Fuck out of here." Now he's driving like he doesn't know where he's going. I got to him. "Kreshon, pull over." He doesn't. "I want to talk to you. Please." Finally he parks on the side of a house. I turn and face him. "You can't have my daughter. She's young but she's not me. I know you, you're probably remembering the times we use to share, and Jayden will never measure up. Her looking like me and fucking like me is two different things."

He eyes me. "Will you keep our secret?"

"What you mean?" For a second, I think I smell gunpowder.

"I don't want you to tell her about us. I'm not going to lie, I care about her, a lot and I'm asking you to hold fast on messing things up."

"What's in it for me?"

"As long as I can keep her, anything you want."

I hate him. It's nothing I can do now, Jayden is the apple of his eye. Plus, I think it's not a big coincidence that I was shot at and he's in the neighborhood. He may kill me if I don't give him Jayden and keep our secret. "I want to buy a bottle of vodka. What you got on you?" He frowns and gives me a hundred bucks from his wallet. "What you want for the money?"

"What you talking about?"

"I know you, and there are always two angles. So what else do you want?"

He unzippens his pants and pulls out his dick. I spit on it first, and suck him like I never have before. At the end of the day, he will never be able to confuse anybody for me, not even my daughter.

JAYDEN
PUSSY PLAN

After that shit that happened on 16ᵗʰ street and my aunts coming over, I stayed in my room until I came up with a plan. I wouldn't even go out when the girls were fighting. I needed to get my mind right and I finally did. With the captions on while I watched the movies, I saw two that changed the course of how I viewed my business. They were *The Mack* and *The Game*. The Mack made me realize that I wasn't a pimp with silky suits and long nails. I was out of my league trying to bitch slap somebody to sell pussy for me on 16ᵗʰ street. The best idea I got came from the movie *The Game*. On that movie people would pay for experiences they wouldn't have otherwise. Isn't the same true for prostitution? Men don't pay to bust a nut but for having the experience to make a bitch do so.

After taking a long bath and smoothing olive oil all over my skin, I slip into some fresh jeans and a white t-shirt. Then I spray Bvlgari perfume on my neck and wrists. Lastly I place the hearing aids in my ears and comb my hair over them. I hate these things but I don't want to miss a question or response today.

When I'm done, I had Passion get the girls together and told Olive to see to it that everyone was on time. For whatever reason, they didn't respect Passion and it was making it harder to do her job. I think because she doesn't get drunk and high anymore. But that wasn't my problem and I wasn't going to make it. If she wanted to continue to be a part of this team she had better learn to be a team player.

Before I go downstairs, I grab my strategic handbook, which includes my Thirteen Flavors Business Plan. Since I have school Monday through Friday, I work every night on it to be sure it's correct, and I finally believed that it is. I also grab a plastic bag I need for an exhibit, and head out my room. When I get downstairs everyone is in the living room looking at me. Everyone but Olive, Hadiya, Tywanda, Blaq and Passion are scratching themselves.

"Why is everyone itching?"

They all look at Gucci. "She gave us chicken pox."

I'm enraged. "Are you serious?"

"Don't worry, we know how to get rid of it." Gucci says. Her face is as red and pusy as a diseased vagina. I swear I hate this bitch but kicking her out now will be the wrong time.

Right before my meeting starts, there's a knock at the door. "Give me a second ya'll." They stir a little in their seats. I guess they're irritated. I sit my book and bag down and hurry to open the door. When I do, I see Sebastian's blue eyes peering into mine. His wild-eyed brother is to the left of him and he looks like he isn't up to any good. Sebastian and me haven't had a chance to play in a while and seeing him now makes me realize I'm long overdue.

With my hands on my hips I ask, "What you want, Sebastian? I'm busy right now." I focus on his lips. It's a habit even though I hear okay with the hearing aids on.

"Too busy to give me a few minutes of your time?" His voice is strong and confident, like his overall attitude. He stuffs his thumbs in the loops of his belt as usual and stands like a hood cowboy.

"You know how we go, but right now is not good." I'm still mad at him for leaving the way he did the last time I saw him.

The door halfway closes in his face until he says, "So I guess you don't want your phone back then."

I open the door, step out and close it behind me. "What phone you talking about?"

He looks at Luh Rod and says, "Give it to her, man."

With an attitude, Luh Rod rolls his eyes, dips his hand into his pocket and hands me the phone I tossed out the window like a cigarette butt months ago. The moment I see it, I count the money in my head. Sebastian doesn't realize how much seeing my phone made my day. Prior to this moment, we were going to have to start all over from scratch to get the business off the ground. Not a problem anymore. This was probably what Luh Rod was talking about when he said, *"I know you ain't coming all this way about that shit."* The day I walked over their house to stab him.

"Here. I think you dropped this out of your window." Luh Rod says, holding my phone out of reach.

I lean in and snatch it so quickly, I yank him a few inches forward. "How you get this? I hit the power button but it doesn't come on. *Please don't let it be broke.* Maybe it needs charging.

He shrugs. "Why you need to know how I got it? You want it or not?"

"He got it from your bushes." Sebastian offers. "Said he saw you throw something out a while back and figured you didn't want it. He ain't hard up for no phone though, so I made him give it back. It's yours right?"

I feel like hurting him, but the ice in Sebastian's eyes tell me it wouldn't be a good idea. I'm preparing to go inside when an all black Mitsubishi Diamante pulls up in the driveway. The moment I see the car, the blood feels like it drains from my body. I have the door open an inch, when a black nigga with a basketball player physique and killer eyes jumps out leaving his car door open. He's so close to me now, my nose is tucked in the pit of his underarm. "Your name, Jayden, bitch?"

I swallow air. "Who the fuck are you? And why are you pulling up in my driveway like you police?"

"Bitch, I'm asking the mothafuckin' questions. Are you Jayden or not?"

I'm about to lie but something tells me he knows the truth already. So in a low voice I say, "Why?"

He grabs both of my shoulders and pulls me toward him. My breasts are pressed against his stomach and I can feel his stiff dick on the side of my hip. I look up at him and can see spit leaking out of the corners of his mouth. Was he foaming? "Where is my girlfriend? I know you know so don't even think about lying to me."

"I don't know who you talking about." I'm being honest. "I think you got the wrong person. Maybe you looking for my neighbor down the street." I'm willing to put this crazy nigga on anybody else but me.

"Do you know a bitch name Tywanda or not?"

The moment her name rolls off of his tongue, I know it's over for me. When I laid eyes on her, I knew she belonged to somebody. But I never thought they'd come looking for her. "Yeah, I know her, but she ain't here."

"Bitch, you think it's a joke? Her mother told me she gave her this address. So either tell me where she at, or I'ma blow your eyebrows to the back of your head."

When I look down at his waist, the dick I thought was poking me in the stomach is actually the brown handle of a gun. "Please, I don't..."

My words are halted when he yanks me by my hair, forcing my head backwards. The cartilage in my neck snaps, causing a cracking sound. He moves his head closer to my face and I swear he's about to chew my nose off. The spit leaking out of the corners of his lips, are threatening to drizzle on my face and I want to faint and wake up on another day.

"Before you open that mouth you better know that I'm not fucking around with you. I been with Tywanda for five years and I'm gonna marry her. I was gonna put a baby in her and everything." *How romantic.* "But now she telling me she not coming home because she tired of me hitting her." He continues and the juice in his mouth finally touches my nose. *Yuck.* "Now I don't intend on letting you or nobody come in the way of that. So I'ma ask you again, where…is…she?"

"She not here. Why don't you leave me your number that way if she calls, I can give her your information." I smile hoping he'll believe me, but the way his nose waves up in the middle, I figure he doesn't.

His eyes turn a shade blacker as he reaches for the dick on his hip. I'm about to say goodbye, when the evil in his eyes turns to fright. He releases my hair and when I back up, I see sprinkles of blood on the gray of my doorstep. He moves away from me, holding his side and blood oozes between his fingers and over his nails. He looks down at the wet mess coming from his body and then at me. "What did you just do to me?"

"Don't worry about all that," Sebastian says, no weapon in hand, "why don't you go back to where the fuck you came from. She says your bitch ain't here, so it mean she ain't here."

He must've realized it was either Sebastian or his brother because he's about to go for his gun, when both of them draw their weapons quicker than a bird can flap his wings. Sebastian's voice is deep but sure. "My man, why don't you get back in your car and get yourself checked out. You not gonna last much longer leaking like that."

The monster gives them looks that could've meant anything from, *this ain't over* to *when I see you again, I'm plucking your teeth out.* Either way he gets the picture because he speeds off. When his car is out of sight, I look at the blood on the pavement and back at them.

"What did ya'll do?"

Sebastian flicks a blade. "Saved your life." He hands it to Luh Rod who turns the water hose on connected to my house, rinses the blood off and hands it back to Sebastian. They do this type of thing all the time. A light bulb immediately goes off in my head. I need their help and am willing to pay. "Sebastian," I step close to him, "I have a business proposition for you."

"What kind?"

"Do you think you and your brother would be interested in doing security for me? I got a business and I need somebody like both of you to look after our backs. Plus I'll pay you a lot of money," since I'm relatively broke right now I say, "well, I'll pay a lot of money once my business gets off the ground."

"I don't need no money." Sebastian's voice is masked with disappointment. He taps Luh Rod on the shoulder and says, "Let's roll, man. We got some place to be."

I feel my temperature rise. Not because I'm angry, but because I realize without them, anything is liable to happen to us on the streets. To my point if they weren't standing here a moment ago, I would've been fertilizer for my mother's bushes. And what was to stop him from coming back?

I walk in their direction. I have to swallow my pride because they are the last pieces to my puzzle. When I get close enough to Sebastian in my softest voice I beg. "Please don't leave. It ain't like ya'll can't use the money, I be seeing you running around here all the time with nothing to do. But I need you Sebastian and I'm begging you to help me out."

"So because we be rolling around here that makes us desperate?" He seems insulted. "You think that little of me?"

"I'm not saying that."

"You not saying nothing I want to hear." He taps Luh Rod on the arm. "Let's go, man." I watch them walk away, taking my sense of security with them.

●━━━━━━━━━━━━━━━━━━━━━●

Thirteen Flavors is sitting on the floor in my living room while I go over my plan. The scratching shit is making my skin crawl. Fuck Gucci! Anyway, I'm still on edge and every time I hear a car near my house, my heart jumps. I didn't bother telling Tywanda that her crazy boyfriend tried to kill me, because for my plan to work, I need all of the girls on dick. I mean deck. And I got something for her nigga anyway.

"First off I need everybody who doesn't have the chicken pox to stay the fuck away from Gucci and the rest and sit over here. At least until I can be sure the shit is gone." The house divides into the diseased and pure. "Good. Now that that's done, we're changing things up a little. First we're going to be working out of the house." I see a few of them sigh in relief. "We're also changing the business model a little. We're not selling sex, we're selling the experience."

I knew Gucci would be the first person to flap her jaws. "What is the *experience*, Jayden?" She scratches her face, which is usually very pretty. "Because you and I both know the only thing niggas paying for these days is pussy. If they get an experience out of that, so be it."

"That's not true, Gucci! They can get sex anywhere, from there own mothers if they tried hard enough. What we'll be offering is a chance to make their fantasies come true."

"And how we gonna do that?" Foxie inquires scratching her legs. "Because if I don't have to fuck, I damn sure ain't trying to."

"We sell the experience by finding out what it is they *really* want. And for the record, pussy will always be involved so keep yours clean." I look at all of them. "All of ya'll better keep that thing right." Blaq clears his throat and I wink. "Don't worry, baby, we making money off of boy pussy too."

I hold the phone up Sebastian gave me in the air and smiles rip across the faces of those who know what it was. "Using the client base we already have, we'll capitalize on their weakness and charge big bucks."

"I don't understand." Hadiya says. She isn't familiar with how we use to roll.

"I'll explain in a second." I open my Business Plan book and hand Olive a piece of paper. On it has five questions that she has to ask each of our clients.

"Olive, you are going to interview our clients. When the interview is over, based on the questions on this paper, we'll arrange to make their fantasy come true. But they must pay in advance for our services. If they don't pay up front we don't fuck with them."

Olive looks at the list. "I can't read your handwriting."

I take a pen and paper and hand them to Passion. "Why don't you write this on a newer sheet and Olive will read it when you're done." She does her best to read my handwriting and successfully makes the transfer. When she finishes Passion hands Olive the paper and I study her facial expressions carefully, waiting for her nod of approval. The questions are simple, but the responses will pay off greatly if we do our jobs correctly.

Reading from the sheet she says, "*What kind of flavor turns you on?*" Olive reads out loud. "*Do you prefer one or more flavors? What kind of kinky thing would you like to do but have never done with your flavors? Where would you like your flavors to meet you? What days are you free?*" She looks up at me when she's done. "It sounds good, but a lot of men will be too nervous to answer these over the phone. We are talking about underage girls, Jayden. They stand to do a lot of time if they are caught with us."

"Yes we are talking about underage girls, that's why we're going to test the theory on the ones who call every night. I already got a few people in mind. One manages a real estate agency and the other is a loyal customer who has slept with every girl in my crew when we first started the business. Their names are Spikes and Clay, and that's just them. Do you know how much this phone rang when I wasn't answering? At least fifteen times a day. And the thing is, our ads aren't even in the grocery stores anymore. I'm telling you they'll pay big. We're offering a niche service, ladies."

I look at all of them. "So how much do you think we can make?" Gucci asks, always the greedy bitch.

I'm not about to tell that whore that I need $250,000 in a matter of months. And to make that sort of cash, each girl needs to bring me about $22,727. "And I'ma need everyone to grind 26 days out of a month. Depending on how hard you work there's no reason you can't stack paper. Basically your salary is totally up to you." Olive rolls her eyes, still hating that I'm giving them cash.

"What about when we get our periods?" Catherine asks, her voice loud and strong like she's still in the penitentiary. "I know you don't expect us to fuck when we like that."

Olive jumps on it. "As long as your pussy not closed up, you still gotta work. If a bitch took a vacation every time she leaked, she'd never get paid."

She frowns and folds her arms into her chest. "And how we supposed to do that? Niggas not trying to fuck when they know you on your cycle."

"First of all some freaks might request it." I dig into the plastic bag and pull out a sponge. "But on the days you do have a situation, and your john isn't feeling it, use this."

"What the fuck is that?" Gucci asks through squinted eyes.

"A natural sea sponge." I hand it to Olive who told me how they work earlier last week.

"And how are we supposed to use it?" Hadiya asks.

"You cut this about twice the thickness of a tampon. Unless you want a stank infection before you stick this in your pussy, rinse it thoroughly because it might have grains of salt or sand in it." She reaches into the bag and grabs the non-applicator tampon. "You put it on this and stuff it inside of you with KY Jelly.

"Now your pussy gonna dry up, so you girls who never get wet, better apply a little extra. We don't want you scratching up clients' dicks." She points it at all of them. "And never, *ever*, work dry because the condom will break. If a nigga bucks the KY jelly, tell them it turns you on when it's slippery and shit like that. I'm not gonna tell you how you run your business, just make sure when you on your period that you use this."

"But won't it get stuck in my cooch?" Johnna asks.

"I'll say this, fishing it out afterwards will be a little tricky but you'll get use to it over time. Squat down and stick your fingers up there. If you still can't get it, call me. I'm on hand to help you out whenever you need it." The girls look at each other. Olive never misses an opportunity to play with some pussy even if it's gross. "Any questions?"

Silence.

"Good. Lighten up, it's all about the Benjamin's." I say.

———————————————————————

I just came back in the house from the ice cream parlor. I have the munchies. I'm standing in the middle of the bedroom in the black one-arm dress I wore when me, Passion and Olive went to a bar earlier. We had a little celebration party alone, without the other girls. I place the vanilla cone to my lips, tilt it and lick the edges. So sweet. It reminds me of the ad we did for Thirteen Flavors. I'm so excited because finally we're back in business.

When I'm done I ease out of my dress and in my bed looking up at the ceiling…again. I charged my phone up and it worked. I have my client list back and am actually about to have my hearing surgery and save my house. When I see my personal cell phone light up. I stuff the hearing aid in my ear, roll over and answer.

"How you doing over there without me?" Kreshon says.

I look at the phone like it isn't mine. He never talks to me like that. "You must be drunk."

He breathes into the phone. "Stop fucking with me, Jayden, I don't play that shit."

What was he talking about? "Play what shit?"

He's quiet for a minute. "I was thinking about you and I was calling to tell you that. Why you gotta come at me from left field all the time?"

Although I'm thrown off at how he's acting, I'm interested in what he has to say. "What were you thinking about? When you were thinking of me?"

"I was just thinking what would a little girl like you do with a man like me? I couldn't answer the question myself so I had to call you to get the answer."

I blush. He's considering my proposal. "I don't know, are you gonna make it your business to find out?"

"Your voice real big for a little girl," he pauses, "I hope it can hold weight. Can it?"

I hate when he refers to me as a child, especially since its obvious that he's making the decision to get with me. "I have a big voice for a big girl."

He chuckles. "Your mother say anything about me?"

I frown. "Why would she?"

"No reason, she just seemed a little confused when she met me. I'll be glad when she stops fucking with that alcohol so she can get her mind right. She straight tripping. I figured she was filling your head up with all kinds of shit."

"My mother got her own business. She not checking for mine."

"That's good. I want to take you out, you gonna let me?"

My pussy throbs. "You know I'ma let you. When we hooking up and where we going?"

"How about I surprise you. I'll call you when I want you to be ready. When I do bring a toothbrush, you won't need nothing else."

I guess the bakery business is doing well. "Kreshon, I can't stay out overnight, I got stuff to do at home."

"Not even for a nigga who trying to show you a good time? You that rich and famous that you can't take a break for a moment? Even Hugh Heffner takes breaks."

I like the reference to Mr. Playboy himself. "Why can't we just hang out for the day?"

"You know what, maybe I made a mistake by reaching out to you."

I think about Olive and Passion. If I left I knew they had me and I didn't want this opportunity with Kreshon to pass me by. Thirteen Flavors was my plan but Kreshon could be back up. Especially since he was willing to put his money on me. Before he hangs up I say, "I can get away. For one night. But after that, I gotta come right back home, cool?"

"Good, I'll call you later."

When he hangs up I'm about to flip my clit again when I hear something being thrown at my window. My heart drops when I realize it could be Tywanda's boyfriend coming back to finish me off. I ease off of the bed and crawl to my window on hands and knees. When I get there, I slowly raise my head, until my eyes can see outside. When I see Sebastian's blue eyes peering at me within the darkness, I hop up, unlock the latches and open the window. "What's up?"

"Ask me again." He says, his brother at his side.

I try to hide my smile but I know it's impossible. That doesn't stop me from playing uninterested. "Ask you what, Sebastian?"

"Ask me what you asked earlier."

I smooth my hair down. "Will you and your brother work for me. Or with me?"

"Yes," he pauses, "but I'm not doing it for money."

"I'm trying to get paid!" Luh Rod says, nudging his arm. "Everybody not royalty like you."

Sebastian pushes him a few feet away and he stumbles to the ground and I wonder what Luh Rod means. "Like I said, I'm not *just* doing it for money." He looks at his brother who's back on his feet brushing his pants off.

"So what you doing it for?"

"I'm doing it for you." He walks away. "To undue some of the things I almost did."

I wonder what he means but don't care. He says yes. I close the window and lean up against it. Now, I'm really ready for business.

GUCCI
EAR HUSTLING QUEEN

Gucci is squatting and pissing on the side of the house when Jayden and Olive come out in the backyard. Although there are five bathrooms in the house, with fifteen people living in Concord, it didn't matter. When she hears the juicy conversation, capable from her ear hustling abilities, she clenches her vagina walls to prevent any more liquid from flowing out. She didn't want to alert them that she was there.

"I'm telling you, Tywanda's nigga looked like he wanted to eat my ovaries, Olive. He was mad as shit. And I started to tell her about it, but I need her mind focused. The nigga was crazy and if it wasn't for Sebastian and Luh Rod, I'm afraid I wouldn't be here right now."

"I hear you, but don't you think she'll find out anyway? She'd been running around the house telling everybody who will listen that he won't return calls. Turns out she was going back to him anyway."

"Probably, but right now it's all about money. Fuck love stories. If any of them niggas gave a fuck about my bitches, they wouldn't pledge their pussies to my cause."

Grimy bitch. Gucci thinks. All she cares about is the buck.

"I guess you're right, I just hope it doesn't come back to bite you later."

If I have anything to do with it, not only will it come back to bite her red ass, it will chew it off. Gucci thinks, wiping her wet cooch with her fingers.

●━━━━━━━━━━━━━━━━━━━━━━●

Tywanda is lying on the living room floor picking the meat out of yesterday's crabs. Gucci crawls in and acts like she's interested in Braveheart, the movie she's watching when even the floors know that she's faking. But Tywanda is smart, and smelled her ass before she even came into her space. "What do you want, Gucci? I'm watching TV."

"I wanted to tell you something pertaining to your nigga but since you wanna lie on the floor and eat crabs that don't belong to you, I guess I'll go back to what I was doing."

Tywanda hops up like her ass is on fire. Besides, she'd been trying to reach her ex-boyfriend for weeks but was unsuccessful. "What is it?" She's holding a crab leg and looks as wild as a two year old. "You know something about my man?"

"I overheard Jayden say he came by here not too long ago. I guess she sent him on his way and didn't tell you. As you can clearly see, the bitch is loyal to no one. And since we both selling pussy, from one whore to another, I just wanted to let you know. Whether you like me or not." She was about to walk away until she turns back around and says, "Oh, and them crabs you chewing were mine. You owe me five dollars. I'll collect that from you later."

Jayden is in her room when Tywanda comes in. She knows the moment she's seen her eyes that's something is wrong. Her face is wet with tears and she looks exhausted. Jayden...always on her job, hops up and says, "What's wrong, baby? Who fucking with you and throwing you off your game?"

Tywanda stands in the middle of the room stuck. "Jayden, did my boyfriend come by here? Because nobody in his family has been able to find him."

Jayden looks at her as if she turned the channel from her favorite TV show. "Oh...yeah...he came by." Who the fuck told her that shit? She thinks. "But I had to check the situation." Jayden says. "Don't worry, it's over now and you safe. I know you weren't fucking with that nigga anyway."

"What happened?" Tywanda sobs.

Jayden reaches out for her and she slides into her bed. She rubs Tywanda's back and her chin leans on Jayden's shoulder. "I wanted to protect you, because I care about you. But since you're asking I'ma be straight. The nigga asked me for money for you and I wasn't willing to pay him at first." She rubs her chin. "You deserve more than that. Think about it, since you been working for me, haven't you gotten everything you wanted?" Tywanda's baldhead nods up and down. "Damn right, look at how much money you been clocking under Jayden's watch. The nigga wanted you for his own financial purposes, not for your wellbeing. That's why I didn't tell you. I want you to stay focused on our personal goals." She maneuvers her chin so that she's looking into her eyes. "And you know what, in the end he said if I gave him one hundred dollars, that he'd leave you alone for good. We talking about a bill, Tywanda. That shit was lightweight and he took it. First he was asking for big money but when he saw it wasn't working, he lowered his price. All the way down.

For one hundred dollars he promised to leave you alone. He didn't give a fuck about you. He never did.

Tywanda's cries pulled from her gut. "Are you serious?"

"I wouldn't lie to you about shit so real." Jayden wipes her tears. "I'm the only one who cares about you, that nigga don't. Remember that."

Tywanda rests back on Jayden's shoulder. At least I have you. She thinks. Jayden smiles when she isn't looking because she knows the truth and the shit she just said are on opposite ends of the planet. But she made it so that she would never find out.

WHAT REALLY HAPPENED

Craig was at his Grandmother's 80th birthday party getting his life on in her large home in Virginia. He'd bought her the new mobile chair she wanted and a few new wigs so she could set them old bitty's straight at church. She was the queen bitch at Mt. Zion Baptist Church. He came out like a hero and drank heavily from the five Hennessy bottles he brought with him in self-appreciation and celebration. So when Jayden, Sebastian and Luh Rod strolled into the party holding gifts boxes as empty as MC Hammer's bank account, claiming to be cousins, he was none the wiser.

Jayden was a predator. She stayed at the party for five hours waiting for the right time. So when she saw him on curve due to the alcohol, she approached him with ill intent in mind.

"I been trying to get up with your ass all night. Follow me?"

The moment he saw her red face and fat ass he forgot where he'd seen her before. The juice killed his smart brain cells and his guard was down. It didn't take long for her to lead him outside to Olive's van with the promise of a good dick licking. Once inside, the moment he pulled his pants down and leaned back, Jayden had sliced his dick off at the root and ripped his throat. The rest was history.

JAYDEN
PICK UP CHICKS

The rain beat against the van hard. I don't have my hearing aids on but I know because when I touch the window, I can feel its rhythm. Sometimes I feel like going deaf is a curse and other times I think it's a blessing. I can see so much more when I look instead of listen at the world around me. I'm excited about hanging out with Kreshon tonight and I hope he sees that although I'm young, I'm ready to do grown women things if he continues to take care of me. I don't put all my shoes in one closet, I want to make sure no matter what, I'm taken care of.

When I focus on the road ahead of us, I notice we're stuck in traffic. We're on our way to make sure the girls' hair is tight and that Blaq has a fresh cut although he hates not being able to ease into the salon chair too. I was able to negotiate his need to be feminine and my desire for him to be masculine, when I told him he could dress like he wanted around the house.

Things are looking up for me. My business plan is in full effect, money is rolling in and we have exactly twenty clients confirmed over the next few days. If everything continues this way, I'll have my deposit for my ear surgery next week.

I'm sitting in the back with Hadiya next to me. When I look over at Passion who's sitting to my left, she seems different. I hope she isn't fucking with the shit again because I love that she's clean. She's the only person besides me who's interested in getting a high school diploma and going to college next. But I also know she thinks about my sister a lot. On more than one occasion, I caught her in Madjesty's room, sleeping on her bed...under her sheets. I never talk to her about it because I'm hoping over time that whatever love she has for her will go away.

When I see Catherine, Tabitha and Tywanda talking and pointing out of the window, I look over at Hadiya. "What they doing?"

I focus on her lips. "Some guys in a limousine just pulled up to the side of the van." She whips her hair on the left side and leans forward to look out of the window. "I think they trying to get us to stop. You think they holding paper?"

I didn't know but I was going to find out. "Metha, pull the van over up the street." I look at the white limo again. "I wanna see what these niggas want."

Metha's been ragging me about the sex business for the longest and it was starting to work my nerves. She says pretty girls should get respectable jobs. My question to her is what should ugly girls do? Needless to say she doesn't want to listen to me. As she decreases speed, I notice that my girls are looking at me with hopeful eyes. They can't wait to work and I love it. They should be holding on a couple of thousand themselves as much as they've been working. When the van stops, I hop out and Hadiya is right behind me, holding a white umbrella over my head. Her own hair gets soaked.

Just as I expect, the limo stops and out comes six guys. They're young like us, but I can tell they have a little change. It dawns on me that they're probably basketball players looking to have a little fun. The one who approaches me first has a quiet swag about him. He's chocolate and doesn't seem to be perpetrating like the others. Water falls on his black shirt like drops of crystals, but he's focused and I like him already.

"Damn, all of them bitches in that mothafucka fine as shit!" One of his friends yells and gropes his dick.

"Nigga, shut the fuck up and show some respect." Mr. Swag says to him. He gives his attention back to me. "What's your name, beautiful?"

I'm not in the mood for games. I have too much shit to do today. "My name is Jayden but I'm not available to you. Now lets get to what you really want to know."

"Damn, you sure know how to burst a nigga's bubble. And quick too." He smiles and winked. "But I feel you though." He looks at the van and when I look behind me, I see all of the hopeful looks on my girls' faces. They resemble little orphans waiting to be chosen. "Are all of your friends off limits? Or just you?"

"It depends on which one you looking at."

He eyes Passion who steps out of the line of his view. "For real I see a few of them that I like. What would you say if I'm up for two?"

"Well you have to pay what they weigh, but I don't see that being a problem. Do you?"

He frowns a little, looks back at his friends and then at me. "It's like that?"

"Let me give it to you straight. I'm a pimp and these are my bitches. You heard of wholesale well I'm into WHORE-SALE. I sell 'em by the dozen. I'm not about to play with you or waste your time. Now you flagged down my van, so I figure you want to have a good time. I can make that happen if you got money. So my question to you is what you trying to do?"

He looks at me and my girls. Then he reaches into his pocket and pulls out a roll of money, which looks decent enough. "So you saying, I can have anyone I want right?"

"Anyone." He eyes me and licks his lips. "But me."

"If that's the case," He walks past me and picks Tywanda. They always pick Tywanda. "Then what we waiting on?"

———————●————————————————————●———————

All of the furniture in the living room in the presidential room of the Embassy Suite is pushed against the wall. Tywanda has Mr. Swag in the middle of the floor on his back with his dick in her mouth. He lost his coolness. Damn. She is on all fours and the arch in her back sends her ass through the roof like downward dog in Yoga. One of Mr. Swag's homies has his finger in her ass as he beat his dick. Foxie, Queen, Na-Na, Hadiya and unfortunately Gucci handle their businesses with the others. Sex is everywhere and the vibe was just right for making money.

I was in the only available chair in the room and Passion is sitting between my legs. I'm scratching her scalp with the comb as we watch the show. She claims her head itches but I think all the sex going on has her wanting to feel something, even if it is only her head.

Earlier I had Metha take all but six of my crewmembers and Passion to their hair appointments. Olive went with them to make sure things went smoothly. The other six girls that the basketball players chose, had their appointments rescheduled for later that night, after they handled business. Luckily I had a stylist who could whip a hairstyle into submission under two hours. She said since nobody was getting any serious hardware like weaves or braids that it wouldn't take her anytime at all. With the appointments rescheduled, we jumped into their limo and made it to their hotel at the Embassy Suite in less than twenty minutes. They reserved the Presidential Suite and I'm surprised at how big the room is.

When Tywanda turns over on her back and rises up on her feet and hands while Mr. Swag hovers over her face, I was about to lose it. She places her tongue in his ass hole as he beats his dick. Tywanda turned her sexy body into a human table as she handled her business and I'm sure every nigga in here wanted a taste. Horny now myself, I start scratching the front of Passion's scalp so that the back of her head is in the center of my crotch. I wind into it a little at a time to go unnoticed. Every time she moves, I force her head deeper into my pussy until I rub out a nut and breathe heavily on a sly.

"Jayden," she asks after awhile. "You okay?" She looks up at me. The front of her hair is smooshed.

"Yeah...why you say that shit?" I frown.

"Because it felt like you were grinding on my head."

I push her away and throw the comb in her face. "Then do the shit yourself ungrateful, bitch!"

She looks at me strangely but leaves it alone. After the performance Tywanda put on, Mr. Swag and his friends can't wait to pull out the bottles and turn on the music. I'm chill because I have five thousand dollars in my hand. And that's money I didn't count on. Thirteen Flavors worked the room like good Sex Specialists should and there wasn't a frown in the house.

Unlike the other girls who were playing socialite, Gucci has been eye-fucking the wad of cash in my hand all night. I swear I don't know how much longer I can tolerate this bitch. "Gucci, while you're looking over here, you could be over there making some paper."

"Looks like you got all the paper over there." She rolls her eyes and steps off.

When she's gone I say, "You miss this shit?" I'm hoping she says no. "Sex, money and mayhem?"

I focus on her lips. "I miss the money, but not the lifestyle." She doesn't seem confident.

"How come I don't believe you?" She shrugs. "Passion, I know you liked to fuck more than any of the girls from the old crew, so you telling me you don't miss all of this. It ain't like you have a friend coming over to bang your back out. How do you deal with that shit?"

She looks at me. "You want the truth or something like a lie?"

"I want to hear what's on your mind."

"I haven't really thought about having s-sex," she stumbles a little, "since me and Wags broke up, I feel like I don't deserve it."

Hearing his name causes my heart to sink. Wags, who me and Madjesty also called Mr. Nice Guy when we were kids, was a wonderful person who died too soon and I wondered how she knew his name. "Did you say Wags?"

She laughs a little. "I meant, Mad." Her face lights up when she says her name. "She told me her name was Wags when we first hooked up, that's why I didn't know she was your sister." *Madjesty is so fucking disrespectful.* "I remembered you telling me you had a sister named Madjesty when we first met but she lied to me." She seems sad. "And I lied to her too."

"You gotta stay away from my sister, Passion. She's fucked up." I look ahead. "More than you realize."

"Were you serious about what you said back then? That she raped you?"

"I wouldn't make up something like that."

"So, how did she do it?"

"I guess the same way she fucked you without you knowing she was a girl." I'm irritated with this line of questioning. "You still see her?"

"I haven't spoken to her or nothing like that," she admits. "She probably wouldn't want to hear from me anyway since I stood her up. Told her I would meet her at the Amtrak train station but I didn't show. I know I broke her heart and I spend a lot of time wondering what would've happened had I met her there."

My face is red. "How is school and staying clean?" I don't want to talk about Madjesty because we will never agree. Plus I need her to do the right thing and stay sober. Something told me if Madjesty was in her life she wouldn't. Plus she would probably choose her over me.

"I can't lie, everyday is a struggle, Jayden but I'm trying."

While the girls work the room, I notice that Mr. Swag has lost Tywanda to one of his friends who now has two of my girls in his arms. When I look at where his eyes are positioned, I see Passion staring in his direction. The nigga is greedy as shit! He just had her lick his asshole, what he want with Passion? He makes his way over to us and looks down at her. "You still don't want to be my friend?" He opens his hand and flashes a blunt. "We 'bout to have a good time if you down in the bathroom."

"She's not available." I say.

He closes his hand and frowns. "Why not?"

"Because I said so and you paid for what you wanted already. My suggestion to you is that you get your money's worth and go enjoy yourself. Your friend looks strong but not strong enough to handle two."

He looks at me like I'm a rash on his nuts. "How about you let the lady talk for herself."

"Why she gotta do that, when I'm doing a perfectly good enough job for her?"

"Look, if it's like that," he reaches into his pocket and hands me another G, "you can have that. I'm just trying to get to know her that's all. You making it deeper than it has to be." I don't trust him and my eyes must've said it all because he raises his hands and says, "I have nothing but the best intentions for her."

This makes me more nervous. Passion has a tendency to fall in love. "Look, I'm not one of the girls available." Passion interrupts. "So how 'bout you go back over there and find one who is."

Wow. She has changed. Or she really is in love with my sister. I feel like I gotta shit just thinking about the idea. He looks at the bills he gave me and I reluctantly hand him a thousand back. "Your call," he walks away and over to his friends. He picks up Tywanda and throws her over his shoulder, as they disappear into one of the bedrooms. I guess he's tired of sharing after all.

With a wide smile on my face, I place my hand on her knee. "Don't worry about that shit, Passion. That nigga wouldn't have done you right anyway. All he wanted to do was fuck you. Love is over rated," I look at the door they went in, "just stay focused on your schooling and stuff."

Something I say bothers her because she gets up, and storms out without saying anything to me. I start to check her for leaving with an attitude, but I let her have it. As long as she keeps her mind on business, all is well in my world.

●━━━━━━━━━━━━━━━━━━━━━━━━━━━●

Kreshon picks me up at my house in his Lexus. He must've just had it cleaned because it shines like a new nickel. I loved the way some niggas kept their cars fresh. It reminds me of money. "Kreshon, you talked to Shaggy?" I ask as we cruise down the highway.

"No, why you ask?" He adjusts the dial on his stereo and looks at me. "He reached out to you or something?"

"No but I'm trying to reach him." I place my seatbelt on when I notice he's speeding faster. "I don't know where he is but I bet you do. Plus he raped my sister. It's urgent that we speak." I scratch my scalp.

He looks over at me and back at the road. "I thought you didn't fuck with your sister like that. Weren't you the one who called me over to the house to pick her up?"

"That don't make a difference, Kreshon. Can you make that happen for me?"

He looks over at me. He seems annoyed. "What are you saying, Jayden?"

I place my hand on his lap and massage his thigh. "Can you find him for me, and take care of him?"

He presses his hand over mine and. "What the fuck is up with you and hurting people? You look like you would be one way, but you turn out to be another. Did your mother fuck you up that bad as a kid?"

"If I say yes, will it affect your response in any way?"

"No."

"Then it doesn't make a difference."

"That makes you dangerous." I'm silent. Sometimes he acts scared. "I can find him but when I do, what you want me to do with him?"

"At first I want you to bring him to me."

With a raised eyebrow he asks, "After that?"

"I'll think of something. Don't worry, he'll be fine with me."

•————————————————————————•

We drive for six hours before finally landing in the city of New York. I heard big things about the city but seeing the high buildings, billboards and lights, gave me inspiration. I'd never been anywhere except Texas, DC and Maryland, but those places couldn't compare to the beauty where I am now.

Kreshon parks the car and he grabs my hand, taking me into the hotel. When we walk inside, it smells of sweet incense and the neon lights over the bar, along with the trendy furniture, makes me feel like I'm in a club. I feel alive. I know then with or without Kreshon, I will be back to this place.

We check in and walk to our room. I can't wait to see what he has in store for me while we're in town. I remove my red toothbrush from my purse and place it in the bathroom on the counter. I'm so excited and can't bring myself to calm down. That is until I come out of the bathroom, only to see this nigga laying face up on the bed, TV surfing. "So what we gonna do?" I stand over of him. He's so attractive. So sexy. "You wanna go to the bar or something?" I feel myself excitedly moving around and I try to stay still.

He frowns. "What is up with you and this drinking?"

"What's up with you not?"

"We chilling right now so relax."

I throw my ass in the seat next to the table. It plops down forcing him to look at me with a smile. I'm trying to figure out why he brought me all the way to New York, just to look at him on the bed, while he eyes at me every so often. When three hours pass and we hadn't moved from the spot, I'm angry and confused.

Fuck this nigga. He's too weird and plays too many games for me. I grab my purse off of the table I'd been dating since we got here and walk into the bathroom to make a call. It doesn't take me any time to get Olive on the phone. "Girl, where is Metha at?" I look at the door and roll my eyes. "I might need her to come scoop me up from New York."

"What's wrong?" She sounds worried. That's why she's my bitch. "He hurt you or something?"

"Not even close. More like this nigga is so boring he hasn't even come close to me."

"I'm sorry, girl. Well, you know Metha don't stay here. I think she took your truck with her like you said she could when she isn't working but I can come get you if you want."

I laugh. "I'm not trying to have you drive that big ass bus out here."

"It's not that serious, Jayden. Whether you know it or not, I'm in New York all the time."

"I'm good, just try to reach her if you can, and if you do, give me a call back."

"No problem."

"Before you hang up, how's Passion? She seemed out of it when I left her earlier."

"She the same. Real quiet. And her little crew been upstairs like five times to check on her but she won't even answer the door for them. I think she's missing your sister even more."

I'm worried more than ever. Had I not been with this loser, I could've tended to my business. One things for sure, I won't make the same mistake again. After ending the call, I walk out of the bathroom and he's standing in front of me with his arms crossed over his chest. "What you in there doing?"

I push past him, sit at the table and throw my purse on top of it again. "Why?"

He stands over me. "So what, you mad at me or something?"

I look up at him with my lips poked out. I hate feeling like this. "Are you gonna take me home or not? This shit is a complete waste of my time."

He smiles and I want to scratch his eyebrows off. "What's so fucking funny?"

"You're very cute. So cute it's hard to believe you were my man's daughter."

"Just because my daddy died, don't mean he's not my father."

"I'm not saying it like that, Jayden."

"I know. Just watch how you say things when it comes to him."

"Fair enough."

Why is he still standing over me? "You ready?" He finally asks.

"For what, Kreshon?"

"To go see New York?"

I try to act uninterested, but it's the only thing I wanted to do since we'd gotten here. "Yeah, I guess so." He laughs, extends his hand and I reluctantly accept.

One minute we're in a cab, and the next we're in front of a helicopter charter service. Kreshon talks to a man and we're led out back to a landing strip where a red helicopter waits. I'm overwhelmed with excitement because the last time I'd been in the air was on the flight from Texas to Maryland. But this helicopter was just for us. After a few more minutes, we're shown our seats and are strapped inside. When we're settled, he gives us headphones, which I think I don't need until he says they'll protect my ears too. Before we even get in the air, I'm excited. Kreshon places his hand over mine and smiles in a way that melts my heart.

The next thing I know we're lifted in the air and taken over the beautiful city. New York is stunning. I admire the green lady holding the lamp in the sky and the big bridge with tiny cars running over it in different colors. I'm so taken that I can feel heat rising between my legs. We didn't stay up in the air too long, but in the end, I can truly say I saw New York.

Thirty minutes later, we're back in a limousine and he has a serious expression on his face. Always in money mode, my mind switches to how he's able to afford all of this. I still hadn't found out who stole my father's money. "How did you get money for that?"

He shakes his head and grins at me. "You never miss an opportunity to let me down do you?"

"I'm waiting."

"First of all I don't own the helicopter and that shit back there was light weight. Under five hundred bucks. Secondly my bakery is doing well, Jayden. So well we've landed a major contract to make cupcakes for large hotels like the Hilton. You don't have to be a dope boy to make a good living, even though I made my fair share of paper in that business too."

I remember how small the bakery is and wonder how he'll be able to fill big orders in that place. "Not taking nothing from you but your store looks too small to bake for a company that huge. How you gonna be able to keep up?"

"With the advance they gave me, I can open another shop. I can open five more if I need to. Instead we're building out the space and adding more ovens."

Although I think the bakery thing is sort of gay, anything that's bringing in paper to me is a good thing. It ain't like he's not hitting me off with money anyway. "So where we going now, Kreshon?" I'm hoping he'll take me to a ritzy restaurant, or some place like it.

"Thinking of ordering in. I'm kind of tired and we have to get up early so I can have you home in time. Since you have to go tomorrow."

"Kreshon, I want to go out and I want you to go with me. You bringing me all this way for a helicopter ride is sick. I'm trying to grab some drinks and enjoy my time with you." I nudge him with the side of my body. "Now if you not willing to do that, take me the fuck home tonight because there ain't nothing else we can say to each other."

"You know what, if that's what you want to do lets go have a nice time."

I smile. It seems like lately, I always get my way.

●━━━━━━━━━━━━━━━━━━━━━━━━━━━━●

Kreshon took me to a beautiful high-class restaurant and I couldn't believe how fly it is. There are dark colors of burgundy played off of cream accents and the waiters smile every time you look their way. We sit at our table overlooking the city on top of the roof and he orders for me since I can't read the lips of our waiter. I have a glass of moscato and he has a bottle of champagne. He looks nervous drinking, like he isn't comfortable with the taste. But it doesn't take him long to get into the flow because before long he ordered another bottle of champagne since he drank the first by himself. Now's he talking loud and his eyes seem to lighten up. He's no longer uptight. He looks just fine to me. I like drunk sex. We're going to have fun tonight.

I'm looking at the flashing colors of the city when I hear, "Damn, I can't wait to get you to that fucking hotel, bitch!" His comment is out of the blue. I'm taken off guard at how he talks to me and I wonder why he is so bold all of a sudden. My pussy doesn't care what the reason is and can't wait to take him up on his offer.

"What you gonna do to me once you get me there?" As I'm waiting on his response, the table is bouncing a little.

"I'm gonna choke the shit out of your dumb ass. And then stuff this dick in your mouth."

Two things stand out to me that he said. Number one, he's going to choke the shit out of me and stuff *this* dick in my mouth. Something about the word *this* made me think we had a bigger problem than I realize. As the table continues to jerk, I look under it and Kreshon's pants *and* royal blue boxers are down at his ankles. The real kicker is, that his dick is in his hands getting choked out. A pile of cum rests on the dark colored carpet under the table, which makes me believe he's busted a few times already.

I look around and back at him. "Kreshon, what are you doing?" I'm trembling. It's the scariest thing I ever seen in my life. And considering all of the things I witnessed, that's saying a lot. I guess mainly because I never saw this coming. At all. "What's wrong with you?"

"What you mean, Harmony? I'm just taking you out like you want-ed." His eyes are now red like he's possessed. "Ain't nothing wrong."

I see the devil flash before me. This nigga is really tripping. "Kreshon, I'm not Harmony. I'm her daughter Jayden." Now I wish he would look at me like a little kid again. "Why do you have your pants down?"

"Listen, bitch, I'm bout to get up and put something in your mouth, and it betta be all meat on my dick. No teeth."

I look behind me when he starts to rise for an exit. A lady who's at the table across from me, with an older man gasps when she sees his na-ked ass. I see two bodyguards rush toward us after seeing my face and looking at the woman. Before I know it Kreshon is knocked face first into the bottle of champagne and something he called Crème Brule that he ordered for dessert. I guess I knew why Metha said to be careful with him. Why didn't she just tell me that shit? It's so stupid. I would not have pressed him out to drink had I known. He obviously turned into some kind of sick freak when he drank. There was no way I was going back to DC with his ass. I was going to have to take Olive up on her offer to come get me after all.

MADJESTY
NO GREATER LOSS

I've been standing outside of Concord Manor for an hour. Just staring at the door, trying to decide if I should knock or not. These days I don't understand what's going on with my life. Why am I so cursed? The moment I learned how to love, I lost soon after that. Tisa, Mr. Nice Guy, Glitter, Passion, Jayden and then Cassius, lost them all.

I still don't understand what happened when I regained consciousness after I had my baby. All I know was I was pushing and trying my best to bring him into the world. I remember seeing my grandmother and her friend Arizona. I remember smiling when I saw he was a boy and telling them his name was Cassius. I couldn't have taken more than a fifteen-minute nap, but when I opened my eyes and saw the police, I knew something was wrong, or that they were coming to take me back to the institution.

Turns out Arizona, my grandmother's friend, stole my baby and sold it for money to buy crack. *I'ma kill this bitch when I find her.* If I can find her. We didn't get the cops involved because it needed to be handled in the streets. The moment they left, we looked everywhere for her. In crack houses, jails, abandoned buildings and even hospitals. We found nothing. My grandmother was so dead set on helping me look for her that she didn't bother to put on her wig. Her natural shoulder length gray hair was pulled back into a ponytail and I didn't see her use any drugs.

We spent weeks trying to find Arizona until one day Bernie came home and said, "Why the fuck you gotta look like a boy? Everybody's talking about you! Walking around with me, having people thinking I'm gay and shit! I need time alone, get the fuck out of my house." She was crying when she said it and I think losing my baby on her watch made her feel guilty. So she didn't want me around anymore. I told her where my friends lived even though I wasn't going to their houses. I wanted her to be able to reach me if she got news on my baby.

I left feeling she was the last person who gave a fuck and now I had nothing. No one. I need to look into the eyes of somebody who cares about me, preferably blood related, which is how I ended up at Concord.

I think the liquor made me *unsmart* for coming here. Hold up...is that a word?

I take another swig from the Henny bottle and walk up to the door. I think I'm moving straight, but every time I place one foot out in front of the other, I seem to sway from left to right. Somehow I make it to the door and when I get there, I knock three times. Nobody answers at first, so I knock harder and lean on it. I almost fall inside and when the door opens, I see a guy wearing an orange nightgown. He must be gay. What's going on here?

"Sorry, little ass boy, but we only accept clients by invitation only." He looks me over. "And judging by how drunk you are, I'm not sure even if you had coins, that you would be able to handle it." He's about to slam the door in my face until I push it back open with a strong hand. I didn't realize I had that much strength in me. Guess I really want to see Jayden. He frowns. "You must have a problem. If you want me to solve it for you, put your hand on this door one more time and your wish is my command."

"I came to see my sister." I point at him but my hand falls down. It's too heavy. "Where the fuck is she?" I try to look behind him, but he's kind of tall.

He frowns. "You know somebody up in here? That's related to you? Or did you just crawl off the bottom of someone's shoe?"

I want to answer him honestly but I don't know what my twin will say. Did she still claim me as her brother? Or sister? Or was she done with me forever, after how I treated her? "My sister is Jayden. And the doorknob you holding belongs to my house."

He looks confused. "Wait, you really know Jayden?" I don't speak. "How come she ain't tell me she had no brother?"

He's getting on my nerves. I didn't have to answer to him or anybody else for that matter. "Go get Jayden."

He rolls his eyes and disappears into the house. He's gone for what seems like an eternity. When the door finally opens, I'm looking into the eyes of the love of my life. As if time never separated us, my heart pounds in my shirt. When I look down, I can see it moving. She's wearing a red dress, that cuts low in the front and her long hair falls over her shoulders. I can smell her perfume; its sweet and I control myself because I want to grab her and yank her out of here.

"Denise, w-what are you doing here?" Had I known I'd see her again, I would've dressed nicer. Looked cleaner. Been sober. "You live here now?"

She gazes at me, like she feels sorry for me. "Hi, Wags. How you been?" Her eyes look into mine. "You okay? Are you hurt?" She looks me over. "Do you need anything?"

I must look pathetic. "I been fine." I pull my red hat further over my eyes. "Don't worry 'bout me. I'm alive." I step closer. I want to touch her but I'm not sure if I'm allowed.

She smiles. "Well you look good."

I examine her face. Her skin and her clothes. Something about her has changed. She looks...well...clean. Like she's not using. "You don't mess around no more?"

She shakes her head. "Not for a long time. Not since what happened to you."

I hate that me getting raped was the last thing she remembers about me, about us. "Passion, I wanted to say..."

"I miss you, Madjesty." She calls me by my name. I like how it sounds. "And I still love you." My heart feels like thunder in my chest. "I think about you most nights and I can't get you out of my mind. I feel like I should've been stronger for you. Did more for you. Fought for you." She looks down. "I was a punk and I never forgave myself for watching Shaggy rape you." She's pouring out her heart and I'm trying to catch it but the liquor has me bent. I'm confused and not thinking clearly. "I guess what I'm trying to say is, I don't know how it would be, to be with a girl, but I'd like to give it a try with you."

What's left of my heart melts. I'm sure if I ask, she'll run away with me to Texas now. But I don't want my feelings hurt again, so I need to be sure. I need to be cautious. "You don't know how much what you just said means to me."

"I hope it means you'll give me a try." She swallows. "Madjesty, I do have to know something before we go any further, did you do that to your sister?"

I feel like a monster. Jayden actually told people that shit? I step back, sip my Henny and observe her. "Fuck are you talking about?"

Her eyes flutter like butterfly wings. "She said, well, she told us you..."

"*Us?*" I frown. "Who the fuck is us?"

She looks back into the house. Who's in there? I imagine it's my mother, her friends and anybody else with ears. I want to get out of here but I can't move. "She told me and a few other people you raped her. At first I wanted to know if it was true but now that I see your face, I know it's not." *I want to steal this whore in the eye.*

"Bitch, get the fuck out of my face." I'm angry. She ain't nothing but a slut anyway. If she loved me she would've came to the train station like she promised. I don't owe her shit, certainly not an explanation. "Go get my sister, Passion."

She steps out and toward me. I step back. "Don't walk up to me." I can't look at her. "If you do I'ma hurt you." She's so beautiful. I point at the door. "Get, Jayden."

"Madjesty, please don't do this." She's crying and the muscles in my stomach pull. I don't want to hurt her but she's chosen sides already. She believed I raped Jayden. *Wait. I did rape her.* I have to get away from her. I don't want to think about this.

"Don't do this to me, Madjesty. I've been waiting here all this time, hoping I'd see you. Dealing with all this fake shit around here. Since you don't have that phone anymore, there's no way for me to get a hold of you. Please let me make it right. Let me treat you how I know I can. Let me take care of you."

I look at her. So she'll know I'm serious. "Either get my sister or I'ma hurt you."

I can tell I've taken the life away from her. *Good.* She runs into the house. Her ass looks fatter than I remember and I think I'm crazy for excusing her. I'm about to run after her, when Jayden walks out. She wears a blank stare. Her hair looks longer and runs further down her back, and the jeans she's wearing hugs her hips. I know right away that she can't keep the dudes off of her if she tries. She's beautiful.

"You know what's funny, Madjesty, I always wondered what I would do to you if and when I ever saw your face again. I even wondered was it possible to love a person who made it obvious that they didn't give a fuck about me. And you know what, I think I have my answer now."

I can tell the moment she speaks that I lost my sister but I want to fight for her anyway. I want her to know that I'm sorry about what I did. And that I'm sorry that I never got the chance to be there for her when her father died. I didn't like him, but I know how much she cared about the dude. "Jayden, before you say anything I just want to say that I'm sorry. I'm so fucking sorry. I violated you in the worst way because I wanted somebody to pay for what happened to me. It was a weak move and one I'll never forget." She seems to focus on my lips more than she did when we were kids but she doesn't respond.

"I did something to you because I was mad that I thought you chose Shaggy over me. So I flipped out. To this day I have nightmares about that day, Jayden. I can't sleep thinking about it. And I only want you to know how sorry I am."

"And you think I can sleep without remembering? Without seeing your face? Without the memories of your body on top of mine? You think the days have been easy for me? If you think that then you're wrong, you have altered my life. Forever."

"I know it's been hard. And I know you're fucked up and that's why I'm here. I want us to be there for each other. Jayden, so much shit has happened in my life."

"It's always about you. Never about me." She says.

"Do you remember when we were in Texas and ma came home after one of her drunken nights?" I ask.

"Which night you talking about?" She says and I think I see a hint of smile on her face but it leaves too quickly for me to be sure.

"It was the night when she threw a coffee cup at my head, and gashed my face open. I got in bed with you because we didn't know if she would come into our room and finish both of us off." The memory hurts too much and I usually don't like pulling them out, but if I'm going to win my sister back, I must go deep. "I pissed on myself and you held me in your arms. You told me it was okay, because at least we had each other. Do you remember?"

She looks down at her feet and I think I'm getting through to her.

"I'm still the same person, Jayden." I touch my chest; unfortunately it's with the hand holding my liquor bottle. It splashes on my Jordans. "And I need you back."

I think she wants to try and work on our relationship. Hate seems to disappear and then she eyes the bottle in my hand. "So you been drinking?" I see disgust on her face and my stomach rumbles. "You came here drunk?"

"Just a little bit, Jayden."

"You know what I remember when we were kids?" She gives me a dirty look. "I remember the day I needed to talk to you. I was gone for three days and when I got back, it seemed like nobody cared. And do you remember what happened when you called?" I shake my head no. "You didn't want to come home because you were hanging with Mrs. Brookes at the grocery store. I never forgot about that but I wanted to be a sister for you anyway, despite how you treated me. I needed you that day."

"Jayden, please don't give up on our relationship."

"You did that, not me." She exhales. "I never told anybody this and I don't know why I'm telling you now. But during the three days I was gone, I was raped by a man." My mouth drops. "So what you did to me in my room, on that floor, only added to my pain." She's crying and I walk up to her but she pushes me back.

I'm losing her. I had a line into her and now it's gone. I think about my son. Her nephew. And how she may never get to know him. "Jayden, I need you right now. Let's put it all behind us." She shakes her head.

"Just hear me out. I was pregnant and had a son. A cute little boy." I want to cry but I hold back, especially when I see her face lights up. And then it goes dark again. "And somebody stole him from me, over my grandmother's." She seems confused. "I know it's a lot but I found my grandmother a while back. Anyway I had the baby over there and he was stolen from me. Sold for drugs. Now you can't begin to understand what I went through when that happened. I love him…his name is Cassius. But if losing him is the cost I have to pay for doing what I did to you," I can feel my stomach churn just saying the words and I try to hold it together, "if that's the cost I have to pay, for what I did, I'm willing to pay it if you come back into my life."

She's blank for a minute. No emotion. No expression.

"You know you're really selfish. So fucking selfish!" She starts laughing. "I always knew that even though we shared the same blood, we weren't alike. And now I'm seeing proof. You must be crazier than I thought if you think you can come here and everything will be forgiven. You violated my fucking trust, Madjesty, and you violated my body. The only reason I came to the door is to make it clear. We are sworn enemies. And the next time we see each other again, one of us will die."

●━━━━━━━━━━━━━━━━━━━━━━━━━●

I can't say what happened from the point I got the door slammed in my face at my sister's, but the next thing I know some girl is sitting on my face and moaning. She's grinding on my mouth and her juices, which smell foul, are pouring into my nose making it tough for me to breathe. So I grab her by her cold thighs and toss her off my face. When I sit up, I'm on a brown leather sofa, looking at her angry face down on the floor.

"What the fuck is wrong with you?" She asks, her words slurring. She looks drunker than I feel. "How you gonna stop moving that tongue when I was just about to nut?"

Ugghh. This bitch is trash. And she smells like trash too. Her brown skin is splotchy and her hair short and curly. When I take a look at her titties and ass when she stands up, I can see why I picked her.

"Look, I'm sorry, but I don't know who you are and I don't remember hooking up."

She turns around to walk to a chair and I see toilet paper hanging out of her ass. *Damn!* "You didn't say all that when you pulled up on me at my friend's house! Matta of fact, you were begging me to eat this pussy." *Doubt that, bitch.* "And now you wanna fake?"

"Where am I?" She doesn't answer. I try to stand up but my head is begging me to stay put. When I look around nothing looks familiar.

And then I hear the voice of my family behind me. "Don't tell me you're that twisted that you can't recognize my house." Krazy K says sitting on the loveseat across from me. Sugar is on his lap and the way her head rests in the pit of his neck, I can tell she's asleep. "Especially after the wild ass night we just had."

I look at Toilet Tissue Booty again. She found a cream sheet somewhere and covers her body with it. It didn't do anything to prevent her fat ass from peaking out. "Bitch, don't look at me now." She says to me. "You should've finished your business and I would've gotten you next." She rolls her eyes and stomps away.

"Where is your foster mother first of all?" I ask Krazy.

"Out of town."

I laugh. "Secondly please tell me who that bitch is." I'm whispering trying not to wake up Sugar, even though I want to see her face.

He rubs Sugar's leg when she moves a little. I can tell they're in love and the relationship is killing me. Making me sick inside. I didn't want Sugar ten months ago but I guess I felt comfortable knowing that someone out there would always be hopelessly in love with me. Which is funny considering I just dumped the baddest bitch I'd ever seen in my life, after she confessed her love.

"You met her when we went to Dynamite's house to pick up some money. She was with her son I think, but she took one look at you and rolled out with you." He laughs a little. "I think the nigga was salty about it but he handled it like it was medium. You don't remember that shit?"

I must've been in the drunk zone again. I pull my cap down. "So wait, we picked up cash from *my* Dynamite?" I point at myself. "The shorty I took from the mental institution, who can pick locks? She got a house?"

"Yeah, her son lives there now. He's nice but I could tell he wasn't happy about her leaving the crazy house. Kept asking why they let her come home and all kinds of shit like that. The only reason we left her was because he said she would be okay. I got fifty bucks that he'll be taking her back before the week is out."

"How old is her son?"

"Slim had to be 'bout twenty. I asked Dynamite how old she was and she said thirty five." My mouth drops. I wouldn't give Dynamite any older than twenty. Tops! I guess crazy looked good on her.

Sugar finally wakes up and when she does, she's staring directly at me. She still looks like somebody different. More confident. More sexy. She's still staring at me, when Krazy moves her chin until her eyes are focused on his. When they are, he kisses her sloppily in the mouth and I feel like a freak watching them, so I look down at my kicks. He doing the shit for me I know it.

"Anyway, before you got extra drunk, you were telling us that one of those bitches stole your kid. Who was it?"

I talk too much when I'm drunk. I didn't even want them to know I actually had the baby, let alone open up about how I felt now that Cassius was gone. My son is gone. My baby is gone. I didn't even get to spend time with him.

"Yeah, it's a fucked up situation." I tug at my cap. I need another drink.

"So what we gonna do? We definitely can't let the shit go down like that. Little shorty needs to be with you. With us." Krazy continues.

"You okay?" Sugar asks pushing her red glasses on her face. "I can't imagine what you're going through right now."

Although she's talking to me, she's holding onto Krazy like he's a bag of money. I really thought that she'd always be obsessed with me. I'm getting the impression that when it comes to love, I'm selfish. I want it all but sometimes I'm not willing to give anything in return.

"Mad, you listening to me?" Sugar gets off of Krazy and walks in my direction. "What's wrong?"

I look past her and stay away from her eyes. "Krazy, you mind if I talk to Sugar alone for a second? I want to ask her something."

He doesn't seem too interested in leaving us alone but he says, "Sure, it ain't nothing. I'm 'bout to go wake the nigga Kid up anyway." He points at me. "We still hitting the club later right?" I nod. Whatever I can do to get him out of my face, works for me at the moment. "Cool," he takes one more look at Sugar as if he's about to lose her. "Let me know when ya'll done." He looks back at me and walks away. When did these niggas get crazy and in love? Kid was always the one hitting this pussy. Shouldn't he have first dibs?

Sugar moves closer. "Let's go over there," I say. We walk to the couch, "I need to sit down anyway, I'm still out of it." I take a seat and she sits next to me, no space between us. "So how have you been?" Her eyes avoid mine. Why isn't she looking at me? "Sugar, what's up with you?"

"I still love you, Mad." This marks the second time a girl told me she loved me in one night and still I want more. I'm a greedy ass nigga. "I don't think that'll ever change, but you made it known a long time ago that you would never be into me like that." *Why she gotta bring up old shit?* "So I had to deal with it. And one way I did it, was by finding someone who loves me, more than I love him."

That's deep but the jealousy juices in my body haven't simmered. "Krazy makes you happy?"

"He's good to me." She touches my hand. "And I've never had that before." She laughs a little, I guess at a personal joke. "You remember the last time we were on the subway?"

Oh shit. This must be the *Ghost of the Shit Madjesty Did In The Past* night. "Yes."

"We were doing greatest fears." She continues. I swallow air but wish I had Hennessey instead. "It was my turn and they asked me what my greatest fear was." She looks sad now. "I was scared to answer." She stares into my eyes like she's peeking into a window. "But eventually I told you that I didn't want to be alone. Ever. And I told you I loved you." *Fuck.* This girl is done with me for sure now. Where's my drink? "And I asked you if I could be your girl."

"Come on, Sugar. Let's not go there."

"Please," she touches my arm and I can feel electricity, "I've always wanted you to know how that night made me feel. So just give me a second. Please."

I look around and spot an empty Hennessey bottle on the floor. For sure I knew the shit belonged to me. Just as I thought, I'm a greedy ass nigga.

"You shut me down quick…told me I was your friend and I ran out of the subway before you could finish your sentence. I was wrong for loving you when Glitter was your girl." Her eyes water and hearing Glitter's name made me feel worse. She was my first *official* love and she was murdered right in front of me. She's the reason my hair stays red, in remembrance, always.

"I never told anybody where I went, but I fucked a nigga who I bumped into on my way off the train. Never met him a day in my life before that night. He took me out to eat and thirty minutes later his nut was all over my face." She laughs. I'm disgusted. "I found out a month later I was pregnant but got an abortion soon after that. I don't even remember his name. He made me feel cheap and worthless and I thanked him for it."

I'm confused. "Why?"

"Because it's what I deserved." She looks into her hands. "It reminded me of the girl I am. I'm the one who fucked everybody in Mad Max remember?" She throws her hands up. "Why would somebody like you want me?" I don't know who she thinks I am but it's obvious she thinks too highly of me. I guess she doesn't know I raped my sister, I'm supposed to be in a crazy house, I cut off my breasts, my father is an escaped convict and I think I'm a nigga. "I'm never gonna be the girl worthy of love, from somebody like you."

"Like me?"

"Yeah." She giggles. "Everybody wants Mad. Nobody want's Sugar. Look at how easily it is for you to get somebody. They see your face, that smile and the cool way you walk and its over. I jumped out of my league when I came at you and it put our friendship in jeopardy, so for that I'm sorry."

"You don't give yourself enough credit. You a bad bitch…Now."

Her face brightens. "So you would give me a chance?"

Part of me wants to say yes. I want to tell her that I'd wipe my face off, drop to my knees and lick her clean if she wants me too. But Sugar is my friend and she's really in love with me. I'm mad at the world and fucking with her now would be wrong. Not only that she's with Krazy, a nigga I love like a brother. Unless I have good intentions for her, which I don't, it would be playing with her heart.

Before I can let her down easily, there's a knock at the door. "It's the pizza man. I got it." Krazy yells coming from the back room, eyeing us on the way to the door.

He's gone for only seconds when a dude rushes into the house. When I hear his voice, chills run up my spine. I hop off of the sofa and look around the living room for something to protect myself with. I can't find shit. I hadn't been in Krazy's crib in a long time because his foster mother was white and acted like she hated niggas, even though she picked one to live in her home.

Finally remembering where I am, I head for the kitchen to dip out the back door. But he's gaining on me knocking tables and chairs down in the process. It's the man who changed my world and he's ready to take my life again. I'm able to reach the door, but the moment I walk out of it, he jumps on my back forcing me facedown into the grass. I manage to turn over and look into his eyes and they are filled with hate. I feel inferior when I'm around him.

Weak.

Useless.

Feminine.

"I bet you didn't think you'd see me again did you, bitch?" Shaggy says, spit escaping his mouth and sprinkling into my face. He's trying to reach for his pocket and I keep hitting his arm. I can feel his gun against my body and if he grabs it, it'll be over. I know what he's trying to do, shoot me. Kill me. "It's because of you, my father is not alive! Did you know that, bitch? Huh? I been trying to get your ass for months and I finally got a hold of that grandmother of yours. She told me everything I needed to know. Including your friends' addresses." He's grinning. "After I kill you, I'm coming for your sister next."

When I see the shine of the gun in his hand, and the barrel moving toward my face, I know it's over.

"Don't kill me, I just had our son." His eyes widen and he lets his guard down. That move allows Sugar to jump on him, forcing his body deeper into mine.

She's clawing at his eyes like she's picking meat from a crab. It's because of her I'm able to get from up under him. "Run, Mad! Run!"

I jump up, with my body and face in tact. She saved my life. I look back at her. "I don't want to leave you!"

"Get out of here, Mad!" She's riding his neck like a horse. "Please, otherwise this will be for nothing!"

By now Krazy and Kid rush outside and they're helping her hold Shaggy. When she moves, Kid and Krazy stomp him like they're doing a dance. "Mad, get the fuck out of here!" Krazy yells kicking him in the neck. "Go!"

I know at that moment, unless they kill him, that it will be a long time before I can show up here again. I feel guilty for putting my friends in danger. I can't go home, Jayden doesn't want me. I can't go to my grandmother's; she acts differently and told him where to find me. I guess there's only one place for me to go and that's hell or the streets. And you know what, I'm for whatever takes me first.

KRESHON

BRINGING THE MAN

Kreshon is smoking a jay with one of his homies at a lounge. When his phone lights up and he see's Jayden's name, he contemplates not answering but his buzz is strong enough to handle her vibe. "What's up, Jayden?" He presses a finger in his ear to hear her over the music. He's still embarrassed about his performance in New York and now that he's drinking again, he is determined to do whatever he can to win her over, again.

"Can you speak up? I can't hear you."

There the bitch goes with the not hearing me shit again. He thinks. "I said, what's up!" He says just a little louder.

"Have you found, Shaggy? I been waiting for a while and I need to see him. And before you lie to me, I already know you keep in contact with him, Kreshon. So where the fuck is he? You're starting to make me believe you're hiding him for personal reasons."

He shakes his head. "You don't know what the fuck you talking about." He grabs his beer from the table and steps away from his homie. "I'm sick of you jumping to conclusions."

"Well prove me wrong. Find him for me, like yesterday."

Click.

"Fuck!" He yells out, startling the girl next to him with her pink tongue in the Corona bottle. He moves away from her and makes another call. It rings once before it's finally answered. "Shaggy, I need to see you."

Silence.

"Shaggy, you hear me?"

"Yeah…what's up?"

"Nothing but why are you dodging me? Plus I know you need the rest of the money we picked up from Jace's crib. If anything, I'd think you'd want to get up with me."

Kreshon is disloyal but it isn't his fault. He has always been that way. The blame rests on Jace's cold bones where it belongs. His weakness was never being able to determine who was for him or who was against him. Not only had Kreshon fucked his bitch Harmony when they were younger, stole his money and the drug connect to get back in the game, now he had his sights on his daughter. He was grimy in every since of the word.

Metha didn't know exactly what Kreshon did to wrong Jace, but having gone to a few Alcohol anonymous meetings, with him, she had a good idea about his character. She faked like his friend to play him close when Jace was alive, because he thought so highly of him. But she would rather befriend Saddam Hussein then Kreshon because at least she knew where he was coming from. She tried to warn Jayden without putting her own life in danger since he was back in the drug business but the girl simply didn't want to listen. Now she was on her own.

"I was going to call you today, when I had a little more time." He lies.

"I must've been feeling you on that shit so I hit you up first. Now when we gonna hook up?"

"In a few days. But look, you not working for that bitch Jayden are you? Because she been calling my folks house every other day trying to get a hold of me."

"Outside of the funeral, I haven't spoken to the bitch. That's on my dick."

"Good, because me and you both had something to do with the money being taken from Jace. So if you sell me out to her, I'm bringing you with me."

"First off why should we even care what that bitch thinks? She ain't nobody's boss. Just call me in a few days so we can get together. I have that package for you too, outside of the money. Let's make paper again, all that other shit you talking is noise."

JAYDEN

OUT SMART OUT RUN

When my mother comes downstairs from her nap, her eyes widen when she sees me sitting at the living room table alone. On the table is a bottle of vodka, a cup, a sheet of paper and a pen. She pulls her robe close and walks closer to me. "What is this about?" She points at my set up.

"This being the pen?" I ask and cross my legs. She licks her lips and nods at my bottle. "Oh…you're asking what's up with this." I point at the liquor. "This is yours soon enough, ma."

"Can I have it now?" She reaches without my okay.

I pull it back. "Sit down, ma. I need you to do something for me and then you can have all the liquor you want."

"Jayden, what is this about?" She's frustrated and moves around in place. She's a fucking drunk ass fein. "I don't have time for this."

"Yes, you do, ma. You stay upstairs, eat, drink and sleep. With my money. Now I need your help and I need it now."

She rubs her arms like she needs to get warm. She looks like and addict and I feel slight hate for her at the moment because I need her on her boss shit right now. I need her responsible, if only for a few seconds. "Can you tell me why you want me to sit at the table with a blank sheet of paper?"

"Because I asked you to." I respond. "This is about you doing something I need you to do for once in your life. Now I have the ability to make all your days from here on out go smooth." I raise the bottle. "I finally get what you need to be happy and I'm not going to fight you anymore. Now do you want a drink or not?"

"I thought you wanted me to stay clean."

"You've been drinking everyday since Kreshon came over, ma. I know it and you know it too."

She quickly takes a seat and I slide the sheet of paper and pen over to her. "I want you to sign Harmony Phillips, twenty times on this."

Her eyebrows pull together. "What…why?"

"Because I'm paying all of your bills and I need your help. That's why. " I nod toward the pen and paper. "Sign your name twenty times."

She's ten signatures in and I pour her a healthy glass of vodka and push it in her direction. She picks it up and is about to kiss the rim when I place my hand on her wrist. "You have ten more times to go." She places it down and signs until she's reached the number. I have her do it again and again until she's signed over one hundred times and has had over five cups of vodka. Straight up. No ice. No juice.

When she's done, I take her upstairs and dress her in the professional outfit I bought for her. I grab her fucked up purse and my new black bucket Louis Vuitton and we head out the door. We jump in the back of the truck and Metha drives us to our destination.

"What's going on, Jayden?" My mother's head falls and rolls. "I thought you wanted me to stay clean. Why would you get me like this?"

"Ma, we talked about that already at the house. Remember? Like I said, I know you been drinking when you're supposed to be going to the meetings." I shake my head. "I found the bottles under your bed."

She rolls her eyes. "What's going on with you and Kreshon?"

I lean back and look at her. "Not one damn thing." Although I need his help on a little project, after he got locked up in New York for indecent exposure, I was playing him at arms length. He kept trying to take me out but I would always make excuses. That nigga was straight weird and after Shaggy was found I plan to focus on Sebastian.

"You need to know about us."

"What do I need to know?" I exhale.

"That at one time, he loved me." She looks a drunken mess.

Who cares? "Ma, you need to relax and stop tripping on the past. Besides, you were with daddy remember? So Kreshon was anything but in love with you."

She laughs. "Yeah, okay…where are we going now? And why do you have my purse?"

I don't answer. I'm not in the mood anyway. When Metha finally stops, we're in front of a bank. I walk her inside doing my best to hold her up on my body. When we reach the counter, a white girl with green eyes greets me. "Welcome to Bank Of Maryland, how may I help you?"

I put on my most professional airs. "My mother would like to open an account. Can you help us please?"

My mother looks at me and says, "Jayden, I told you I don't need no fucking bank account." The moment she opens her mouth, the smell of alcohol rolls off of her breath and smacks me in the face. I'm sure the green-eyed lady has the same experience. "Now take me out of here." She turns to leave but I yank her back towards me.

"Is she able to handle business today?" The green-eyed lady asks observing her. "Because she seems inebriated."

"Drunk?" I laugh. "Trust me she's anything but drunk. And she's able to handle business," I pause, "but let me talk to her in private for a moment." I take her out of earshot and say, "ma, I need you to open this fucking bank account. I know you not use to having one, but if you don't get it today I can't help you out anymore. Shit is that serious."

She sways and I'm tempted to knock her over. "You don't even have any money to put in the account. What the fuck I'm going to open it with…air?"

"I have fifty six thousand dollars in my purse right here," I slap my bag and her eyes light up. "There's no need in your looking like that, because this money is for me not for you."

She rolls her eyes. "What do you need that amount of money for?"

I look away from her. "I can't tell you."

"If you can't tell me then I guess we'll just leave."

I sigh. I don't have time for this shit. I decide to tell her because she'll probably forget in the morning anyway. "I have to have surgery on my ears because you were either drunk, high or diseased when you had me. The procedure costs fifty thousand dollars and when I went to see the doctor today to give him the down payment, he said he won't accept this amount of money from me because I'm a minor. It has to come from you by way of a cashiers check. I'm not old enough to open an account on my own, ma. So I need you to do this. Not only that, I'm raising the money for the house and we'll probably need to pay the courts with a check, too. We need an account for more than one reason."

"So that's why you keep looking at my lips, because you can't hear? I was starting to worry if you were going to try and fuck me or something. It's weird to be looking in peoples mouths when they talk to you."

"Ma!"

"I'm serious!" She looks like she wants to laugh and I'm beyond angry. Who laughs at their daughter when they are to blame? "But, Jayden if you raise that kind of money and open a bank account, it'll be a problem. Trust me. The IRS will come running. Not only that, I won't be able to collect welfare anymore. The government knows all."

"Ma, I'll take care of you if you do this for me. Fuck welfare. I can give you what they pay you for up to a year when we leave out of here."

"How are you going to do that?" She yells and the green-eyed lady looks our way. I smile at her to throw her off our trail. "You don't need to worry about that," I whisper, "but if I could raise fifty grand, you better believe me when I say I have us."

I'm not certain, but she looks jealous. "If I do this, I don't want you riding me about the alcohol meetings anymore. And I'm not trying to be a prisoner in my own house. I come down when I want and how I want."

"Ma, you have to go to the meetings until Katherine Sheers gets off of our case. Just do it long enough for her to go away."

"I been drinking all my life, Jayden. I'm not going to be able to do it."

"Well maybe stay sober on the days before the meeting...I don't know. I will tell you this, if you don't go to those meetings, they'll take me out of the house and you'll lose your checks anyway. This process is for me and you." She seems angry. "Ma, please, I'll look out for you. I promise."

"How?"

"For starters I'll give you all the alcohol..."

"And money," She adds.

I roll my eyes. "And cash you want."

With my promise to feed her alcohol habit and grease her palms, I hand her back her purse and we find ourselves in front of an older black male manager. She caused a slight scene when she almost slipped on the shiny floors on the way over to the chair, but luckily we were able to move past the moment. Once she's sitting down, the manager is focused on my mother's red eyes. I know I should've brought her some shades. I gave her too much to drink. I didn't have any other choice because when I asked her to open the account before, she said she wouldn't. This was the only way I knew how.

"Before we begin," the bank manager says, "I need to be sure you're familiar with *Capacity To Contract.*"

I shake my head no. He looks at my mother again. "Capacity to Contract basically means that people who enter into agreements must be in the right state of mind. So if someone is intoxicated they can't. And looking at your..."

"Mother." I tell him.

"Well looking at your mother it seems that she is. Under her condition, she can't know what she's doing and that could cause problems later. So I'm sorry but I'll have to ask you both to leave."

"Sir, my mother is fully aware of what's going on." I put my arm around her and pinch her hard. I need her focused. "Right, ma?"

She doesn't respond and he lowers his eyes. "I'm not sure that she does."

This was the worst-case scenario for me. I didn't want to be handicap for the rest of my life. I didn't want to lose my home. God please help me with this. I don't know what else to do.

For the first time ever God answers me when my mother says, "Listen, mothafucka, I have over fifty thousand dollars to place in your bank right now." She scared me to death with her outburst but it's worth it.

"Which means I'm ready to do business today." She stabs her finger on his desk. "Now if you aren't interested in my money, I'd love to hear what your boss has to say about that before we leave."

He adjusts his tie and says, "There's no need to do all of that. If you're sure you're capable, I don't see any reason why we can't continue." He pauses and looks at the green-eyed lady. I know she put him up to it. He looks back at us, "Wait, what is that dripping sound?"

"Not sure but can you make sure I have access to her account." My mother looks like she doesn't agree but remains silent. "I'd also like a bank card. Here is my school ID, I reach into my purse. My name is Jayden Phillips."

The manager keys in some more information and is once again distracted. "What is that noise? It's very irritating." I'm not sure what he's talking about until I feel something splash on my ankles. When I look down I see that my mother is pissing in her seat and it's smacking against the hardwood floors making extra noise.

My heart kicks up speed and I look at the manager and grin. He doesn't see what's going on because he would've certainly thrown us out now. Thinking on my feet, I place my new Louis Vuitton purse on the floor and kick it under her seat. It catches her urine before it splashes to the floor. In the process, it wets up my money and everything else inside. My mother did that nasty shit on purpose. I know she did.

"I don't hear anything." I tell him.

He listens harder. "I don't hear it anymore either." He shrugs. "Maybe it's just me."

When he finishes setting up the account, we ask for a cashiers check for twenty-five thousand dollars. I don't want to give the doctor the entire fifty thousand even though I have it, just in case I need it for an emergency. When it's time to give him the cash, I reach into my purse and place the urine soaked bills on the table. I'm so disgusted that I want to scream and it takes everything in me to keep a straight face.

"Wow, why is some of your money wet?" He frowns as he takes it in his hands.

I shrug. "I guess that's what happens when we make it rain on 'em." I give him my biggest grin.

GUCCI

IT'LL MAKE YOU FEEL GOOD

Passion lay in Madjesty's bed crying her eyes out. All of the kissing Jayden's ass and fake being her friend was all for nothing. Passion was the one to answer the phone when it rang, she was the one who always ran to the door first. And when she finally saw Mad, she accused her of something her heart knew she didn't do which caused her to lose her forever.

When the door opens, in crawls Gucci with a smile on her face. "I heard about what happened with Mad the other day. I mean, I know you don't fuck with me like that, but I hate that that happened to you. I'm so sorry, Passion. I know how you felt about Mad's cute ass."

Passion doesn't look at her. Instead she remains balled up like a baby. "I don't want to talk, Gucci. Leave me alone."

Gucci sits on the bed and rubs her thigh. "I hate what's become of our friendship. We use to be so close, Passion. Shit, I'm the one who gave you the nickname Passion and everything. Before me you were Denise. And the way you're treating me hurts my feelings."

Passion rolls over and looks at her. There she goes making a moment about her again. "What does you giving me my nickname have to do with anything?"

"I'm just saying that we go way back to straightening combs and hair grease. And I miss that."

Passion wipes her eyes. Her heart is on her sleeve and she's vulnerable to any kind of attention now. She wasn't getting it from Jayden because she was all about her money. She wasn't getting it from Olive because she was all about Jayden. And her friends in the house seemed to abandon her a little since all she wanted to talk about was her ex-boyfriend who was actually Jayden's sister. The whole thing was weird and freaked everybody out.

"I miss her so much, Gucci." Tears travel down to her chin before falling onto her breasts. "I feel like I can't breathe or move. What can I do to get her back? I can't even find her."

Gucci's eyebrows rise. "I got an idea but you might not be willing to do it."

She sits up. "What is it?"

"How about you help me get the girls together and we take over the business. If you ask me, the reason ya'll can't be together is Jayden's fault anyway. I mean, ain't she the one who lied and said she raped her?" She nods her head in agreement. "The shit is so ridiculous anyway? How a girl gonna rape another girl? You need to get it together and help me make this bitch pay!"

Passion frowns. "All you want to do is hurt Jayden. I'm not down for that shit, Gucci. I want my nigga back. Not no pussy business."

She's so mad she wants to steal Passion in the face. "Why are you taking up for this bitch even now?"

"Because what's going on with me and Mad don't have nothing to do with her. That's why."

Gucci didn't want to do it but she activates another plan. She stands up, reaches in her pocket and pulls out a cellophane wrapper. It has a brown powder inside. She places it on the desk next to the bed. "I think you need to get your mind right, so I bought that for you."

Passion picks it up and her body trembles so hard it falls to the bed. She can smell its sweet scent from where she is. "Is that…"

"Heroin."

She licks her lips and her pussy tingles. "I can't do that, I'm clean." Still she can't take her eyes off of it. Why can't she take her eyes off of it?

"Passion you're a mess right now. What's the use of being clean if you not happy? The least you can do is feel a little better until you can sort things out." Passion doesn't budge. "If you don't want it I'll take it out of here." She reaches for the pack but Passion grabs Gucci's hand so hard, her fingernails dig into the skin on the top of her causing it to bleed. Gucci is in pain but loves every bit of it.

"Leave it." She says. "I want it."

"Let me see you do it." Gucci begs. She doesn't want anybody talking her out of it later.

Passion thinks about all the hard work she's been doing in high school. She thinks about her dreams for college and the dreams she and Jayden share for the future. Then she thinks about not having Madjesty or never seeing her again. Suddenly her dreams don't matter anymore without Mad. She needed her to make her life complete. So she unwraps Gucci's gift carefully. Then she places it against her nose and inhales. Instantly a rush of warmth takes over her and she feels orgasmic.

Gucci takes Madjesty's shirt off of Passion, freeing her breasts. She massages the left and then the right titty. Passion would have never allowed this shit if she had been in her right mind. Prior to fucking with

Madjesty, she was totally disgusted at the idea of being with a woman. And she wasn't for being with another chick now but the drug had her twisted.

Before long Gucci weaseled her hand between her legs as she flipped her clit. Passion was wet and back to her old shit. She made a decision that she would never separate from her favorite drug again. And she had Gucci's sneaky ass to thank.

JAYDEN
GET SHIT TOGETHER

I adjust my hearing aids and cover my ears. I know what I'm about to say won't be popular with a few of the girls but I want to hear everything they have to say once I make my announcement. I'll be happy when I'm able to get my surgery in a few weeks so I won't have to bother with these things at all.

When I open Gucci's bedroom door, I see her, Olive, Na-Na, Queen and Foxie practicing a routine for a client who wants to experience an orgy at the gym. They're naked and their bodies are twisted together like a pretzel. "Gucci, I don't believe you want to eat Na-Na's box." Olive coaches before they know I'm there. "You have to make me believe you. I don't believe you and chances are, our client won't either."

"Maybe you don't believe me because I don't want to eat her out." She wipes her mouth with a sock and throws it down. The room she shares with Queen and Na-Na is a mess. "Plus she keeps making garlic eggs for breakfast and I told her it comes out in her pussy juice but she don't listen to me."

"I don't want to eat you out either! And for your information I don't smell nothing." Na-Na protests, placing her fingers in her box and touching her nose. "I don't smell nothing."

"You can never smell yourself before somebody else do." I say. "And what I tell you about the garlic shit, Na-Na?" I step fully inside. From where I stand, I can smell garlic rising off of her body too. "No fucking with garlic before dealing with a client. That shit spits out your pores and we already had a complaint about that."

Na-Na picks her dress up and stands in the middle of the floor. Embarrassed. "But I hear garlic is good for you."

"I don't give a fuck what you hear, no garlic before a date." I look at everyone. "Now that that's out the way I need to talk to you about something. I'm going to need you, you and you to move into a room with Johnna." I say to Gucci, Na-Na and Queen. I focus on Foxie next. "And I'm going to need you to move in with them too."

"Wait, why do I have to move?" Foxie says. "What about Hadiya? Me and her share rooms together. Why can't she leave?"

"Because I got another plan for her." Foxie's nose twitches. "Questions?" I continue.

She folds her arms to her chest. "No."

"Good, because I need this move done today."

Gucci's jaw drops. "Why we gotta move in with that white bitch, Jayden? She cool and all but you know blacks and whites don't get along too well. It's a biological fact. Making them type of arrangements is just begging something to happen."

I approach her. "For one thing that white bitch you talking about earns more money than you since she's been here and I never have to hear her mouth either. She does what I say immediately no questions asked. Don't play the racist card with me bitch because you can kill yourself. There's one language in this house and it's PUSSY! Secondly this is my house, Gucci." I point to myself. "Mine...so if I tell you to move you take what you can grab and do it quick."

"But I don't want to. That's five people to a room. We gonna be pushed together."

"Johnna's room is big enough. Plus I'm having bunk beds brought in tomorrow as well as a full. Since she's been in there before you guys, she keeps the full." They sigh. "We already did the measurements so it will work."

"But, Jayden I wish you would've talked to us about that first. You don't just up and make decisions like that. It ain't fair."

Olive shakes her head. "Gucci, you do know Jayden's your boss right? Because I think you get it fucked up sometimes."

She rolls her neck and slaps her hands against her hips. "I know who she is. That's why I'm being real with her. If she makes moves without talking to us, the girls will be unhappy. It's bad for business."

"Which girls you talking about?" I ask.

"All of us."

Olive walks out. I know what she's thinking before she even opens her mouth. She's thinking that because I give them too much say-so around here, now they're trying to run over me. "If you don't like how I wiggle, pack your shit and go, Gucci. It's that simple." I pause to give her another chance to put her titty in her mouth and get tossed out on her ass. "Any more questions?" She doesn't take the bait.

Since I've dealt with them, I'm about to go and find Passion when I hear Hadiya yell, "Jayden, some old lady just pulled up out front of the house. You want me to let her in?"

I can't see my face but I know I go bright red. I rush to the window and she's approaching the house with her clipboard in hand and ugly face on her shoulders. I rush downstairs to tell Hadiya to lock the doors but

Mrs. Sheers is already in the foyer. "Next time don't open the door unless I tell you." Hadiya runs to her room crying. "What's up, Mrs. Sheers?"

"You don't seem to happy to see me, Jayden." *I'm not.* "How are you today?"

"I'm fine." I don't smile. I barely move. "How can I help you?"

She flings her black leather purse over her shoulder, slides on her glasses and says, "I hear your mother hasn't been to the sobriety appointments I set up for her. Any reason why?"

"First off I'm the child remember?" She doesn't respond. "And as far as I know, the program is voluntary. So if my mother doesn't show it shouldn't be too big of a deal right?" As I'm standing in front of her, I'm hoping that my girls don't walk out here naked, causing her to be more suspicious about this house. The only time the girls put clothes on was when they were getting dressed for a job. They walk around naked. We all walk around naked.

"It is voluntary…but I hoped your mother would do a little better with her commitments. Like you have. I'm hearing your grades are great and that you are a candidate for a few scholarships for college if you keep this up."

I already know my status in school. Ever since I decided to stay focused, and keep my promise to my father, I didn't back down. "I'm not my mother's keeper, Mrs. Sheers. Your concern was me going to school and I'm doing that, so why are you still bothering us?"

"I'm not bothering you. And you're right, my main priority is you kids. If it's any consolation I'm not here for you. I'm here to check on Madjesty and after that, I'll be leaving." She looks upstairs.

"Mrs. Sheers, it's no consolation. And Madjesty is sick with the flu. I told you that."

"Madjesty isn't upstairs." Gucci says walking into the foyer. "At least I didn't see her."

My face is numb. This bitch is doing this shit on purpose. "She is upstairs, Gucci. And why don't you go up there and let me talk to Mrs. Sheers alone." She smirks and walks away. I can't wait to handle that bitch. When she's gone I say, "My mother said she told you that Madjesty was ill."

"I know and as I explained to your mother, I need to lay eyes on her to be sure. Things happen all the time to children when the social workers turn their backs. I don't intend on letting that happen with you girls. And if you've seen some of the dead children I've buried in my day, you'd thank me." I know she's being real but something says where we're concerned it's just petty bullshit.

Without my okay she treks up the stairs and toward Madjesty's room. I'm so nervous I forget the code word. I worked so hard for this moment and now it was all in vein. Sweat forms on my forehead and I wipe it quickly. I have to get myself together and quick.

Before she opens the door, I throw myself in front of it and say, "You can't go in there. She's been so sick that if you open this door, you may contaminate the whole house." When Gucci walks out of the room next to Madjesty's, half naked with Na-Na, Queen and Foxie following her like baby chickens, I want to choke the bitch. They disappear downstairs and Mrs. Sheers doesn't break her stare until they're out of sight. "Who are they?"

"My cousins." She opens her records and look at the sheet. "I don't remember any cousins."

I frown. "Just because we're poor doesn't mean we don't have family." I pause. "If I say they're my cousins then they're my cousins. What else you want me to say?"

Mrs. Sheers shoves me out the way and opens the door anyway. This bitch has been calling for Madjesty religiously and every time me or my mother tells her that she's sick, she never believes us. I guess its cuz we're lying. When she turns the knob, I know it's over until I see a body under the blanket. The person's back is faced our direction with a sheet pulled all the way up to their neck. They're wearing the red wig I bought months ago and the black baseball cap. If she doesn't see her face, whoever it is will pass for Madjesty instantly.

I walk in front of Mrs. Sheers, trying to block her view. "See...I told you, she's in bed."

"Well I want to talk to her." She tries to step in front of the body when I snatch her wrist forcing the gray curls on top of her head to whip. She looks at my hand until I squeeze tighter. "You are our social worker, not our owner, Mrs. Sheers. If I said my sister is sick, she's fucking sick. So unless you have a warrant, you need to get out of her room and leave her alone. I'm not going to tell you again, and I don't believe I have too."

She snatches away from me. "Jayden, I know something is going on around here." She looks at the stand in, Madjesty's back again. "And when I find out, you and your mother are in for it."

"Mrs. Sheers, I'm tired of looking at your bush. Please leave." She stomps down the stairs.

When she exits, I walk into Madjesty's room, where I haven't been since we were cool and gaze out of the window. I see Mrs. Sheers crawl back into her car and speed off. When I focus on the body, I see Passion lying in the bed instead of Olive. She's so stiff she looks like a corpse.

What's going on?

"She gone yet?" Olive asks coming out of the closet.

I shake my head and smile. "How did you pull this off? I forgot the code word."

"You know I'ma handle my business regardless, Jayden." She closes the door. "But I can't lie, that was a close call."

"How did you know I needed you?"

"I just left the bedroom when they said the lady was coming. Remember?"

I didn't. "Girl, I was so scared that I totally forgot to use the code word maroon." I sigh. "She won't stop getting in the business."

"To be honest, I think you'll always have a problem with her. You better tighten up around here and quick because one false move and she won't hesitate to throw you in a home." My head hurts just thinking about the possibility. "I'm not gonna lie though, that plan you had for the wig was genius. You really are covering your tracks."

"More than you know." I plop on the edge of Madjesty's bed. Just being in here makes me miss her more. It makes me sick too because I also hate her.

"Why use, Passion?" I whisper. She hadn't budged since we'd been in here. "Why didn't you jump in the bed and pretend to be Madjesty like the plan called for?"

"I don't know if you looked at your girl lately but she's been in coma like sleeps. I think she's taking sleeping pills or something. She may even be on heroin again."

"Naw, I think she's fucked up because Mad came here awhile back and dumped her. She ran in the house crying and everything."

"I heard." She shrugs. "Well maybe she's trying to sleep her problems away." She scratches her curly bush. "Anyway I didn't move her because by the time I'd try to get her out of the bed, the old bitty would've seen a body on the floor. I had to think on my feet."

Times like this make me love Olive even more. Wanting to see Passion's face, I stand up and walk to her front. Her skin is ash gray and it doesn't have the glow it once did. This bitch is using again. I'm disappointed. I'm about to try and wake her myself, when Hadiya runs in and says, "You have a phone call." She's holding the white handset in her hand.

"Who is it?"

"It's some man. He says he's from Bank of Maryland and that your mother just took a bunch of money out of the account."

My heart is heavy. "How much she take?"

"He didn't want to tell me at first but I recognized his voice. He's the client you set me up with the other day." *Wow. A small world.* "After a little persuading eventually he said she took..." She's hesitant.

"How much?"

Her voice is low but I have the hearing aids on. "Twenty thousand dollars."

I can kill my mother. Two days after I open the banking account, she betrays me. It's not like I wasn't giving her money. She didn't have to take shit. I mean how much liquor can you drink? Now I'm going to have to come up with the cash quick for my surgery. Every day my hearing gets worse and without the aids, I wouldn't hear anything at all.

I don't know what to do with her right now. I'm trying. Trying to help her and to be the daughter I know she needs, but each day she proves to me that she doesn't want my love. I'm glad she thinks she has the upper hand on me though, because I have a few tricks up my sleeve she won't see coming. She's going to pay greatly.

GUCCI

KICKED OUT

Gucci plops on the lawn chair in the backyard with a funky ass attitude. Queen, Na-Na and Foxie follow hoping she calms down. Nobody is trying to fuck up their sweet deal but they can already see it's about to happen. Foxie is sitting on a chair alone, while Queen is sitting on Na-Na's lap and because she doesn't have any panties on, her pussy rubs against her thigh.

Gucci is fuming so much about having to share a room with Johnna that her underarms are dripping with sweat. The tissue that she uses to wipe them off, crumbles. The truth is she didn't have anything against the white girl. That was just an excuse to call the situation out. Her real gripe was with Jayden and how she seemed to take the side of everybody who kissed her ass. All of her plans didn't do enough drama. Telling Tywanda backfired in her face because she was more loyal to Jayden than ever. And every time she told them Jayden didn't respect them, they didn't stay mad long like her. She could hold a Grudge longer than the movie.

"Now ya'll see what the fuck I'm talking about," Gucci announces, "Jayden don't give a fuck about nobody but them new chicks. The messed up part is, we the ones who helped her build the original Thirteen Flavors." The girls weren't hype enough for her yet. She needed to kick up some more shit in order to get more people on her side.

"Maybe there's a reason she told us to move in with Johnna. I mean think about it, she never told us to leave our room before." Foxie says. "And you should see how pretty Johnna keeps her room. She really takes care of the place."

"Geez, Foxie, you getting in the bed with Johnna or are you gonna sleep on your own bunk?" Gucci fires. "She told us to get out because she don't fuck with us." Gucci wants to slap her into submission but she wouldn't prove her point that way. "How come you still taking this bitch's side when she made it clear she don't take yours?"

"Gucci, we making more money than we ever have in our lives. I'm about to buy a car next week and everything. All I want to do is stack paper, get high and stay fresh. Don't you?"

Gucci squints. "I been knowing you since we were kids. You just met this bitch a little over a year ago at school. Are you that pressed where you will forget our bond just to make some extra cash?"

Silence.

Gucci looks at all of them. "I'm telling you now, at some point this bitch is going to get rid of us. I know you sitting pretty thinking this mansion is yours but it ain't. Remember she told us that our niggas can't even come over. We can either get smart and wake up or be dumb and wait till the other bra drops." She pauses. "If we wait, how we gonna make our paper then?"

Queen responds. "I don't know."

"I know you don't know but I do. From here on out when we go on dates, we collect as much information as possible from our clients. If you don't have any appointments, talk to Olive to see if she can schedule you more. Let her lick your pussy or you suck hers if you have to, just as long as we are in there." She pauses. "When we get enough numbers, we'll bounce and take her business with us."

HARMONY
DAMAGED GOODS

Jayden can suck my ass if she thinks she can keep me sober for two whole days before meetings. I don't have a man. I don't have kids who respect me and I don't have hope. To be honest, I can't even find a decent piece of dick nowadays. Niggas come too quick. My fuck game is too thorough for my own good. Without liquor, I'd probably be dead by now, so in my opinion it's the only thing keeping me alive.

Not only that, the place Mrs. Sheers made me go for alcohol rehab was Green Door – Adult Mental Health Clinic and it was an absolute mess. Christina Zahm, the doctor they put in charge of my case, hates me and I hate her. She's too condescending, with her pale skin and degrees on her wall. Personally I think the more degrees you earn, the more out of touch with reality you are. She needs to spend a day in my world and I bet her a blowjob she'd feel cheated by all of the bullshit she learned in college. All Christina wants is for me to be in an in-house program. And if Jayden saw this nurse pushing me out of the hospital in a wheel chair, after my recent alcohol poison situation, she'd think Christina was right. I wonder if she forgives me for spending twenty thousand dollars that she had in the bank, for hotel fees, drinks and fun.

When we get outside, the cool air brushes my hair back and I smile. Why? Because the night sky catches up with me and all I want is another drink. Between losing Jace and finding out I'm HIV positive, I think my life can't get any worse. That is until I found out I was pregnant with another child. Can you imagine? Me? Pregnant, with another baby. Any kid dumb enough to enter my drunken womb to come into the world, deserved to die.

I noticed my belly growing a long time ago but I thought it was because of all of the alcohol I drank. I had no idea that I was pregnant with a stranger's child. The doctors in the hospital set me straight. Now all I want to do is kill it. Fuck an abortion. Death by drinking is the best idea I have.

When we get outside, the nurse can't wait to dip the chair, forcing my ass flat on the concrete. After giving her a few choice words and lifting up my blue dress to show her my bare ass, I feel its time for me to get away from the scene before they lock me up.

After waving my thumb back and forth, I finally hail a cab. I have a few crumpled bills in my pocket and I can't wait to spend them. I couldn't get more because apparently Jayden walked into the bank, said she was me and closed the account.

When I reach my destination, the neighborhood's friendly liquor store, I give the cab driver a few bucks and ask him to stay but he doesn't. Once inside, I spend every dime for a bottle of strawberry 20/20. With my paper bag firmly in the palm of my hand, I walk outside and lean on the side of the store. There are a few regulars outside and all eyes are on me. I feel like Halle Berry as they crowd around for a sip of my shit. No haps though. I'm selfish when it comes to my sauce.

The rain pouring down is bugging the hell out of me, as I tilt the bottle to my lips. Suddenly I can't help but feel and overwhelming sense of dread. I have HIV. I lost my first love. And I'm an, *"alcoholic"*. To make things worse, I'm pregnant and I just stole money from my daughter, the only person who ever helped me.

I'm trying to wash my problems away when I hear, "What you over there crying about?" The voice is strong an authoritative. But what is he talking about? I'm not crying. "You too cute to be crying over a nigga who's probably fucking another bitch right now anyway."

I touch my face and my eyes are wet. It's not raining after all. When I look over at the voice, I see a twenty-something man smiling in my direction. He isn't driving a fancy car and doesn't appear to be a baller like Jace. He's wearing blue pants with dried paint all over them. Basically he's ordinary…plain. And then it dawns on me, I'm a washed up drunk, with two kids who hate each other, a baby in my belly and a fresh case of HIV. Who am I to judge?

"It's been a long time since I've cried over anyone, especially a man." I explain. I remember something else he says. "And did you call me cute?"

He smiles and leans up against his sliver Altima. "You heard me right."

I grin. "I think you have zero taste, but okay." I call myself looking in his eyes, but they keep focusing on his ears instead. I'm bent already.

"You alright? Because you look like you about to fall."

"Not really," I confess, "So how 'bout you help a bitch out?"

"With a ride?"

"Fuck no! With another drink."

He laughs. *What the fuck is so funny?* "How about I give you a ride to wherever you want to go and then you can get a drink there. I just want you to be safe."

I walk closer to him. He's very handsome with his dark brown skin and pearly white teeth. His energy tells me he's a nice guy, and it's a shame he's run into me. "Instead of taking me where I want to go, how 'bout you keep me as long as you want and then drop me off wherever."

He smiles. "Life for you is that easy?"

"It wasn't always that way." I think about my kids...my pregnancy...Jace. And HIV. "It is now."

"So what's your name?" I ask.

"Lonnie J and it's a pleasure meeting you."

"Let's see if you feel that way later."

━━━━━━━━━━━━━━━━━━━━━━━━━━━━━━━━━━━━━

We end up in a diner where everybody who walks by me smells like weed. They serve food that's cold and tasteless but after eating the hospital meals for days, I welcome the change. "So, where were you on your way to?" I ask. I chew the eggs in my mouth and fork up some grits to get rid of the box taste. "Before you ran into me?"

"I just got off work," he stirs his black coffee and his spoon bangs against the edges. "So before I saw your beautiful face, I wasn't about to get into anything but my bed. So what's your name?"

"Harmony Phillips." I keep eating.

"Wow you gave me the first and last name." He sips his coffee. "You must be famous with a name like that."

"I don't know about all that, but you can say I've lived the life of a porn star."

Coffee comes flying out of his mouth and nostrils. He wipes it with the back of his hand and looks at me hard. "You playing right?"

"I don't do a lot of playing, I don't have time." I chew some more box and grits. "So let me tell you what I want to do." I ate the rest of my food and make him wait. It looks like he's holding his breath. "I want to go to the liquor store again, go back to your place and fuck. After that if you decide you want to have this conversation again, you know, with me being a porn star and all, we can do that. But to be honest, the only thing on my mind right now is getting on top of you and riding you like it's nobody's business. You with that?"

He clears his throat and places his coffee cup on the table. "Look, maybe I gave you the wrong impression about me. I have freakish ways but I'm not a whore." Never heard a man refer to himself as a whore in the same breath. Interesting. "I like what I like but I'm not rushing to do anything. If that's how you move, that's on you. It's just not my way."

He's getting on my nerves but there's something about him that makes me humor the situation. "What you looking for then? Because I'm gonna tell you right now, you not gonna get some dream girl over here, or somebody who's looking to take care of a man. I'm a loner. I'm the shit the street sweepers didn't clean and I like it that way. I hope you can understand that."

"You being real heavy with me when you don't have to be. So let's do this," he motions for the waiter, "how 'bout we get you another order of eggs and grits, since you licking the plate," it isn't until he says that, that I realize my tongue is on the plate, "and get to know each other better. Okay?"

I place the plate down and look at him. He's cool and all I can think about is how sad it is that I couldn't have met him at a better time in my life. When I was young and impressionable. Unfortunately he met me during the most diseased time of my life.

KRESHON

TRUNK CLOSE

Kreshon speeds down Martin Luther King Jr., Blvd in Washington D.C, listening to Chuck Brown on CD. Jayden had been on his mind ever since he last saw her in New York. He was beyond embarrassed when the officers told him what he'd done and what he was charged with. He had nightmares of the expression on Jayden's face as he whipped out his dick in the restaurant. That's why he didn't fuck with liquor anymore because while some just got drunk after having too many, he became a pervert. To make matters worse, he started drinking again...every night. Prior to that night, he had five years clean and now it was all or nothing. Metha knew that because they had alcohol anonymous meetings together and now he wasn't coming anymore. But as long as he could win Jayden over, in his book, it would be worth it.

When he makes it to the carry out, he parks his car and gets his and Jayden's food order. When he's done, he makes his way to Concord Manor. The moment he pulls up, he sees Jayden is waiting for him in the foyer with a smile on her face. Her long hair is dripped over her shoulders and her pink silk nightgown clings to her recently oiled body. He sits in the car for a minute, just admiring her body from a far. She looks foreign. So sexy, yet so familiar. He takes in what he knows was true all the time, Jayden looks like Harmony did when he first met her. When he was in love with her.

When he can't take it anymore, he grabs the bag of food from the car and eases out. "You looking good, baby." He shakes the bag. "I got the food you wanted. Hungry?"

She frowns and doesn't seem too interested in the meal. "Did you get what else I ordered?"

He grins although he's irritated with her impatience. "You wanna do that now?" He looks into her house. "With all them niggas in your crib?"

She steps out of the doorway, barefoot. "Kreshon, I told you what I need. Now if you can't be that for me, you betta get another bitch who can deal with slackers. I want what I want and I always have a reason for it. The last thing I'm worrying about are the niggas in my house. Now do you have it or not?"

He frowns and the arm holding the bag hangs by his side. "Go put your shoes on. I'll show you what you want to see."

"I'll be fine. I walked miles with no shoes for most of my life, I don't have a problem with walking a few feet."

She follows him out of the door and toward his car. He takes his time taking the keys out of his pocket, to activate the automatic trunk button. When it flies open, she walks hesitantly toward the back. Peering inside, she twinkles. Inside, hogtied with a tennis ball stuffed in his mouth is Shaggy, the man she wanted dead. The man whose disloyalty ruined her life and destroyed her bond with her sister. "I'm glad we finally meet again, Shaggy. Talk that shit now."

●━━━━━━━━━━━━━━━━━━━━━━━━━━━━━━━━━━━●

Shaggy is in the basement face down on a mattress on the floor. The ropes on his wrists and ankles are tied with ropes connected to the opposite side of the wall. He's face down, naked and gagged. Kreshon is standing on the opposite end of the basement with his hands on his waist. He doesn't know what sadistic shit she has planned, but he's scared about the outcome. Besides he fucked with Paco, Shaggy's father, and didn't want his son to go out like this. Now it was out of his hands. Ever since he met Jayden he'd done some crazy shit. Like stuffing Mr. Grover in his trunk, bringing Shaggy to her and even trying to kill her mother when he saw her walking down the street one day. Even though minutes later, she had his dick in her mouth, being with her was beginning to be too heavy.

"So you like to fuck people against their will, Shaggy?" She walks around him before bending down to remove his gag. "I asked do you like fucking people against their will?"

"Jayden, I swear to God I didn't know she was your sister that night, man." He lies. "And I didn't rape her. She wanted to have sex with me."

Jayden knew he was lying immediately. If she knew nothing else about Madjesty, she knew she didn't want a man to be anywhere near her. "So you telling me my sister wanted to fuck you?"

He nodded. "Yeah, I don't know what she told you but it's the truth. I don't know why she would lie to you."

"Gag this nigga." She tells Kreshon who does it even though he's freaked out.

Jayden walks to the edge of the room. She picks up a gas torch and a long grey iron fire poker from a table. She burns the tip of the poker until it turns orange. She parts his ass cheeks with one hand and rams it in and out of him until blood is everywhere. When she remembers what

Madjesty did to her, she pushes it into him so many times, she pierces the wall of his anal cavity. Before long, he bleeds to death.

KALI

THE 'A'

Kali sits outside in the backyard of a house they rented in Atlanta, with his fist nestled in the center of his palm. He'd been calling Jace for months and it bugged him that he had the audacity not to return his calls. It wasn't like he'd been waiting the entire time for his call. Kali found Atlanta to be quite the money pit, especially for his career of choice…a hired killer. It didn't take long for Kali's name to ring bells and before long, he was known as the man you needed to call if you wanted to get rid of a problem. All of that was good and sweet, but he still had business back home.

When he hears the sliding door open behind him, he reaches for the hatchet until he sees Ann standing over top of him, with a glass of ice tea in her hand. She made it obvious on more than one occasion that although Kali was brokering the deal with Jace for her life, she wasn't interested in going home without him.

"I made you this," she extends her arms. "It has extra honey in it, the way you like it." He looks at the cup and turns around. She takes a few sips to avoid waste and stays put. "Kali, what's on your mind? You're scaring me. These past couple of days you've been quieter than usual."

"Ann, the last thing I'm worrying about or care about is scaring you." He looks around the yard, frustrated. "I can't believe this nigga Jace acting like I'm not good to my word. Don't he know what I'd do to you, if he doesn't come up with my money? And Shaggy? Haven't I showed him the limits I'm willing to take to avoid being fucked with?"

Suddenly the tea seems bitter so she sits it on the table beside him. "Kali, I don't want to get in your head because I know you don't like it."

"Ann, that's your problem, you still think you know me. You could never get in my head. You think too highly of yourself."

She clears her throat. "I didn't mean it that way. It just that I pray every night that you won't hurt me if Jace doesn't come through with what you're asking. I feel like you and I have a bond outside of Jace now, and I want to make that work. Think about it, you haven't had to tie my hands or force me to do anything I don't want to. I willingly turn myself over to you every night. And I willingly give you my heart."

Kali wasn't about love when it came to Antoinette. Yes he was feeling her, which shocked him more than he realized. And on most nights he could even tolerate her but the situation he had with Jace was about business, not pleasure. "Ann, I hear you, but all I can suggest is that you pray a little harder. Truth be told, I don't know what I might do until he fucks up his end of the deal." He removes his cell from his pocket and dials a number he hasn't called in years. It rings two times before it's finally answered.

"Kreshon, what's up with you?" Kali says.

Kreshon laughs and finally responds, "What the fuck you doing calling me? We thought you were dead."

"I'm not even gonna get into all of that because this will be quick. Me and your man had an arrangement and I'm getting the impression he's not going to honor it."

"What the fuck that got to do with me?"

He's arrogant and he figures he's drinking again. "Kreshon, where is Jace?" He says, irritated with his lack of seriousness. Since he's so lackadaisical, Kali makes a note to see him too when he touches down.

Kreshon laughs. "Nigga, you mad funny."

"I bet it won't be funny when I murder his trophy wife." He looks at Antoinette, who doesn't feel as comfortable as she did in the past, that he won't hurt her. "Because I guarantee you there won't be shit to laugh about when I blow the features off her face."

"Truthfully I don't give a fuck what you do to his bitch. And to be honest, Jace wouldn't either."

He frowns. "And why is that?"

"Because you were spotted in Atlanta a long time ago, nigga. We knew where you were and we knew you were fucking her. When it got back to Jace he didn't care anymore." Kreshon feels dumb for being caught slipping until he says, "and even if you did kill her, he still wouldn't care because we buried my man months ago."

Kali is outside but he feels like he can feel the earth spinning. Sure he wanted the money Jace owed, that had always been one of his gripes. And yes he wanted Shaggy's head on a stick for what he did to his only child. But a part of him, the part he would never admit out loud, loved the dude and didn't want to see him fall. He felt the man deserved a soldier's death, by his hands if nothing else. He would've placed a bullet in his head a long time ago if it was only about the money and called it quits. Jace was the first person who treated him with respect when they were kids, and he was the first nigga who gave him a break when he needed one.

"How he die?"

"He contracted HIV. We think he had it for a minute but we not sure. Any nigga who fucked with Harmony, has turned themselves in for a check up, I suggest you do the same." He says as if he didn't just participate in a new blowjob by her recently.

"I hope you're taking your own advice. At one time you wanted to marry the bitch."

He laughs. "I got myself checked homie and I'm good over here. My suggestion to you is that you worry about yourself."

Kali isn't worried. He was checked after he left her alone, when he went into a clinic under another name to find out why he had a strange pain in his arm. When his labs came back clean, he hadn't fucked with her since. Nor did he have a desire too. That's more that could be said for most dudes.

"You seen my daughter?"

"What am I...your best good girlfriend?" Kreshon responds.

Kali sighs in frustration as he presses the phone to his ear. "I'm asking you a fucking question, nigga. Either you answer it or you don't." He pauses. "And take caution with how you speak to me. Don't let the state lines fool you, I'm still a killer."

Silence.

"I didn't see her but Jayden said she came by the house not too long ago. She don't fuck with her too much anymore and I'm not sure why. Anyway, the last I heard, she was pregnant and had a kid." Kali is rocked physically by the news. "I think one of Bernie's friends stole it from her for crack. Since then I been seeing her roaming around D.C. looking like she could use a bath or too. I tried to pull up on her to give her some paper, but she ran the moment she saw my face."

"So you saying she living on the streets?"

"Don't know and it ain't my problem." He pauses. "Oh, and if you worried about Shaggy you don't have to be anymore. The debt is settled. So there ain't no reason for you to harbor any ill will."

This piece of news makes him grin. "How can I be sure?"

"I saw to the shit myself." He lies. Jayden laid down the murder game, not him. "And since I did, I need for you to leave Jayden alone."

Behind his words Kali can feel his reason. "Let me find out you fell in love with a kid. Your man's daughter at that. If he was alive I'm sure he'd have a problem with how you carrying shit."

"Well thank God he's not and I didn't say I'm fucking her. I just want you to know that I'm fully vested in Jayden and everything she does. I won't have anybody coming at her in a way that may cause her harm. You hear what I'm saying?"

Kali thinks the man is hilarious and decides to play on it. "That's cool and everything, but there's still the debt that Jace owed. Him being dead doesn't mean that the debt is negated. Just that there's a new debtor."

Kreshon sighs in frustration. "You can't be serious, man. That's not her beef."

"If I serve it to her, she gonna eat it."

"Stay away from her, Kali. I'm warning you."

Kreshon hangs up and Kali sits back in his seat. Kreshon popping them bubbles didn't do anything to ruffle his feathers. He was a gangster. He and Kreshon both know who the real killer is. Since his man was dead, the only thing on his mind is Madjesty. He's worried that she's five seconds from being a statistic. And where is Harmony? How could she allow her daughter to live on the streets? What the fuck did he mean she looked like she needed a few baths? If there was one thing that could be said for Madjesty, she always kept herself fresh so something had to be wrong. And if Shaggy and Jace was dead, she had no other enemies.

There was nothing left to do, he had to get to D.C. and he had to do it quickly. His mind is heavy but he has a daughter and judging by what Kreshon told him, she needs him more than ever. In the beginning he didn't want her, but now that she entered his life, part of what he did was for her, including trying to find Shaggy and murder him for raping her. Money came and went, but blood, when it was his, lasted forever.

"We gotta get out of here." Kali says to Ann when she walks in front of him.

Since he used the word we, which meant he wasn't going to kill her even though he learned that Jace was dead, she put fire to her ass and got things in order before he changed his mind and chopped off her head. She didn't have the details so when they walk into the bedroom she asks, "What happened?" She stuffs her suitcase.

"Jace is dead." He throws a few things into his bag and looks at her. "Why you looking like that?"

"How he die?"

"HIV." Ann stumbles backwards but she tries to pull it together. If he's infected, what was to stop her from being positive too? "Don't look all crazy," Kali suggests, "you don't have that shit."

"How do you know?"

"Because that pussy too good that's why." He grins.

She wasn't at ease. "Kali, I'm scared."

He sighs, stops packing and pulls her toward him. "If you're really worried, we can get that thing checked out when we get back but for now we gotta bounce. Cool?" He releases her and she continues packing.

"You know, I didn't know how I was going to take it…if Jace finally died." She stuffs her colorful panties into her bag. "But now that he's gone, all I can do is smile." She demonstrates her pleasure with a grin.

"I hope you won't be that happy if something was to happen to me."

The grin is gone. "Kali, you just don't get how much I fucking love you." She never used that word before and he's off guard. "I think you believe in your mind that just because Jace had money, that he was the nigga for me. If that's what you thinking let me stop you right now. Jace was weak and if there's one thing I hate in this world, it's a weak man." She walks over to him. "But you're strong," she rubs his face, "and you're dangerous. All of the things I adore. I was born to ride with a man like you. Even if you had to convince your daughter to fake a seizure in the nail salon to make me realize it," she giggles, "believe me when I say I'm glad that you did."

Kali sees something in her eyes he never saw in another woman's before. Sure he Cave Man'd a few bitches into being with him. And yes he knew how to lay the dick like a plumber did copper pipes, but Antoinette had seen the worst of him. She'd been there when her life depended on it and everyday she woke up with a smile on her face, just because he was by her side. He didn't know if she would last much longer but for some reason, when it came to her, he was willing to try.

JAYDEN

TO THE RESCUE

I love how Sebastian drives. Safe. Secure. He's focused and moves down the road at a comfortable speed. I can go to sleep if I try. Every so often he looks at me in the rearview mirror, and I smile. When I look at the passenger seat, Luh Rod seems to be in a world of his own. He has ear buds stuffed in his ears and he's rocking to his own music. I call them Young Guns because they know how to handle themselves with weapons.

Although shit is looking up for me because my money is rolling in, and Shaggy got the death he deserved, right before we threw his body in the Anacostia River, there are still a few other things I have to handle.

I tug on the red scarf wrapped around my neck when I feel it tighten. I think I should be nervous even though I'm very calm. Too calm. Am I some sick sort of serial killer? I don't know. When we finally park, I look at the address in my hand and the number on the house. Satisfied I'm in the right place, I glide out of the truck with Sebastian and Luh Rod closely behind me.

When I reach the house, I knock once on the door and when someone answers, I knee her in the stomach forcing her to the ground. Sebastian and Luh Rod lift her up and grip her under her arms, before shoving her inside and to the sofa. She's screaming loudly and her mouth is open so wide I can see her tonsils. I close the door, walk up to her and look down at her pathetic-addict-face. Disgusted, with a clinched fist, I crash it into her jaw. Her gold wig slides backwards, her cheeks jiggle and she immediately goes silent.

As she moans I say, "A baby was born here not too long ago." She looks scared. "That baby was taken out of this house by someone you know. A friend maybe, and accomplice possibly." I focus on her face, wondering if I should finish her off or let things play out. "What do you know about it?"

I read her lips. "Oh my, God is this about Madjesty?" She wails, "I told her I didn't have anything to do with Cassius' disappearance. He's my great grandchild for heaven sake." She's weeping. "I even tried to help her find him. Did she tell you that?" She swallows her blood but it doesn't matter because another blow from me fills her mouth up again.

"Listen, bitch, Madjesty may have believed that shit you just said but I don't. Now you know where my nephew is and I'm sure of it. Either tell me where he is, or there won't be enough of you to bury. Where...is...Cassius?"

"Okay, okay," she says, her white teeth are now red. "Miss, I think there's been a mistake. You have the wrong impression about me. I don't know anything about where the baby is otherwise I would've taken her to him. Please, this is a great mistake. You gotta believe me. I loved him the moment I saw his face. It hurt me too when he was stolen."

I sigh. I hoped this situation would go better. A little easier. I look at Sebastian and Luh Rodd. "Don't let her go." I remove the scarf from around my neck, approach her and stuff it inside her mouth. Then I take the knife out of my pocket, climb on top of her and slice into her ear. I go past the cartilage and bone, until it's completely hanging off. It's a bloody mess, in the palm of my hand. She's screaming as much as she can but all I hear is a dry tone. A stuffed tone. Courtesy of the material in her mouth.

When her ear is off, I throw it in her lap and wipe my hand in her hair to get it clean. "Now you know that I'm serious. I know what kind of person you are, somebody like you raised me." Sebastian looks at me that time, although his eyes avoided mine up until this point. "Now I'm going to slice off every part of your body until you tell me exactly where my nephew is. Please know that I wouldn't come over here, until I was ready to see things through. You've been researched. I know more than you think."

Once I found out this bitch took Madjesty's baby, I contacted Kreshon and he told me where she lived. Apparently they did some surveillance on her a while back and found out she was having sex with Kali, her own son. So unless she was giving me my nephew, there was nothing this whore could tell me that I would be interested in, except the truth.

Her eyes roll around in her head. "I'm going to take this out of your mouth, but if you get too free, I'm going to pluck your eyes out next. Okay?" She nods and I remove my scarf.

"Please, don't hurt me anymore. This shit hurts so much! I'll show you exactly where he is." She weeps a little. "Just promise me you won't hurt me anymore. Please."

When we make it to a run down building in D.C. I'm sick to my stomach. Just imagining Cassius being anywhere in that place makes me ill. Sebastian holds a gun in the bottom of Bernie's back, as we shove her up three flights of stairs by force. When we finally get to the door she points and says, "He's in there."

"You want me to go in first?" Sebastian says. "I don't trust this bitch."

"We all going inside. Let's see how things pan out, "I tell him before knocking on the door.

Eventually someone responds, "Yes!"

"It's her." Bernie whispers. "She has the baby…can I go now?" Luh Rod crashes his elbow into her nose silencing her.

I cover the peephole and look at Bernie. Calmly I say, "Tell her to open the door."

In a shaky voice she says, "It's me, Arizona. Bernie. Open the door, girl. Some crazy shit happened to me and I need to talk."

"Oh shit! Who bothering you now?" Arizona pulls the door open without a dispute.

When she does, Sebastian pushes Bernie to the floor and she falls on her face, rolls over and rubs her chin. The blood from her ear trickles on the floor. Arizona tries to run into the back of the apartment but Luh Rodd catches her and hits her in the back of the head with a closed fist. He pulls her back into the living room.

"You sneaky, bitch! Niggas told me not to fuck with you and now I see why!" Arizona screams at Bernie.

"They were about to kill me." Bernie cries. "Look at my ear! I didn't have no choice!"

"Bitch, you don't have no ear there!" She yells. "And it was your idea to sell her baby the moment she came to the house. Why you acting like its all me?"

I'm so angry my skin is hot. Why would Madjesty trust this bitch? Everything about her smells foul. "Put them on the sofa." I look at Arizona. "Who else is in your house?" She doesn't respond. "If I go back there and see somebody else, I'ma have them slice out your heart."

"Nobody's back there." She says. "Just the baby."

I slowly walk down the hall and toward the door. I can't believe I can hear his voice so clearly from where I am. When I turn the knob and go inside, I don't see the baby because of all the dirty clothes and trash bags piled high on the floor. It reminds me of when we were kids and I make a promise that my nephew will never have to live like this again.

After some time, I spot a wooden crib. I walk toward it when I hear his cry. I remove a plastic bag that's inches away from his head. He could've suffocated and I would've lit this building on fire! It ain't like I didn't do it before. When I remove it, I see the cutest baby boy I've ever seen in my life. He's crying until he sees my face and I can't help but smile. Oh my God, he's perfect! He has the curliest hair and yellow skin and his eyes are so big that they look like black marbles. The wider his smile grows I see he's all gums.

Carefully I reach down and pick him up and he feels like heaven in my arms. He smells sour but I don't worry, because I'll clean him up when we get home. "It's okay, baby. I have a room all ready for you, I hope you like it." I'm thinking of the place I kicked Gucci and them out of.

With him in my arms I walk back into the living room. The two addicts look at me. I look at Sebastian and say, "Finish them." And I walk out the door and to the car, with my nephew securely in my arms.

JAYDEN
CLOSET FREAK

After getting my nephew back from that addicted monster and seeing how Sebastian handled business, I was in the mood to see about his sexy ass. Lately everything has been about work between us and although we weren't playing the way that we use to, I thought about him most of the time. After getting dressed in my sexiest black jeans and cute pink fall sweater, I walk to his mobile house. I could've gotten Metha to drive me but she bugs me out at times. Always worrying about what I'm doing and who I'm doing it with.

When I get to his house, I spray some Bvlagari perfume on my wrists and knock on his door. After about six raps, I hear some movement inside but he doesn't open the door. I go to the side of the house and try to look into the windows, but they're too far up. I can't see. So I look on the ground, find a rock and throw it at the window. I hear loud footsteps and I go to the door again. He throws it open. I focus on his lips.

"What's up, Jayden?" He's wearing grey sweatpants and his shirt is off. Those blue eyes fuck me up every time. "I'm into something right now."

I run my fingers through my hair. "I was coming to ask if you wanted to grab something to eat." I lick my lips and run my fingers over my hips. "I'm hungry…are you?"

He smirks. "You sure food is the only thing you want?"

I look at his chest and run my fingers over it. He grabs my wrist and squeezes. "Jayden, I got company. So you gotta bounce." He lets me go.

I feel like he punched me in the stomach. "W-what you mean I gotta bounce? Do you remember who the fuck I am, nigga?"

He crosses his arms over his chest. "I don't give a fuck who you are. I'm off the clock."

"So you can take my money and then treat me like shit?"

He looks angrier than I ever saw him. "When your father was alive, he hired me and my brother to look after you." My legs feel like jelly. "We use to check on the house, to make sure shit was okay like he asked. To make sure the nigga Kali wasn't after you. Jace was a straight up dude and we respect him…even to this day."

"So you were lying when we first fucked, about liking me? You were working for my father all the time?"

"Yes but I didn't know that was going to happen. Having feelings for you and all. On my dead mother who died in a lightning storm in that house over there, I never played you like that. When Jace died, me and Luh still looked after you but shit got weird after your house was broken into. That's when you came and begged me to take your paper remember? You sought out me and my brother not the other way around. And what I do on my spare time don't have nothing to do with you. If you don't want us to work together anymore just tell me now. Because believe me when I say, I don't need your money."

I still need their help but I'm so confused. Why didn't my father tell me? "I didn't say I don't want to work with you."

"Good...now you gotta go. I'm being rude to my company."

I'm so mad. Why do I feel like I want to hurt him right now? "Why are you doing this?"

He sighs. "You know what, you a cool girl, Jay. And at one point like I said, I was feeling you. So what I'm about to say is not personal. I just realized you're not somebody I want to be with in that way anymore. You don't need a nigga. You the boss, so lets keep it like that." He seen the worst side of me and now he's turned off.

"And the girl who's in your house is somebody you want to be like that with?" And then I think about all of my girls. I remember the way him and his brother be looking at them. "Wait, you not fucking one of my bitches are you?" He slams the door in my face.

———————●———————

I went to get my truck and came back to his block. I wait until the sun goes down in front of his house. Morning is around the corner now, when a short pretty white girl, with dark brown hair waltzes out of the trailer. She looks drunk and I love people that way. You always get the truth out of them. But I'm so hot I can feel the heat steam from my body. I open my truck door and rush toward her right before she enters a white Kia.

"Excuse me, can I talk to you for a second?" I ask in a really sweet voice.

She turns around and I realize she's even prettier than I thought. Fuck this bitch. "Sure, what's up?"

"Are you fucking with Sebastian?"

I focus on her lips. "Oh my, God, he's so cute but I only just met him through his grandfather. He's in town from Saudi Arabia tonight. He came by to take him back home but Sebastian doesn't want to leave his little brother. And since they have the same mother but not father, his grandfather doesn't want Luh to go." She really talking. Damn. "I was supposed to convince him to come back but I'm not sure if it worked." Suddenly she looks scared. "Wait, are you like his girlfriend or something?"

"No, and what do you mean you met him through his grandfather?" I lean in.

"His father is some type of royalty in that country."

"So you're saying he's rich?"

She laughs. "That's an understatement, if Sebastian goes home, that'll make him the only heir. He'll be a millionaire." She grins again. "Wait...who are you if you're not his girlfriend?" She seems scared. "Why are you asking so many questions?"

"Don't worry about that shit, bitch." I move closer and place my hand in her soft head. It smells like lavender. I ease my fingers through the edge and pluck a strand of hair out.

"Ouch!" She yells before I slap her in the face. Her skin reddens.

I put my hand back in her hair and pull out another strand. Instead of screaming she covers her mouth. She takes the pain like a good bitch should. "I don't know who you are but you better never let me see you around here or Sebastian again. Are we clear?"

"Yes..." she's crying, "please don't hurt me no more."

I walk away leaving her alone. If Sebastian wasn't giving me that dick nobody else was going to have it either. Besides, I just found out Sebastian is Mr. Biggs, but I'll have to let him believe I don't know it.

MADJESTY

AT THE END OF THE RAINBOW

My body roams the street but I spend most of my time in my head. I lost my son and had nightmares about how his life might end up. Will somebody kill him? Rape him? Or leave him to die? I went by Bernie's house the other day to see if there was any more news and she wouldn't answer the door. When I looked through the windows, it looked like she moved.

Since Shaggy tried to kill me I disconnected from everyone to keep them safe. My mother, sister and even my friends. Hungry and damn near broke; I went into a diner off of Martin Luther King Jr. Blvd in DC. My head is swaying a little because of the buzz I'm feeling and I have to feed my liquor. My bottle is only half full, so I know I need to come up with some cash quick before my buzz dies out for good.

After buying a glazed donut, I sit down at the table and try to force it down my throat. If it didn't sting going down and get me drunk, I found I didn't want it. Some kind of way I finish it all and decide to take a nap right here, at the table. In the restaurant. The moment I shut my eyes, I hear somebody screaming.

I look at the table across from me and this lady has nothing but hate in her eyes as she yells at some kid. "Why did you do that, huh?" Her glitter fingernails dig into the flesh of his forearm and he looks scared. In some ways, he looks like me when I was about ten years old. "That was your sisters toast not yours! I'm tired of your fat ass stealing food!"

The kid is quaking but manages to say sorry. I'm hoping that will be the end but she doesn't stop. She pushes his head into the window so hard; his cheek leaves a print on the glass. "Greedy fucking, bastard! All you do is eat me out of house and home. That's why you got three asses now! Never know when to push back!"

Not sure when I got up but when she turns around I'm in her face. "What the fuck do you want?" She asks me. "I don't have no change and even if I did, I wouldn't give it to you."

He looks more scared now that I'm here. And I swear I heard him say, "Please sit down, stay out of this." Except his mouth doesn't open.

"Why you hit him like that? He got feelings too in case you didn't know."

"Fuck are you worried about what I do to him for?" She says.

"Yeah, lil, nigga. Why you in our business?" I'm focused on her but the voice behind me causes me to turn around. When I do, I see a six foot-something man looking down at me. His baldhead seems to glow and his brown eyes darken. He throws something on the table but I keep my eyes on his. I don't want to die right here. I rather die in front of the AMTRAK train.

"I was just…"

"You were just what, punk?" He frowns. This shit won't end well, I'm positive.

"Look, I was just thinking that it was wrong for her to be hitting him like that."

"Why is how she disciplines him, any business of yours?"

"It's not." I clear my throat and my voice cracks. "I'm sorry okay?"

He backs up. "Wait, you a girl?" He looks at the lady slapper and back at me. Before I can respond he snatches off my cap, exposing my wild curly hair. If he took my pants down, it would've had the same effect on me. I'm embarrassed and feel stripped. "You over here stepping like you a nigga when you ain't nothing but a little ass bitch." He gropes his dick. "I usually fuck little things like you." *What does that mean? He fucks dogs…cats…birds?*

My mind goes back to Shaggy and I feel stiff. I feel like I'm scared all of the time. Like I can't defend myself like I use too. "If you don't care if she hit your kid, then I don't either." I try to take my cap from him but he won't let go. "Please give me my shit back."

He's talking to his girl but stops to laugh at me. "Get the fuck out of my face." He eases into the booth, taking my hat with him.

I can feel all kinds of rage brewing inside of me. I look at the lady slapper, their son and the man. Since dude is my size now because he's sitting down, I decide to go for it. While he places a forkful of spaghetti in his pie hole, I swing on him, forcing it out of his mouth. It doesn't look like it caused any damage, until I see his lip bust open and blood oozing on his jeans. I smile. Until he moves toward me like the booth is on fire.

Standing over top of me again, I brace myself for what he's about to do next. Instead of knocking me out, he takes his full hand and mushes it in my face, forcing the back of my head into the edge of the table. The pain ripples across the back of my head, from my left ear to the right. Thinking he's about to do it again, since he grabs two fistfuls of my shirt,

I kick him in his dick forcing him to let me go. He balls over and screams out in pain.

He's going to kill me now. I hop up, grab my hat, his keys and wallet, and hit it towards the door. I'm running so fast I knock over a little girl holding her mother's hand. Once outside I hit the button on his alarm and see yellow lights bling in the back of a white Mercedes.

"Bitch, I'ma kill you!" He yells coming quickly behind me. He can't get me. I can't let him get me. "I promise I'ma get you!"

Once I reach his car, I hop inside and bump the truck in front of me trying to get out of the parallel parking space. When I'm finally free, he's hanging on the driver's side door causing it to fly open. I keep my hands on the steering wheel and raise my left foot to kick him in the face. He falls in the middle of the street and I pull away from the scene, looking at him in the rearview mirror.

I'm laughing the entire way until I look to my right and see somebody staring at me from the passenger seat. He's Chinese and probably black, sporting a Mohawk. His jean jacket looks a little dirty and I figure he's trying to find money for drugs.

"What the fuck you doing in here!" I yell hitting the steering wheel, looking from him to the road ahead of me. "Who are you?"

"Who are you?" Somebody says from the backseat.

I adjust the rearview mirror and see a black girl with big hoop earrings and even larger eyes. Her hair is pulled into a ponytail and soft loose curls round out her face. Who are these people? This is my lick!

"I'm not fucking around." I yell. "Either tell me who you are, or get the fuck out of my car."

"You tell us first!" The Chinese kid says, "We were here before you were."

Not trusting them, I drive a few more miles up before pulling over and parking behind and abandoned convenience store. "Look, this is my car," I say looking at both of them." I tap the keys in the ignition. For the moment I believe the shit. "You see, I got the keys and everything."

"You must think we crazy." The dude says. "We saw the owner of this car the moment he went into the restaurant. That's how we knew we could hit this Benz."

"And we saw the same man hanging from the door before you kicked him in the face." The girl adds. *They had me.* "So who are you?" She looks at me like she doesn't trust me.

There's no use in me hiding. I might as well come out with the truth. "The nigga who owns this car hit me back at the spot. So I took the keys to his car." I'm keeping the possession of his wallet to myself. "Now since I'm driving and I don't know you niggas, I want ya'll to get out now."

"We can't leave." The girl says, "We gotta bring…"

"Shut the fuck up, Gage!" he says to her. "We don't know this chick."

How did he know I was a girl?

"I know, but if she throws us out, we won't be able to look through the car and find something useful to sell. We need the money, Spirit. We don't have a choice."

Now I'm completely interested.

"It's like this," Spirit says to me, "we have a situation back at our spot. So how about we go through this car, split what we find and part ways."

"What if I don't want to share shit with ya'll? I got the keys so that makes me in charge."

"Then I'll do whatever you want me to do." Gage responds rubbing my shoulders sexually. A sensation smacks me and for a second I lose it. But I don't want somebody like this. Even if she's pretty.

"You can take your hands off of me now." She throws herself back in her seat. "If you want a business arrangement with me, I got an even better idea."

●━━━━━━━━━━━━━━━━━━━━━━━━━━━━●

We found his address from a piece of mail in his glove compartment. He's stupid. He lives in a nice community, in a house somewhere in Bowie Maryland. Spirit looked at the GPS and was able to direct us here. Once we make it into his house, I park and we jump out. Using the keys I open the door and they're right behind me. I know we don't have much time because he'll be on his way soon. I figure since he has to call the police, make a report and call a ride, we have at least twenty minutes to spare. Minimum.

Once we arrive at the door Spirit says, "Wait a second, let me check to make sure nobody is here." He runs through the house and from the back he yells, "We good. Let's hurry up, grab what we can and get the fuck out of here."

I rush to the bedroom, find a pillowcase and stuff everything I can inside. After looking around, I steal a Rolex watch, a gold chain and five one hundred dollar bills. I'd pay to see the look on his face when he comes back to find all his shit gone. While I look for things I can sell, Spirit and Gage grab food and raid the medicine cabinets. What's up with them?

Once we are loaded up, we walk into the living room and a beautiful tall black girl is staring at us. She's wearing a navy blue suit, which shows her curves despite being professional. I know this bitch is going to call the police. "So it's like that huh?" She asks, her gold purse drops to the floor. It thumps loudly. "I been calling him all day and it's like this?"

Silence.

"I see he gave you his car," she points toward the window, "so he must really not give a fuck about me no more."

"I don't know what you..." Gage says, the cans in the pillowcase she's holding clank against each other.

"Ain't no use in you lying," she cries, interrupting her, "I'm just disappointed. I figured he'd at least be man enough to tell me he's leaving me to my face." She wipes the snot from her nose but a strand falls over her lips and doesn't break. "So what did he do, pay ya'll?"

I'm stuck but luckily Spirit is on it. "Yeah, Grant sent us," he continues, remembering the name on the mail we found in the car. "Matta fact when we left him in the restaurant, he was with his kid's mother."

Her eyes widen and she stumbles back. "So those *are* his kids!" She cries. "He spent all night telling me that the bitch was lying when she called here last night asking for child support! He claimed that she was just another groupie trying to put kids on him, since he's lead in a popular Go-Go band. I should've known after all of the things she knew about me, that he was lying. I feel so stupid!" She stomps in place. "So used!" She picks up her purse and throws her body into the green velvet sofa. "I fucking hate him! And I hate me, for giving him my heart."

When she cries hysterically, Gage places her pillowcase on the table, jogs to the kitchen and returns with a bottle of water. She's nurturing and I can't help but like her. She hands the water to her and rubs her back. "Please don't cry. I don't like it when women cry over men," tears roll down her face and I wonder what kind of evil went on in her life. "Don't worry about him, he's a dog anyway. Trust me, any man who cheats on you doesn't deserve your soul."

"You should take your own advice." Spirit says. Gage frowns.

The woman looks at Gage and smiles through her pain. "You're so young to be so wise." She touches her hand. "Thank you for the water."

This is all well and good, but the only thing on my mind is getting out of here before this nigga comes back.

"And don't worry, I know what I have to do. You're right, he doesn't deserve me. He doesn't deserve anyone." She looks at Spirit and me. "I know he sent you for his clothes, but did he tell you about the money he has stashed under the floor in my laundry room? I bet he didn't." *Fuck no.* "Take that too."

We waste no time rushing toward the laundry room. I look at the floor and immediately see a tile out of place. We lift it up and find a Gucci box full of money. "Wow," Spirit says, "we haven't had a come up like this since never."

"We definitely going to be able to get the stuff for Fierce now." Gage adds.

He shoots her a glare and then looks at me. "Not in front of her."

Although we're not friends, I feel like an outsider. "Look, I'm tired of you keep hushing her every time she talks to me. I'm not interested in what ya'll got going on anyway. I got business of my own. We can part ways and be done with it."

"I'm sorry, it's not like that. It's just that…we been burned before by letting people into our circle."

"I'm not people and like I said I got my own shit. So ya'll go your way, and I'll go mine."

We're just about to leave until I hear a familiar voice. *"How did my car get here?"* He says anxiously.

"Don't play games. I already know about everything and I know you sent them to help you move out. It's cool though because I'm not taking it anymore. They had your keys and your car."

"I don't know what the fuck you talking about. All I want to know is how my car got here."

The next thing I hear caused us all to jump. It was the sound of two gunshots followed by two thuds and then complete silence.

LONNIE J
PUSSY TRAP

Lonnie J parks his car in front of his tree-lined house in Maryland. His wife and daughter were probably inside waiting on him and he's guilt ridden. He never wanted to cheat and he definitely didn't think it would be on a regular basis, but there he was with the scent of Harmony Phillips still on his body in his driveway. He'd been fucking her on and off since they first met and he couldn't get over how flexible she was in the bedroom. The biggest disaster was that he'd been married for only three months and she was a stay at home mom, taking care of their seven year old daughter who was stricken with diabetes.

He sighs and pops open the ashtray in his car. He slides on his wedding ring and grabs the two shopping bags in the backseat. Once he's to the house, the alarm chimes. He opens the door and notices its extra silent. That is until he hears a blood-curdling scream. "Lonnie J, where have you been? I been calling you all day!" His wife yells from the back of the house. "Leila just went into insulin shock."

He drops the bags on the floor and rushes to the back of the house. When he makes it to his daughter's room, he sees her weak body. "You were supposed to bring the insulin pump home! Why didn't you?" She's sobbing.

Because he was fucking with Harmony but he couldn't tell her that though. It would kill her. "I'm sorry, baby. I…I got caught up at work," he lies. "Did you call 911?"

"They're on their way but I'm so scared!"

"Don't worry, baby. I got an idea, she can use mine!" Lonnie J who also suffers from diabetes runs to the bathroom to get his kit. And then he remembers, he hadn't picked up his prescription either, which includes new needles. Since he gave one to himself earlier, he takes it out of the trashcan and washes it off. Then he grabs a bottle of insulin and with it firmly in his hand; he scampers back to his daughter's room. He sets up the insulin and gives her what she needs through her veins. His wife is angry but relieved, had he not finally showed up, she would've lost her mind. The ambulance comes later, checks her levels and asks the family if they want her to go to the hospital even though she's fine.

There insurance coverage is low and he can't afford the trip so they decline. While she recuperates in bed, he grabs the prescriptions and returns home. When he walks into the room, his wife is on the floor drinking coffee out of a red mug.

"Here it is right here." He raises the white bag and places it on the table next to her bed. Then he eases on the floor and sits next to her. His wife places her head in his lap. "I'm so sorry, baby. I…I fucked up majorly." He rubs her hair as she looks at her sleeping daughter in the bed.

"I know you're busy, honey." She wipes her tears. "I really do. You work hard for us and because of it, I'm able to stay home and take care of our sick child. But you can never let us down like that again. I almost lost the most important person in the world to me, next to you. If it happens again, I will leave you for good. My ex-husband proposes to me everyday and he will jump at the opportunity to take care of us." That comment sends him over the edge. Her connection with her ex-husband was one of the reasons he fucked Harmony to begin with. "Never again, Lonnie J."

He doesn't respond. He makes a firm decision at that moment to leave Harmony alone. And it is a pledge he vows to keep.

●━━━━━━━━━━━━━━━━━━━━━━━━━━━●

A Month Later

Every muscle in Lonnie J's body aches because he worked eighteen hours straight painting rehabilitated houses. When he opens the door to his house, he can tell something is off. He walks toward the back. "Janelle," he calls for his wife, "Leila!" He yells for his daughter. He doesn't get any answers. "What the fuck is going on?" He says to himself.

When he walks into the kitchen to grab a beer and opens the refrigerator, he sees a note on top of a six-pack of Budweiser. The letter says, 'I KNEW YOU'D FIND ME HERE'. He smiles, takes it out and closes the refrigerator door. With the beer in his hand, he sits down and drinks half of it before even reading it.

Lonnie J,

I wanted to murder you. That's what I told my mother I would do. But then I knew the thought of losing us and living with what you did would hurt even more. Before you lie to me, just know that I know it was you. You were the only man I'd ever been with since my divorce, the only man I wanted to be with.

And for my loyalty, my daughter is now infected with HIV. I haven't even gotten myself checked yet. I hate you.

The letter drops out of his hand and falls to the kitchen floor. He can't catch his breath. He looks down and reads the rest from afar.

That needle you used on her was infected with the virus. And for that you are as low as they come. I've taken your revolver with me. Stay the fuck away from me and her or I will kill you.
Your Possible Murderer

Lonnie J throws the beer down on the table, the suds from the can falls out and dampens the letter. How could she be infected? How could he be infected? Sure he fucked Harmony raw but she was the first person he stepped out with since he'd been married. Originally he wasn't going to sleep with her at all. All he wanted to do was give her a bite to eat and drop her off home. He even told her he wasn't interested when she tried to give him some pussy the first time he met her. But soon, like all men, he fell victim to her seduction. He knew nothing about her...outside of her name. He didn't even know where she lived. But he would find her before it was all over and it wouldn't be nice.

JAYDEN
ROCK A BYE NEPHEW

"Passion, open this fucking door!" My fist bangs so many times against the wood, my knuckles are throbbing and red. "We got a job tonight and I need you to get the girls ready." All this bitch does now is wake up and get high before going back to sleep. The only reason I didn't throw her out was because Olive begged me not too and her pussy still works.

"She not coming out," Hadiya says walking behind me, "Passion has been out of it for a while, Jayden." Her voice is soft but confident and I can hear it thanks to the aids I'm wearing. "You don't have to keep asking her to do something she obviously doesn't want to do. Let me get the girls ready, since all I do is watch the baby now anyway. I don't mind doing a little extra around here."

I back away from the door but I continue to stare it down like it's her face. I can't wait to see this bitch. And since she wants to stay in the bed and cry like a whore, I'll treat her like one by putting her back on the books and giving her the worst jobs.

Frustrated, I turn around and face Hadiya. "Okay, I'ma let you get the girls together. That'll be your job for now on but never at the expense of my nephew. When I'm not here to take care of him, he comes first. If I see a single hair rubbed off the back of his head because you kept him in the crib too long, or if he has anything resembling a diaper rash, I'm going to hurt you. Now are you sure you want to do this?"

She jumps in place and claps her hands. "Yes! And I won't let you down I promise."

"I know you won't." I roll my eyes. Everything is so ridiculous around here now.

"But I have one question, can you please let the girls know I'm in charge? Because If you don't they'll never listen to me. You see how Gucci and them treat Passion around here. They'll only do me worse since they think I'm the new girl on the block."

Although she's right, I hate that I have to do this right now. Why can't she use her people skills? I push past her and go downstairs and in my loudest voice available yell, "Bitches, get down here now!"

Within a minute I'm looking at all of my girls. "Passion is not on house duty anymore. She not feeling well and won't be working with you tonight or helping you get ready from here on out."

"Humph," Gucci starts filing her nails, "If you ask me, she ain't been feeling well for the past few days. Why you just finding out now?"

I whip my head in her direction. "I didn't ask you shit now did I, bitch?" Everyone gasps and she drops her file. I focus on everyone. "Like I was saying, Passion is not feeling well, and because of it, Hadiya is now in charge."

"I knew that bitch would suck herself into position sooner or later." Foxie says. "Congratulations, ass kisser, you've made it to the major leagues."

Hadiyah steps close to her. "So what you mad it's me and not you?"

"First of all you better get out of my face, bitch." Hadiya backs up. "Second of all I never wanted the fucking position of babysitter. But everyone knew you would, boot licker."

"Call it what you want but you will give her your respect." I say. "As a matter of fact, make it the same respect you give me if not more."

Gucci laughs and Olive shakes her head. I hate that she may have been right all along about letting the girls think we are friends. I'm starting to realize they won't respect me until I give them a reason and I might have to make a few examples in the process.

"If that bitch comes near my room, I'm going the fuck off." Foxie promises. "That's all I'm saying, Jayden. No disrespect to you, but this Indian has been in my shit ever since she joined the squad. On my cousin, I'm not having it no more."

I walk over to her. "What did you just say?" She steps back. "Don't say it under your breath, say it to my face."

"I didn't say nothing directly to you, Jayden." She hesitates. "I just don't like that bitch that's all."

"Then you better learn too. Matta fact you better learn to love her!" I look at all of them. "I'm tired of the fighting and shit going on around here. At some point ya'll gonna realize that everybody in here selling pussy and if there's any hang ups about it, the door is behind you. I've been real lax with ya'll but I also have the ability to snap." I look at Hadiya. "Make sure the lineup for tonight is ready. If they not, I'm holding you accountable."

———————————————————

I'm sitting in a chair in my bedroom rocking the baby, when my mother comes home. I'm so mad, I squeeze the baby too tight and he whines. I loosen up my grip. I haven't seen her in forever. And now she shows up drunk? And what was up with her fat ass stomach? I look at her and back at the baby whose gripping my index finger. She steps into the room quietly and looks down at me. The room lights up with the scent of liquor and shit.

"Whose baby?" She points at him. She's swerving a little.

"His name is Cassius." I say calmly. I don't want to flex on her with the baby in my arms.

She approaches us and the baby frowns. "I mean who does he belong to?"

I look her square in the eyes. "He belongs to me."

The moment she stands over us, her body trembles. "What you doing with Madjesty's baby?" How the fuck does she know he's hers? "Why is he here?"

I stand up and yell, "Hadiya!" The baby cries when I startle him but when she comes inside, I hand him over to her. "Its time to feed him, when you're done, take him to his room so he can get some sleep."

"No problem. Do you need anything?"

"No, just keep an eye on him. Yesterday you fed him without burping him and he had vomit on his cheeks." Hadiya reddens. "Don't let it happen again."

When she's gone Harmony says, "What are you doing with Madjesty's baby? I might be a drunk but I know my offspring when I see it."

I walk up to her. And she steps back but I grab her. To my surprise my hand wraps around her forearm and my fingers touch each other. She's so skinny its foolish. "You are so foul, Harmony. I knew you didn't give a fuck about nobody but yourself, but you outdid yourself this time."

"So I'm Harmony now? Not your mother anymore?"

"How could you steal my money and show your face here, when you knew what the cash was for? I did nothing but try to love you and it was all for nothing."

She laughs at me. "I can show my face here as much as I want because unless you have forgotten, this is my house." She tries to walk away but I snatch her back.

When she calls herself fighting me, I'm surprised at how weak she is. I slap her in the face and across the neck and her blows feel like kisses. It's like I'm overpowering a child. I have her up against the wall and she can't move when she tries. If only I realized I had this much power as a kid, I would've never let her hurt me. "Listen and listen good, you will never take advantage of me again. Ever. Do you hear what I'm saying?"

"Are you going to let me go?"

"I need you to hear what the fuck I am saying. You don't want me to love you anymore, so I won't." She seems sad. "I can't forgive you for what you've done and if you continue to fuck with me, I might hurt you."

She doesn't respond because when I look behind her, in the doorway are cops. Four of them to be exact and I think they're here for me. Because of what I did to Bernie and her friend Arizona. Who the fuck snitched? Was it Sebastian? Or Luh Rod? My thoughts are all over the place until I remember the baby. Technically my mother isn't supposed to be around small children after fucking the boy in the bushes. Did they see the baby? My mind is all over the place until the Asian cop walks up to my mother and grabs the handcuffs from his pants, "Harmony Phillips, you are under arrest."

She backs up and her eye sockets stretch open. "For what?" She looks at all of them. "What did I do?"

"For the solicitation of porn of a minor."

They focus on me. "Young lady, do you have anybody who can stay here with you?" I'm stuck. This is the moment I feared where I would be ripped from my home. I don't want to live in some group home or be thrown into foster care. I can take care of myself. I always have. And what about my nephew? Where is he going to go?

"Young lady, do you have someone who can stay here?"

I'm about to lose it until Olive walks in and says, "I'm twenty and I can stay here with her." It's not until that moment that I breathe.

THIRTEEN FLAVORS
PROJECT SCHOOL FREAK

Greg wipes his forehead with the red and white doo rag in his lap for the tenth time, since he left the house thirty minutes ago. His white face is flushed and he's extremely anxious. He didn't know what was in store for him, but he was certain after listening to his friends who used Jayden's services on a regular, that it would be well worth the money. Normally he dumpster dived so this was a treat.

All he was told by the girl known as O, who picked up his money, was to drive past Harry Truman middle school at exactly 12:00pm. He's exhausted but the excitement wouldn't allow him to get a minute sleep the night before. When he reaches the middle school, he's thrown off when he sees two girls leaning on the fence and kissing each other in navy blue school uniforms.

Tywanda's tongue is dipped into Foxie's mouth as she pulls her closer to her body. Foxie appears unable to hold back, as she snakes her hand under Tywanda's pleated dress. And Tywanda's arms are draped over Foxie's back. Greg almost crashes when he sees the peach fuzz on Tywanda's pussy. Although his dick stands at full attention in his khaki's, he manages to pull himself together so he can enjoy the show. After all, he paid top bucks for the experience and didn't want it going to waste. When he pulls up alongside of them, he rolls down his window and says, "You girls need a ride?"

Tywanda, whose tongue is still in Foxie's mouth looks at him and says, "I'm not supposed to ride with strangers. How do I know you won't hurt us?" She's in full character.

He pops the locks, pushes the passenger door open and says, "Get in." Although the fantasy was just as he imagined, he didn't want to misspend too much time on wordplay either.

Tywanda and Foxie hold hands as they ease into his car. Within five minutes, he's parked behind a grocery store, with his pants hanging down at his knees. Tywanda is hovering over his lap, kissing him deeply in the mouth, while Foxie has her lips wrapped around the length of his dick.

Greg grips Tywanda's meaty ass cheeks as she suckles his tongue. She's a hard-worker but she loves to fuck too. He can't believe his dream is finally coming true and is so real. When he was growing up, bitches like Tywanda and Foxie never gave him the time of day. Now, he's sitting in his car with two baby-faced whores and reliving his schoolyard dreams.

Since Foxie is sucking his dick, Tywanda's ass rests on the top of her head and the syrup from her pussy falls into her hair. She would tell the bitch about herself later but knew starting something with Tywanda now could start a fight. Besides, Tywanda was 'Team Jayden' and would tell everything she did.

Feeling like he's about to cum, Greg pushes Foxie out of the way. The edge of the steering wheel bangs her in the face and he could care less. He wants to be inside of Tywanda for this part of the game. Tywanda's wet minty kisses has him geeking and he can no longer wait.

While they do their thing, Foxie sits in the passenger seat with her arms crossed over her chest in brat-like fashion. She hates how Tywanda has full use of each ass cheek while she, on the other hand, would be lucky if she could swirl her waist. Yes she could suck the veins out of a dick, but when it came to fucking, outside of Passion, Tywanda was Queen Pussy.

"Fuck, you for feeling so good!" Greg proclaims digging into her tightness.

He looks over at Foxie who seems off the job. Since he paid for them both he says, "Suck my chest or something. Make yourself useful."

Her eyebrows rise. "What? I'm not doing that nasty shit." She says, as if she didn't do worse.

Tywanda breaks her kiss and gives her 'The Look'. Foxie showed her ass on a job before which is why she hated that Greg requested them together. She wants to be done with this shit so she can collect her share of the money when she goes back home and go about her business. But the jealous look in Foxie's eyes tells her relief may be a long time coming.

Realizing Foxie isn't being a team player; Tywanda tightens her cave over School Freak's dick and massages him with her jelly walls. His mouth opens and she nibbles on the side of his neck giving him an extra treat. She can tell by the pulsation in his dick that he's almost there. If she keeps this up, they'll be home by the afternoon.

On the verge of busting, he opens his eyes and looks into her brown ones. He's almost there so he extends his hand to Foxie again, who looks like a pouty teenager instead of the slut he paid for. Why hadn't she sucked his hairy nipples like he asked?

Realizing all is about to be lost, Tywanda pulls his face to hers and squirms her tongue into his mouth and gives him the whirlwind experience. In less than twenty seconds, it's all over. He splashes his glue into her body. Since the rules say once you bust you're done, his experience is officially over.

"Shit!" He yells, holding her waist. "That shit was so fucking good."

"Glad you liked it, but how about you prove it to me by giving me a little extra." She extends her hand and wiggles her fingers.

He winks at her, reaches into his pocket and removes his wallet. Then he hands her one hundred dollars, which she stuffs into the pocket of her pink bra. Now that she's been blessed with a few extra dollars, Foxie looks at her with a hung jaw. Tywanda pushes her mouth back in place. "You better handle that thing before it falls off and you lose it."

Foxie just knew Tywanda was going to split the money but outside of a few licks on his nuts, she didn't fulfill her obligation. It was Tywanda who deserved Most Valuable Team Player.

They are just about to get out of the car until Greg says, "The other girl is cheaper, but you are clearly better." Tywanda lifts off of him and pulls down her dress. She sits in Foxie's lap and she's even more pissed now. She doesn't want that stingy bitch anywhere on her.

"What girl?"

"I think her name is Gucci or something. She has a pretty face but she's not about her business like you and your boss. I should've stuck to the professionals."

Tywanda looks at Foxie and shakes her head; she can't wait to give Jayden the news.

HARMONY
LOCK DOWN

This metal bed is cold under me as my new view is changed from the inside of a luxurious mansion to an evil place with bars. I can't believe what they're charging me with. I can't believe they think I'd actually be that dumb. Turns out the electrician who I paid to install cameras in my home, for my own sneaky purposes, broke into my house and took the tapes. Now I know who robbed us but when I try to tell the detectives they aren't listening. What's fucked up is when he first installed the cameras I didn't have the money to pay him. But when he came back and Irma was there, he got his cash so our debt was settled. What was his thing now?

Don't get me wrong, I'm half guilty. Yes I sold the sex tapes of me, Jace and a few random men having sex in the house to a porn company. But I was on probation for fucking the boy in the bushes outside of my house and would've never sold the tape of one of my daughters raping the other that the detective claimed. I was thrown back when I envisioned Madjesty on top of Jayden. I'm not the best mother but I would never want either of them to go through rape, like I went through.

Tired of being ignored, I get up and move to the bars. I place my hands on them and stick my face through the crack to look down the hall. "Can someone please let me use the bathroom?! I think I gotta shit in here!"

"Bitch, shut the fuck up," one of the guards says, "you been running your mouth nonstop since you got here." She's a slender bitch with a lot of mouth and no hair and I guess something to prove.

"Well unless you want me to shit on these floors, you better open this gate. I'm a human being you know...not an animal."

"If you shit on the floors while I'm in here, I'ma kick your head off your shoulders," my cellmate says. The dark-skin pretty chick is evil, breathes too hard and seems mad at me for no apparent reason. I want out of here.

With my hands back on the bars again I yell, "Let me out of here! Please! I gotta go to the bathroom."

When the CO stands up, she's stomping quickly in my direction with her club swinging from her hand. I know her name is Tamira after hearing it earlier today. When I see her face, I back up but it doesn't stop her from reaching in, snatching me by the face and banging it against the bars. My forehead accepts a wicket blow and I feel off balance. "Listen bitch, I got a lot going on today and anybody who sold porn of their daughters raping each other is the least of my worries. Now either you shut the fuck up or I'ma have somebody hurt you."

"But I didn't do it." I whisper, as the dirty bars press against my lips. My teeth feel like they're being pushed backwards. "I think it was the electrician, he's the only one who knew about the cameras."

"So you admit to installing cameras in your daughters' room?" I nod. She grips me tighter. "You a sick bitch. Now either shut the fuck up or I'm going to put this stick in your mouth." She pushes me back and I go flying into the cell and against my mate.

Oh...oh, there's going to be a problem now. Just as I suspect my cellmate takes her fist and hits me square in the middle of my back. A tingly sensation runs down my tailbone like I'm having an epidural and enters the back of my legs. I turn over preparing to fight her but she stomps on my face with the bottom of her shoe before she bends down and grips a fistful of my hair. When I look up I see the guard smiling and its clear she won't help me out.

I know I'm about to die until my cellmate says, "Oh shit, what's going on with you." She backs up and looks down at me.

"You're beating my ass! That's what!" I yell.

She backs further away and when I place my hand between my legs, I feel blood oozing everywhere. And then I smile. She successfully beat the baby out of me. I guess going to jail was a good idea after all.

●━━━━━━━━━━━━━━━━━━━━━━━━━●

Once again I'm in my favorite place, the hospital. My wrist is chained to the bed and I can barely move. I'm angry. I'm mad. Until a doctor walks in with the baby I spit out of my pussy. "Hi, I'm doctor Shakia Bright. I know you want to see your precious child." She hands him to me. He's a cute little boy with a button for a dick and a pudgy navel.

"We can't let you keep him too long." The doctor says, "He's a very sickly child."

I look at the white lady with the piercing blue eyes. She's the first kind person I'd seen since being arrested. A little boy is all I ever wanted and I know I don't deserve the moment. I don't deserve him. I didn't even take care of the twins. I need a drink. Badly. "Please, let me keep him for a few more seconds."

She looks like she wants to dispute but I beg her with my eyes. She nods and I say, "Thank you." I really mean it.

I run my hand softly over his hair and kiss him gently on the forehead. When I remove my lips, you would've thought I was about to eat his face off, the way she snatches the baby out of my arm. I'm quiet. I'm broken. I'm hurt.

After he's taken from me and placed into a glass box, I roll over and cry. "Do you have anyone to care for the child? Any next of kin?" The doctor asks. *Fuck you.* "Mam, I know this hurts but with you being incarcerated, if your baby makes it, we need to know what you want done with him."

I think of Jayden and the whorehouse she's running out of Concord Manor. I think about my sisters and how they'd probably fry him before giving him any love. I think about how I don't even know who the father is. "No. I don't have any family. If he makes it, I'll put him up for adoption."

She gasps. "Miss, are you sure? As sickly as he is, even if he survives, he'll need the love of his family to pull through."

I can't hear her anymore. There's one question I must know. "Is he HIV positive?"

"Yes." She says softly. I weep. "Mam, are you sure about adoption?"

I fucked up his world before it even has a chance to begin. I won't hurt him further by being his mother. "Yes, I am."

She shakes her head and says, "If you say so. I'll bring in the paperwork later."

I plummet deeper into depression with the birth of my son. So deep that I can see hell. I can touch it if I try hard enough. Life for me is over and I welcome the day when I don't have to breathe anymore. I hope it comes sooner than later.

MADJESTY
THE HOLE

This place is dark and cool. Not much light is here with the exception of the candles on the opposite wall from us. I'm sitting on the floor, leaning up against the wall with a box of shrimp fried rice in my hand. Spirit is to my left and Gage is to my right and they're tearing into the chicken wings.

Since I got up with them we spent a lot of time in this abandoned building in D.C. that they called The Hole. We stayed here even though after we left Mr. Mercedes house, we were up about two thousand dollars apiece. But I didn't want to give anybody my money for a hotel room because right now all I wanted to do was drink and stack my paper. In case I found my baby and had to take care of him.

It's fucked up how we came up on the money, by being in the presence of a murder-suicide but it wasn't like we pulled the trigger. We just made the best of a tragic situation. After his girlfriend killed Mr. Mercedes, right before she killed herself, we wiped the house and the car down of our fingerprints and decided to get away together. We'd been together ever since.

Spirit and Gage were the ones who told me about The Hole and tonight I would be meeting the rest of their friends. They're real hush-hush about their circle and I think most of them are on the run from something or somebody. For instance I found out that Gage hitchhiked from New York to be with her boyfriend Wicked. Although Gage's face lights up whenever she talks about him, it's obvious that Spirit doesn't fuck with the relationship. After we shared a bottle of henny, I found out why one night.

We were sitting in a diner, busted when Spirit said, "Gage, Wicked is my boy, but you know he never gonna do you right. He treats you like shit and I know he hit you before."

"That's a lie."

"You know it's not. Plus he fucked with everybody in the family and he does it in your face at that." Spirit continued. I wasn't sure if he liked her for himself, or if he just wanted her away from Wicked. "Stop taking up for him. It's not necessary when you're with me."

"You always saying stuff like that but you not the one who's with him. I love him, Spirit, and if you're my friend you're going to have to respect that. He makes me happy and I'm in D.C., because he brought me here. Had it not been for him, I would've never met you." She paused, drinking her Coke. "Don't make me choose between you and him because it won't be you."

Spirit seemed sad. "I would never do that to you. You're the closest person to me in the family and I don't want to see you hurt. And the nigga Wicked will hurt you."

I found out that day that family to them was the same thing as a gang to me. Except they had a father, a mother and kids, which I think is way too weird. But since I didn't have a life anymore, I had time on my hands to humor them. To see what they were about.

That day at the diner didn't change how Gage felt about Wicked, but it did give me an idea of what I was in store for. It's also the reason I'm nervous about meeting the rest of the crew tonight.

After Spirit and Gage came back with the money we'd stolen from Mr. Mercedes, they were able to buy antibiotics from a place in Virginia for Fierce, one of their members who was sickly. The rest of the family made the trip to Virginia to get the stuff and Spirit and Gage hung back with me. Their crew had been gone for four days and I wasn't sure how I felt about them coming back and seeing me in their spot.

"I see you look nervous," Spirit says, slapping his hand on my shoulder. "You gonna love the family though. We wouldn't have you here if we thought otherwise."

"He's right, just remember to never, ever, ask people about their past unless they're ready to tell you on their own. We're here because we have a life we want to run away from. Things that haunt us in our sleep." She cries again. Why is she always crying? "That's why we adopted new names and abandoned our old ones." She wipes her tears away and grabs a chicken wing.

"How do you want us to refer to you?" Spirit asks. "A bitch or nigga?"

"I'm a nigga, so I'd prefer to keep it like that."

"You got it." He laughs.

"Ok, so what name you gonna go by?" Gage says.

I think about it for a few seconds. There's something fly about leaving the past in the past and starting all over. But I think my real name reflects how I feel and where I am in my life. I haven't slept in a bed in weeks; I don't have a home and the only thing that stays fresh on me are my sneaks and my underwear. I'm angry all the time. "Mad." I nod. "I think I'm keeping Mad."

"If you like it I love it." Spirit says.

━━

We just cracked opened another bottle of Hennessy when Wicked, White Boy, Fierce, Daze and Killer walk in with a white girl who seems out of place. She has red hair and she's wearing a white dress that looks like she just left the prom. A little dizzy, I use the wall to stand up, brush off the back of my pants and ready myself to greet the squad. They embrace Gage and Spirit without acknowledging me. It's cool though.

When they're done Spirit says, "Wicked, I want you to meet one of the realest niggas I know." He walks him over to me and I reach out to shake his hand. He doesn't accept.

Wicked is a white boy with a baldhead and dark gray eyes. "Cool tat." He says pointing to my right hand. "Who's Cassius?"

"My son." I look down at the tattoo which reads, '*Cassius Phillips Lost But Soon Found*'.

"That's hot." He doesn't ask more questions about him. "I heard it's because of you, we had money to help our friend." He pulls over another kid who's very scrawny. "This man right here." He taps him on the back. "Fierce, say hi to the person responsible for saving your life."

Fierce seems shy but he manages a, "Hi," along with a weak wave. He's a black kid who looks timid.

"What it is," I say waiting for the rest of the introductions. I pull my cap over my eyes.

Spirit continues, "This is White Boy," when a black kid as dark as an Opal Stone steps up I'm thrown off. "But we call him WB."

"Don't worry about it, buddy." He laughs I guess picking up on my facial expression. "I get that most times when people meet me. Since I'm extra dark and I tell people my name is White Boy, I always throw them off." His energy is infectious and I like him immediately.

"Now this is our father, Daze." Spirit continues. A black teenager steps up and he looks a little older than everybody else.

"Welcome." He says to me, although I don't believe he means it. "This is the mother of our family, her name is Killer." Killer is a beautiful light skin girl with heroin tracks up and down her body...not just her arms. "She's the love of my life," and he points a finger into my chest, "and she's off limits."

I step back and all of them hang against the walls looking at me. I'm sipping some Hennessey until I see Gage's face. She's focused on her boyfriend Wicked who is in another world with his new friend. "Who's the white girl?" Spirit asks. "She hasn't been introduced yet." Wicked's arm hangs over her neck and he's whispering in her ear.

"My bad," he says with a smile, "we found this beauty at the train station on the way back. She was alone and crying after her fiance' stood her up at the alter. We took a vote and everybody agrees. We like her so we'll keep her." Gage is standing behind me and I hear her crying softly. Not caring about his girlfriend's feelings, he claps his hands together. "Since we got the formalities out the way, let's party."

An hour later there was weed, liquor and other drugs I stayed away from circling around The Hole. Everybody seems lighter and I feel like I'm in a different world. They told me that they only use the building on certain days, because the police usually run them out every chance they get. When I asked where they go during the times they can't stay there, Spirit's response throws me off.

"Underground. We call it the Catacombs."

●━━━━━━━━━━━━━━━━━━━━━━━━━━●

When I wake up my head is banging. I feel like its about to explode and I think once again, I'd overdone it. When I look around I see every-body is still asleep. Since I don't know where the bathroom is, I grab my Jordans and put them on. I don't care how long I've gone without taking a shower, when it comes to keeping my tennis shoes and my underwear fresh, I don't fuck around. When I'm done, I stand up to try and find a bathroom. Once on my feet, I see the white girl with the red hair laying on the floor, with blood all over her dress and face. Her legs are wide open along with her eyes. She's as dead as MC Hammer pants.

"Spirit." I say in a low voice. He doesn't move. "Yo, Spirit, get the fuck up."

He finally shifts and when he does, I point in the direction of the girl. "What the fuck!" he says scrambling to get off the floor.

His response wakes up everyone else and they all scream after seeing her body. Daze walks up to her, places his hand on her neck and says what we already know. "She's not breathing." He looks at all of us and shakes his head but then his eyes rests back on me.

He walks to my direction and says, "What's that on your shirt?"

"What?" I look down and I see blood all over my hands and clothes. "Wait a minute…"

"What you do to her, man?" he looks like he wants to hit me.

"I…I don't know." I wasn't even interested in her.

"What do you mean you don't know?" He persists. "She's dead and you have blood all over your clothes." This has happened to me before. All I can think is damn; I picked a hell of a time to go into the Drunk Zone.

GUCCI
CAUGHT UP

Gucci gropes her boyfriend's dick when he pulls up on the side of Concord Manor. She just finished tonguing his asshole, while he jerked off in the back of his car after a movie. He parks. "You are so fucking sexy. You know that's how you got me, with that pretty ass face of yours," Tito says to her. "Your pussy is good but when I look into them eyes, my dick gets hard every time."

She blushes. "Thank you, baby, whatever I can do to keep you I'm on it."

"I don't think you can take all the credit for that, your mother had something to do with it too." He pauses and rubs her hair. "So when we gonna get that place we talked about, Gucci?" He strokes the side of her face. "I'm tired of having to share you with this bitch." He nods at the house. Although Tito wants to live with Gucci, it's not because he loves her. She's been tricking out on him since they first got together.

"I'm working on it right now, trust me. The moment I get a few more of her clients, we're out of here." She kisses him on the lips and suckles his tongue like a lollipop. "And then we'll get to have the life we always wanted. And maybe even a baby." Yeah right, bitch. He thinks.

While she talks to her boyfriend in the car, Sugar passes to approach Concord Manor. She goes to the door, takes a deep breath and knocks twice. She's been worried sick since no one has been able to get a hold of Madjesty. It doesn't take long for a girl to open the door that she recognizes from school. "Ain't your name Passion?" She points. "I think we go to high school together."

Passion rubs her arms rapidly like its freezing. "So...who's asking?"

Sugar senses her attitude and backs down on the pleasantries. "I'm sorry, my name is Sugar. And I'm looking for Madjesty, is she here? Or has anyone inside heard from her?"

Passion grows angry. Madjesty was the love of her life and since she'd been rejected recently, she plummeted into drugs. So a bitch coming to the house asking where she was did nothing but worsen her mood. "What do you want with Madjesty?" She looks the pretty girl with the red glasses over. Madjesty would fuck her for sure. She thought.

"I'm one of her best friends and the last time I saw her, some guy name Shaggy was trying to kill her. And I really want to make sure she's okay." Passion shivers upon hearing the news, she has no idea the Jayden used a calculator for the situation. In other words, the problem was already solved. "Don't worry," Sugar responds, seeing her body language change, "we were able to hold him off but he got away before the cops came. He could be anywhere which is why we're scared for Madjesty."

Her body relaxes. "I see," she sighs, "I don't know where Madjesty is." Her voice lowers. "I wish I did though." She looks behind her, steps out and closes the door. She doesn't see Gucci approaching before she makes her next statement. "If you find Madjesty tell her that her sister has her son. And she says as long as she has him, she'll never see him again."

Sugar's mouth drops. "Are you serious? Can I see him?"

Gucci hides in the bushes to ear hustle some more.

"I'm very serious and you can't see the kid. I would tell her myself but Mad hasn't come back here since I last saw her a while ago. But please get the message to her. And if you find her, tell her I still love her too." Sugar didn't know about all of that, but if she found Madjesty, some of her message would get to her. She had what folks called, selective memory.

When Sugar moves to her car, she sees Gucci in the bushes and smiles. Although Gucci gives her a grin, she can't wait to let Jayden know that her precious little two-faced friend Passion has finally stabbed her in the back.

●━━━━━━━━━━━━━━━━━━━━━━━━━━━━●

Gucci marches into the house eager to tell everything she's discovered about disloyal ass Passion. But when she gets inside, Jayden is sitting at the table with a no nonsense look on her face. A small burgundy cloth napkin is covering a pile of something she can't see on the table, and a mallet used for crabs is on the side. Standing against the walls are all of Thirteen Flavors along with her crew, Queen, Na-Na and Foxie whose nose is red due to crying. The Young Guns are in the background, waiting for their queue from Jayden.

"Hello, Gucci. I've been wondering when you were going to come into the house. Jayden crosses her legs and whips her hair over her shoulder. "Come over here. We've been waiting for you."

She walks closer to the table almost swallowing her throat in the process. "What's up, Jayden?" She looks at her friends, trying to read their expressions. "Is everything good?"

"I don't know, you tell me." Jayden stands up and smooth's the sides of her red shirt with her hands, "are you not happy with our arrangement here? Haven't I treated you with respect despite not liking your sneaky ass? Didn't I allow you to stay in my home, eat my food and use my water? I treated you better than that bitch you have for a mother and yet you continue to bite my hand. Even tried to set me up when Mrs. Sheers came over, by telling her Madjesty wasn't upstairs, when you knew what it meant to me."

Suddenly Gucci knows what's going on and she grows uneasy. Some kind of way she was ousted and it hurts thinking that it was a member of her crew. "Jayden, you know I love it here. Girl, I was just telling my mother how happy I am now that I live with you. I'm thinking about going back to school with you and Passion and everything." Beads of sweat dance across her forehead. "If anything you been an inspiration in my life and I thank God every morning for you." She's laying it on thick and some people can't bare to listen.

Jayden giggles. "Is that why you steal from me? Because you're so happy here? Because I inspire you?" She snaps her thumb and Queen and Foxie grab their friend forcefully. The way they grip her forearms hurt more than anything. She feels like they are being unfaithful which is what Jayden wanted.

On Jayden's command they pull her to the table and when she's there, Jayden lifts the cloth napkin revealing a pile of broken glass. While Gucci was licking ass and nuts outside the movie theater, she was inside smashing a glass bottle into tiny fragments. Just…for…her.

"I will give you credit, the client you stole from me says although your price was cheap and your services okay, you do have a pretty face." Jayden runs her finger alongside her jaw before stuffing her finger in her jaws, opening her mouth wider. "Let me see if I can change your looks a little."

With Queen and Foxie holding her steady, Jayden presses her face down and into the broken glass. Blood shoots from her skin as glass slivers wedge into the sockets of her eyes. She screams for relief from her friends but they are loyal to Jayden's plan. Besides, Jayden told her time and time again not to fuck with her and Gucci wouldn't listen. Now she was paying with her looks, the only thing she had left in life.

When Jayden is done, the skin on her face hangs off like shreds of ground beef. The pain is so excruciating, she's on the verge of passing out. Sebastian and Luh Rod step over to Gucci and throw her to the floor. Jayden stands over her and wipes the blood off of her hands and onto Gucci's shirt.

"I told you not to fuck with me, and you thought it was a joke. Now this shit is on you." She looks at everyone else. "This is going to be a common fucking thing around here if my money is fucked with. If you feel like you can't deal with my playbook, leave now. While you still can because after this, the door in and out is locked." Gucci's sniffling from the floor does not solicit walkers. "That's what the fuck I thought."

Olive pulls Jayden to the side and whispers directly into her ear. Jayden can hear her clearly. "'Bout time you put shit on the map, but if you ask me, you gonna have to do that a few more times." She looks at Gucci's crew.

"At this point I don't give a fuck anymore. That shit been long overdue."

"Can I give you a suggestion?"

As much as Jayden hates somebody telling her what to do, she would be lying if she didn't say Olive wasn't on point with her advice. It was like she was her council. She also knew that at some point she would have to tighten the purse strings on her girls, but not until she collected the two hundred fifty thousand dollars which she almost raised. She would not have done Gucci so bad had her mother not gone and got herself locked up. Now she was going to have to pay to get her out, since Mrs. Sheers called everyday asking where Harmony was. She couldn't risk her clients going astray. She was in deep shit. Two of her most frequent clients called earlier in the week and wanted to make appointments. Neither could meet up with Olive to give the money first, which was required, but she decided to let Spikes and Clay pay when they met up with her girls since she trusted them.

"What do you want to tell me, Olive?"

Olive is so close to Jayden their breasts touch. "You sure you don't want to kill this bitch?" She looks down at her. "I have a feeling leaving her alive, will be a mistake."

Jayden considers what she said, but the thought of her walking around with a fucked up face was too juicy for her to pass up. "Naw, I think I'm good." She looks at the Young Guns. "Sebastian, take this bitch anywhere but here." She looks at everyone else. "The rest of you ready for work."

As her homegirl is getting thrown out on her ass like recycled plastic, Foxie feels like a traitor for not warning Gucci that Tywanda was on to their plan. But she feared had she said something, all of them would've been implanted in the crime. If anything Gucci deserves a medal for taking one for the team. And to prove her loyalty, she would make Jayden pay by taking control of the girls herself.

PROJECT GYM RAT
THIRTEEN FLAVORS

Tonio Strong couldn't wait to shut his friend Alexander down today. He'd been cool with him for most of high school and Alexander was always bragging about how many women he'd fucked and how irresistible he was to most chicks. With his sculpted muscles and model good looks, he wasn't lying. Tonio's puny body and pimple face was always an obstacle but today, as he walked into the gym, everything would change.

"Damn, this bitch is crowded." Alexander says. "I hope we can get a treadmill."

"I see two over there," Tonio responds, scanning the gym for the girls he paid for. The moment he sees them jogging wearing tiny blue shorts and white t-shirts with no bras, he almost cums in his pants. He isn't concerned with the two men on the stationary bike right behind them because he doesn't know they're threats. Sebastian and Luh Rod are always on point ready to protect the girls if need be.

"Nigga, please tell me you see them bitches over there," Alexander says geeking at the way their bodies jiggle in their outfits. "Let me go lay down my game on these whores and show you how its done."

Alexander flexes his muscles and walks over to the women. "Ladies, I don't even know why you're in here because both of you are already in perfect condition." When they stop running on the treadmills they hop down and he can see the browns of Passion and Foxie's nipples. "I feel like I'm in love. My only question is which one of you…"

"We're not interested." Passion says wiping her face with a towel, as she makes her way to Tonio. Foxie follows her lead. "But you on the other hand, I'd love to get to know." They grope him.

"Damn, Passion, I was going after him too." Foxie says pulling his hand toward her.

Alexander's ego is receiving blow after blow so a dark look takes over and he wants to do them harm. "You bitches can't be serious!" He yells so loud he's spitting. "You choosing this nigga over me?"

"Who the fuck are you that we would even be interested?" Passion asks him. "If I say we ain't with it we ain't with it." She drapes her arm

over Tonio's shoulder and it falls to his back. Her wet breasts press against his chest. "Because I'm all about your friend right now."

"Well I guess we'll have to share him then won't we?" Foxie says, grabbing the rim of his gym shorts and pulling him closer to her.

Insanely jealous, Alexander grabs Passion's arm forcefully, "I don't know what you two bitches are up to but this shit ain't funny." He acts as if his friend is stealing his wife. "Ain't nobody ever…" His words stop when he receives a ten-pound dumbbell to the top of the head courtesy of Sebastian. At first Tonio is worried for him until Passion and Foxie grab his hand and leads him to the back of the locker room. They leave Sebastian and Luh Rod to clean up his messy friend.

Once in the men's locker room, they go into a bathroom stall. Passion pushes him on the toilet and slides his shorts down to his ankles before dropping to her knees. Foxie, always the lazy slut, massages his shoulders and suck on his earlobes while she does all the major work. The moment Passion grabs a firm hold of his bat and slides him into her mouth, he wants to explode. But he paid top dollar for this experience and tries to occupy himself with other thoughts to delay his orgasm.

I gotta get an oil change. Passion sucks his tip. *I…I gotta…I gotta get a haircut.* Passion spits on his dick two times, jerks him hard and stuffs him into her mouth again, no gag. *I gotta take my mother to church in the morning.* Passion slides two fingers under his nut sack and jiggles them slightly. *I…gotta. I gotta.* Fuck it! It's too late; he feels a warm sensation take over. Going with the flow he stands up and pushes his dick into her face. The back of her head slams against the stall as his entire body presses against her. He doesn't let her breathe until cream shoots into her mouth and he exhales. She accepts every drop.

"Fuck!" he says looking down at her. "How the fuck you do that shit so good?"

Passion holds her hand out and says, "Don't tell me how you like it, show me." He reaches into his shoe, takes out a wet twenty-dollar bill and slaps it into the palm of her hand. Since she hears all the time how much Tywanda makes in tips, she feels slighted.

When Passion gets blessed, Foxie holds her hand out too. "You wanna do something to show me love?"

Both he and Passion look at her crazy. "Not for nothing, baby, but I wasn't looking for a massage. Your girl put it down; you were just her hype man. Thanks anyway." He walks out leaving them to it.

Passion and Foxie walk into the girl's locker room to clean up. Foxie uses the opportunity to get into her ear. "Ain't it fucked up what Jayden did to Gucci? She was in the hospital for one week and they still didn't fix her face right. The only good thing is she's going back to school."

Passion splashes some water on her shoulders. "I don't want to talk about Gucci, and you shouldn't either."

"Do you even care that Jayden has changed for the worst? She ruined her life. Gucci lost her boyfriend behind her ugly mug and everything. It's sad, Passion. I mean, we grew up together, what are we gonna do to help?"

"Gucci wasn't fucking with me before she got her face chopped. As a matter of fact it's because of her I started back getting high. You know it and so do I." She throws some water in her mouth to wash off her tongue. The niggas spunk tastes like onions. "So I don't see why I should be coming to the rescue for her. If you ask me, she almost got what she deserved."

"Did you know Jayden had something to do with Madjesty dumping you?" She lies.

Passion turns the water off and now Foxie has her attention. "That don't make sense, Jayden don't even talk to Madjesty no more. Plus she got her baby and she won't let Madjesty see him."

"She stopped ya'll from being together before the baby shit. I'm telling you they were cool and that's why Madjesty came by the house that day she broke up with you. Jayden told her if she loved her she wouldn't fuck with you no more." She continues to lie. "If you don't have a problem with Jayden getting over on your relationship, I won't either."

The recent episodes Passion is having with drugs fuck up her mind. "You know this for a fact?"

"I swear to Jesus Christ our savior. When you were fucked up all that time, and wasn't getting out of bed, Jayden told Madjesty not to fuck with you when she was calling the house. She wasn't even concerned about the baby. It was all about keeping you away from Madjesty."

Passion begins to cry and she couldn't lie, in her lovesick haze, Foxie was making a lot of sense. Whenever she wanted to talk about Madjesty, Jayden had a problem. She knew she shouldn't have trusted that snake. "So what we gonna do?"

"I say we go on strike. Make her remember that she needs us…not the other way around." She says with a smile. "How many girls do you think you can get on your side in the house?"

"If I try real hard, at least four of them."

"That's cool because Jayden is saving up for something and we about to put that shit on pause right now." She grins. *"Once we put the bitch in her place, we'll remind her who's really in charge."*

THIRTEEN FLAVORS
GAME ESCALATED

"I hear what you're saying, baby." Tywanda says standing naked in front of Spikes, one of Jayden's frequent customers. The small motel room smells stale and feels hot and she and the others want to leave. "But our mommy said once you bust, you gotta pay. Normally Jay makes customers pay up front but you are a favorite so she sent us out anyway. So what's up with our money? You were satisfied right?"

"Of course." He says rubbing his baldhead before licking his lips. His hairy toes stick out of the covers on the edge of the bed. "I'm gonna be dreaming about that shit for days."

She grins although she hates him. "Then pay us. Be fair."

Spikes wipes the sweat off of his face with the edge of the sheet. He just experienced an hour of great sex from Tywanda, Johnna and Jay-O and now he was faking on the payout. Had Jayden not been hard pressed to get her mother out of jail, she would not have allowed her heart to get in the way of business. Her policy was to always have Olive pick up the cash the day the appointment was scheduled before the girls went out. But Spikes couldn't make the meet up time because he claimed he was coming from out of town and that he would give the money to the girls. He lied.

"Why don't the three of us get in bed and do our thing again." He says. "And when I'm done, ya'll can ride with me to the ATM and I'll pull out $600.00. That's $200.00 a piece you can pocket for yourselves."

The shit is laughable to them because with Jayden's price of $600 per girl, each of them stood to make $300.00 anyway. "Let me get this straight before I crack off on you. We asking for our money and you saying you don't got it or don't want to give it to us? Which one is it?"

Silence.

Since he failed to answer, the girls begin to get dressed. "So I take it you're not willing to accept my offer." When they don't answer he gets angry. "Jayden doesn't own your pussies, you do." He pats the bed. "Come on, get back in the bed and let's finish it off." The girls frown.

"What happens next is on you." Tywanda grabs her cell phone and goes into the bathroom. The girls shake their heads at his upcoming fate.

Jayden's pimp game is solid these days and nobody is fucking with her. When Tywanda returns she says, "You 'bout to be a dead nigga. My mommy is on the way."

He jumps out of bed, gets dressed. "I'm not fucking with you bitches." He grabs his wallet and moves to the door. The moment it opens he's met with a thump to his eye socket courtesy of the handle of Sebastian's .45. His body plummets to the thin carpet and his head knocks against the bed railing. "What's going on?" Spikes yells rubbing his head. "What's happening?"

Sebastian and Luh Rod rush into the room and lock the door. No one says anything and when he tries to leave again Sebastian smacks him back down. "Don't get up again." He warns. "Stay right where you are. And wait."

After thirty minutes of suffering silence there is a knock at the door. Jayden walks in with a blank expression on her face. Her fashionably holey jeans wrap over her voluptuous thighs. When she snaps her fingers, Sebastian and Luh Rod grab Spikes and throw him on the bed. They maintain their hold on him although he struggles to get away. Jayden doesn't say a word and the silence is killing him. He continues to buck the Young Guns until she eases out of her jeans. The room is so silent you can hear eyes wink. Standing in front of him with her white jacket, orange lace thongs and black stilettos, he can't stop his dick from hardening. He'd been wanting to fuck the boss for a minute so this was a welcoming treat. But when he focuses on her eyes, he sees the evil.

She reads his lips. "Jayden, he laughs, "You know me and you go way back. I'm not trying to knock your game. I patronize your business before you got the new girls. Remember how much money I use to spend with you for Passion alone?"

She places a finger over his lips and eases out of her thong. Luh Rod is glued to her hairless pussy, which seems to be whispering his name. Shit is beyond sexy until everyone sees the seat of her panties is carrying a blood soaked pad. She balls it up in her hand and says, "Open your mouth, Spikes."

He looks at the underwear. "Jayden, what are you doing?"

Sebastian hits him in the eye with the telephone. Blood spurts from his skin and wets up the hairs on his chest. "Fuck!" He screams wiping his eyebrows.

"Open your mouth." Jayden says calmly. It was either going to be her way or his. Although one led to death.

With a strong desire to live and see his mother's eyes again, he opens his jaws. Jayden stuffs the mess in his mouth and pushes his lips closed.

The metal taste from her blood and the cotton from the pad dry his tongue out.

"Spikes, I'm having a bad week." She rubs his hairy, bloody chest. "A real bad one." She leans over him naked from the waist down. "Now you're going to give me my money and let me go on my way. If you don't I will take out everything I'm going through on you. And I can promise you this, you'll cry for death but it will never come."

He mouths as much as possible with the obstruction in his mouth. "Can I talk?" She nods yes and he uses his tongue to push the panties out. He swallows to clear his tongue. "Jayden, I only can take out $600.00 a day. That's what I was trying to tell your girls." He lies. "I wasn't trying to get over on you."

She stands up straight, looks down at him and frowns. "Well you're going to stay in this hotel for four days and each day you'll withdraw $600.00. Starting today."

His eyebrows rise. "That's $2,400.00 I only owe you $1,800.00."

"No...that's the new price for fucking with my money and tasting my bloody pussy. And to make sure it goes down as planned, my boys over here will be watching after you. Understood?"

A lone tear fell from his eyes. "Yes."

The Next Day

Jayden is riding in the van on the way to confront her next broke client. It's the second time in a week she was stiffed by a regular. After she got her money, she was done giving pussy away on tick. She would have never done it in the past, except her mother's problems caused her not to think straight. When they were pulling up to the destination Jayden turns around to Tywanda, Passion and Tabitha and says, "Take off everything but your shoes." They waste no time getting naked. "Park in the front of that real estate building, Metha. Over there."

She looks at her through the rearview mirror. "Jayden, can you tell me what's going on?" She looks at the girls stripping. "Why are they getting naked?"

Jayden twists in her seat. "For once in your life can you do something I ask you to do? Just park in the front."

"But it's next to a fire hydrant." She points to the red chipped mess.

"That's why you're driving, if the cops come, move this bitch."

Metha shakes her head because Jayden was becoming worse by the day. She was all about money and often didn't think about what her actions meant for other people. When she parks Jayden and the girls glide out. *People's jaws drops when they see the sexy spectacle outside. She struts through the real estate building's double doors and past the receptionist.*

"Mam, what's going on?" *Jayden ignores the four-eyed bitch.* "You can't be in here! I'm calling the police."

"Help yourself." *Jayden says.*

She could care less as she heads for Clay's elaborate office. It was obvious that they treated the boss well. Through the glass office, his eyes pop open when he sees the performance Jayden is putting on for his employees. Although he wants them to go away, they walk though his office door and close it behind him. Passion sits her naked ass on a stack of papers on his desk and crosses her legs. Her pussy juice smears a client's mortgage papers. Tywanda stands in front of the window and waves at some passerby's and Tabitha sits at a chair across from him with her legs wide open. Jayden remains standing by the door. Her eyes never leave his. She focuses on his lips.

"You got five seconds to tell me what the fuck is going on." *He whispers harshly.*

Jayden ambles toward him and slaps his face. "Where is my money, Clay? We made an arrangement, you fucked my girls, so where is my paper?"

"I don't know what you're talking about." *He looks around at his employees. Some look disgusted, some are turned on and others are taking pictures.* "You're going to get me fired."

"Fuck Fired. You're going to get locked up. The receptionist out front already says she's calling the police. The clock is now ticking. Now I want my money and I want it now, Clay. If you don't give me every last dime, I'll tell the cops all the kinky shit you did to my girls."

"Like what?"

"Like how you made me suck your dick, while your dog licked your toes." *Passion says.*

"Or how you had me stick my finger up your…"

"Stop!" *He raises his hand, interrupting Tywanda. He looks at his employees outside and then Jayden again.* "Okay, this shit you pulled worked. You got me in a bind. So how 'bout you give me your address and I'll bring your money."

"I'm not leaving without cash in hand, Clay. You fucked us once, I won't let you do it again." *She looks around.* "And you better do it quickly too. The crowd out there is getting larger."

He shoots her an evil look. "You gonna get what's coming to you."

"I know…starting with my money."

Clay unlocks a box under his desk and hands her the money he owes from the petty cash fund. Paid in full, Jayden takes her bitches and strolls out the door.

HARMONY
NASTY OLIVE

Jayden spent good money on an attorney to get me out of jail and on bond. Although my fate is still up in the air, the attorney feels confident that he can get the charges thrown out of court. The reason was when the videotape was sold to the company, I was in the hospital suffering from stab wounds, so I could not have made the sale. Secondly the owner who purchased the tape from the electrician is afraid of losing his company, so he's cooperating with authorities. The one stipulation the judge placed on me is that where at first the alcohol meetings were voluntary, now they are mandatory.

When I walk outside the jail, I see Olive is in front of Jayden's truck and the girl I know as Metha is behind the wheel. "What's up?" I say walking up to her. "Where's Jayden?"

She leans up against the truck. "She's not coming. She sent me instead."

I look her over. "Why?"

She stands up straight. "Let's get in the truck."

"No thank you." I say turning around to walk back inside. "I'll find my own way home."

I'm strutting down the block until I'm yanked by my shirt and thrown into the truck. "What the fuck is wrong with you?" I yell at her. "I'm sick of people putting their hands on me."

"Then do something about it, bitch." I swallow. "Listen, drunk, your daughter may care about you but I don't give a fuck if you die today or tomorrow as long as it's soon." She pauses. "You are the nastiest mother I've ever known in my life. You stole money from her bank account, you probably abused her as a child and you don't give a fuck that all of your responsibilities are now hers. So let me say this to you as plain as possible, I care about her. As a matter of fact I love her, and I won't see her hurt. And if she is hurt, you better hope I'm not around because I will kill you."

I gasp.

I analyze her like a computer program. "My daughter will never love you like you want." She seems to lose her steam. "If I know nothing else, I know love sick when I see it."

"I don't know what you're talking about. Jayden is just a friend."

"Sure you do." I laugh poking her buttons. "And like I said, if you are sniffing up her tree, you're wasting time. She loves dick all the way around the board. Just...like...her...mammy."

At first she's angry but then she gets serious. "Maybe you're right, but even if she does reject me when or if that time comes, it still won't stop me from killing you." She taps the back of the driver's seat. "Metha, can you take us back home, I appreciate it." She pauses and looks back at me. "Oh before I forget some man named Lonnie J came by the house looking for you. He said you met him in front of a liquor store. I'm not sure, but judging by the look in his eyes he wants to kill you too."

FOXIE
PUSSY UPRISING

Foxie couldn't stop the grin from spreading across her face because with Passion's help, she was able to convince Queen, Na-Na and Catherine to strike with them to force Jayden to do what they wanted. They were asking for more money, two days off during the week instead of one and to be able to have their boyfriends over. The girls were standing in the living room waiting for Jayden when Olive walks down the stairs.

"I told her ya'll wanted to talk. I don't know what's going on with you chicks, but whatever you got planned it's not going to go down well." Olive crosses her hands over her breasts. "She seemed real irritated over the phone."

"Olive, why do you always have something to say about Jayden when she not even here? If it don't go down as planned, we'll just leave." Foxie says in a condescending tone. "But I can tell you one thing, we not taking her shit no more."

Olive laughs. "Passion, are you actually down with whatever plot they have brewing? Don't let them rope you into this shit. Turn around while you still can."

"Olive, just leave me alone." She says under her breath.

Olive throws her hands up in the air and says, "Okay, it's your funeral."

When Jayden finally walks through the door with Sebastian and Luh Rod behind her, she knows immediately something is going on when she looks at all of their faces. She doesn't have time for this shit. She places her purse on the counter and walks over to them. "I heard ya'll wanted to meet with me, so where are the rest of Thirteen Flavors?"

"They're upstairs, we wanted to talk to you about something in private. The rest of them are not included." Foxie quarterbacks. "So we asked them to stay in their rooms."

She nods her head and places her hands on her hips. "Okay, you got the mike, so what's up?"

Foxie steps up. "Jayden we feel like what you did to Gucci was wrong. That girl's entire life is ruined and it's all your fault."

Jayden raises her eyebrows. "And?" She says real calmly looking at everyone at her side.

"And if you don't treat us right, we're not working for you anymore. We deserve respect, Jayden. You weren't the only one who built this business from the ground up. You made this money off of our backs. And now I feel like you look at us like we're property." Foxie continues.

You are. She thinks. "What are you asking for?"

"For starters I think you should pay for Gucci's plastic surgery."

"Not happening." She shakes her head. "Next?"

Foxie clears her throat. "I think you should give us more money, two days off during the week and allow us to have company over." She pauses briefly to catch her breath. "If you say no, we'll leave and we're already packed."

Jayden looks at the floor and back at them. She walks past all of the girls and stops at Foxie, "I want to be clear, every last one of you feel the same way right?"

Passion can barely answer the question, "Jayden, I do think you are a little too harsh on us. I feel like you're our pimp and we're hoes." You are. Jayden thinks. "If you say we're partners we need to be partners and it should feel that way. So yes," she swallows to prevent from passing out, "I'm with them."

One by one everyone said the same thing, either she changed her ways, or they weren't working for her anymore. "I need some time to consider your proposal but please know that this is your home. I would never throw you out." She picks up her purse and goes upstairs without another word and Olive follows.

They were expecting thunder and rain. Foxie turns to Passion and says, "See, I told you we had that bitch right were we wanted. She may can get rid of Gucci, but she can't get rid of all of us." Foxie continues as if her fuck game was top notch. "What do you think she's going to do, Passion?"

Passion wipes the sweat off of her forehead and looks at all of them. "I think shit is about to hit the fan and if I were you I'd get out while you still can."

●──●

When the girls woke up the next morning, Passion was nowhere to be found. But the others thinking Jayden would change her ways decided to stay around. She made everyone a large breakfast and afterwards they watched a new movie in the living room. She laughed with them and even joked around on the funny parts. When it was nighttime, they placed Usher's C.D. on the stereo, Jayden's favorite, and danced to his old songs. Things seemed to be going smooth and Foxie was happy she made a decision to stay. Besides, since she moved there she saved up over fifteen thousand dollars although she spent every dime on drinking and drugging. Jayden didn't say she would submit to their proposal but it was looking good.

At about seven o'clock that night there was a knock at the door. Olive smiled at Foxie and her crew who was sitting on the sofa and answered it. When she opened the door a white boy from an unmarked delivery service was on the other side. He handed Olive a large brown box, which she walked carefully upstairs. An hour later, everybody accept Foxie, Na-Na, Queen and Catherine exited the house.

As they're sitting on the sofa, Queen leans over to Foxie and says, "You think we should leave too? That's kind of weird that the rest of Thirteen Flavors rolled out without us."

Foxie is filing her nails next to her on the sofa. She rolls her eyes and exhales. "Damn, why is you worried about what everybody else doing? Huh?" She pauses. "It ain't nothing to be worried about, we got that bitch in the pocket. You saw how she was kissing our asses earlier today. Not only that, the bitch is so scared we're going to leave that she made us a big ass breakfast."

"Right, if she was going to do something I would've thought she'd poison the food." Catherine says, "but when she ate it too, I knew we were all good."

"What you think?" Queen asks Na-Na.

"I think we good," Na-Na replies, "and as long as that bitch pays me, I'm not going nowhere."

Later on that night Jayden baked an apple pie. They all ate a slice with a scoop of vanilla ice cream; but she refrained from eating this time although she faked like she did. Full and tired, they all went to sleep in their rooms. They couldn't even make it upstairs they were so exhausted. When they closed their eyes, they were in a deep sleep, enhanced by the pills in the dessert. They should've left when they had the chance.

While she was comfortable in bed, Catherine rolled over once and felt a prick on her left thigh. She was too tired to get up, so she tried to rub it and go back to sleep.

Foxie felt a sting on her back that caused a pain to rush down her tailbone. Na-Na was pricked on her neck and Queen on her face. The sensation was so great for all of them that after about twenty minutes they woke out of their drug-induced stupor and tried to get out of the room. But when they turned the doorknobs, they wouldn't open. They were all locked inside. Cries rained in the hallway and for the weak at heart it was the most painful thing to hear.

"Jayden!" Foxie screams banging on the door. "Please let me out. Something bit me and I...I can barely move."

Jayden walks in the hallway so that from behind the closed doors, they all could hear her emotionless voice. "If I were any of you I'd be laying down and reserving my energy because you were just bitten by a black widow spider, one of the most dangerous in the world. And unfortunately for you, it's bred in Maryland. In a minute you'll feel abdominal pain, tremors and before long you won't be able to breathe. In other words, you'll die."

Foxie cries against the door. "Jayden, please don't do this. I'm so sorry. I don't want to die. I'll do whatever you ask me too. This was Gucci's fault. She put me up to it!"

"Foxie, maybe you don't understand how serious I am about my money. I will never let you or anybody else get in the way of that. You jumped out of the window when you called this fake ass strike and because of it, you have to suffer. Your cohorts too."

•━━━━━━━━━━━━━━━━━━━━━━━━━━━━━━•

The next morning Jayden arranged to have their bodies taken out of the house and Harmony was there when it happened. The white boy who dropped the spiders off collected them safely. When the last body was removed, she turns to face her daughter. "Jayden, what's going on with you? What happened to those girls?" When she looks into her daughter's eyes, she seems zoned out. "I don't recognize you anymore. Is it because of what Madjesty did to you? I just found out about it when I was locked up."

A tear rolls down her face. "Harmony, get the fuck out of my face, the Jayden you knew died a long time ago. It's sad that you're just noticing now."

MADJESTY
WET BRIDGE

We're sitting under a bridge in Washington D.C. and I'm trying to figure out what just happened. Rain is pouring down around us and all I can think about is how a few days ago, I had the blood of a white girl on my body. "I keep telling ya'll I don't know what happened to her." I say mainly to Daze and Wicked who won't let it go. "If I wanted to fuck with the bitch, on my eyes you wouldn't have been with her." I look at Wicked. "She was looking at me the whole time so it wouldn't have been a problem."

"What you trying to say to me, nigga?" Wicked asks stepping to me.

We're arguing back and forth and I'm considering taking out the knife I have to jab him when Gage says, "We all know what happened in that building and who killed her." She steps between us. "And the fact that we're trying to put it on Mad, is not fair."

I frown. They no more than me. "What are you talking about?"

"Don't open your mouth, Gage!" Wicked demands pointing his index finger at her. "If you do I'll never fuck with you again."

She rolls her eyes. "You know what, you use to be everything to me but after you brought that girl into our fold, I don't give a fuck anymore. I'm tired of being your number two, Wicked. I'm done!" Everyone looks shocked. "Now Mad has been nothing but real with us since she got here and she deserves more from us."

"She." He points at me. "This nigga is a bitch?"

I don't have time for this, so I drop my pants where I am. Through the peephole in my boxers I show them the strap-on that never leaves my body. If they gonna accept me then they gonna accept me. I'm tired of hiding who I am. Overall I'm a good person and its time that the people around me recognize that shit. "Yes, I'm a female physically but not mentally. So you see, your theory of me raping her is flawed. I couldn't have." I pull my jeans up.

"You could have, she just might not have enjoyed it." He laughs and I think about Jayden. He's right.

I hate this feeling. I hate this person. And I hate being ridiculed for who I am. So I run over to him and knock him off the top of the hill under the bridge, where he rolls down below. He almost rotates into the street but jumps up just in time. He's not able to stay up long because I hit him again. The moment he tries to move for me, this time I sock him in his left eye. Either he's weak, or not as strong as I thought he would be because I'm getting the best of him. I don't stop beating this dude until I have blood on my hands. For the second time this week.

Spirit and Gage finally break up the fight. I push them both away. "You know what, shit has been real but I'ma go at this shit on my own." I grab my backpack and look at Spirit and Gage. "I'ma get up with ya'll when I can."

"Don't go, Mad." Gage pleads. "You belong here with us. I can feel it."

"I ain't no gay," Spirit adds, which causes Fierce to shuffle a little, "but I'm with her. I don't think you should leave right now either, especially with this shit over our heads. You need us as much as we need you."

"So you choosing this bitch over me?" Wicked asks.

Silence.

He steps closer to them. "We have been through everything together. When we didn't have food, I was the one who went out to get it. I'm your brother." He looks at Spirit. "And I'm your lover." He touches Gage on the cheek. "So I need to know right now who's family you all belong to. Mine? Or the outsider?"

Daze steps to Wicked's side, along with his girlfriend Killer. Fierce goes with them to, although he doesn't look like he wants too. I'm thinking he has his answer when Spirit and Gage stand with me along with WB.

"Wow, White Boy," Wicked shakes his head, "you chose that easily, huh? Damn, you sure you didn't suck that plastic thing between her legs the night Rose was killed."

"Remember what you just said, because that's one of the reasons I'm choosing them. The fact of the matter is you're too reckless, Wicked. You've gotten us in trouble many times before. We all we got and it's important that we stay smart. Yet you don't get it anymore. You bring the wrong people into our circle and one of the times you did that, Gage got raped. As far as Mad is concerned, she brought to the group, not took from it."

Wicked looks like he wants to kill him. "I didn't know that dude was a convicted rapist when I took him to the Catacombs."

"Because you didn't care." Gage whispers. "He had liquor and drugs and that's all you saw." Wicked is breathing so hard he looks like he's going to fall down again.

"So this is how ya'll really want it?" Silence. "Okay, do what you want, but you can't bring her to the Catacombs." He points at me.

"We got our own spots down there." Spirit says. "You don't own the Catacombs, you know that. They belong to no one. She's welcome with us if she wants to come." Spirit says. "That's on her."

Daze places his hand on his shoulder. To be honest Wicked seems more like the leader than Daze. "Let's go, man." Daze says, "Ain't nothing for us under here." He shakes his head and the four of them walk away. I don't move until I see them enter the rain and disappear into it.

"You okay?" Gage asks touching my hand.

I shake it off. "Yeah I'm good." I walk back to where we were sitting and they follow. "Tell me about what you wanted me to know about who may have killed the girl."

She exhales and WB begins. "One day Wicked brought a dude he met at church to the Catacombs. Normally we don't do that without everyone getting to know them first. That's why we were hesitant about bringing you in, and hesitant about talking to you. But you gave to the group instead of taking from it." She pauses. "Anyway, we usually hang out here or in the building if the cops aren't fucking with us on the days it rain. It gets nasty in the Catacombs when it rains. But since he met him at church, during one of the soup kitchen feedings, he thought he could trust him." She shakes her head. "Doesn't he know how many pervs hang out in the pews on Sunday?"

"We all told him that although dude talked real soft, that something behind his eyes expressed something different." Spirit continues. "But he didn't want to listen. He never listens to us. He ain't nothing but a fucking bully. We all under twenty but he swears he's in charge, even over Daze who's twenty-six." He leans against the wall under the bridge. "The night he brought him to the Catacombs, all he kept saying was that he was good people and that we should trust him because he did."

"What is the Catacombs ya'll keep talking about?"

"In Roman Times they use to bury the dead in tombs under the city, we liked the name so we used it." Spirit continues. "We're the dead. The children everybody forgot."

"And don't give a fuck about." Gage adds.

"So how old was he? The man who Wicked brought to the Catacombs?"

"About thirty something." Gage responds, crying again. "I think. His name is Mystery."

I put my arm around her and she stops immediately. "Well what happened?" I ask Spirit. "Once he got there?"

"The next morning one of our members, Sunny Day, was raped and killed. Someone from another family lost a member too. His head was decapitated."

"There are other families in the Catacombs?"

"Plenty." Spirit replies. "It's like a secret society."

"The dude who adopted the name Mystery, that Wicked brought in, was nowhere to be found." WB goes on. "First we thought whoever killed our member Sunny Day, killed him too. But a few days later he was spotted wearing Sunny Day's jean jacket. She loved that jacket, it had a sun stitched on the back and everything. She would've given her life for it." He shakes his head and it's obvious he can't continue. "She would not have let him have it without a fight. A good one at that."

"Sunny was WB's girl." Spirit explains. "That day was hard on all of us. Wicked wouldn't accept the responsibility even though he brought him into our fold. To this day we've never fully forgiven him for it."

"The real kicker is Mystery tried to act like he was hurt about what happened to Sunny Day too." WB says. "But when we asked for her jacket back, he wouldn't give it to us. The dude is crazy for real!" He rubs his head. "We told him he was cut and to stay the fuck from around us, now he just stalks us. He'll show up some place he knows we'll be, fight us or even try to hurt us. He knows about The Hole, so I wouldn't be surprised if he showed up there and killed Rose when we all went to sleep."

"Can't we call the police?" I ask.

They look at me like I'm delusional. And I realize I am. "We never, *ever* get the police involved in our business. You have to remember, we are wanted for different reasons. So we deal with everything in the underworld on our own." Spirit says.

"Always." WB adds.

I'm thrown off. "I got it, so what are your stories? Before you got here?" I ask.

WB starts. "My birth name is Nathan. I was brought here from Africa when I was one year old. A cool white family raised me for ten years and when they died from carbon monoxide poison, I was placed into a foster home. They beat and ridiculed me for being this dark, so I ran away when I could. All they wanted was the money to take care of me." He exhales. "It took some time for me to escape, but that's how I ended up here. With you lovely people." His personality comes back and I'm grateful.

That's deep. "What about you?" I ask Spirit.

"I was born to a Chinese father and a black mother. I don't say my name anymore because in the culture your name brings with it spirits, whether good or bad from the past. I will say that I killed somebody in defense of my baby sister. For now I'll leave it at that."

Since I killed a girl in a motel with my bare hands, I understood him. "What about you, Gage?"

"My real name is Lazo. I come from a rich black family who disowned me when I got pregnant by Wicked. One of the reasons is that he's white and the other reason is that he's poor. My parents are the kind of people with enough money to destroy lives. So like my mother demanded, I had the abortion. That wasn't enough; they threatened Wicked's family and said if they caught him around me again, that they would see to it that he came up missing. We had no choice at the time, we were in love so we ran away together. We haven't seen our families since."

Wow. That's deep. "What about you?" Gage asks me.

I exhale. I hate my story. "I was born to an alcoholic whore. For most of my life she had me thinking I was a boy." They look confused. "I did a lot of things I'm not proud of and I hurt a lot of people. So now I'm here."

"Are you serious? About thinking you were a boy?" Spirit asks, leaning in.

"Yeah, I was dumb in school and I'm not the brightest now." I realize. "But I'm smart on the streets and I'm starting to get to know people better." I decide against telling them about Jayden. "And I'm here because I don't have any place else to be and to be honest," I look at all of them, "for the first time I feel like I'm around people like me."

"That's real." Gage responds.

We were just about to talk some more when I see Fierce jogging back toward us. He trots up the hill and seems out of breath. "You know you not supposed to be running, Fierce." WB says anxiously. "You cool, man?" He looks concerned.

"I'm fine." He's wet from the rain but sits next to me "I decided to hang out with you guys instead. I feel safer." They grip him into a manly hug. It's all love here now. He looks at me. "I'm sure at this point everybody gave the rights of passage by giving up the past, so let me. Mad, my real name is George. I was the youngest kid in my family and was raped by all of the men in my house. My father, my three brothers and even my uncle. I was thirteen when I passed out in front of a record store because I lost so much blood through my anus." He shakes his head. "I woke up in a hospital, all stitched up. They told me I would be released to my family but I couldn't take it anymore. So I ran away, met this family and the rest is history."

"What about your moms?" I ask.

"She wasn't no good. Since my mother drank alcohol while pregnant with me, I suffer from asthma."

I think of my mother who drank when she was pregnant with me too. I wonder what illness I have because of it. That I don't know about.

"This family was the first family who ever cared about me and they've been helping me stay alive ever since."

I look at all of them. "I had friends like this before," I remember how happy Sugar, Krazy and Kid look with out me recently, "but we weren't as strong. We called ourselves Mad Max."

"For real?" I respond.

"Well if the name isn't being used, I like it." Spirit says.

"Me too." Gage adds. "How about we call ourselves that, and adopt a new name. Since we starting over because of you."

WB and Fierce seem to agree to. "Mad's Max it is!"

"You know what, we're thrown away kids." Gage says looking at us. "The abused, the troubled but we're not worthless. As long as we have each other, we'll never be down again."

I don't know where life is going to lead me now. I'm on the run for a crime I didn't commit. I still miss my sister and I think about my son every time I breathe. But I need to work on me. And if this family can help me, I'm willing to ride with them.

"Oh, before I forget, we have to watch Wicked." Fierce says seriously. "He's talking about getting revenge and it sounds to me like he wants it in blood."

KALI
MAD MAN HUNT

Kali becomes one with the leather seats of Ann's car as she cruises slowly down the street, giving him the mental space to think. Since they'd been back from Atlanta, she visited her family and friends and told everybody she wasn't kidnapped. Most of them thought she was selfish for not letting them know sooner but she didn't care. The only thing on her mind was Kalive.

As Kali focuses on the road, his mind is on Madjesty. He almost lost his head a few days ago when he saw the news. They flashed a picture of his daughter and some other kids leaving an abandoned building, where a girl name Rose Midland was found murdered. A witness snapped the picture and handed it over to the authorities and all of them were wanted for questioning regarding the crime. The others were mysteries, but since Mad's fingerprints were found on a wall, they wanted her by name.

"You know how to get there right?" He looks over at her as she maneuvers her black BMW, a birthday gift from Jace when he was alive. "I'm not trying to get lost fucking with you."

"I got it, Kali. I know where I'm going." She says softly.

When they finally reach Concord Manor he knocks on the door and Jayden opens it. Although only a year had passed since he last seen her, her body filled out and her eyes told him she was different. She looked like the poison he tasted when he was a kid. She looked like Harmony before the liquor took the life out of her.

"What do you want, Kalive?" Jayden asks crossing her arms. Her game face is in position and she doesn't seem scared of him anymore.

Kali pushes her out of his way and rips through the house on a mission. He went into every room, and searched every nook and cranny. All of the doors gave him access but one and it was locked. He walks back down the stairs and into the foyer, surprised she didn't follow. "Where is Madjesty? And why is that room upstairs locked?"

"I don't know where she is and that room is locked because this is my house."

As he breathes her in, he can see why Kreshon is trying to cuff her young ass. She is bad to the bone. "This shit is serious. I'm trying to reach her and I been by my mother's place and she's not even there. So if you know where she is, you better tell me now."

Jayden seems uneasy when he mentions Bernie. Why? It's the only time the game face she wears comes off. "You came to the wrong place."

"If I know nothing about Madjesty, I know she'll always stay in contact with you." He looks around. "And where is that mother of yours?"

"My mother is at a sobriety meeting and as you can see I'm all alone. You should also know that if Madjesty was anywhere near here, she wouldn't be welcome. Besides, the police have been here to question us and everything about her. I know about the girl she killed in some abandoned building. She left her bloody fingerprints on the wall there. She'd be majorly dumb if she came back to Concord Manor." She throws her game face back on. "I'm busy now, anything else?"

"I'll be back and if…"

When he hears a baby cry the smug look on Jayden's face is wiped off. Kali grins. He knows without her telling him that his grandson is in that house. But what was he going to do about it? Take him and roam the streets with him? No that wouldn't be smart. First he had to find his daughter and see what was up with her. So in his book the safest place for the kid to be at the moment was there.

"I'll be back, Jayden. You can bet that phat ass of yours on it."

JAYDEN
PARTY LIGHTS

I'm in the middle of my living room. Looking at the women of my stable. A lot of things were going on today. I received my Learners Permit since I just turned sixteen. We're having a major party tonight and I invited the richest men who ever used my services. I'm having surgery tomorrow and I raised every dime of the two hundred fifty thousand dollars I needed. It was all upstairs. I would present it to the banks when I got back and not a moment sooner, first I have to have a meeting with my mother and Olive.

A lot had changed. For starters, I took money out of my bitch's hands. Anything they needed I provided but they would never, ever, get a dime from me again. Its funny, when you treat a bitch with respect she's ungrateful but when you treat her like a dog she loves you for life.

Before the party, I examine each of the ladies and Blaq. They look good, but Tabitha, Jay-O and Tywanda seem a little too drunk for my taste. Ever since Catherine, Foxie, Queen and Na-Na mysteriously disappeared and Passion went on the run, they indulged a little too much. I know they wondered if they'd be next and the only thing I could say is this. Don't fuck with my money, follow the rules and I won't fuck with you. My star bitch was also letting me down. Tywanda had gained a significant amount of weight and it was starting to look bad on her. In fact as I'm looking at her now, she was on her third donut. I'm tired of her misusing her body, so I slap the food out of her mouth.

"You better watch what the fuck you eat, Tywanda." I point in her face. "You getting a little chunkier than my taste."

I'm about to approach the others about their alcohol, when I receive an email from one of my guests on my phone.

'J,

Although I am in receipt of your invite, I respectfully decline. This due in part to one of your employees sanitary issues, who I enjoyed working with in the past. I will not be able to indulge her or your services anymore.

Best Wishes,

Mr. Rich.'

I feel the blood rush to the surface of my face. What did he mean sanitary issues? I need a response so I write, *'Can you please elaborate'?*

I wait nervously for his response. He's one of the reasons I decided to throw the party in the first place and now he isn't coming.

While I'm waiting, Hadiya walks up to me and I focus on her mouth. "Cassius is in bed fast asleep, can I get you anything?" She looks at me and licks her lips. "Anything at all?"

I don't respond. A second later, he sends another email. *"The Bald Headed Wonder."*

I know who he's talking about now. I'm hot. Pissed off, I yell, "I need everybody in the foyer now!" When they are in front of me I say, "I need everyone to drop their underwear." Blaq looks relieved until I say, "You too."

One by one, they all submit. When everyone including Blaq is naked below I say, "Olive, go into the kitchen and get me a cup of ground coffee and a hot rag. I wait for her to return. Walking up to Jay-O, I ease a finger inside of her pussy and sniff she's fine. I wipe my fingers, stick it into the coffee and go to Tabitha followed by Johnna. All of them are official. I even sniff Blaq's nut sack and he's cool. It isn't until I get to Tywanda, that there's a problem. Her body smells of shit and piss and if she tells me she washed up I'll probably kill her right where she stands. Lately all she cares about is clubbing and getting high. So what her nigga is dead, get over it already!

"Follow me, Tywanda." I walk upstairs and into the public bathroom. When we are inside, I close and lock the door. "Get undressed and get into the tub."

"Jayden, what's this all about?" She asks.

When she's undressed, I open the cabinet below the sink, grab the bleach and throw it on her body, the way my mother use to do us when we were kids. She screams but she takes every bit of it while covering her eyes. When I'm done I say, "I got a call today from a customer, who said you weren't taking care of your personal hygiene. I run a respectable establishment, bitch. And if you can't see fit to push back from the bar long enough to wash your clit, I will cut it off." She trembles. "Am I understood?" She nods. "Now get it in order, before I decide you're better off to me dead."

Me, Olive and Harmony are sitting at the dining room table before the party. "Harmony, I can't speak with you long because of my event tonight. But I need you to give Olive guardianship over me."

Her eyebrows rise. "I'm not doing that shit." She says, wearing the lavender robe she always wears. "What about my welfare checks?"

"You are and you will. Fuck welfare!" I say. "I don't have the energy to argue with you anymore. You've officially stolen my love and what's left in its place is rage, and hate for you. But even still I don't want to see you out on the streets. Unless you won't do what I say."

"You couldn't put me out on the streets anyway, this is my house."

"Harmony, this is your house for now. I have the money upstairs to pay Laura and Ramona off. It's done. Now either sign these documents and give Olive custody of me until I turn eighteen or I'll leave, take my money with me and tell Mrs. Sheers I don't live here. If that happens since Madjesty isn't here anymore, your checks will stop all together."

She reluctantly signs.

———————————————●———————————————

The party is going full swing until I get a call that causes me to breakout in hives. "The cops are going to be there in fifteen minutes. They have pictures of men running in and out of your house tonight. I guess for some party. Be careful and be ready." He hangs up. It's great to have a policeman as a client.

I quickly run through the house on full alert. "Code THIRTEEN! Code THIRTEEN!"

Olive is on it and she quickly searches the house for the list while I put out everybody who didn't live there. I'm positive that Gucci had something to do with this and she'll regret it sooner than later. Olive was right, I should've taken her face and her life together. Fifteen minutes later my girls are changed and the men are gone but part two of my plan isn't in effect yet.

"Jayden, what's going on?" My mother asks walking up on me. "I'm not trying to be involved with no police. I'm already on paper."

I look over her head like she's an animal. "Sebastian and Luh Rod, take my mother downstairs and keep her there until shit cools down. However you gotta do it works for me. Draw blood if you need too." They grip her by her arms and pull her down the stairs fussing and screaming. She's not going to ruin this shit for me. When they are in the basement, I lock them in with the key, so the cops won't be able to go downstairs and slide it into my pocket.

I approach Olive and she says, "I reached some of the people on the list but the others wouldn't answer the phone. Probably because school is tomorrow."

"Fuck!" I rub my throbbing temples. "Did you tell them that they need to come over soon as possible? And that it was our agreement?"

"Some of them said they would try but it doesn't sound too good."

I feel faint and look around. "Where is Hadiya?"

"She's dressed already so she's bringing the baby down in a second." She touches my hand. "I think we're going to be okay no matter what happens. Try not to worry."

Nervous out of mind anyway, I go to deal with the police. The moment I step outside, I see the cops pulling up in front of the house. One of them is black and his body is built like a sack of rocks. He moves quickly toward me, flashes his badge and asks, "Are you Jayden Phillips?"

"Yes." I say softly. "What do you officers want?" I focus on his lips.

He smirks. "I'm sure you already know but I'll entertain you. For the moment anyway." He laughs. "We received a report that you are running a prostitution ring out of your house. With underage girls. Is this correct?"

I laugh even though I want to cry. "No, sir. I think you are mistaken, I'm running a babysitting service out of my house."

He looks at other officers with him before focusing back on me. "We were told you would say that. However, we received these pictures of men coming in and out of your home." He shows me the photos and I feel my temperature rise. "So who are these people?"

I take a photo from him. "Friends of my mother's." I give it back. "We are allowed to entertain aren't we?"

"You're trying to be smart?"

"No, sir I'm not trying to be anything. I'm very intelligent. Now my mother and her friends are gone so if there isn't anything else, I'm busy."

He frowns and says, "Not so fast, this is a warrant," he flashes a piece of paper at me which I scan quickly, "this way officers." They push past me and rush into the house. I know I'm done. I wait outside and contemplate running away but where will I go? When I didn't hear as much drama as I thought I would, I walk inside. What I see makes me want to drop to my knees.

Sitting in the living room was my girls in cute colorful pajama pants and some of the kids on the list. Teddy bears and other toys we had stashed for this day are thrown around the floor and Hadiya is rocking my nephew. I realized a long time ago that there was a possibility that one of my bitches would hate and tell the police, so I greased the palm of all of the parents on the list I created a while back. Gucci didn't know about this part of the plan. They live in the neighborhood and every month they get a few bucks to give me access to their children in the event the police raided my home. I call it insurance and I hoped I didn't need to use it but I clearly did.

Officer Sack of Rocks walks up to me with his peers behind him. I read his lips. "You're real cute aren't you?"

"I don't know what you're talking about." I shrug and try to look innocent.

"I'm sure you do. Where is your mother?"

"I told you officer, she isn't here. But we are all over the age of 16 and therefore able to watch ourselves. And Olive here is an adult so we're even better."

He is so mad at me his eyes redden. He checks Olive's ID and calls it in. Everything checks out. "Why is that door over there locked?" He points at the basement.

"Because we keep it locked."

"But we have a warrant."

"Sir, the warrant you flashed was for the living areas and the rooms. Did you and your officers check those areas?" He's silent. "Sir...did you?" I already know he did. "The basement is rented out and is not ours to let you in."

"You may have won this round, but you better hope I never have to come back here again. I'm not sure if you have somebody in the police department working on your side but I always get my man," he eyes me, "or bitch. Remember that."

Present Day

Green Door – Adult Mental Health Care Clinic
Northwest, Washington DC

Christina sat back in her chair and exhaled. Harmony led a life fit for a movie. "So when did she have you sign over guardianship? To her friend?"

Harmony leans back in her chair. "Last week."

"Wow, I'm so taken back by you." She sighs. "Just when I think I've heard it all, you tell me a little more."

"It's my world, I don't make it rotate."

"I know...but of course you told me some things that I might have to share with the authorities. Like the murders your children committed and those types of things like that." She makes notes on her chart. "Our client confidentiality agreement goes but so far you know."

Harmony grins. "You won't do that."

She giggles. "Why not?"

"Because I came in here drunk and your employees saw me. Remember, she asked was I okay before I even walked in. And if you needed her to call the cops," Harmony responds. "If I have to, I could always say that I have no idea what you're talking about. Besides, without bodies you can't prove a thing."

Her forehead creases. "You came in here drunk on purpose. Didn't you? Just to fuck with my mind"

Silence.

"I really had hopes for you Harmony but its obvious that you will always be what you are, a sad woman who abused her children and herself. I feel sorry for you."

Harmony stands up. "Don't feel sorry for me. I finally know what I have to do and I owe it all to you." She walks to the door. "Christina, if there's any consolation, you did make me realize a lot about myself. I should never have had any children. I didn't have the right to bring them into my fucked up world. If I knew back then what I know now, I would've taken that gun out of Constance hands and killed myself instead." She sighed. "Have a nice life. You not too bad after all."

JAYDEN
THE REAL

The music sounds so good driving in my new white Benz even though I'm still impacted by the surgery. And for some reason the night sky looks sexy. I bought my car when I turned sixteen. At first I was angry that nobody came to pick me up from the hospital after my ear surgery. I got over it when I realized life for me can't get shit but better. Plus Olive went to visit her family in Virginia and most of Thirteen Flavors were too busy enjoying their one day off.

They told me Metha quit when I was in the hospital, a punk move since she could've told me to my face but fuck that bitch. She told Olive that her conscious wouldn't allow her to work for someone who sold sex. This after you took my money? Really? Fucking slut! I'd given her so much cash over the course of our relationship; you'd think she'd be more grateful. She better keep her mouth closed, or I'm coming for her too. The messed up part was that she was the one person who kept it real with me, with the exception of Olive. I gotta take care of my nephew and run my bitches with an iron fist. I have no time to think about my driver.

I'm driving down the street until I pull up at a light and a cutie in a red Suburban smiles at me from my left. He isn't as sexy as Sebastian, or even Kreshon for that matter, but he's cute enough to make me notice. "Pull over for a second, baby. Let me talk to you."

"I got something to do tonight, maybe next life time." He grins and I speed off.

I don't entertain him because I have to check on my house. There will be plenty time for playing. When I pull up in front of Concord, before I even open the door, I hear yelling from the inside. "You not the boss of me, bitch! Jayden may have said you are in charge tomorrow, but it's my day off tonight!" Tywanda yells. "I'm sick of all this fake shit around here anyway." She's probably talking to Jay-O who I put in charge since Hadiya is out of town, either way right now I don't want to be bothered.

I decide at that moment that I'm not going inside. Instead I park my Benz and grab my truck. I want to be in my father's energy and since this was once his car, it makes me feel safe. I put Hadiya and Cassius up in a hotel in Atlanta so she could visit her family. Since the baby is not here, I might as well take advantage of this time off. I drive up the street not sure where I'm going. When I see *Strawberry Lounge*, I decide to pull over and have some wine. To my surprise when I walk inside with my fake ID, the place is packed. I'm kicking it at the bar until a nigga with a fitted blue New York Yankee cap pulls up on me. His expression is straight but his eyes tell me exactly what he wants...pussy.

"Sexy." Is all he says to me at first and then he licks his lips.

"Thanks." I play with the rim of my wine glass. "I appreciate it."

"You with somebody?" He looks around the dark club. "Because I don't want to get myself all excited about you, only for a nigga to claim you later. I'm jealous that way."

"I'm single when I want to be, which is most of the time."

"Fucking with me you not going to be single for long."

I blush and whip my hair around my shoulder. One of my curls drops into my glass. He grabs a napkin, takes it out and wipes it off. "That's all your hair ain't it?"

"Why don't you tell me?"

He steps up to me, runs his fingers through my hair and smiles. "Sexy ass, bitch." He shakes his head. "I know for a fact somebody claiming you."

"Let's just say I've had a tough couple of weeks, and right now I'm here with you, so lets enjoy the moment. Who cares about anybody else? Fair enough?"

He smiles. "I feel you, so how about we get out of here and get some breakfast." He tugs his cap and it reminds me of my sister. That's when I see it. Something about him is off. "I just want to get you alone in a place not so loud."

I know what this is about and for real, I don't have time for the long version. I like to fuck and he's cute enough for me to let him hit, and since I like to have sex in my bed I decide to take him home. "If you want a little quiet, how 'bout we leave this spot and go to my place."

He grins. "Hold up, shawty. It ain't about all that with me. Let's grab something to eat, have some conversation and if you still wanna dip back to your crib, I'm with that all the way."

●━━━━━━━━━━━━━━━━━━━━━━━━━━━━━━●

We eat a nice breakfast and an hour later, the only thing on my mind is sex. I like how he carries himself and he appears low key. When we make it back to my house, the moment I place my key into the door, I know something is off. He steps up close to me and I can't move. It's completely dark inside and when I turn around to look at him, there's a frown on his face. He pushes me inside and my body slides on the floor and into someone's legs. There is a lot of whimpering and the feeling of fear is so strong, it gives me chill bumps. When I smell strong alcohol and a Frito scent, I know its Tywanda. The door slams and the light flips on. I see Tywanda and Jay-O tied back to back on the floor, and their mouths are covered with duct tape.

I look at the nigga I brought home. "What's going on?" He's been with me the entire time, so I try to figure out when he planned this robbery. I'm about to reach for the knife in my pocket but he's watching me now. It's not the right time.

"Shut the fuck up, bitch. I'm running this shit...now where is the fucking money?" His voice is flat and emotionless.

"What is this about?" I'm confused and the sound of my girls whimpering puts me on edge. "I don't have shit in here you would want. I promise!"

"Stop fucking playing games! I know you wouldn't be in this big ass house without holding paper." He looks around. "Give me the money or I'ma shoot so many holes in you, you'll need a blood transfusion!"

"I wouldn't fuck around with you." I cry. "I don't have anything in here!"

"Is that why you switched from a Benz to an Escalade? Because you don't have no paper?" How does he know that? I met him at the bar, not here.

While I'm trying to sort it all out, another man whose face I do recognize appears from the back. He's eating a crab leg. "What took you so fucking long? I was about to kill these bitches and bounce." He throws the shells on the floor.

"I wanted to give you enough time to find the paper. And when you texted me that you didn't, I came here."

I finally remember where I saw the other dude. He was smiling at me at the light on my way to the house in a Suburban. It all makes sense now. They must've followed me home and when I didn't come inside they split up. One came with me and the other to my house.

"Hey, beautiful, remember me?" he asks. "I wish we could've met under different circumstances. But that's how life goes."

"Look, I don't have anything here. Please don't hurt me or my girls."

The dude who smiled at me on the road, grabs me by the hair and forces me up the stairs. Then he moves me toward my mother's room. My heart rate kicks up. I don't want them to harm her. "Look...my room is over there." I point, wanting them to stay away from her. "I got a little money there. Let me give you what you need and you can go about your business."

"Bitch, we already know your peoples is in there." When they open my mother's door, her face is beaten so badly she looks disguised. It's a crime scene. Something from CSI. Blood is everywhere. On the walls, the carpet and even the curtains. They beat her like they hated her. This shit is personal.

He releases my hair and I try to run over toward her but they stop me by pulling me back. "Mommy...say something to me!"

She isn't moving and I can't breathe. I can't see straight. Both of them are now in the room with me. "Your mother took a bullet to the stomach. She'll probably live if you tell us where the dough is because you can call the cops. We brought you in here to know how serious we are. Now we gonna ask you again, where is the paper?"

"In my room. Oh my, God its in my room. Please don't hurt my mother anymore. She's sick."

"Then take us to the stacks!"

"I will." I try to stop crying. "Just let me talk to her first. To tell her I love her in case she dies. Please."

"We don't have time for that shit."

"If I don't check on my mother I won't remember the code to the safe." I look at them seriously. "And then you can just kill me anyway. If you could've found the money you would be gone already. You need me." I cry again. "Matter of fact, kill me now." I call their bluff.

They look at each other and my date says, "Hurry up, bitch. If I see you being slick, I'ma flatten you and her together."

I rush toward her and drop to my knees. I can barely see her facial features and I wipe some of the blood out of her eyes. "Mommy, are you okay?" I ask lifting her head. "I'm so sorry about this, please forgive me."

"Make it quick, slut." Mr. Smiles says. "We ain't got time for all of this shit."

"One more second. Please." When she opens her eyes I smile. "Hi, mommy. I never wanted you to be hurt like this. I only wanted you to do better and now this is all my fault." I know she has HIV but I don't care at the moment. I just want her to survive.

"Jayden, be careful with my blood." She says in a low voice. "D-do you remember that time...when you were gone for three days?" I nod. "I looked....everywhere for you." I'm on pause. I never knew this until now. "I went to the cops and everything," she moans in pain, "I even tried to stop drinking for a whole day. It didn't work and I felt like a failure when I couldn't find you and I hated myself even more for letting you down. So I took it out on you and that made me a coward. I pit you and your sister against each other, repair the relationship if you can," She cries out in pain again and clenches her stomach. "Please forgive me, Jayden. And take care of yourself and Mad..." Her eyes close.

"Mommy," I wipe the tears off of my face and her blood smears everywhere. "Talk to me. You always pull through, mommy. Do it again now, when I need you. Please."

"Hurry up, bitch." My date says.

I feel so much hate toward them and it's hard to control. On the sly I take the knife out of my pocket, flick it open and coat it with her blood. When I see them moving toward me, I cut one of them on the thigh and the other on the knee. They're so angry they beat me until I forget who I am. Forget where I'm at. When they're done, they pull me toward my room by my hair. Both of them are hobbling. Good!

"Where the fuck is the money?" Mr. Smiles asks holding his thigh.

"In the bathroom." He grabs me by the hair again and pulls me in the bathroom. Once there, he throws me on the tub. My tooth hits the edge and falls down my mouth. I swallow it. "Get the money, bitch." He says, breathing hard. "Now! I'm tired of fucking around with you and your drunk ass mother." *Wait...how did he know my mother is a drunk?*

When I get there, I try to see through all of the blood but its everywhere and coat's the white bathtub like paint. I rub it out of my eyes and turn the hot water faucet. I have the same set up for my safe as my dad. I decided to have it installed after my mother let me down with the banking account. I thought this shit was safe. I thought it was fail proof. "Bitch, what the fuck are you doing?"

I look back at them. "Getting your money."

"Well you better not try no other slick shit. After what you just did, I don't have no problem killing you."

"Fuck ya'll!" I turn the hot water to the right and then the left and the safe opens. "See, it's all in there."

They push me out of the way and climb on top of each other going for the stacks I saved up. Everything I earned from Thirteen Flavors is all inside. "Oh, my fucking God!" My date says. "There has to be at least two hundred thousand dollars in there." *There's more.* Three hundred thousand to be exact. "We gonna be set behind this shit."

"What we gonna do about her?" Mr. Smiles asks.

He raises his gun and I say, "Wait."

I cough out blood. "Don't kill me yet...I want to say something. It's important."

"Make it quick!" Mr. Smiles says.

"I just want to say that I gave both of you a little case of HIV. Courtesy of my mother. Enjoy what's left of your life, bitches!" I laugh hysterically.

Boom!

SUGAR
MAD STATE OF MIND

Gucci walks through the hallway on the way to the bus stop. These days are tough since she decided to go back to school, thanks to Jayden who left her totally disfigured. She scares everything from dogs to birds when they see that face. She's almost to the bus stop when Sugar stops her. "Hey, aren't you that girl I waved at in front of Jayden's house? At Concord Manor." She looks over her mutilated face. "What happened to you?"

Gucci wants to use the toilet right where she stands after the mentioning of Jayden's name. Every night in her dreams, Jayden cuts up her face again. "A lot happened to my face and yes it's me. What do you want?"

"Have you seen Madjesty?" Sugar asks like she always does to anybody who ever laid eyes on Madjesty in life.

"No." She shrugs. "But if you find her, tell her that her mother was killed. Some niggas ran up in the house and robbed them." Gucci is smiling, especially since her plan to tell the cops she was having a whore party failed. "Her funeral is tomorrow at New World Church in Lanham."

Sugar doesn't think Madjesty would care but if she's lucky enough to run into her, she would definitely tell her the news. "Wow, I'm sorry to hear that." She lies. Madjesty was so fucked up in the head, that she knew her mother was to blame and figured her death was the best thing for her friend. "Is Jayden still going to school here?" Sugar persists.

She frowns. "No, she's in some high saddity private school out Virginia. Where her classes can be used toward college credits or some shit like that." Gucci still has plans for Jayden but for now things would have to wait. "I hear the night her mother died, somebody shot Jayden in the arm. I wish they caught her face, like she did mine."

"Wow." Sugar shakes her head.

"I just hate that Denise was involved in any of the shit, even though I tried to warn her about her in advance."

"Denise is Passion's real name right?" She remembers Madjesty talking about her all the time.

"Yes." She shakes her head. "They found her naked body in some bushes behind a strip club. They said some john followed her outside and raped and killed her. She had teeth marks all over her body and her head was hanging off. I don't believe it was the john though."

"Why not?"

"Because she also had a spider bite mark on her leg. And I remember Passion making a comment about Jayden saying that some people who handle spiders are immune to their venom after awhile. It's mighty funny how she went out. Seems familiar."

"Jayden doesn't strike me as somebody who would kill."

"I'm not surprised, you don't know her. Some of my friends are missing too and we can't find them either. I'm not worried though, sooner or later Jayden will get what she deserves. And I'll be there to see when it happens." Gucci walks off leaving Sugar alone.

●━━━━━━━━━━━━━━━━━━━━━━━━━━━━━●

As she always does every Friday night, Sugar cruises downtown D.C. to find her friend, although she always comes up empty-handed. This time she almost shits her pants when she saw Madjesty with some gay boy, a black kid who was very dark, a mixed kid who looked Asian and a very pretty girl. They were all grungy but had character about them and she could see why Madjesty chose to roll with them. They are walking out of a McDonalds and they seem to be deep in conversation when Sugar approaches.

When Sugar gets closer, she can't get over how good Mad looks even at her worst. She stands out. It appears that she's been in the streets and with the exception of the red hair hanging from up under her cap and her clean sneakers, she would've walked right past her. Sugar throws the car in park and walks over to her.

Madjesty is just about to run thinking that the police was on to her, until she sees Sugar's face. "Mad," Sugar says looking her over. "What's going on with you?"

"Who is this?" Gage asks Madjesty. She's ready to kill if need be. "Is she cool?"

Madjesty doesn't respond right away. She hates that Sugar sees her like this until she remembers that they are her new family and this is her new life. "She's cool, give me a second though." Madjesty steps over to her, out of earshot from her friends. "What's up, Sugar?"

"What are you doing, Mad? And what are you doing with them?" She looks at the group of misfits and back at her. "You look so dirty."

"Are you looking for me for a particular reason?" Sugar nods yes. "Then get to what you want."

"Mad, your mother has died."

Madjesty's lower body can no longer stand and she falls down. The new Mad Max thinking she was struck by Sugar, begin to whip her ass. They didn't come up for air until Madjesty demands that they stop. Finally catching wind, Mad stands up and walks over to Sugar where she's balled up and in pain. She helps her up. "I'm sorry about that shit. They thought you hurt me."

"Why would I do that?" She says. "I love you."

Mad's heart flutters. "I know but they're my family and they're just worried that's all."

"What about us? We're your family too."

Silence.

Sugar looks at them and contemplates fighting back but she knows she's outnumbered and as brainwashed as Madjesty appears, she's liable to help them. "Mad, like I said, your mother died and her funeral is tomorrow at New World Church in Lanham." She walks to the car and writes down her number. "Me and Krazy got a place together, he left the foster home. If you want to stay with us, you can."

Madjesty takes the card and stuffs it in her back pocket. She has no intentions on staying with her or anyone else for that matter. She took to the streets well. Besides, she has a commitment to her new family and she can't be around Krazy and her all day, while they play out their love. Her new family chose her and she decided to choose them too. "Naw, I'm good."

Sugar seems despondent. She hoped things would turn out differently if she found her. Now she knows that she's wrong. One things for sure, since she sees how bad she's doing, she thinks the baby is fine right where he is and decides not to tell her about her son. Or that Jayden was shot and Passion was killed.

Sugar walks away until Madjesty says, "Thank you." She swallows. "I wish you and my nigga Krazy the best too. I love ya'll both."

Sugar looks at Madjesty's new family. They are an odd bunch but she can tell they care about her. And she does too. Sugar doesn't want to tell Madjesty that although she's grungy, she has more swag in her little finger than Krazy did in his entire body. And that they spend most of their time arguing about if she loves him or Madjesty. She definitely won't tell her that she's prepared to leave him if Madjesty gives the word. Instead she let's it go, hoping that one day Madjesty would come back to her on her own terms.

As Sugar pulls off, Madjesty thinks about her mother dying. She was sure all the love she had for her was gone, but she was surprised to learn that it didn't. Losing her stung because it marked the end of one part of *her life and the arrival of a new era. She remembered when Harmony said one day she would realize how much she loved her, she guessed Harmony was right after all. She would have to make a decision to go to funeral or not. With her being wanted she figured the best thing may be to stay away, but for now she wasn't sure.*

JAYDEN
DEAD WEIGHT

Jayden was burying her mother tomorrow, yet she had to sit across from her aunts Ramona and Laura and look at their smug faces. When they learned that Harmony was dead, they actually did a dance in the lawyer's office. Just thinking about their disrespect enraged her.

Olive was holding Jayden's hand because she knew today was tough. After all the time knowing her, she finally got full details of what went on in her life as a child and she was surprised she was even breathing. To her, Jayden was the strongest person she knew and she would always be in her corner. Although she was dead broke, Jayden still had her girls and she sunk her teeth into her rich boyfriend. Sebastian went to visit his grandfather in Saudi Arabia, but couldn't wait to come back to make sure she was okay. He hated that she was shot on his watch. It wouldn't happen again.

"Since it's obvious that your mother's passing has altered the agreement, we are going to ask the courts to turn over the house." Her aunts' lawyer says. "A.S.A.P."

"Why is the agreement altered?" Jayden asks.

He smirks at the foolish child. "Because you don't have the money to buy them out and your mother died without a will in place."

"Says who?" Jayden responds nodding to her attorney.

On queue he says, "Here is Harmony Phillips' will." He slides it over to them. "That copy is yours to keep. As you can see from the highlighted areas, she left Jayden everything."

When Jayden spoon-fed her mother liquor the day they went to the bank, at some point she exchanged the blank sheets of paper for a will. Olive was the witness and when Harmony was done signing, she gave Jayden full power of the estate once she came of age.

The aunts are still smiling. "So what she left the will." Ramona shrugs. "She still doesn't have the money."

"Here's a cashiers check for two hundred fifty thousand dollars." He continues. They aren't smiling anymore. "That takes care of their portion of the house." He slides it to their attorney.

Laura snatches it from him and eyes it like it'll turn to water. "But...how..."

"It doesn't matter how. You wanted your money and now you have it." He points to Olive. "This is Jayden's legal guardian, that is Harmony's will and there is your money. Even in death Harmony fulfilled her obligation. Anything else?"

Ramona shoots up. "This isn't fair! Mama, left that house for us before she died! We want the house not the money!"

"Wrong, your mother and my grandmother, left it to her first child, Harmony Phillips. If she would've wanted it any other way, we wouldn't be here."

"I want you out of that house!" She looks at Jayden. "I don't understand how you raised the money!"

"So that's what this was always about." Jayden says. "You never thought we were going to raise the money. Sadly you are mistaken." Jayden and Olive rise. "Since we have nothing else to discuss I'm out of here. I have more important things to tend to, like the burial of my mother."

●━━━━━━━━━━━━━━━━━━━━━━●

When Jayden walks outside her grandfather is there waiting. She runs into his arms and he hugs her tightly, sniffing her hair in the process. Pushing her back softly he asks, "Are you okay now?"

"Yes. Thank you, grand daddy." Although he loves to hear her acknowledge him, he prefers to be called by his name. "Please, call me Rick."

Jayden feels it a bit strange but continues. "I just want to say how much I appreciate what you've done for me. I feel bad for how I talked to you at my aunt's house. It's because of you, I can say I officially have a home."

"Don't worry about that, I just want us to work on our relationship. Okay? The money I gave you is lightweight."

They say their goodbyes and he watches them get into her Benz and drive off. Jayden doesn't know that he orchestrated the hit on her house. She isn't aware that he gave the order to kill Harmony but to shoot his granddaughter in the arm, to spare her life. She also isn't aware that the money he spent on the house and the attorney, all came out of the duckets she earned from Thirteen Flavors. There's a reason why Jace didn't fuck with his father and Jayden would be late in finding out. He had a lot of shit with him. He had motives and they were many. He was the worst man money could buy.

Epilogue

It was sunny but breezy the day Harmony Phillips was laid to rest. It was said that she couldn't have looked prettier if she tried. Her funeral was small and only the people who cared about her, showed their faces. Which means there were very few. Still, no one grieved but her daughter.

Large black Michael Kors shades covered most of Jayden's face, as she walked slowly out of the funeral home, holding Cassius in her arms. Kreshon moved slowly at her side, his smoke gray suit hanging effortlessly off of his toned body.

When they reached the curb, Luh Rod opened the passenger door. He paused when he saw a group of teenagers in the distance. His hand touched his weapon and his senses were heightened because something felt off. They were standing in the middle of the street and seemed to be focused on them. He put his hand over his eyes to shade them. "You know them mothafuckas up there?" He pointed in their direction. "They look like they scoping us out." He was always extra cautious whenever his brother was not around. He was still in Saudi Arabia.

Jayden looked up the street and through her tinted lenses, saw a strange group. They looked like derelicts. Vagabonds. They were dressed in dark colors and the looks on their faces were blank. But it was the one in the middle, with the black New York Yankees cap pulled over her eyes, and the red curly hair flying in the wind, that made her uneasy.

Madjesty stepped out of the bunch and toward Jayden. The clean white sneakers seemed to light up her steps like Michael Jackson's Beat It video. When there was no more than ten feet between them, she stopped. Her eyes were locked on Jayden's, until she saw the beautiful little boy who she seemed to protect and caudle. His hair was curly, just like Mad's. And the smile on his face was contagious enough to force a grin onto hers. Bliss lasted all of a few seconds, until it was replaced with confusion.

"Whose son is that?" Madjesty pointed at him but looked at her sister. "Whose kid, Jayden?" He looked like her baby but she'd drank so much Hennessy that she couldn't be sure. Was she just like her grandmother? Unable to identify her own child?

Jayden stepped back a little and Kreshon placed a hand on her shoulder for support. "You didn't come to the funeral, but you have the nerve to question me? Why the fuck would you disgrace this day like this?"

"I didn't give a fuck about that bitch in there!" She pointed at the funeral home. "I told you that shit! So me not showing up don't mean shit. My only problem was that she didn't die sooner."

A tear crawled from under Jayden's shades and she wiped it away. "I can't believe you just said that."

"I'm not gonna listen to you talk to her like that!" Kreshon spit.

"Then close your fucking ears, nigga! I ain't hardly talking about you." Madjesty yelled. When Mad Max heard the noise, they inched closer until she raised her hand, forcing them to stop. "I need to talk to my sister for a minute, alone." She looked at Kreshon and the dude with dreads who had his gun trained on her. "I know ya'll want her to be safe, but I'm not gonna ask you again. A minute with my sister please." When they didn't move she said, "Either shoot me or get the fuck out of my face."

"Well you speaking to your sister is going to be a problem," Jayden said, "because I stopped being related to you the day you raped me."

Madjesty looked at the little boy. Her stomach swelled with guilt. She knew he couldn't understand what was just said, but what if he did? This wasn't how she wanted to be remembered.

"Just a few minutes. Please."

Jayden looked at Kreshon and said, "Get in the truck. I'm coming."

"You sure?"

"Yes." She looked at Luh Rod. "You too."

They disappeared into the truck leaving them alone.

"I told you I'm sorry about what I did to you and I think about it everyday, Jayden. But you made it clear you don't fuck with me and I'm not gonna kiss your ass anymore." Jayden was hurt, something in her was now ready to make amends. Maybe it was the plea Harmony made to her on her dying day. "What I'm asking you now don't have nothing to do with us. I haven't been whole since I lost my kid. I been doing some fucked up shit, just to make it go away in my mind and it's not working. So I'm asking you, whose kid is that?"

"This is my son." She pulled him closer. The little boy wrapped his arms around Jayden's neck. "I haven't seen you in a while so you didn't know about it." She opened the door of the truck and was preparing to strap him into his car seat.

"You know how long I've been looking for my kid? I know you heard how hard I've been trying to find him, Jayden." Tears flowed slowly from her eyes. She looked at him again. "If I find out you have *my son in your arms and you not telling me, I'm gonna hurt you. I don't want to take him from you and I'm not even gonna act like I can take care of him right now. I just want to know he's safe. And be a part of his life." She looked at him again, and slowly walked away. "So I'ma ask you again, is that my son?"*

"No, he's my baby." She said softly. "Now can you leave us alone? I just buried my mother and all I want to do is go home and get some rest."

Madjesty unhurriedly walked away. She almost reached her friends until she heard Jayden say, "Let me strap you in, Cassius. It's time to go."

Madjesty was inflamed. Jayden stole her son and lied to her face. She was about to confront her, when a blue compact car pulled slowly out of a parked spot. It seemed like time stopped as the driver pulled up in the middle of the street, next to the truck and parked. Lonnie J appeared from behind the driver's seat with red eyes, Madjesty turned white. So what Harmony was killed. His daughter was infected with HIV and he wanted to kill her spawns too. He lifted his shirt and pulled out two .45 automatics and fired at the Escalade. His shots spread evenly from the front to the back.

"Get the fuck down!" was the last thing Luh Rod said before metal rain crashed into the truck. He lifted his weapon and fired back but it was like Lonnie J had fifty niggas with him. And since he was caught off guard and without his brother, he was ill prepared.

Madjesty dropped to the ground and tried to pull on the door to free Jayden and the baby but it was locked. Whoever the attacker was meant business and wasn't leaving until he took lives. Although it seemed like the assault lasted forever, it was only a matter of seconds and then the car pulled off leaving death in his wake.

Madjesty defecated her pants when she realized she might have lost her son and her sister. Her stomach knotted up and cramps ran through her body. Part of her life returned when she heard Cassius's loud cries. If he was whimpering, even if he were injured, it meant he was alive. Madjesty stood up, crashed the window with her elbow and unlocked the door. Blood and body parts were splattered everywhere but she didn't care. She hoisted the baby from his car seat and held him in her arms. Then she tried to reach for Jayden who was slumped over in the back seat but she couldn't get a good hold of her.

"Give me the kid." Gage said walking up behind her. Madjesty didn't let him go until she inspected his little body for wounds. Although blood was everywhere it didn't belong to him. Relieved, she handed him to Gage as the rest of Mad Max looked up and down the street worried that the gunman would return.

Madjesty rushed into the truck and a prickly sensation took over her body. Everything in her told her that Jayden was dead but she didn't want to believe it. Once inside, she eased behind Jayden and placed her head in her lap. "Oh my, God." Madjesty cried out rocking her slowly. Sticky blood was everywhere. "You can't die on me, Jayden. I need you. Please don't do this shit to me."

Spirit and WB checked Kreshon and Luh Rod's pulses. "They're dead, Mad. We gotta get out of here before the police come."

"I'm not leaving my sister!" She yelled. "Do you hear what the fuck I'm saying? I'm not leaving her!"

The sirens scared her friends and made them more nervous about the situation. "Mad, I know you fucked up and I can't say I understand what you're going through right now. It would be disrespectful." Fierce said. "But if you stay here, you gonna go to jail. Now you wanted for murder and this ain't a good look to prove your case."

"You think I give a fuck about the police? Huh?" Mad spit. "Fuck the police! This is the only family I got left."

"Wrong." Gage said softly looking at the baby. "You got a son. And he needs you out! Not behind bars. And you got us! If you stay here they gonna pin this shit on you and what happened to that white girl back at The Hole. We gotta dip and we gotta dip now."

"We not going to leave you." Spirit said trembling. "But if you stay, we gonna get locked up too. And I didn't tell you everything about my past, Mad. But if they get me, I'm never coming home. They throwing away the key!"

"What you gonna do, Mad?" WB said looking up the block again. He was contemplating running on them mothafuckas.

"Ya'll just take the baby...I'm staying." When they didn't move she yelled, "Go 'head."

"Mad, we not leaving you and we not taking your son. What you gonna do is put him back in the car seat and come with us. The police are coming and he'll be okay. We need to act like we were never here." Spirit said, wiping their fingerprints off the doors.

Mad was going to scream on them again until Jayden said, "Mad, you gotta go."

When her sister spoke her eyebrows rose. "Oh, shit! Oh shit!" She smiled. "You alive."

Her voice was low and heavy. "Yes, but you gotta leave. Please."

"Where were you shot?

"In my leg but I'm gonna be okay." She said although she couldn't be sure.

The sirens were so loud now it was obvious they were on the other block. "Mad, please let's go. Your peoples said she's good." Gage said putting the baby back in the car seat. "This not good."

Madjesty looked at Jayden and said, "I'm so sorry for everything. I love you so much."

"I know. Now go…please."

Madjesty kissed Cassius on the forehead and left the scene. She would've taken him with her but she was on the run. Keeping the kid would have complicated things. Reluctantly she ran away with her new family, leaving her old family behind.

THE END

COMING SOON

MAD MAX

CHILDREN OF THE CATACOMBS

CARTEL PUBLICATIONS
PRESENTS

The Cartel Collection
Established in January 2008
We're growing stronger by the month!!!
www.thecartelpublications.com

Cartel Publications Order Form
Inmates ONLY get novels for $10.00 per book!

Titles		*Fee*
Shyt List	_____	$15.00
Shyt List 2	_____	$15.00
Pitbulls In A Skirt	_____	$15.00
Pitbulls In A Skirt 2	_____	$15.00
Pitbulls In A Skirt 3	_____	$15.00
Victoria's Secret	_____	$15.00
Poison	_____	$15.00
Poison 2	_____	$15.00
Hell Razor Honeys	_____	$15.00
Hell Razor Honeys 2	_____	$15.00
A Hustler's Son 2	_____	$15.00
Black And Ugly As Ever	_____	$15.00
Year of The Crack Mom	_____	$15.00
The Face That Launched a Thousand Bullets		
	_____	$15.00
The Unusual Suspects	_____	$15.00
Miss Wayne & The Queens of DC		
	_____	$15.00
Year of The Crack Mom	_____	$15.00
Familia Divided	_____	$15.00
Shyt List III	_____	$15.00
Shyt List **IV**	_____	$15.00
Raunchy	_____	$15.00
Raunchy 2	_____	$15.00
Raunchy 3	_____	$15.00
Reversed	_____	$15.00
Quita's Dayscare Center	_____	$15.00
Shyt List V	_____	$15.00
Deadheads	_____	$15.00

Please add $4.00 per book for shipping and handling.
The Cartel Publications * P.O. Box 486 * Owings Mills * MD * 21117

Name: _____

Address:_____

City/State:_____

Contact # & Email:_____

Please allow 5-7 business days for delivery. The Cartel is not
responsible for prison orders rejected.

CARTEL PUBLICATIONS
BRINGING OUR STORIES TO LIFE
WWW.THECARTELPUBLICATIONS.COM